No Frills, Just

A Letter From Th

CW00405134

Dear Readers,

The releases of classic tales from the pen of H.Rider Haggard have proved to be the most popular of our programme of titles. This famous author has been sorely neglected in the last few decades with only the perennially popular "King Solomon's Mines" and "She" being perpetually in print. The author spun approximately 50 tales of romance and adventure that can be comfortably termed as Pulp Fictions. We wish to reassure all readers of our titles that this author remains at the forefront of our publishing strategy,and that it is our intention to reissue the bulk of his work.

Are you a pulpster for the millenium ? Pulp Fictions continues its search for artistic/writing talent with the entries for the initial competition being of a uniform high quality. The closing date for our next competition is 30th June 1999. See back pages for more details.

If you would like to join our regular mailing list to receive news of available and forthcoming titles then simply fill out the coupon in the rear of this book to receive our free catalogue and regular news of new titles from the land of Pulp Fictions. There is a Prize draw twice a year, the lucky winner receiving free copies of Pulp Fictions novels. Could it be you ?

Better Read Than Dead !

The Chief Archivist
Pulp Fictions
c/o Pulp Publications Ltd
Po Box 144
Polegate
East Sussex
BN26 6NW

Pulp Fictions - The Collection

"Fantastic Fiction, Fantastic Fun . I'm addicted to Pulp Fiction!" - James Herbert

The Lair Of The White Worm by Bram Stoker.
(ISBN: 1-902058-01-1)
Murders In The Rue Morgue and Other Stories by Poe
(ISBN: 1-902058-02-x)
The People Of The Mist by H.Rider Haggard
(ISBN: 1-902058-00-3)
She by H.Rider Haggard
(ISBN: 1-902058-03-8)
Ayesha - Return of She by H.Rider Haggard
(ISBN: 1-902058-04-6)
She & Allan by H.Rider Haggard
(ISBN: 1-902058-05-4)
When The World Shook by H.Rider Haggard
(ISBN: 1-902058-07-0)
Kidnapped By Cannibals by Dr Gordon Stables
(ISBN: 1-902058-06-2)
Journey To The Centre of the Earth by Jules Verne
(ISBN: 1-902058-08-9)
The Mysterious Island Part One: "Dropped From The Clouds" by
Jules Verne
(ISBN: 1-902058-13-5)
Allan and the Ice Gods by H.Rider Haggard
(ISBN: 1-902058-11-9)
The Green Rust by Edgar Wallace
(ISBN: 1-902058-10-0)

Coming Soon - May 1999

The Mysterious Island Part Two: "Abandoned" by Jules Verne
(ISBN: 1-902058-14-3)
Dr.Nikola -Occult Adventurer by Guy Boothby
(ISBN: 1-902058-17-8)
The Boats of The Glen Carrig by W.Hope Hodgson
(ISBN: 1-902058-15-1)

ALLAN
AND THE
ICE-GODS

A Tale of Beginnings

By
H. RIDER HAGGARD

A fire mist and a planet,
A crystal and a shell,
A jelly fish and a Saurian
And caves where the cave men dwell;
Then a sense of law and beauty,
And a face turned from the clod—
Some call it Evolution,
And others call it God.

WILLIAM HERBERT CARRUTH.

"No Frills, Just Thrills"

This edition published 1999 by
Pulp Fictions
A Division of Pulp Publications Ltd

ISBN 1-902058-11-9

c. Pulp Publications Limited 1999.

All rights reserved. This publication may not be reproduced,
stored in a retrieval system, or transmitted,
in any form or by any means, electronic, mechanical,
photocopying, recording or otherwise without the
prior permission of the publishers.

This book is sold subject to the condition that
it shall not, by way of trade or otherwise, be
lent, re-sold, hired out or otherwise circulated
without the publisher's prior consent in any
form of binding or cover other than that in which it
is published and without a similar condition including
this condition being imposed on the subsequent purchaser.

Every effort has been made by the publishers to contact
relevant copyright holders. In the event that an oversight has occurred
the publishers would be delighted to rectify any omissions
in future editions of this book.

Printed and bound by: W.S.O.Y in Finland
Cover Template Design copyright - The Magic Palette
(all rights reserved)

Book Introduction copyright David Pringle.

Allan and the Ice-Gods
— Introduction by David Pringle

Although it did not appear until two full years after his death on 14th May 1925, *Allan and the Ice-Gods* (Hutchinson, May 1927) was not quite the last of Rider Haggard's novels. It had been preceded by the posthumous *The Treasure of the Lake* (1926) — also an Allan Quatermain story — and it was followed by a final pair of posthumous titles, *Mary of Marion Isle* (1929) and *Belshazzar* (1930), both unrelated to the Quatermain series. We know that Haggard liked to write well ahead of his approximately annual publishing schedule and to store his finished manuscripts in a safe, so it comes as no great surprise to read in Morton Cohen's excellent biography of the author that *Allan and the Ice-Gods* was written as early as 1922. What comes as much more of a surprise is to learn from Professor Cohen that this far-out adventure tale of a modern-day hero who takes an hallucinogenic drug which allows his consciousness to plunge backwards through time, entering the mind of an Ice-Age man, was actually plotted in collaboration with Rudyard Kipling, eminent author of *The Jungle Book* and *Kim*:

> "In the course of their association, Kipling suggested the idea for at least one of Haggard's tales (*When the World Shook*), he took a considerable hand in five others (*The Ghost Kings*, *Red Eve*, *Allan and the Ice-Gods*, *The Mahatma and the Hare*, *The Way of the*

Spirit), and he read (or was read) at least six stories in manuscript... For this much we have evidence...

"Kipling seems to have given Haggard the most elaborate assistance on *Allan and the Ice-Gods*, which they worked over on Haggard's visit to Bateman's [Kipling's home] in February 1922. The evidence rests in a group of seven pages (four quarto sheets) containing detailed plotting, alternating between Haggard's and Kipling's handwriting... [and] a list in Kipling's hand of the characters of the tale, with accompanying phrases that either explain the meaning of their names or give a thumb-nail description... On the reverse of one page, Haggard wrote: 'Synopsis of story drawn up by Rudyard K & myself at Batemans (Feb. 1922) H. Rider Haggard.' Of particular interest is the fact that the larger part of the writing is in Kipling's hand..."

— Morton Cohen, *Rider Haggard: His Life and Work*, London: Macmillan, 1960; 2nd edition, 1968, p204-206

It would be a mistake to make too much of that, however — to regard *Allan and the Ice-Gods* as essentially Kipling's novel. It may contain some of Kipling's ideas, but the style is pure Haggard; and, after all, Haggard himself had earlier been an inspiration to Kipling — the latter testified in his autobiography that the idea for the Mowgli stories in *The Jungle Book* (1894) had suddenly flashed upon him while he was reading the episode of the "wolf brothers" in Haggard's Zulu romance *Nada the Lily* (1891). Also, Kipling may well have been influenced by the tale of Hendrika the baboon-woman in Haggard's earlier novel *Allan's Wife* (1889) — an interesting female model for both Mowgli the wolf-boy and Edgar Rice Burroughs's Tarzan the ape-man (the latter was first presented to the world in 1912, in the pages of an American pulp magazine, *All-Story*). The give-and- take between these turn-of-the-century popular writers was considerable, although Haggard, who was nearly a decade older than Kipling and wrote his first Allan Quatermain story, *King Solomon's Mines*, in 1885, takes precedence over most.

It was an extraordinary era for popular fiction, this period from the 1880s to the First World War which the critic Roger Lancelyn Green has called the Age of the Storytellers. At exactly the moment when Haggard was enjoying his first flush of success with *King Solomon's Mines*, in 1885, Robert Louis Stevenson was writing his celebrated novella *Strange Case of Dr Jekyll and Mr Hyde* (published January 1886) and Arthur Conan Doyle was scribbling his "shilling shocker" *A Study in Scarlet*, about the adventures of a near-superhuman detective called Sherlock Holmes (foolishly rejected by the leading publisher of shilling shockers, Arrowsmith, it languished for over a year until its appearance in *Beeton's Christmas Annual*, 1887). At almost the same moment, too, a very young Herbert George Wells was conceiving the ideas, and writing the early drafts, of what would become his first great success in the field of scientific romance, *The Time Machine* (in book form, 1895; but the crude prototype was serialized as "*The Chronic Argonauts*" in the *Science Schools Journal*, 1888). Five authors, above all others, were to dominate the Age of the Storytellers, and those five were Stevenson, Haggard, Doyle, Kipling and Wells. Between them, they bequeathed to the 20th century, to its legacy of popular prose fiction and film, so many of the great and enduring characters, ideas, themes, situations and genres.

One of the new sub-genres which arose in that period was the tale of prehistory, the adventure story set in the remotest conceivable human past. In many ways, this type of tale blended well with those that explored the "wild man" or feral-child theme, alluded to above: both sub-genres were imaginative responses, however muddled, to the 19th-century discovery of fossilized hominid remains, such as the famous Neanderthal Man, and to the new biology of evolution by Natural Selection, as expounded by Charles Darwin. The colourful and conventional historical romance, full of knights in armour or Romans in togas, had been a popular genre for a long time, at least since the days of Sir Walter Scott's *Ivanhoe* (1819) and Bulwer Lytton's *The Last Days of Pompeii* (1834), but the *pre*-historical romance — inspired more by the sciences of archaeology and paleontology than by any written records, and thus more a form of science fiction than of historical fiction — was a new thing in the late 19th century.

There were French-language precedents (one can find French precedents for most 19th-century trends in popular fiction) — an 1861 novel called *Paris avant les hommes* (Paris Before Men) by Pierre Boitard seems to have been the first — but in English the tale of prehistory really got underway in the 1890s and the decades following. Examples of the form include *A Son of Noah* by Mary Anderson (1893), From *Monkey to Man* by Austin Bierbower (1894), *The Story of Abby Stanley Waterloo* (1897), "A Story of the Stone Age" by H. G. Wells (serialized in *The Idler*, May- September 1897), *The Pagan's Progress* by Gouverneur Morris (1904), *A Woman of the Ice Age* by Louis Pope Gratacap (1906), *Before Adam by Jack London* (1906), *The Red Feather* by Theodore Goodridge Roberts (1907), *Wolf: The Memoirs of a Cave Dweller* by Peter B. McCord (1908), *Longhead* by Charles Henry Robinson (1913), *Stories of the Cave People* by Mary E. Marcy (1917) and *In the Morning of Time* by Charles G. D. Roberts (1919). Rider Haggard's friend and erstwhile collaborator, the folklorist and amateur anthropologist Andrew Lang, had been one of the earliest in the field with his amusing short story "The Romance of the First Radical" (1886).

Thus Haggard was contributing to an already well-established genre when he came to write *Allan and the Ice-Gods* in 1922, and few of his ideas were "original." There had been many tales of small primitive tribes struggling with dangerous environments, savage beasts and their own atavistic impulses. Even his framing device, of a hero's slip backwards in time into an earlier incarnation of himself, was well-worn: Jack London had utilised something similar in *Before Adam*. But Haggard's narrative has the virtue of being more vivid than most, more deeply imagined. Once past the opening couple of chapters, with their rather heavy-handed humour and elements of authorial self-parody (the ageing Allan Quatermain in terrified flight from his own particular cut-price version of She-Who-Must-Be-Obeyed, Lady Luna Ragnall), the reader is gripped by the prehistoric characters, the descriptions of their world, and the set-piece action scenes. There are many good things: the mammoth and the hairy ape-man trapped inside the glacier, where they are mistaken for "ice-gods"; the making of the great axe by Pag the Cunning Dwarf; the hero's duel-to-the-death with the old tribal chieftain, Henga; the trapping of the wolves and the killing of the sabre-tooth; the coming of the golden-haired, heartbreaking Laleela in her dugout canoe; the fight with the aurochs; and so on. The character of Pag, in particular, dominates the novel; he is another of Haggard's wise and wonderful dwarfs (compare Hans the Hottentot in *The Ivory Child* — of whom, we learn in the final chapter, Pag is almost certainly a "pre-incarnation" — or Otter, the stunted but formidable Zulu warrior in *The People of the Mis*t).

Prehistoric romance has remained popular since Haggard's contribution to the form; in fact, it has gained a whole new lease of life in the last couple of decades thanks to Jean M. Auel's bestselling series of "Earth's Children" novels (*The Clan of the Cave Bear* [1980], etc) — compare Auel's Ayla, the stone- age blonde, with Haggard's Laleela. Among the lesser-known recent examples of prehistoric fiction are Philip José Farmer's *Hadon of Ancient Opar* (1974) and it sequel *Flight to Opar* (1976), action-adventure yarns which readers of Haggard's novel should find particularly interesting. Although they are billed as prequels to Edgar Rice Burroughs's "Tarzan" novels, set circa 10,000 BC and involv-ing a sophisticated civilization which flourishes around an inland sea in central Africa, a civilization which founded Tarzan's lost city of Opar, they are also, as it turns out, sequels to *Allan and the Ice-Gods*. The characters of Laleela and Pag recur — renamed by Farmer "Lalila" and "Paga"— and are imagined fleeing southward to Africa from the European locale of Haggard's novel. Pag, or Paga, carries with him the marvellous axe which he fashioned from meteoric metal.

When I interviewed Philip José Farmer many years ago, in 1976, he had this to say:

"My Oparian civilization is not founded just on elements from Burroughs. It represents an amalgamation between Burroughs and Haggard. This huge axe-head made from meteorite iron actually first appeared in Haggard's *Allan and the Ice-Gods*. There are two characters in the first novel, *Hadon of Ancient Opar*, who appeared in Haggard's book, Lalila and the Paga — or Pag, as he was called in Haggard's novel. Now the hero of Haggard's novel has died in my novel; he gave the axe to Pag, who in turn has given it to Kwasin [one of Farmer's heroes]. Kwasin will have this huge axe through the series, and eventually it will go to Hadon's son, who, after the great catastrophe, will emigrate to the south and found the city of Kor which appeared in Haggard's *She*. And this axe, if you're familiar with the Allan Quatermain novels, later on fell into the hands of Umslopogaas, the great Zulu hero, who shattered it in the city of Zu-Vendis, you remember [the reference is to the climax of

Haggard's *Allan Quatermain*, 1887]. So... I'm tracing the history of this axe from Haggard to Burroughs and back to Haggard and I'm incorporating Haggard's lost cities into Burroughs's lost cities."

— Philip José Farmer, interviewed by David Pringle on 14th June 1976.

Unfortunately, Mr Farmer (who is now 80 years of age) did not write a third "Opar" novel, and so we never did get to learn the story of Pag's axe in full; but the notion of it surviving to become Umslopogaas's great war-axe, the dreaded skull-tapper known as "Woodpecker," is pleasing, and I am sure Haggard himself would have appreciated it.

— David Pringle, January 1999

CONTENTS

ix

SENSATIONAL OFFER

Always Welcome!
Always Useful!

GENUINE LEATHER

WALLET

Strongly, handsomely stitched, 8 card windows, deep currency pocket, coin purse pocket.

ONLY $1.00

FREE Your name engraved in Gold Leaf. Here is the greatest Wallet bargain ever offererd.

ORDER YOUR WALLET RIGHT NOW.

Send $1.00, plus 20% Federal Tax, Total $1.20 and we pay postage. Or order C.O.D. pay postman $1.20 plus postage and fees.

F. R. NOVELTY WORKS, Dept. 67-A
71 EAST BROADWAY, NEW YORK 2, N. Y.

Allan and the Ice-Gods

A TALE OF BEGINNINGS

CHAPTER I

ALLAN REFUSES A FORTUNE

HAD I the slightest qualifications for the task I, Allan Quatermain, should like to write an essay on Temptation.

This, of course, comes to all in one shape or another or at any rate to most, for there are some people so colourless, so invertebrate, that they cannot be tempted ; or perhaps the subtle Powers which surround and direct, or misdirect us, do not think them worth an effort. These cling, like limpets to a rock, to any conditions, moral or material, in which they may find themselves, or perhaps float along the stream of Circumstance like jelly-fish, making no attempt to blaze a path for themselves in either case, and therefore die as they have lived, quite good, because nothing has ever moved them to be otherwise, the objects of the approbation of the world, and let us hope of Heaven also.

The majority are not so fortunate ; something is always egging their living personalities along this or that road of mischief. Materialists explain to us that this something is but the passions inherited from a thousand generations of unknown progenitors who, departing, left the curse of their blood behind them. I, who am but a simple old fellow, take another view which at any rate is hallowed by many centuries of human thought. Yes, in this matter, as in sundry others, I put aside all the modern talk and theories and

plump for the good, old-fashioned and most efficient
Devil as the author of our woes. No one else could
suit the lure so exactly to the appetite as that old fisher
in the waters of the human soul, who knows so well
how to bait his hooks and change his flies, so that they
may be attractive, not only to all fish but to every mood
of each of them.

Well, without going further with the argument, rightly
or wrongly that is my opinion.

Thus, to take a very minor instance—for if the reader
thinks that these words are the prelude to telling a tale
of murder or other great sins, he is mistaken—I believe
that it was Satan himself, or at any rate one of his
agents, who caused my late friend, Lady Ragnall, to
bequeath to me the casket of the magical herb called
Taduki, in connection with which already we had shared
certain remarkable adventures.*

Now it may be argued that to make use of this *Taduki*
and on its wings to be transported, in fact or in imagination, to some far-away state in which one appears for
a while to live and move and have one's being, is no crime,
however rash the proceeding. Nor is it, since if we can
find new roads to knowledge, or even to interesting
imaginings, why should we not take them ? But to break
one's word *is* a crime, and because of the temptation of
this stuff, which I confess for me has more allurement
than anything else on earth, at any rate in these latter
days, I have broken my word.

For, after a certain experience at Ragnall Castle, did
I not swear to myself and before Heaven that no power
in the world, not even that of Lady Ragnall herself,
would induce me again to inhale those time-dissolving
fumes and look upon that which, perhaps designedly, is
hidden from the eyes of man, namely, revealments of
his buried past, or mayhap of his yet unacted future ?
What do I say ? This business is one of dreams, no more,

---

* *See* the books called "The Ivory Child" and "The
Ancient Allan."

though I think that these dreams are such as are best
left unexplored, because they suggest too much and yet
leave the soul unsatisfied. Better the ignorance in which
we are doomed to wander than these liftings of corners of
the veil, than these visions which excite delirious hopes
that after all may be but marsh-lights which, when they
vanish, will leave us in completer darkness.

Now I will get on to the story of my fall ; of how it
came about and the revelations to which it led, that I
found interesting enough, whatever others may think of
them.

Elsewhere I have told how, years after our joint adventure in Central Africa, once again I came into touch with
the widowed Lady Ragnall and allowed myself to be
persuaded in her company to inhale the charmed smoke
of the *Taduki* herb, with which she became familiar when,
in a state of mental failure, she fell into the hands of the
priests of some strange African faith. Under its influence
the curtain of time seemed to swing aside and she and I
saw ourselves playing great parts as inhabitants of Egypt
in the days of the Persian domination. In that life,
if the tale were true, we had been very intimate, but
before this intimacy culminated in actual union, the
curtain fell and we re-awoke to our modern world.

Next morning I went away, much confused and very
frightened, nor did I ever again set eyes upon the stately
and beautiful Lady Ragnall. After all that we had learned
or dreamed, I felt that further meetings would be awkward. Also, to tell the truth, I did not like the story of
the curse which was said to haunt the man, in whatever
generation he might be born, or perchance re-born, who
had aught to do with her who, in it, was named Amada
and filled the rôle of priestess of Isis, the goddess whom
she betrayed. Of course, such ancient maledictions
are the merest nonsense. And yet—well, the truth is
that in our separate fashions we are all superstitious,
and really the fate of Lord Ragnall, who had married this
lady, was most unpleasant and suggestive ; too much so
to encourage anyone else to follow his example. Further,

I had come to a time of life when I did not wish, even in
dreams, for more adventures in which women were concerned, since such, I have observed, however entrancing
at the moment, lead to trouble as surely as sparks fly
upwards.

Thus it came about that when Lady Ragnall wrote
asking me to stay with her, as she did on two subsequent
occasions, I put her off with excuses which were perfectly
valid, although at this moment I forget what they may
have been, it being my firm intention never again to
place myself within reach of her beauteous and commanding personality. You see, in that dream we
dreamed together, the story came to an end just as I
was about to marry her, the Princess and High-priestess
Amada, who was, or appeared to be, Lady Ragnall's
prototype. Indeed, on regaining her senses she, whose
vision lasted a second or two longer than did mine, let
it slip that we actually had been married in some primitive
Egyptian fashion and, although I knew it to be nonsense,
I could see clearly enough she believed that this event
had happened.

Now even when the scene was laid a long while ago,
it is extremely awkward to foregather with an imperial
woman who is firmly convinced that she was once your
wife, so awkward that in the end it might have proved
necessary to resume what she considered to be an established if an interrupted relationship.

This, for sundry reasons, I was determined not to
do, not the least of them being that certainly I should
have been set down as a fortune-hunter ; also, as I have
said, there was always the curse in the background,
which I hoped fondly would recognise my self-denial and
not operate in my direction. And yet—although to
think of it makes me feel cold down the back—if perchance
that dream were true, already it was incurred. Already
I, Allan, the Shabaka of former days, am doomed " to
die by violence far from my own country where first I
had looked upon the sun," as its terms, recorded in the
papyrus from Kendah-land of which I read a translation

at the Castle, provide with antique directness and
simplicity as the lot of all and sundry who have ever
ventured to lay hands or lips upon the person of Amada,
High-priestess of Isis.

To return. In reply to my second letter of excuse, I
received a quaint little epistle from the lady to whom it
had been written. It ran thus :

" O Shabaka, why do you seek to escape the net
of Fate, when already you are enveloped in its meshes ?
You think that never more, seated side by side, shall we
see the blue *Taduki* smoke rise up towards us, or feel its
subtle strength waft our souls afar. Perhaps this is so,
though assuredly even here you are doomed to acknowledge its dominion, how often I do not know ; and will
you find it less to be feared alone than in my company ?
Moreover, from that company you never can escape, since
it has been with you from time immemorial, if not
continuously, and will be with you when there is no more
sun

" Yet, as it is your wish, until we meet again in the
past or in the future, farewell, O Shabaka.

                                                   " AMADA."

When I had finished reading this very peculiar note,
of which the envelope, by the way, was sealed with the
ancient Egyptian ring that my late friend, Lord Ragnall,
had found and given to his wife just before his terrible
fate overtook him, literally I felt faint and lay back in
my chair to recover myself. Really she was an ominous
and, in her way, rather creepy woman, one unlike all
others, one who seemed to be in touch with that which,
doubtless by intention, is hidden from mankind. Now
it came back to me that when first I met her as the Hon.
Luna Holmes and was so interested in her at the Ragnall
Castle dinner-party before her marriage, I was impressed
with this ominous quality which seemed to flow from her,
as, had he been more sensitive, her future husband
should have been also.

During our subsequent association in Africa, too, it had always been with me, and of course it was in full force through our joint experience with the *Taduki* herb. Now again it surged up in me like an unsealed fountain and drowned my judgment, washing the ordered reason on which I pride myself from its foundations. Out of this confusion another truth emerged ; namely, that from the first moment I set my eyes on her I had always been attracted by and in a kind of hidden way " in love " with her. It was not a violent and passionate sort of affection, but then the same man can love sundry women in different ways, all of which are real enough.

Yet I knew that it was very permanent. For a little while her phantasies got a hold of me and I began to believe that we always had been and always should be associated together ; also that in some undeclared fashion I was under deep obligations to her, that she had stood my friend, not once but often, and so would stand while our personalities continued to endure. True, she had been Ragnall's wife, yet—and this through no personal vanity, since Heaven knows that this vice is lacking in me—of a sudden I became convinced that it was to me that her nature really turned and not to Ragnall. I did not seek it, I did not even hope that it was so, for surely she was his possession, not mine, and I wanted to rob no man. Yes, in that instant there the fact loomed before me large and solid as a mountain, a calm, immovable mountain, a snow-capped volcano, apparently extinct, that still one day might break into flames and overwhelm me, taking me as its captive upon wings of fire.

Such were my reflections during the moments of weakness which followed the shock I had received from that remarkable letter, outwardly and visibly so final, yet inwardly and spiritually opening up vast avenues of unexpected possibilities. Presently they passed with the faintness and I was my own man again. Whatever she might or might not be, so far as I was concerned there was an end of my active fellowship with Lady

Ragnall, at any rate until I was certain that she was
rid of her store of *Taduki*. As she admitted in her
curiously-worded communication, that book was closed
for our lives, and any speculations concerning the past
and the future when we were not in being, remained
so futile that about them it was unnecessary to
trouble.

A little while later I read in a newspaper under the
head of " Fashionable Intelligence " that Lady Ragnall
had left England to spend the winter in Egypt, and
knowing all her associations with that country, I marvelled at her courage. What had taken her there ? I
wondered ; then shrugged my shoulders and let the
matter be.

Six weeks or so afterwards I was out shooting driven
partridges. A covey came over me, of which I got two.
As I thrust new cartridges into my gun, I saw approaching
me, flying very fast and high, a couple of wild duck that
I suppose had been disturbed from some pond by the
distant beaters. I closed the gun and lifted it, being
particularly anxious to bag those wild duck, which were
somewhat rare in the neighbourhood, especially at that
season of the year. At that moment I was smitten by
a most extraordinary series of impressions that had to
do with Egypt and Lady Ragnall, the last things I had
been thinking of a minute before.

I seemed to see a desert and ruins that I knew to
be those of a temple, and Lady Ragnall herself seated
among them holding up a sunshade which suddenly
fell on to the sand. This illusion passed, to be followed by another, namely, that she was with me, talking
to me very earnestly and in a joyful, vigorous voice, but
in a language of which I could not understand one word.
Yet the burden of her speech seemed to reach my mind ;
it was to the effect that now we should always be near
to each other, as we had been in the past.

Then all was gone, nor can these impressions have
endured for long, seeing that when they began I was
pointing my gun at the wild duck and they left me

before the dead birds touched the ground, for automatically I went on with the business in hand, nor did my accustomed skill desert me.

Setting down the fancy as one of those queer mental pranks that cannot be explained, unless in this instance it was due to something I had eaten at lunch, I thought no more about it for two whole days. Then I thought a great deal, for on opening my newspaper, which reached the Grange about three o'clock, that is, exactly forty-eight hours after my telepathic experience, or whatever it may have been, the first thing that my eye fell on among the foreign telegrams was the following from Cairo :

"A message has been received here conveying the sad intelligence of the sudden death yesterday of Lady Ragnall, the widow of the late Lord Ragnall, who as a famous Egyptologist was very well known in Egypt, where he came to a tragic end some years ago. Lady Ragnall, who was noted for her wealth and beauty, was visiting the ruins of a temple of Isis which stands a little way back from the east bank of the Nile between Luxor and Assouan, where her husband met with his fatal accident while engaged in its excavation. Indeed, she was seated by the monument erected to his memory on the sand which overwhelmed him so deeply that his body was never recovered, when suddenly she sank back and expired. The English medical officer from Luxor certified heart-disease as the cause of death and she has been buried where she died, this ground having been consecrated at the time of the decease of Lord Ragnall."

If I had felt queer when I received Lady Ragnall's mystical letter before she left for Egypt, now I felt much queerer. Then I was perplexed ; now I was terrified, and what is more, greatly moved. Again that conviction came to me that deep down in my being I was attached, unchangeably attached, to this strange and charming woman, and that with hers my destiny was intertwined.

If this were not so, indeed, why had her passing become
known to me of all people, and in so incongruous a
fashion ?—for although the hour of her death was not
stated, I had little doubt that it occurred at the very
moment when I shot the wild duck

Now I wished that I had not refused to visit her,
and even that I had given her some proof of my regard
by asking her to marry me, notwithstanding her great
wealth, the fact that I had been her husband's friend,
and all the rest. No doubt she would have refused ;
still, the devotion of even so humble an individual as
myself might have pleased her. However, regrets
came too late ; she was dead, and all between us at an
end.

A few weeks later I discovered that here I was
mistaken, for after a preliminary telegram inquiring
whether I was in residence at the Grange, which I answered
on a prepaid form to the address of some unknown
lawyers in London, there arrived at lunch-time on the
following day a gentleman of the name of Mellis, evidently
one of the firm of Mellis & Mellis who had sent me the
telegram. He was shown in, and without waiting for
luncheon, said :

" I believe I am addressing Mr. Allan Quatermain ? "
I bowed, and he went on :

" I come upon a strange errand, Mr. Quatermain, so
strange that I doubt whether in the course of your life
which, as I have heard, has been full of adventure, you
have ever known its equal. You were, I believe, well
acquainted with our late client, Lord Ragnall, also with
his wife, Lady Ragnall, formerly the Honourable Luna
Holmes, of whose recent sad death you may perhaps have
heard."

I said this was so, and the lawyer went on in his
dry, precise way, watching my face as he spoke :

" It would appear, Mr. Quatermain, that Lady Ragnall must have been much attached to you, since a while
ago, after a visit that you paid to her at Ragnall Castle,
she came to our office and made a will, a thing I may

add that we had never been able to persuade her to do.
Under that will, as you will see presently, for I have
brought a copy with me, she left everything she possessed,
that is, all the great Ragnall property and accumulated
personalty of which she had the power to dispose at
her unfettered discretion, to—ahem—to *you*."

"Great heavens!" I exclaimed, and sank back into
a chair.

"As I do not wish to sail under false colours," went
on Mr. Mellis with a dry smile, "I may as well tell you
at once that both I and my partner protested vehemently
against the execution of such a will, for reasons that
seemed good to us but which I need not set out. She
remained firm as a rock.

"'You think I am mad,' she said. 'Foreseeing this,
I have taken the precaution of visiting two eminent
London specialists, to whom I told all my history,
including that of the mental obscuration from which I
suffered for a while as the result of shock. Each of these
examined me carefully and subjected me to tests, with
the result—but here are their certificates and you can
judge for yourselves.'

"I, or rather we, read the certificates, which of
course we have preserved. To be brief, these stated
that her ladyship was of absolutely sound and normal
mind, although certain of her theories might be thought
unusual, if not more so than those of thousands of
others, some of them eminent in various walks of life.
In face of these documents, which were entirely endorsed
by our own observation, there was but one thing to do,
namely, to prepare the will in accordance with our client's
clear and definite instructions. While we were writing
these down she said suddenly :

"'Something has occurred to me. I shall never
change my mind, nor shall I remarry, but from my
knowledge of Mr. Quatermain I think it possible and
even probable that he will refuse this great inheritance'
—a statement, sir, which struck us as so incredible that
we made no comment.

" ' In that event,' she continued, ' I wish all the real property to be realised and together with the personalty, except certain legacies, to be divided among the societies, institutions and charities that are written down upon this list '—and she handed us a document—' unless indeed Mr. Quatermain, whom, should he survive me, I leave my sole executor, disapproves of any of them.'

" Do you now understand the position, sir ? "

" Quite," I answered, " that is, no doubt I shall when I have read the will. Meanwhile, I suggest that you must be hungry after your journey and that we should have lunch."

So we lunched, talking of indifferent matters while the servants were in the room, and afterwards returned to my study, where the documents were read and expounded to me by Mr. Mellis. To cut the story short, it seemed that my inheritance was enormous ; I am afraid to state from memory at what figure it was provisionally valued. Subject to certain reservations, such as an injunction that no part of the total, either in land or in money, was to be alienated in favour of Mr. Atterby-Smith, a relative of Lord Ragnall whom the testatrix held in great dislike, or any member of his family, and that for part of the year I must inhabit Ragnall Castle, which might not be sold during my lifetime, or even let, all this vast fortune was left at my absolute disposal, both during my life and after my death. Failure to observe these trusts might, it seemed, invalidate the will. In the event of my renouncing the inheritance, however, Ragnall Castle, with a suitable endowment, was to become a county hospital and the rest of the estate was to be divided in accordance with the list that I have mentioned, a very admirable list, but one which excluded any society or institution of a sectarian nature.

" Now I think that I have explained everything," said Mr. Mellis at length, " except a minor and rather peculiar provision as to your acceptance of certain relics, particularly described by the testatrix in a sealed

letter which I will hand to you presently. So it only
remains for me, Mr. Quatermain, to ask you to sign a
document which I have already prepared and brought
with me, to enable me to deal with these great matters
on your behalf. That is," he added with a bow, " should
you propose to continue that confidence in our firm
with which the family of the late Lord Ragnall has
honoured it for several generations."

While he was hunting in his bag for this paper,
explaining as he did so that I must be prepared to face
an action brought by Mr. Atterby-Smith, who had been
raging round his office " like a wild animal," suddenly
I made up my mind.

" Don't bother about that paper, Mr. Mellis," I said,
" because Lady Ragnall was right in her supposition.
I have no intention of accepting this inheritance. The
estate must go for division to the charities, etc., set down
in her list."

The lawyer heard, and stared at me.

" In my life," he gasped at last, " I have known mad
testators and mad heirs, but never before have I come
across a case where both the testator and the heir were
mad. Perhaps, sir, you will be pleased to explain."

" With pleasure," I said, when I had finished lighting
my pipe. " In the first place, I am already what is
called a rich man, and I do not want to be bothered with
more money and property."

" But, Mr. Quatermain," he interrupted, " you have
a son who with such wealth behind him might rise to
anything—yes, anything." (This was true, for at that
time my boy Harry was living.)

" Yes, but as it chances, Mr. Mellis, I have ideas upon
this matter which you may think peculiar. I do not
wish my son to begin life with enormous resources, or
even the prospect of them. I wish him to fight his own
way in the world. He is going to be a doctor. When
he has succeeded in his business and learned what it
means to earn one's bread, it will be time for him
to come into other people's money. Already I have

explained this to him with reference to my own, and
being a sensible youth, he agrees with me."

" I daresay," groaned the lawyer. " Such—well,
failings, as yours are often hereditary."

" Another thing is," I went on, " that I do not wish
to be worried by a lawsuit with Mr. Atterby-Smith.
Further, I cannot bind myself to live half the year in
Ragnall Castle in a kind of ducal state. Very likely,
before all is done, I might want to return to Africa,
which then I could not do. In short it comes to this :
I accept the executorship and my out-of-pocket expenses
and shall ask your firm to act for me in the matter.
The fortune I positively and finally refuse, as you observe
Lady Ragnall thought it probable I should do."

Mr. Mellis rose and looked at the clock. " If you will
allow me to order the dog-cart," he said, " I think there
is just time for me to catch the afternoon train up to
town. Meanwhile I propose to leave you a copy of the
will and of the other documents, to study at your leisure,
including the sealed letter which you have not yet read.
Perhaps after taking independent advice from your own
solicitors and friends, you will write me your views in a
few days' time. Until then this conversation of ours
goes for nothing. I consider it entirely preliminary and
without prejudice."

The dogcart came round—indeed it was already waiting—and thus this remarkable interview ended. From
the doorstep I watched the departure of Mr. Mellis and
saw him turn, look at me, and shake his head solemnly.
Evidently he thought that the right place for me was a
lunatic asylum.

" Thank goodness that's done with ! " I said to
myself. " Now I'll order a trap and go to tell Curtis
& Good all about the business. No, I won't ; they'll
only think me mad as that lawyer does, and argue with
me. I'll take a walk and mark those oaks that have to
come down next spring. But first I had better put away
these papers."

Thus I reflected and began to collect the documents.

Lifting the copy of the will I saw lying beneath it the sealed letter of which Mr. Mellis had spoken, addressed to myself and marked : " To be delivered after my death, or in the event of Mr. Quatermain predeceasing me, to be burned unread."

The sight of that well-known writing and the thought that she who had penned it was now departed from the world and that never more would my eyes behold her, moved me. I laid the letter down, then took it up again, broke the seal, seated myself, and read as follows :

" My dear Friend, my dearest Friend, for so I may call you, knowing as I do that if ever you see these words we shall no longer be fellow-citizens of the world. They are true words, because between you and me there is a closer tie than you imagine, at any rate at present. You thought all our Egyptian vision to be a dream, no more ; I believe it, on the other hand, at least in essentials, to be a record of facts that have happened in bygone ages. Moreover, I will tell you now that my revelation went further than your own. Shabaka and Amada were married and I saw them as man and wife leading a host southward to found a new empire somewhere in Central Africa, of which perchance the Kendah tribe were the last remnant. Then the darkness fell.

" Moreover, I am certain that this is not the first time that we have been associated upon the earth, as I am almost certain that it will not be the last. This mystery I cannot understand or explain ; yet it is so. In some of our manifold existences we have been bound together by the bonds of destiny, as in some we may have been bound to others, and so, I suppose, it will continue to happen, perhaps for ever and ever.

" Now, as I know that you hate long letters, I will tell you why I write. I am going to make a will, leaving you practically everything I possess, which is a great deal. As there is no relationship or other tie between us, this may seem a strange thing to do ; but after all, why not ? I am alone in the world, without a relative of any kind. Nor had my late husband any except some distant cousins, those Atterby-Smiths whom you may remember, and these he detested even more than I do, which is saying much. On one point I am determined —that they shall never inherit, and that is why I make this will in such a hurry, having just received a warning that my own life may not be much prolonged.

"Now I do not deceive myself. I know you to be no money-hunter, and I think it highly probable that you will shrink from the responsibilities of this fortune which, if it came to you, you would feel it your duty to administer for the good of many to the weariness of your own flesh and spirit. Nor would you like the gossip in which it would involve you, or the worry of the actions-at-law which the Atterby-Smiths, and perhaps others unknown, would certainly bring against you. Therefore it seems possible that you will refuse my gift, a contingency for which I have provided by alternative depositions. If a widowed lady without connections chooses to dispose of her goods in charity or for the advancement of science, etc., no one can complain. But even in this event I warn you that you will not altogether escape, since I am making you my sole executor, and although I have jotted down a list of the institutions which I propose to benefit, you will be given an absolute discretion concerning them, with power to vary the amounts and add to or lessen their number. In return for this trouble, should you yourself renounce the inheritance, I am leaving you an executor's fee of £5,000, which I beg that you will not renounce, as the mere thought of your doing so offends me. Also, as a personal gift, I ask you to accept all that famous set of Caroline silver which was used on grand occasions at Ragnall, that I remember you admired so much, and any other objects of art that you may choose.

"Lastly—and this is the really important thing— together with the Egyptian collection I pass on to you the chest of *Taduki* herb, with the Kendah brazier, etc., enjoining you most strictly, if ever you held me in any friendship, to take it, and above all to keep it sacred.

"In this, Friend, you will not fail me. Observe, I do not direct you to make further experiments with the *Taduki*. To begin with, it is unnecessary, since although you have recently refused to do so in my company—perhaps because you were afraid of complications—sooner or later you will certainly breathe it by yourself, knowing that it would please me much and perhaps, when I am dead, hoping that through it you may see more of me than you did when I was alive. You know the dead often increase in value at compound interest, and I am vain enough to hope that this may be so in my case.

"I have no more to say. Farewell—for a little while.

"LUNA RAGNALL.

"P.S.—You can burn this letter if you like ; it does not in the least matter, as you will never forget its contents. How interesting it will be to talk it over with you one day.

"L. R."

CHAPTER II

BACK TO THE PAST

IT is unnecessary that I should set out the history of the
disposal of the great Ragnall fortune in any detail. I
adhered to my decision, which at last was recorded with
much formality, though, as I was a totally unknown
individual, few took any interest in the matter. Those
who came to hear of it for the most part set me down as
mad ; indeed, I could see that even my friends and
neighbours, Sir Henry Curtis and Captain Good, with
whom I declined to discuss the business, more or less
shared this view, while a society journal of the lower
sort printed a paragraph headed :

" The Hunter-Hermit. Ivory Trader who Mocked at
Millions ! "

Then followed a distorted version of the facts. Also
I received anonymous letters written, I do not doubt, by
members of the Atterby-Smith family, which set down
my self-denial to " the workings of a guilty conscience "
and to " fears of exposure."

Of all these things I took no heed, and notwithstanding
wild threats of action by Mr. Atterby-Smith, in due
course the alternative clauses of the will came into
operation, under which, with only a rough list to guide
me, I found myself the practical disposer of vast sums.
Then indeed I " endured hardness." Not only had
collieries and other properties to be sold to the best
advantage, not only was I afflicted by constant interviews with Messrs. Mellis & Mellis and troubles too
numerous to mention ; in addition to these I think that
every society and charity in the United Kingdom, and
quite eighty per cent of its beggars, must have written

or sought interviews with me to urge their public or private
claims, so that in the end I was obliged to flee away and
hide myself, leaving the lawyers to deal with the
correspondence and the mendicants.

At length I completed my list, allotting the bulk of
the money to learned societies, especially such of them as
dealt with archæological matters in which the testatrix
and her husband had been interested ; to those who
laboured among the poor ; to the restoration of an abbey
in which I had heard Lady Ragnall express great interest ;
and to the endowment of the castle as a local hospital
in accordance with her wish.

This division having been approved and ratified by
an Order in Court, my duties came to an end. Further,
my executor's fee was paid to me, which I took without
scruple, for seldom has money been more hardly earned ;
and the magnificent service of ancient plate was handed
over to me, or rather to the custody of my bank, with
the result that I have never set eyes upon it from that
day to this, and probably never shall. Also I selected
certain souvenirs, including a beautiful portrait of Lady
Ragnall by a noted artist, painted before her marriage,
concerning which there was a tragic story whereof I
have written elsewhere. This picture I hung in my
dining-room, where I can see it as I sit at table, so that
never a day passes that I do not think twice or thrice
of her whose young loveliness it represents. Indeed I
think of her so much that often I wish I had placed it
somewhere else.

The Egyptian collection I gave to a museum which
I will not name ; only the chest of *Taduki* and the other
articles connected with it I kept, as I was bound to do,
hiding them away in a cupboard in my study and hoping
that I should forget where I had put them—an effort
wherein I failed entirely. Indeed, that chest might
have been alive, to judge from the persistence with which
it inflicted itself upon my mind, just as if someone were
imprisoned in the cupboard who wished to get out. It
was packed away in the bottom part of an old Chippendale

bookcase I had taken over as a fixture when I bought
the Grange, which bookcase stood exactly behind my
writing-chair. Now this chair, that I am using at the
moment of writing, is one of the sort that revolves, and
heedless of the work I had to do, continually I found
myself turning it round so that I sat staring at the
cupboard instead of at my desk.

This went on for some days, until I began to wonder
whether there was anything wrong : whether, for instance,
I had placed the articles so that they could fall over,
and my subconscious self was reminding me of the fact.
At length one evening after dinner this idea fidgeted me
so much that I could bear it no more. Going to my
bedroom I opened the little safe that stands there and
took out the key of the cupboard which I had stowed
away so that I could not get at it without some trouble.
Returning, I unlocked that faded mahogany door of
the eighteenth-century bookcase and was surprised when
it opened itself very quickly, as though something were
pushing at it.

Next moment I saw the reason. My unconscious
self had been right. Owing, I suppose, to insufficient
light when I put them away, I had set the ebony tripod,
upon which rested the black stone bowl, that formerly
was used in the *Taduki* ceremonies in the sanctuary of
the temple in Kendah-land, whence Lady Ragnall had
brought it, so that one of its feet projected over the
edge of the shelf. Thus it pressed against the door,
and when this was opened of course fell forward. I
caught it, rather smartly I flattered myself, or rather
I caught the bowl, which was very heavy, and the tripod
fell to the floor. Setting down the bowl on the hearth-
rug which was near, I picked up its stand and made a
hasty examination, fearing lest the brittle, short-grained
wood should have broken. It had not ; its condition
was as perfect as when it was first used, perhaps thousands
of years before.

Next, that I might examine that curiosity with more
care than I had yet done, I placed the bowl upon its stand

to consider its shape and ornamentation. Though so
massive, I saw that in its way it was a beautiful thing,
and the heads of the women carved upon the handles
were so full of life that I think they must have been
modelled from a living person. Perhaps that model was
the priestess who had first used it in her sacred rites
of offering or of divination ; or perhaps Amada herself,
to whom, as I had seen her in my *Taduki* dream, now
that I thought of it, the resemblance was great.

The eyes of that face (for both handles are identical)
seemed fixed on me in a solemn and mystical stare ; the
parted lips looked as though they were uttering words
of invitation. To what did they invite ? Alas, I knew
too well ; it was that I should burn *Taduki* in the bowl
so that they might be opened by its magic and tell me
of hidden things.

Nonsense ! I thought. Moreover, I remembered
that one must never take *Taduki* after drinking wine,
or even tea. Then I remembered something else,
namely, that as it happened, at dinner I had drunk
nothing but water, having for some reason or other
preferred it to claret or port. Also I had eaten
precious little, I suppose because I was not hungry.
Or could it be that I was a humbug and had done these
things, or rather left them undone, so that should temptation overtake me its results might not prove fatal ? Upon
my word I did not know, for on such occasions it is
difficult to disentangle the exact motives of the heart.

Moreover, this speculation was forgotten in a new
and convincing idea that suddenly I conceived. Doubtless the virtues, or the vices, of *Taduki* were all humbug,
or rather non-existent. What caused the illusions was
the magnetic personalities of the ministrants, that is
to say, of Lady Ragnall herself, and on my first acquaint-
ance with it, here in England, of that remarkable old
medicine-man, Harut. Without these personalities, and
especially the first of them who was now departed from
the earth, it would be as harmless as tobacco and as
ineffectual as hay. So delighted was I with this discovery

that almost I determined to prove it by immediate demonstration.

I opened the carved chest of rich-coloured wood and drew out the age-blackened silver box within, which now I observed for the first time had engraved upon it a picture, frequently repeated, of the goddess Isis in her accustomed ceremonial dress, and a god, Osiris or Ptah, I think, making incantations with his hands, holding lotus-flowers and the Cross of Life, stretched out over a little altar. This I opened also, whereon a well-remembered aroma arose and for a moment clouded my senses. When these cleared again I perceived lying on the top of the bundles of *Taduki* leaves, of which there seemed to be a large quantity remaining, a half-sheet of letter-paper bearing a few lines in Lady Ragnall's handwriting. I lifted it and read as follows :

" MY FRIEND,
        " When you are moved to inhale this *Taduki*, as certainly you will do, be careful not to use too much lest you should wander so far that you can return no more. One of the little bundles, of which I think there are thirteen remaining in the box, should be sufficient, though perhaps as you grow accustomed to the drug you may require a larger dose. Another thing—tor a hidden reason with which I will not trouble you—it is desirable, though not necessary, that you should have a companion in the adventure. By preference this companion should be a woman, but a man will serve if he be one in whom you have confidence and who is sympathetic to you
                                                "L. R"

" That settles it," I thought. " I am not going to take *Taduki* with one of the housemaids, and there is no other woman about here," and I rose from my chair, preparing to put the stuff away.

At that moment the door opened and in walked Captain Good.

" Hullo, old fellow," he said. " Curtis says a farmer tells him that a lot of snipe have come in on to the Brathal Marshes, and he wants to know if you will come over to-morrow morning and have a go at them. I say, what's this smell in the room ? Have you taken to scented cigarettes, or hashish ? "

" Not quite ; but to tell you the truth I was thinking of it," I answered, and I pointed to the open silver box.

Good, who is a person of alert mind and one very full of curiosity, advanced, sniffed at the *Taduki*, and examined the brazier and the box, which in his ignoranec he supposed to be of Grecian workmanship. Finally he overwhelmed me with so many questions that at length, in self-defence, I told him something of its story and of how it had been bequeathed to me with its contents by Lady Ragnall.

" Indeed," said Good, " she who left you the fortune which you wouldn't take, being the lineal descendant of Don Quixote, or rather, of Sancho Panza's donkey. Well, this is much more exciting than money. What happened to you when you went into that trance ? "

" Oh," I answered wearily, " I seemed to foregather with a very pretty lady who lived some thousands of years ago, and after many adventures was just about to marry her when I woke up."

" How jolly ! though I suppose you have been suffering from blighted affections ever since. Perhaps if you took some more you might pull it off next time."

I shook my head and handed him the note of the Instructions that I had found with the *Taduki*, which he read with attention, and said :

" I see, Allan, that a partner is wanted and that, failing a lady, a man in whom you have confidence and who is sympathetic to you, will serve. Obviously that's me, for in whom could you have greater confidence, and who is more sympathetic to you ? Well, my boy, if there is any hope of adventures, real or imaginary, I'll take the risk and sacrifice myself upon the altar of

friendship. Light up your stuff; I'm ready. What
do you say? That I can't because I have been dining
and drinking wine or whisky? Well, as a matter of
fact I haven't. I've only had some tea and a boiled
egg—I won't stop to explain why—and intended to raise
something more substantial out of you. So fire away
and let's go to meet your lovely lady in Ancient Egypt
or anywhere else."

" Look here, Good," I explained, " I think there is a
certain amount of risk about this stuff, and really you
had better reflect——"

" Before I rush in where angels fear to tread, eh ?
Well, you've done it and you ain't even an angel. Also,
I like risks or anything that makes a change in this mill-
round of a life. Come on. What have we got to do ? "

Then feeling that Fate was at work, under a return
of the impulse of which the strength had been broken
for a moment by the reading of Lady Ragnall's note of
instructions, I gave way. To tell the truth, Good's
unexpected arrival just when such a companion was
essential, and his strange willingness, and even desire,
to share in this unusual enterprise, brought on one of
the fits of fatalism from which I suffer at times. I
became convinced that the whole business was arranged
by something or somebody beyond my ken, that I must
take this drug with Good as my companion. So, as I
have said, I gave way and made the necessary prepara-
tions, explaining everything to Good as I did so.

" I say ! " he said at last, just as I was fishing for
an ember from the wood fire to lay upon the *Taduki* in
the bowl, " I thought this was a joke, but you seem
jolly solemn about it, Allan. Do you really think it
dangerous ? "

" Yes, I do, but more to the spirit than to the body.
I think, to judge from my own experience, that anyone
who has once breathed *Taduki* will wish to do so again.
Shall we give it up ? It isn't too late."

" No," answered Good. " I never funked anything
yet, and I won't begin now. ' Lay on, Macduff ! ' "

"So be it, Good. But first of all, listen to me.
Move that armchair of yours close to mine, but not
quite up against it. I am going to place the brazier
just between and a little in front of us. When the
stuff catches a blue flame will burn for about thirty
seconds ; at least this happened on a previous occasion.
So soon as it dies away and you see the smoke begin to
rise, bend your head forward and a little sideways so
that it strikes you full in the face, but in such a fashion
that when you become insensible the weight of your
body will cause you to fall back into the chair, not
outwards to the floor. It is quite easy if you are careful.
Then open your mouth and draw the vapour down into
your lungs. Two or three breaths will suffice, as it works
very quickly."

"Just like laughing gas," remarked Good. "I
only hope I shan't wake with all my teeth out. The
last time I took it I felt——"

"Stop joking," I said, " for this is a serious matter."

"A jolly sight too serious! Is there anything
else ? "

"No. That is, if there is anybody you particularly
wish to see, you might concentrate your thoughts on
him——"

"Him! I can't think of any him, unless it is the
navigating lieutenant of my first ship with whom I
always want to have it out in the next world, as he is
gone from this, the brute."

"On her, then ; I meant her."

"Then why didn't you say so, instead of indulging
in Pharisaical humbug? Who would breathe poison
just to meet another man ? "

"I would," I replied firmly.

"That's a lie," muttered Good. "Hullo, don't be
in such a hurry with that coal; I ain't ready. Ought I
to say any hocus-pocus ? Dash it all ! it is like a night-
mare about being hanged."

"No," I replied, as I dropped the ember on to the
Taduki just as Lady Ragnall had done "Now play

fair, Good," I added, " for I don't know what the effect of half a dose would be ; it might drive you mad. Look, the flame is burning. Open your mouth and arrange your weight as I said, and when your head begins to whirl, lean back at the end of the third deep breath."

The mysterious, billowy vapour rose as the pale blue flame died away and spread itself out fanwise.

" Aye, aye, my hearty," said Good, and thrust his face into it with such vigour that he brought his skull into violent contact with mine as I leant forward from the other side.

I heard him mutter some words that he had better have left unsaid, for often enough Good's language would have borne editing. Then I heard no more and forgot that he existed.

My mind became wonderfully clear and I found myself arguing upon all sorts of fundamental problems in a fashion that would have done credit to the greatest of the Greek philosophers. All I can remember about that argument or lecture is that in part, at any rate, it dealt with the possibility of reincarnation, setting out the pros and cons in a most vivid manner. Even if I had not forgotten them, these may be passed over, as they are familiar to students of such subjects. The end of the exposition, however, was to the effect that, accepted as it is by a quarter of the inhabitants of the earth, this doctrine should not lightly be set aside, seeing that in it there is hope for man ; that it is at least worthy of consideration. If the sages who have preached it from Plato down—and indeed for countless ages before his time, since without doubt he borrowed it from the East— are right, then at least we poor human creatures do not appear and die like gnats upon a summer's eve, but in that seeming death pass on to life eternally renewed, climbing a kind of Jacob's ladder to the skies. It is true that, as our foot leaves it, each rung of that ladder vanishes. Below is darkness and all the gulf of Time. Above is darkness and we know not what. Yet our hands cling to the uprights and our feet stand firm

upon a rung, and we know that we do not fall but mount,
also that in the nature of things a ladder must lean
against some support and lead somewhere. A melancholy business, this treadmill doctrine, it may be said,
where one rung is so like another and there are so many
of them. And yet—and yet is it not better than that
of the bubble which bursts and is gone ? Aye, because
life is better than death, especially if it be progressive
life, and if at last it may lead to some joy undreamed,
to some supernal light in which we shall see all the path
that we have trodden, and with it the deep foundations
of the Rock of Being upon which our ladder stands
and the gates of Eternal Calm whereon it leans.

Thus in the beginning of my dream-state, I, the
lecturer, argued to an unknown audience, or perhaps I
was the audience and the lecturer argued to me, I am
not sure—pointing out that otherwise we are but as
those unhappy victims of the Revolution in the prisons
of Paris, who for a little while bow and talk and play
our part, waiting till the door opens and the jailer,
Death, appears to lead us to the tumbril and the knife.

The argument, I should point out, was purely rational ;
it did not deal with faith, or any revealed religion, perhaps
because these are too personal and too holy. It dealt
only with the possible development of a mighty law,
under the workings of which man, through much tribula-
tion, might accomplish his own weal and at last come
to look upon the Source of that law and understand its
purpose.

Obviously these imperfectly reported reflections, and
many others that I cannot remember at all, were induced
by the sense that I might be about to plunge into some
seeming state of former existence, as I had done once
before under the influence of this herb. My late friend,
Lady Ragnall, believed that state to be not seeming,
but real, while I on the other hand could not accept this
as a fact. I set it down, as I am still inclined to do,
to the workings of imagination, super-excited by a
strange and powerful drug and drawing perhaps from

some fount of knowledge of past events that is hid deep in the being of every one of us.

However these things may be, this rhetorical summing-up of the case, of which I can only recollect the last part, was but a kind of introductory speech such as is sometimes made by a master of ceremonies before the curtain rises upon the piece. Its echoes died away into a deep silence. All the living part of me went down into darkness, dense darkness that seemed to endure for ages. Then with strugglings and great effort I awoke again, re-born. A hand was holding my own, leading me forward; a voice I knew whispered in my ear, saying,

"Look upon one record of the Past, O Doubter. Look and believe."

Now there happened to me, or seemed to happen, that which I had experienced before in the museum at Ragnall Castle, namely, that I, Allan, the living man of to-day, beheld myself another man, and yet the same. Whilst remaining myself I could enter into and live the life of that other man, knowing his thoughts, appreciating his motives and his endeavour, his hopes and his fears, his loves and his hates; reading him like a book and weighing everything in the scales of my modern judgment.

The voice—surely it was that of Lady Ragnall, though I could not see her face—died away; the hand was loosed. I saw a man in the cold, glimmering light of dawn. He was a very sturdy man, thick-limbed, deep-chested and somewhat hairy, whose age I judged to be about thirty years. I knew at once that he was not a modern man, although his weather-tanned skin was white where the furs he wore had slipped away from his shoulder, for there was something unusual about his aspect. Few modern men are so massive of body, and never have I seen one with a neck so short and large in circumference, although the feet and hands were not large. His frame was extraordinarily solid, being not more than five feet seven inches in height and by no means fat, yet he must have weighed quite fifteen stone, if not more. His dark hair was long and parted in the middle; it hung down to his shoulders.

He turned his head, looking behind him as though to make sure that he was alone, or that no wild beast stalked him, and I saw his face. The forehead was wide and not high, for the hair grew low upon it; his eyebrows were beetling and the eyes beneath them deep-set. They were remarkable eyes, large and grey, quick-glancing also, yet when at rest somewhat sombre and very thoughtful. The nose was straight, with wide and sensitive nostrils, suggesting that its owner used them as a dog or a deer does, to scent with. The mouth was rather thick-lipped, but not large, and within it were splendid and regular white teeth, broader than those we have; the chin was very massive and on it grew two little tufts of beard, though the cheeks were bare.

For the rest this man was long-armed, for the tip of his second finger came down almost to the kneecap. He had a sort of kilt about his middle, and upon his shoulders a heavy fur robe that looked as though it were made of bearskin. In his left hand he held a short-hafted spear of which the blade seemed to be fashioned of chipped flint, or some other hard and shining stone, and in the girdle of his kilt was thrust a wooden-handled instrument or axe, made by setting a great, sharp-edged stone that must have weighed two pounds or so into the cleft end of the handle, which was lashed with sinews both above and below the axe-head.

I, Allan, the man of to-day, looked upon this mighty savage, for mighty I could see he was, both in his body and, after a fashion, in his mind, and in my trance knew that the spirit which had dwelt in him hundreds of thousands of years ago, mayhap, or at least in the far, far past, was the same that animated me, the living creature whose body for aught I knew descended from his, thus linking us in flesh as well as soul. Indeed, the thought came to me, I know not whence, that here stood my remote forefather whose forgotten existence was my cause of life, without whom my body could not have been.

Now I, Allan Quatermain, fade from the story. No longer am I he. I am Wi the Hunter, the future chief of a little tribe which had no name, since, believing itself to be the only people on the earth, it needed none. Yet remember that my modern intelligence and individuality never went to sleep, that always it was able to watch this prototype, this primeval one, to enter, as I have said, into his thoughts, to comprehend his aims, desires, alarms, and to compare them with those that companion us to-day. Therefore the tale I tell is the substance of that which the heart of Wi told to my heart, set out in my own modern tongue and interpreted by my modern intellect.

CHAPTER III

WI SEEKS A SIGN

WI, being already endowed with a spiritual sense, was praying to such gods as he knew, the Ice-Gods that his tribe had always worshipped. He did not know for how long it had worshipped them, any more than he knew the beginnings of that tribe, save for a legend that once its forefathers had come here from behind the mountains, driven sunwards and southwards by the cold. These gods of theirs lived in the blue-black ice of the mightiest of the glaciers which flowed down from the crests of the high snow-mountains. The breast of this glacier was in the central valley, but the most of the ice moved down smaller valleys to the east and west and so came to the sea, where in springtime the children of the Ice-Gods that had been begotten in the heart of the snowy hills, were born, coming forth in great bergs from the dark wombs of the valleys and sailing away southwards. Thus it was that the vast central glacier, the House of the gods, moved but little.

Urk, the Aged One, who had seen the birth of all who lived in the tribe, said his grandfather had told him when he was little, that in his youth the face of this glacier was perhaps a spear's cast higher up the valley than it stood to-day, no more. It was a mighty threatening face of the height of a score of tall forest pines set one upon the other, sloping backwards to its crest. For the most part it was of clear black ice which sometimes, when the gods within were talking, cracked and groaned, and when they were angry heaved itself forward by an arm's length, shaving off the rocks of the valley which stood in its path and driving them in front of it. Who or what these gods might be Wi did not know. All he knew was that they were terrible, powers to be feared in whom he believed, as his forefathers had done, and that in their hands lay the fate of the tribe.

In the autumn nights when the mists rose some had seen them, vast, shadowy figures moving about before the face of the glacier, and even at times advancing towards the beach beneath where the people dwelt. They had heard them laughing also, and their priest, Ngae the Magician, and Taren, the Witch-who-hid-herself, only coming out at night, who was the lover of Ngae, said that they had spoken to them, making revelations. But to Wi they had never spoken, although he had sat face to face with them at nights, which none others dared to do. So silent were they that at times, when he was well-fed and happy-hearted and his hunting had prospered, he began to doubt this tale of the gods and to set down the noises that were called their voices, to breakings in the ice caused by frosts and thaws.

Yet there was something which he could not doubt. Deep in the face of the ice, the length of three paces away, only to be seen in certain lights, was one of the gods who for generations had been known to the tribe as The Sleeper, because he never moved. Wi could not make out much about him, save that he seemed to have a long nose as thick as a tree at its root and growing smaller towards the end. On each side of this nose projected a huge curling tooth that came out of a vast head, behind which swelled an enormous body as large as that of a whale, whereof the end could not be seen.

Here indeed was a god; not even Wi could question it, for none had ever heard of or seen its like, though for what reason it chose to sleep for ever in the bosom of the ice he could not guess. Had such a monster been known alive he would have thought this one dead, not sleeping. But it was not known, and therefore it must be a god. So it came about that for his divinity, like the rest of the tribe, Wi took a gigantic elephant of the early world, caught in the ice of a glacial period that had

happened some hundreds of thousands of years before
his day, and slowly borne forward in the frozen stream
from the far-off spot where it had perished, doubtless
to find its ultimate sepulchre in the sea. A strange god
enough, but not stranger than many have chosen and still
bow before to-day.

Wi, after debate with his wife, Aaka the proud and
fair, had climbed to the glacier while it was still dark,
to take counsel of the gods and learn their will as to a
certain matter. It was this. The greatest man of the
tribe, who by his strength ruled it, was Henga, a terrible
man born ten springs before Wi, huge in bulk and fero-
cious. This was the law of the tribe, that the mightiest
was its master, and so remained until one mightier than
he came to the opening of the cave in which he lived,
challenged him to single combat, and killed him. Thus
Henga had killed his own father who ruled before him.

Now he oppressed the tribe ; doing no work himself,
he seized the food of others or the skin garments that
they made. Moreover, although there were few and all
men fought for them, he took the women from their
parents or husbands, kept them for a while, then cast
them out or perhaps killed them, and took others. Nor
might they resist him, because he was sacred and could
do what he pleased. Only, as has been said, any man
might challenge him to single combat, for to slay him
otherwise was forbidden and would have caused the
slayer to be driven out to starve as one accursed. Then,
if the challenger prevailed, he took the cave of this
sacred one, with the women and all that was his, and
became chief in his place, until in his turn he was slain
in like fashion. Thus it came that no Chief of the Tribe
lived to be old, for as soon as years began to rob him
of his might, he was killed by some one younger and
stronger who hated him. For this reason also none
desired to be chief, knowing that if he were, sooner or
later he would die in blood, and it was better to suffer
oppression than to die.

Yet Wi desired it because of the cruelties of Henga,

and his misrule of the tribe which he was bringing to
misery. Also he knew that if he did not kill Henga,
Henga would kill him from jealousy. Long ago Wi
would have been murdered had he not been beloved by
the tribe as their great hunter who won them much of
their meat-food, and therefore a man whose death would
cause the slayer to be hated. Yet fearing to attack
him openly, already Henga had tried to do away with
him secretly, and a little while before, when Wi was
visiting his pit-traps on the edge of the forest, a spear
whizzed past him, thrown from a ledge of overhanging
rock which he could not climb. He picked up the spear
and ran away. It was one which he knew belonged to
Henga ; moreover, its flint point had been soaked in
poison made from a kind of cuttle-fish that had rotted,
mixed with the juice of a certain herb, as Wi could tell,
for sometimes he used this poison to kill game. He
kept the spear and, save to his wife Aaka, said nothing
of the matter.

Then followed a worse thing. Besides his son Foh, a
lad of ten years whom he loved better than anything on
earth, he had a little daughter one year younger, named
Foa. This was all his family, for children were scarce
among the tribe, and most of those who were born
died quite young ot cold, lack of proper food, and various
sicknesses. Moreover, if girls, many of them were cast
out at birth to starve or be devoured by wild beasts.

One evening Foa was missing, and it was thought
that wood wolves had taken her or perhaps the bears
that lived in the forest. Aaka wept, and Wi, when there
was no one to see, wept also as he searched for Foa
whom he loved. Two mornings afterwards when he came
out of his hut, near to the door-place he found something
wrapped in a skin, and on unwinding it saw that it was
the body of little Foa with her neck broken and the marks
of a great hand upon her throat. He knew well that
Henga had done this thing, as did everybody else, since
among the tribe none murdered except the Chief, though
sometimes men killed each other fighting for women,

of whom there were so few, or when they were angry. Yet when he showed the body to the people, they only shook their heads and were silent, for had not Henga the right to take the life of any among them ?

Then it was that Wi's blood boiled within him, and he talked with Aaka, saying that it was in his heart to challenge Henga to fight.

" That is what he wishes you to do," answered Aaka, " for, being a fool, he thinks himself the stronger, and that thus he will kill you without reproach, who otherwise, when he is older, will kill him. Also I have wished it for long who am sure that you can conquer Henga, but you will not listen to me in this matter."

Then she rolled herself up in her skin rug and pretended to go to sleep, saying no more.

In the morning she spoke again, and said,

" Hearken, Wi. Counsel has come to me in my sleep. It seemed to me that Foa our daughter, who is dead, stood before me, saying,

" ' Let Wi my father go up at night to make prayer to the Ice-Gods and seek a sign from them. If a stone fall from the crest of the glacier at the dawn it shall be a token to him that he must fight Henga and avenge my blood upon him and take his chieftainship ; but if no stone falls, then, should he fight, Henga will kill him. Also afterwards he will kill Foh my brother, and take you, my mother, to be one of his wives.'

" Now, Wi, I say that you will do well to obey the voice of our child who is dead, and to go up to make prayer to the Ice-Gods and await their omen."

Wi looked at her doubtfully, putting little faith in this tale, and answered :

" Such a dream is a thin stick on which to lean. I know well, Wife, that for a long while you have desired that I should fight Henga, although he is a terrible man. Yet if I do he may kill me, and then what would happen to you and Foh ? "

" That which is fated will happen to us and nothing else, Husband. Shall it be said in the tribe that Wi

was afraid to avenge the blood of his daughter upon
Henga ? "

" I know not, Wife, but I know also that if such
words are whispered they will not be true. It is of you and
Foh that I think, not of myself."

" Then go and seek an omen from the Ice-Gods,
Husband."

" I will go, Aaka, but do not blame me afterwards
if things happen awry."

" They will not happen awry," answered Aaka,
smiling for the first time since Foa died.

For she was sure that Wi would conquer Henga if
only he could be brought to fight him, and thus avenge
Foa and become chief in his place. Also she smiled
because, for reasons of which she did not speak, she was
sure also that a stone would fall from the crest of the
glacier at dawn when the sun struck upon the ice.

Thus it came about that on the following night Wi
the Hunter slipped from the village of the tribe and,
walking round the foot of the hill that ran down to the
beach on the east, scaled the cleft between the mountains
until he came to the base of the great glacier. The
wolves that were prowling round the place, still winter-
hungry because the spring was so late, scented him and
surrounded him with glaring eyes. But he, the Hunter,
was not afraid of wolves ; moreover woe had made his
heart fierce. So with a yell he charged at the biggest
of them, the captain of the troop, and drove his flint
spear into its throat ; then while it writhed upon the
spear, gnashing its red jaws, he dashed out its brains
with his stone axe, muttering,

" Thus shall Henga die ! Thus shall Henga die ! "

The wolves knew their master and sped away, all
save the father of them that lay dead. Wi dragged its
carcase to the top of a rock and left it there where the
rest could not reach it, purposing to skin it in the morning.

This done, he went on up the cold valley where no
beasts came, because here there was nothing to eat,

till he reached the face of the glacier, a mighty wall of backward sloping ice that gleamed faintly in the moon-light and filled the cleft from side to side, four hundred paces or more in width. When last he was here twelve moons gone, he had driven a stake of driftwood between two rocks and another stake five paces lower down, because of late it had seemed to him that the ice was marching forwards.

So it was, indeed, for the first stake was buried, and the cruel, crawling lip of the glacier had nearly reached the second. The gods were awake! The gods were marching towards the sea!

Wi shivered, not because of the cold, to which he was accustomed, but from fear, for this place was terrible to him. It was the House of the gods who dwelt there in the ice, the gods in whom he believed, who were always angry, and now he remembered that he had brought no offering to propitiate them. He went back to the place where he had killed the wolf and with diffi-culty, by aid of his sharp flint spear and stone axe, hacked off its head. Returning with this head he set the grizzly thing upon a stone at the foot of the glacier, muttering:

"It bleeds, and the gods love blood. Now I swear that if I can kill Henga I will give them his carcase, which is better than the head of a wolf."

Then he knelt down, as men have ever done from the beginning before that which they fear and worship, and began to pray after his rude fashion:

"O Mighty Ones," he said, "who have lived here since the beginning, and O Sleeper with a shape such as no man has ever seen, Wi throws out his spirit to you; hear ye the prayer of Wi and give him a sign. Henga the fierce and hideous, who kills his own children lest in a day to come they should slay him as he slew his father, rules the people and does evilly. The people groan, but according to the old law may not rebel, and to speak they are afraid. Henga would kill me, my little daughter Foa he has killed and her mother weeps. I, Wi, would fight Henga as I may do under the law but he is strong as the wild bull of the forest, and if he prevails, not only will he kill me. He will also take Aaka whom he covets, and will murder our son, Foh, and perhaps devour him. Therefore I am afraid to fight, for their sakes. Yet I would be revenged upon Henga and slay him, and live in the Cave and rule the people better, not devouring their food, but storing it up for them ; not taking the women, but leaving them to be the wives of those who have none. I have brought you an offering, O Gods, the head of a wolf fresh slain which bleeds, the best thing I have to give you ; and if I can kill Henga I will bring you a richer one, that of his dead body, because our fathers have always said that you love blood."

Wi paused, for he could think of nothing more to say ; then remembering that as yet he had made no request, went on :

" Show me what I must do, O Gods. Shall I challenge Henga in the old way and fight him openly for the rule of the tribe ? Or, since if I fear to do this I cannot stay here among the people, shall I fly away with Aaka and Foh and perhaps Pag the wise dwarf, the Wolf-man, who loves me, to seek another home beyond the woods, if we live to win through them ? Accept my offering and tell me, O Gods. If I must fight Henga, let a stone fall from the head of the ice, and if I must fly to save the lives of Aaka and Foh, let no stone fall. Here now I will wait till an hour after sunrise. Then if a stone falls, I will go down to challenge Henga ; and if it does not fall, I will give it out that I am about to challenge him and in the night I will slip away with Aaka and Foh, and Pag if he chooses, whereby you will lose worshippers, O Gods."

Pleased with this master argument, which had come as an inspiration, since he had never thought of it before, and sure that it would appeal to gods whose followers were few and who, therefore, could not afford to lose any of them, Wi ceased praying—a terrible exercise which tired him more than a whole day's hunting or fishing—

and remaining on his knees, stared at the face of the ice
in front of him. He knew nothing of the laws of Nature,
but he did know that heavy bodies, if once set in motion,
moved very fast down a hill, going quicker and quicker
as they came to its foot. Indeed, once he had killed a
bear by rolling a stone down on it, which overtook the
running beast with wonderful swiftness.

This being so, he began to marvel what would happen
if all that mighty mass of ice should move in good earnest
instead of at the rate of only a few hands'-breadths a year.
Well, he knew something of that also. For once when
he was in the woods he had seen an ice-child born, a
vast mass large as a mountain which suddenly rushed
down one of the western valleys into the sea, sending
foam flying as high as heaven. That hurt no one, except
perhaps some of the seal-people which were basking in
the bay, because there was no one to hurt. But if it
had been the great central glacier that thus moved and
gave birth, together with the other smaller glaciers to
the west, what would chance to the tribe upon the beach
beneath ? They would be killed, every one, and there
would be no people left in the world.

He did not call it the world, of course, since he knew
nothing of the world, but rather by some word that
meant " the place," that is, the few miles of beach and
wood and mountain over which he wandered. From a
great height he had seen other beaches and woods, also
mountains beyond a rocky barren plain, but to him
these were but a dreamland. At least no men and women
lived in them, because they had never heard their voices
or seen the smoke of their fires, such as the tribe made to
warm themselves by and for the cooking of their food.
It was true that there were stories that such people existed,
and Pag, the cunning dwarf, thought so. However, Wi,
being a man who dealt with facts, paid no heed to these
tales. There below him lived the only people in the
world, and if they were crushed all would be finished.

Well, if so, it would not matter very much, except in
the case of Aaka, and above all of Foh, his son, for of

other women he thought little; while the creatures that furnished food, the seals and the birds and the fish, especially the salmon that came up the stream in spring, and the speckled trout, would be happier if they were gone.

These speculations also tired him, a man of action who was only beginning to learn how to think. So he gave them up, as he had given up praying, and stared with his big, thoughtful eyes at the ice in front of him. The light was gathering now; very soon the sun should rise and he could see into the ice. Look! There were faces, grotesque faces, some of them vast, some tiny, that seemed to shift and change with the changes of the light and the play of the shadows. Doubtless they were those of the lesser gods, of whom probably there were a great number, all of them bad and cruel, and they were peering and mocking at him.

Moreover, beyond them, a dim outline, was the great Sleeper as he had always been, a mountain of a god with huge teeth and the curling nose much longer than the body of a man, and a head like a rock and ears as big as the sides of a hut, and a small cold eye that seemed to be fixed upon him, and behind all this, vanishing into the depths of the ice, an enormous body the height of three men standing on each other's heads, perhaps. There was a god indeed, and looking at him, Wi wondered whether one day he would awake and break out of the ice and come rushing down the mountain. That he might see him better, Wi rose from his knees and crept timidly to the face of the glacier to peer down a certain crevice in the ice. While he was thus engaged, the sun rose in a clear sky over the shoulder of the mountain, and shone with some warmth upon the glacier for the first time that spring, or rather early summer. Its rays penetrated the cleft in the ice, so that Wi saw more of the Sleeper than he had ever done.

Truly he was enormous; and, look, behind him was something like the figure of a man, of which he had often heard but never before seen so clearly. Or was it a

shadow ? Wi could not be sure, for just then a cloud
floated over the face of the sun and the figure vanished
He waited for the cloud to pass away, and well was it
for him that he did so, for just then a great rock, which
lay doubtless upon the extreme lip of the glacier, loosened
from its last hold by the warmth of the sun, came
thundering down the slope of the ice and, leaping over
Wi, fell upon the spot where he had just been standing,
making a hole in the frozen ground and crushing the
wolf's head to a pulp, after which, with mighty bounds,
it vanished towards the beach.

" The Sleeper has protected me," said Wi to himself
as he turned to look after the vanishing rock. " Had I
stayed where I was, now I should be as is that wolf's
head."

Then suddenly he remembered that this stone had
fallen in answer to his prayer, that it was the sign he
had sought, and removed himself swiftly, lest another
that he had not sought should follow after it.

When he had run a few paces down the frozen slope,
he came to a little bay hollowed in the mountain side,
and sat down, knowing that there he was safe from
falling stones. Confusedly he began to think. What
had he asked the gods ? Was it that he must fight
Henga if the stone fell, or that he must not fight him ?
Oh, now he remembered. It was that he must fight,
Aaka wished him to do, and a cold trembling shook
his limbs. To talk of fighting that raging giant was
easy enough, but to do it was another matter. Yet the
gods had spoken, and he dared not disobey the counsel
that he had sought. Moreover, by sparing his life from the
falling stone, surely they meant that he would conquer
Henga. Or perhaps they only meant that they wished
to see Henga tear him in pieces for their sport, for the
gods loved blood, and the gods were cruel. Moreover,
being evil themselves, would it not perhaps please them
to give victory to the evil man ?

As he could not answer these questions, Wi rose
and walked slowly towards the beach, reflecting that

probably he had seen his last of the glacier and the Ice-Gods who dwelt therein, he who was about to challenge Henga to fight to the death. Presently he drew near to the place where he had killed the wolf, and looking up, was astonished to see that someone was skinning the beast. Indeed, his fingers tightened upon the haft of his spear, for this was a crime against the hunter's law, that one should steal what another had slain. Then the head of the skinner appeared, and Wi smiled and loosened his grip of the spear. For this was no thief—this was Pag, his slave who loved him.

A strange-looking man was Pag, a large-headed, one-eyed dwarf, great-chested, long-armed, powerful, but with thick little legs not longer than those of a child of eight years; a monstrous, flat-nosed, big-mouthed creature, who yet always wore upon his scarred countenance a smiling, humorous air. It was told of Pag that when he was born, a long while before—for his youth had passed—he was so ugly that his mother had thrown him out into the woods, fearing that his father, who was absent killing seals further up the beach, should be angry with her for bearing such a son, and purposing to tell him that the child had been still-born.

As it chanced, when the father came back he went to search for the infant's bones, but in place of them found the little babe still living, though with one eye dashed out against a stone and its face much scarred. Yet, this being his first-born and because he was a man with a merciful heart, he brought it home into the hut and forced the mother to nurse it. This she did like one who is frightened, though why she was frightened she would not say, nor would his father ever tell where or how he had found Pag. Thus it came about that Pag did not die, but lived, and because of what his mother had done to him, always was a hater of women; one, too, who lived much in the forest, for which reason or for some other he was named "Wolf-man." Moreover, he grew up the cleverest of the tribe, for Nature, which had made him ugly and deformed, gave him more wits than the

rest of them, and a sharp tongue that he used to gibe
with at the women.

Therefore they hated him also, and made a plot
against him, and when there came a time of scarcity,
persuaded the Chief of the Tribe of that day, the father
of Henga, that Pag was the cause of ill-fortune. So
that chief drove Pag out to starve. But when Pag was
dying for lack of food Wi found him and brought him
to his hut where, although like the rest of her sex Aaka
loved him little, he remained as a slave. For this was the
law, that if any saved a life, that life belonged to him.
In truth, however, Pag was more than a slave, because
from the hour that Wi, braving the wrath of the women
who thought that they were rid of Pag and his gibes,
and perchance the anger of the chief, had rescued him
when he was starving in a season of bitter frost, Pag
loved him more than a woman loves her first-born, or
a young man his one-day bride.

Thenceforward he was Wi's shadow, ready to suffer
all things for him, ready to die for him, and even to refrain
from sharp words and jests about Aaka or any other
woman upon whom Wi looked with favour, though to do so
he must bite a hole in his tongue. So Pag loved Wi and
Wi loved Pag, for which reason Aaka, who was jealous-
hearted, came to hate him more than she had done at first.

There was trouble about this business of the saving
of the life of Pag by Wi after he had been driven out to
starve as an evil-eyed and scurrilous fellow, but when
the matter came before him, the chief, Henga's father,
a kindly-natured man, said that since Pag had twice
been thrown out and brought back again, it was evident
that the gods meant him to die in some other fashion.
Only now that Wi had taken him, Wi must feed him and
see that he hurt none. If he chose to keep a one-eyed
wolf, it was his own business, and that of no one else.

Shortly after this Henga killed his father and became
chief in his place, and the matter of Pag was forgotten.
So Pag stayed on with Wi, and was beloved of him and of
Wi's children, but hated of Aaka.

CHAPTER IV

THE TRIBE

"A GOOD pelt," said Pag, pointing to the wolf with his red flint knife, "for the spring being so late, this beast has not begun to shoot its hair. When I have brayed it as I know how, it will make a cloak for Foh. He needs one that is warm, even in the summer, for lately he has been coughing and spitting."

"Yes," answered Wi anxiously. "It has come upon him since ever he hid in the cold water because the black bear with the great teeth was after him, knowing that the beast hates water; for which," he added viciously, "I swear that I will kill that bear. Also he grieves for his sister, Foa."

"Aye, Wi," snarled Pag, his one eye flashing with hate, "Foh grieves, Aaka grieves, you grieve, and I, Pag the Wolf-man, grieve too. Oh, why did you make me come hunting with you that day when my heart was against it and, smelling evil, I wished to stop with Foa, whom Aaka let run off by herself—just because I told her that she should keep the girl at home?"

"It was the will of the gods, Pag," muttered Wi, turning his head away.

"The gods! What gods? I say it was the will of a brute with two legs, nay, of the great-toothed tiger himself of which our forefathers told, living in a man's skin; yes, of Henga himself, helped by Aaka's temper. Kill that man-tiger, Wi, and never mind the great black bear. Or if you cannot, let me. I know a woman who hates him because he has put her away and made her serve another who has her place, and I can make good poison, very good poison——"

"Nay, it is not lawful," said Wi, "and would bring a curse upon us. But it is lawful that I should kill him, and I will. I have been talking to the gods about it."

"Oh, that is where the wolf's head has gone—an offering, I see. And what did the gods say to you, Wi ? "

"They gave me a sign. A stone fell from the brow of the ice, as Aaka said that it would if I was to fight Henga. It nearly hit me, but I had moved nearer to the ice to look at the Sleeper, the greatest of the gods."

"I don't believe it is a god, Wi. I believe it is a beast of a sort we do not know, dead and frozen, and that the shadow behind it is a man that was hunting the beast when they both fell into the snow that turned to ice."

Wi stared at him, for this was indeed a new idea.

"How can that be, Pag, seeing that the Sleeper and the Shadow have always been there ? For our grandfathers knew them, and there is no such beast known. Also, except us there are no other men."

"Are you sure, Wi ? The place is big. If you go to the top of that hill you see other hills behind as far as the eye can look, and between them plains and forests ; also there is the sea and there may be beaches beyond the sea. Why, then, should there not be other men ? Did the gods make us alone ? Would they not make more to play with and to kill ? "

Wi shook his head at these revolutionary arguments, and Pag went on :

"As for the falling of the stone, it often happens when the heat of the sun melts the edge of the ice or makes it swell. And as for the groans and callings of the gods, does not ice crack when the frost is sharp, or when there is no frost at all and it begins to move of its own weight ? "

"Cease, Pag, cease," said Wi, stuffing his fingers into his ears ; "no longer will I listen to such mad words. If the gods hear them they will kill us."

"If the people hear them they may kill us, because they walk in fear of what they cannot see and would save themselves at the cost of others. But for the gods—that," and Pag snapped his fingers in the direction of the glacier, which, after all, is a very ancient gesture of contempt.

Wi was so overcome that he sat down upon a stone unable to answer, and that first of sceptics, Pag, went on :

" If I must have a god, who have found men quite bad enough to deal with without one above them more evil than they, I would choose the sun. The sun gives life ; when the sun shines everything grows and the creatures mate and the birds lay eggs and the seals come to bear their young and the flowers bloom. When there is no sun, but only frost and snow, then all these die or go away and it is hard to live, and the wolves and bears raven and eat men if they can catch them. Yes, the sun shall be my good god and the black frost my evil god."

Thus did Pag propound a new religion, which since then has been very popular in the world. Next, changing the subject rapidly, as do children and savages, he asked :

" What of Henga, Wi ? Are you going to challenge him to fight ? "

" Yes," said Wi fiercely, " this very day."

" May you be victorious ! May you kill him, thus and thus," and Pag jabbed his flint knife into the stomach of the dead wolf. " Yet," he added reflectively, " it is a big business. There has been no such man as Henga among our people that I have heard of. Although Ngae, who calls himself a magician, is without doubt a cheat and a liar, I think he is right when he says that Henga's mother made a mistake. She meant to have twins but they got mixed up together, and Henga came instead. Otherwise why is he double-jointed ; why has he two rows of teeth, one behind the other, and why is he twice the size of any other man and more than twice as wicked ? Still, without doubt he is a man and not what you call a god, since he grows fat and heavy and his hair is beginning to turn grey. Therefore he can be killed if anyone is strong enough to break in that thick skull of his. I should like to try poison on him, but

you say that I must not. Well, I will think the matter
over and we will talk again before you fight. Meanwhile, as there may be no chance afterwards when
chattering women are about, give me your commands,
Wi, as to what is to be done if Henga kills you. I suppose that you do not wish him to take Aaka, as he desires
to do, or Foh, that he may make a nothing of him and
keep him as a slave."

"I do not," said Wi.

"Then please direct me to kill them, or to see that
they kill themselves, never mind how."

"I do so direct you, Pag."

"Good; and what are your wishes as regards myself?"

"I don't know," answered Wi wearily; "do what
you will. I thank you and wish you well."

Pag lifted a corner of the skin which he had half
dragged off the wolf and wiped his one eye, saying:

"You are not kind to me, Wi. Although I am called
the Twice-thrown-out, and the Wolf-man, and the
Hideous, and the Barbed-tongued, still I have served
you well. Now when I ask you what I must do after
you are dead and I have killed your family, you do not
say 'Why, follow me, of course, and look for me in the
darkness, and if you find nothing it will be because
there is nothing to find,' as you would have done did you
love me. No, you say, 'Do as you will. What is it
to me?' Yet I shall come with Foh and Aaka, although
of course I must be a little behind them, because it will
take time to fulfil your orders, and afterwards to do what
is necessary to myself. Still, wait for me an hour,
even if Aaka is angry, as she will be."

"So you think you would find me somewhere, you
who do not believe in the gods?" said Wi, staring at him
with his big, melancholy eyes.

"Yes, Wi, I think that, though I don't know why I
think it. I think that the lover always finds the loved,
and that therefore you will find Foa and I shall find
you. Also I think that if I am wrong it doesn't matter,
for I shall never know that I was wrong. But as for

those gods who dwell in the ice, *piff*!" and again Pag snapped his fingers in the direction of the glacier and went on with the skinning of the wolf.

Presently this was finished and he threw the gory hide, flesh side down, over his broad shoulders, to keep it stretched, as he said, for a little blood did not trouble him. Then without more talk the pair walked down to the beach, the squat, misshapen Pag waddling on his short legs after the burly, swift-moving Wi.

Here, straggling over a great extent of shore, were a number of rough shelters not unlike the Indian wigwams of our own age, or those rude huts that are built by the Australian savages. Round these huts wandered or crouched some sharp-nosed, surly-looking, long-coated creatures, very powerful of build, that a modern man would have taken for wolves rather than dogs. Wolves their progenitors had been, though how long before it was impossible to say. Now, however, they were tamed, more or less, and the most valued possession of the tribe, which by their aid kept at bay the true, wild wolves and the other savage beasts that haunted the beach and the woods.

When these animals caught sight of Wi and Pag they rushed at them, open-mouthed and growling fiercely till, getting their wind, of a sudden they became gentle and for the most part returned to the huts whence they had come. Two or three of them, however, which were his especial property and lived in his hut, leapt up at Wi, wagging their tails and striving to lick his hand or face. He patted one upon the head, the great hound Yow that he loved, which was his guard and companion when out hunting, whereon the other two in their fierce jealousy instantly flew at its throat ; nor did Pag find it easy to separate them.

The noise of the worrying attracted the tribe, many of whom appeared from out of the huts or elsewhere to discover its cause. They were wild-looking people, all dark-haired like Wi, though he was taller and bigger than most of them, very like each other in countenance, moreover, as a result of interbreeding for an unknown number of generations. In fact, a stranger would have found difficulty in distinguishing them apart except by their ages, but as no stranger ever came to the home of the Beach People, this did not matter.

The greater number also were coarse-faced and crushed-looking, as though they were well acquainted with the extremities of cruelty and hardship, which was indeed the case ; like Wi, however, some of them had fine eyes, but even these were furtive and terror-stricken. Of children there were not many, for reasons that have been told, and these hung together in a little group, perhaps to keep out of the way of blows when their elders appeared, or in some instances wandered round the fires of driftwood on which food was cooking, bits of seal meat for the most part, toasting upon sticks—for the tribe were not advanced enough in the domestic arts to possess cooking vessels—as though, like the dogs, they hoped to snatch a mouthful when no one saw them. Only a few of the smallest of these children sat about upon the sand playing with sticks or shells which they used as toys. Many of the women seemed even more depressed than the men, which was not strange as, like slaves, it was their lot to do the hard work and to wait hand and foot upon their masters, those who had taken them as wives either by capture or in exchange for other women, or for such goods as this people possessed and valued—bone fish-hooks, flint weapons, fibre rope and dressed skins.

Through this collection of primitive humanity—our forebears, be it remembered—Wi, preceded by Pag, marched towards his own hut, a large one more neatly constructed than most, of fir poles from the woods tied together at the top, tent-shaped and covered with tanned skins laid over a roof of dried ferns and seaweed arranged so as to keep out the cold. Obviously he was a person held in respect for the men made way for him, though some of the short little women stood staring at him with sympathy in their eyes, for they remembered that

a few days ago Henga had stolen and killed his daughter.
One of them mentioned this to another, who, being
elderly and cynical, replied as soon as Wi was out
of hearing :

" What does it matter ? It will be a mouth less to
feed next winter, and who can wish to bring up daughters
to be what we are ? "

Some of the younger females—there did not seem
to be any girls, they were all either children or women
—clustered about Pag and,unable to retain their curiosity,
questioned him as to the wolf-skin on his shoulders.
Living up to his reputation, he replied by telling them
to mind their own business and get to their work instead
of standing idle, whereon they jeered at him, giving him
ugly names and calling attention to his deformity or
making faces until he set one of the dogs at them, whereon
they ran away.

They came to Wi's hut. As they approached, the
hide curtain which hung over the front opening was thrust
aside and out rushed a lad of some ten years of age, a
handsome boy though rather thin, with a bright, vivacious
face, very different in appearance to others of the Tribe
of the same age. Foh, for it was he, flung himself into
his father's arms, saying :

" My mother made me eat in the hut because the wind
is so cold and I still cough, but I heard your step, also
that of Pag who lumbers along like a seal on its flippers.
Where have you been, Father ? When I woke up this
morning I could not find you."

" Near to the Gods' House, Son," answered Wi,
nodding towards the glacier as he kissed him back.

At this moment Foh's quick glance fell upon the big
wolf-skin which hung from Pag's shoulders to the ground,
and still dripped blood.

" Where did you get that ? " he cried. " What a
beautiful skin ! A wolf indeed, a father of wolves.
Did you kill it, Pag ? "

" No, Foh, I flayed it. Learn to take note. Look at
your father's spear. Is it not red ? "

" So is your knife, Pag, and so are you down to the heels. How was I to know which of you slew this great beast when both are so brave ? What are you going to do with the skin ? "

" Bray it into a cloak for you, Foh ; very cunningly, with the claws left on the pads, but polished so that they will shine in front when you tie it about you."

" Good. Cure it quickly, Pag, for it will be warm and these winds are cold. Come into the hut, Father, where your food is waiting, and tell us how you killed the wolf," and seizing Wi by the hand, the boy dragged him between the skin curtains while Pag and the dogs retreated to some shelter behind, which the dwarf had constructed for himself.

The place within was quite spacious, sixteen feet long perhaps, by about twelve in breadth. In the centre of it on a hearth of clay burned a wood fire, the smoke of which escaped through a hole in the roof though, the morning being still, much hung about, making the air thick and pungent ; but this Wi, being accustomed to it, did not notice.

On the further side of the fire, attending to the grilling of strips of flesh set upon pointed sticks, stood Aaka, Wi's wife, clothed in a kirtle of sealskins fastened beneath her breast, for here, the place being warm, she wore no cloak. She was a finely-built woman of about thirty years of age, with masses of black hair that hung to her middle, clean and well-kept hair arranged in four tresses, each of which was tied at the end with fibres of grass or sinew. Her skin was whiter than that of most of her race ; indeed quite white, except where it was tanned by exposure to the weather ; her face, though slightly broad, was handsome and fine-featured, if somewhat querulous, and like the rest of her people she had large and melancholy dark eyes.

As Wi entered she threw a curious, searching glance at him, as though to read his mind, then smiled in rather a forced fashion and drew forward a block of wood. Indeed there was nothing else for him to sit on, for

furniture, even in its simplest forms, was not known in
the tribe. Sometimes a thick flat stone was used as a
table, or a divided stick for a fork, but beyond such
expedients the tribe had not advanced. Thus their
beds consisted of piles of dried seaweed thrown upon
the floor of the hut and covered with skins of one sort
or another, and their lamps were made of large shells
filled with seal-oil in which floated a wick of moss.

Wi sat down on the log, and Aaka, taking one of the
sticks on which was spitted a great lump of fizzling
seal-meat not too well cooked and somewhat blackened
by the smoke, handed it to him and stood by dutifully,
while he devoured it in a fashion which we should not
have considered elegant.

Then it was that Foh, rather shyly, drew out from
some hiding-place a little parcel wrapped in a leaf, which
he opened and set upon the ground. It contained
desiccated and somewhat sandy brine, or rather its
deposit, that the lad with much care had scraped
off the rocks of a pool from which the sea-water
had evaporated. Once Wi by accident had mingled
some of this dried brine with his food and found
that thereby its taste was enormously improved. Thus
he became the discoverer of salt among the people, the
rest of whom, however, looked on it as a luxurious
innovation which it was scarcely right to use. But
Wi, being more advanced, did use it, and it was Foh's
business to collect the stuff, as it had been that of his
sister, Foa. Indeed, it was while she was thus engaged,
far away and alone, that Henga the Chief had kidnapped
the poor child.

Remembering this, Wi thrust aside the leaf, then noting
the pained expression of the boy's face at the refusal of
his gift, drew it back again and dipped the meat into its
contents. When Wi had consumed all he wanted of the
flesh, he signed to Aaka and Foh to eat the rest, which
they did hungrily, having touched nothing since the
yesterday; for it was not lawful that the family should
eat until its head had taken his fill. Lastly, by way of

dessert, Wi chewed a lump of sun-dried stockfish upon which no modern teeth could have even made a mark, for it was as hard as stone, and by way of a savoury a handful or so of prawns that Foh caught among the rocks and Aaka had cooked in the ashes.

The feast finished, Wi bade Foh bear the remnants to Pag in his shelter without, and stay with him till he was called. Then he drank a quantity of spring water which Aaka kept stored in big shells and in a stone, her most valued possession, hollowed to the shape of a pot by the action of ice, or the constant grinding of other stones at the bottom of the sea. This he did because there was nothing else, though at certain times of the year Aaka made a kind of tea by boiling a herb she knew of in a shell, a potion that all of them loved both for its warmth and its stimulating properties. This herb, however, only grew in the autumn, and it had never occurred to them to store it and use it dry. Therefore of necessity their use of the first intoxicant was limited, which was perhaps as well.

Having drunk, he closed the skins that hung over the hut entrance, pinning them together with a bond that passed through the loops in the hide, and sat down again upon his log.

" What said the gods ? " asked Aaka quickly. " Did they answer your prayer ? "

" Woman, they did. At sunrise a rock fell from the crest of the ice-field and crushed my offering, so that the ice took it to itself."

" What offering ? "

" The head of a wolf that I slew as I went up the valley."

Aaka brooded awhile, then said,

" My heart tells me that the omen is good. Henga is that wolf, and as you slew the wolf, so shall you slay Henga. Did I hear that its hide is to be a cloak for Foh ? If so, the omen is good also, since one day the rule of Henga shall descend to Foh. At least, if you kill Henga, Foh shall live and not die, as Foa died "

An expression of joy spread over Wi's face as he listened.

"Your words give me strength," he said, "and now I go out to summon the people and to tell them that I am about to challenge Henga to fight to the death."

"Go," she said, "and hear me, my man. Fight you without fear, for if my rede be wrong and Henga the Mighty should kill you, what of it? Soon we die, all of us, for the most part slowly by hunger or otherwise, but death at the hands of Henga will be swift. And if you die, then we will die soon, very soon Pag will see to it, and so we shall be together again."

"Together again! Together where, Wife?" he asked, staring at her curiously.

A kind of veil seemed to fall over Aaka's face, that is, her expression changed entirely, for it grew blank and wooden, secret also, like to the faces of all her sisters of the tribe.

"I don't know," she answered roughly. "Together in the light, or together in the dark, or together with the Ice-Gods—who can tell? At least together somewhere. You shake your head. You have been talking to that hater of the gods and changeling, Pag, who really is a wolf, not a man, and hunts with the wolves at night, which is why he is always so fat in winter when others starve."

Here Wi laughed incredulously, saying:

"If so, he is a wolf that loves us; I would that we had more such wolves."

"Oh, you mock, as all men do. But we women see further and we are sure that Pag is a wolf by night, if a dwarf by day. For if any try to injure him, are they not taken by wolves? Did not wolves eat his father, and were not the leaders of those women who caused him to be driven forth to starve when there was such scarcity that even the wolves fled far away, afterwards taken by wolves, they or their children?"

Then, as though she thought she had said too much, Aaka added,

"Yet all this may be but a tale spread from mouth

to mouth, because we women hate Pag, who mocks us.
At least he believes in naught, and would teach you to
do the same, and already you begin to walk in his footsteps. Yet if you hold that we live no more after our
breath leaves us, tell me one thing. Why, when you buried
Foa yonder, did you set food with her in the hole, and her
necklace of shells and the stone ball that she played
with and the tame bird she had, after you had killed
it, and her winter cloak, and the doll you made for her
of pinewood last year? Of what good would these
things be to her bones? Was it not because you thought
that they might be of use to her elsewhere, as the dried
fish and the water might serve to feed her?"

Here she ceased and stared at him.

"Sorrow makes you mad," said Wi, very gently, for
he was moved by her words, "as it makes me mad, but
in another fashion. For the rest, I do not know why
I did thus; perhaps it was because I wished to see those
things no more, perhaps because it is a custom to bury
with the dead what they loved when they were alive."

Then he turned and left the hut. Aaka watched him
go, muttering to herself:

"He is right. I am mad with grief for Foa and with
fear for Foh; for it is the children that we women love,
yes, more than the man who begat them, and if I
thought that I should never find her again, then I would
die at once and have done. Meanwhile, I live on to see
Wi dash out the brains of Henga, or if he is killed, to
help Pag to poison him. They say that Pag is a wolf,
but, though I hate him of whom Wi thinks too much,
what care I whether he be wolf or monster? At least
he loves Wi and our children and will help me to be
revenged on Henga."

Presently she heard the wild-bull horn that served
the tribe as a trumpet being blown and knew that
Wini-wini, he who was called the Shudderer because he
shook like a jelly-fish even if not frightened, which was
seldom, was summoning the people that they might talk
together, or hear news. Guessing what that news would

be, Aaka threw her skin cloak about her and followed the
sound of the horn to the place of assembly.

Here on a flat piece of ground at a distance from the
huts that lay about two hundred paces from a cliff-like
spur of the mountain, all the people, men, women, and
children, except a few who were in childbed or too sick
or old to move, were gathering together. As they walked
or ran they chattered excitedly, delighted that something
was happening to break the terrible sameness of their
lives, and now and again pointing towards the mouth
of the great cave that appeared in the stone of the cliff
opposite to the meeting-place. In this cave dwelt Henga,
for by right from time immemorial it had been the home
of the chiefs of the tribe, which none might enter save
by permission, a sacred place like to the palaces of modern
times.

Aaka walked on, feeling that she was being watched
by the others but taking no heed, for she knew the
reason. She was Wi's woman, and the rumour had run
round that Wi the Strong, Wi the Great Hunter, Wi
whose little daughter had been murdered, was about to
do something strange, though what it might be none was
sure. All of them longed to ask Aaka, but there was
something in her eye that forbade them, for she was cold
and stately and they feared her a little. So she went
on unmolested, looking for Foh of whom presently she
caught sight walking in the company of Pag, who still
had the reeking wolf-skin on his shoulders, of which, as
he was so short, the tail dragged along the ground. She
noted that as he advanced the people made way for him,
not from reverence or love, but because they feared him
and his evil eye.

" Look," said one woman to another in her hearing,
" there goes he who hates us, the spear-tongued dwarf."

" Aye," answered the other, " he is in such haste that
he has forgotten to take off the wolf's hide he hunted
in last night. Have you heard that Buk's wife has
lost her little child of three ? It is said that the bears
took it, but perhaps yonder wolf-man knows better."

" Yet Foh does not fear him. Look, he holds his hand and laughs."

" No, because——" here suddenly the woman caught sight of Aaka and was silent.

I wonder, reflected Aaka, whether we women hate Pag because he is ugly and hates us, or because he is cleverer than we are and pierces us with his tongue. I wonder also why they all think he is half a wolf. I suppose it is because he hunts with Wi ; for how can he be both a man and a wolf ? At least I too believe that report speaks truth and that he and the wolves have dealings together. Or perhaps he puts the tale about that all may fear him.

She came to the meeting-ground and took her stand near to Foh and Pag, among the crowd which stood or sat in a ring about an open space of ground, where some-times the tribe danced when they had plenty of food and the weather was warm, or took counsel, or watched the young men fight and wrestle for the prize of a girl they coveted.

At the head of the ring, which was oblong in shape rather than round, standing about Wini-wini the Shudderer, who from time to time still blew blasts upon his horn, were some of the leaders of the tribe, among them old Turi the Avaricious, the Hoarder of Food, who was always fat whoever grew thin ; and Pitokiti the Unlucky, with whom everything went wrong, whose fish always turned rotten, whose women deserted him, whose children died and whose net was sure to break, so that he must be supported by others for fear lest he should die and pass on his ill-luck to them who neglected him ; and Whaka, the Bird of Ill-omen, the lean-faced one who was always howling of misfortunes to come ; and Hou the Unstable, a feather blown by the wind, who was never of the same mind two days together ; and Rahi the Rich, who traded in stone axes and fish-hooks and thus lived well without work ; and Hotoa, the great-bellied and slow-speeched, who never gave his word as to a matter until he knew how it was settled, and then shouted it loudly and looked wise ; and Taren, she who hid with Ngae, the Priest of the Ice-Gods and the magician who told fortunes with shells, and only came out when there was evil in the wind.

Lastly there was Moananga the brave, Wi's younger brother, the great fighter who had fought six men to win and keep Tana the sweet and loving, the fairest woman of the Tribe, and killed two of them who strove to steal her by force. He was a round-eyed man with a laughing face, quick to anger but good-tempered, and after Wi the Hunter he who stood first amongst the people. Moreover, he loved Wi and clung to him, so that the two were as one, for which reason Henga the Chief hated them both and thought that they were too strong for him.

All these were talking with their heads close together, till presently appeared Wi, straight, strong and stern, at whose coming they grew silent. He looked round at them, then said,

"I have words."

"We are listening," replied Moananga.

"Hearken," went on Wi. "Is there not a law that any man of the tribe may challenge the Chief of the Tribe to fight, and if he can kill him, may take his place ? "

"There is such a law," said Urk the old wizard, he who made charms for women and brewed love potions, and in winter told stories of what had happened long ago before his grandfather's grandfather was born, very strange stories, some of them. "Twice it has chanced in my day, the second time when Henga challenged and killed his own father and took the cave."

"Yes," added Whaka, the Bird of Ill-omen, " but if he who challenges is defeated, not only is he killed, his family is killed also," here he glanced at Aaka and Foh, " and perhaps his friend or brother," here he looked at Moananga. "Yes, without doubt that is the law. The cave only belongs to the chief while he can defend it with his hands. If another rises who is stronger than he, he may take the cave, and the women, also the

children if there are any, and kill them or make them
slaves, until his strength begins to fail him and he in
turn is killed by some mightier man."

" I know it," said Wi. " Hearken again. Henga has
done me wrong ; he stole and murdered my daughter,
Foa. Therefore I would kill him. Also he rules the
tribe cruelly. No man's wife, or daughter, or robe,
or food is safe from him. His wickedness makes the
gods angry. Why is it that the summers have turned
cold and the spring does not come ? I say it is because
of the wickedness of Henga. Therefore I would kill
him and take the cave, and rule well and gently so that
every man may have plenty of food in his hut and sleep
safe at night. What say you ? "

Now Wini-wini the Shudderer spoke, shaking in all
his limbs :

" We say that you must do what you will, Wi, but that
we will not meddle in the matter. If we do, when you are
killed, as you will be—for Henga is mightier than you,
yes, he is the tiger, he is the bull of the woods, he is the
roaring bear—then he will kill us also. Do what you
will, but do it alone We turn our backs on you, we put
our hands before our eyes and see nothing."

Pag spat upon the ground and said in his low, growling
voice that seemed to come out of his stomach :

" I think that you will see something one night when
the stars are shining. I think, Wini-wini, that one night
you will meet that which will make you shudder yourself
to pieces."

" It is the Wolf-man," exclaimed Wini-wini. " Protect
me ! Why should the Wolf-man threaten me when we
are gathered to talk ? "

Nobody answered, because if some were afraid of
Pag, all, down to the most miserable slave-woman,
despised Wini-wini.

" Take no heed of his words, Brother," said Moananga
the happy-faced. " I will go up with you to the cave-
mouth when you challenge Henga, and so I think will
many others to be witnesses of the challenge, according

to the custom of our fathers. Let those stop behind who will. You will know what to think of them when you are Chief and sit in the cave."

"It is well," said Wi. "Let us go at once."

CHAPTER V

THE AXE THAT PAG MADE

THIS matter being settled, there followed a jabber of argument as to the method of conveying the challenge of Wi to Henga the Chief. Urk the Old was consulted as to precedents and made a long speech in which he contradicted himself several times. Hou the Unstable sprang up at length and said that he was not afraid and would be the leader. Suddenly, however, he changed his mind, declaring he remembered that this office by right belonged to Wini-wini the Horn-blower, who must sound three blasts at the mouth of the cave to summon the chief. To this all assented with a shout, perhaps because there was a sense of humour even in their primitive minds, and, protest as he would, Wini-wini was thrust forward with his horn.

Then the procession started, Wini-wini going first, followed close behind by Pag in the bleeding wolf-skin, who, from time to time, pricked him in the back with his sharp flint knife to keep him straight. Next came Wi himself with his brother Moananga, and after these the elders and the rest of the people. At least they started thus to cover the three hundred paces or so which lay between them and the cliff, but before they reached the cave most of them lagged behind, so that they were dotted in a long line reaching from the meeting-place to its entrance.

Indeed, here remained only Wini-wini, who could not escape from Pag, Wi, Moananga, and at a little distance behind, Whaka, the Bird of Ill-omen, prophesying evil in a ceaseless stream of words. At his side, too, was Aaka walking boldly and looking down at his withered shape with scorn. Of the remainder the bravest, drawn by curiosity, kept within hearing, but the rest stayed at a distance, or hid themselves.

"Blow!" growled Pag to Wini-wini and, as he still hesitated, pricked him in the back with his knife.

Then Wini-wini blew a quavering blast.

"Blow again louder," said Pag.

Wini-wini set the horn to his lips, but before a sound came out of it a large stone hurled from the cave struck him in the middle and down he went, writhing and gasping.

"Now you have something to shake for," said Pag as he waddled to one side lest another stone should follow.

None came, but out of the cave with a roar rushed a huge, hairy, black-browed fellow waving a great wooden club—Henga himself. He was a mighty, thick-limbed man of about forty years of age, with a chest like a bull, a big head from which long black hair fell upon his shoulders, and a wide, thick-lipped mouth whence projected yellow, tusk-like teeth. From his shoulders, in token of his rank, hung the hide of a cave-tiger and round his neck was a collar made from its claws and teeth.

"Who sends that dog to waken me from my rest?" he shouted in his bellowing voice, and pointed with the club to Wini-wini twisting on the ground.

"I do," answered Wi, "I and all the people. I, Wi, whose child you murdered, come to challenge you, the Chief, to fight me for the rule of the tribe, as you must do according to the law, in the presence of the tribe."

Henga ceased from his shouting and glared at him.

"Is it so?" he asked in a quiet voice that had in it a hiss of hate. "Know that I hoped that you would come on this errand and that is why I killed your brat to give you courage, as I will kill the other that remains to you," and he glanced at the boy Foh, who stood at a distance. "You have troubled me for long, Wi, with your talk and threats against me, of which I am hungry to make an end. Now tell me, when does it please the people to see me break your bones?"

"When the sun is within an hour of its setting, Henga, for I have a fancy to sleep in the cave to-night as Chief of the people," answered Wi quietly.

Henga glowered at him, gnawing at his lip, then said:

"So be it, dog. I shall be ready at the meeting-place an hour before the sun sets For the rest it is Aaka who will sleep in the cave to-night, not you, who I think will sleep in the bellies of the wolves. Now begone, for a salmon has been sent to me, the first of the year, and I, who love salmon, would cook and eat it."

Then Aaka spoke, saying,

"Eat well, devil-man who murders children, for I, the mother, tell you that it shall be your last meal."

Laughing hoarsely, Henga went back into the cave, and Wi and all the others slipped away.

"Who gave Henga the salmon?" asked Moananga idly as one who would say something.

"I did," answered Pag, who was walking beside him, but out of earshot of Wi. "I caught it last night in a net and sent it to him, or rather, caused it to be laid on a stone by the mouth of the cave."

"What for?" asked Moananga.

"Because Henga is greedy over salmon, especially the first of the year. He will eat the whole fish and be heavy when it comes to fighting."

"That is clever; I should never have thought of that," said Moananga. "But how did you know that Wi was going to challenge Henga?"

"I did not know, nor did Wi. Yet I guessed it because Aaka sent him to consult the gods. When a woman sends a man to seek a sign from the gods, that sign will always be the one she wishes. So at least she will tell him and he will believe."

"That is cleverer still," said Moananga, staring at the dwarf with his round eyes. "But why does Aaka wish Wi to fight Henga?"

"For two reasons. First because she would revenge the killing of her child, and secondly because she thinks that Wi is the better man, so that presently she will be the wife of the Chief of the Tribe. Still, she is not sure about this, because she has made a plan, should Wi be defeated, that I must kill her and Foh at once, which I shall do before I kill myself. Or perhaps I shall not kill myself, at any rate until I have tried to kill Henga."

"Would you then be Chief of the Tribe, Wolf-man ? " asked Moananga, astonished.

"Perhaps, for a little while ; for do not those who have been spat upon and reviled always wish to rule the spitters and the revilers ? Yet I will tell you, who are Wi's brother and love him, that if he dies I, who love him better and love no one else, save perhaps Foh because he is his son, shall not live long after him. No, then I should pass on the chieftainship to you, Moananga, and be seen no more, though perhaps in the after years you might hear me at night howling round the huts in winter —with the wolves, Moananga, to which fools say I belong."

Moananga stared again at this sinister dwarf whose talk frightened him. Then, that he might talk of something else, asked him,

"Which of these two do you think will conquer, Pag ? "

Pag stopped and pointed to the sea. At some distance from the shore a mighty struggle was in progress between a thrasher shark and a whale. The terrible shark had driven the whale into shallow water, where it floundered, unable to escape by sounding. Now the sea-wolf, as it is called, was leaping high into the air, and each time it fell it smote the whale upon the head with its awful sword-like tail, blow upon blow that echoed far and wide. The whale rolled in agony, beating the water to a foam with its giant flukes, but for all its size and bulk could do nothing. Presently it began to gasp and opened its great mouth, whereon the thrasher, darting between its jaws, seized its tongue and tore it out. Then the whale rolled over and began to bleed to death

"Look," said Pag. "There is Henga the huge and

mighty, and there is Wi the nimble, and Wi wins the day
and will feed his fill upon whale's flesh, he and his friends.
That is my answer and the omen is very good. Now I
go to make Wi ready for this battle."

When Pag reached the hut he sent Aaka and Foh out
of it, leaving himself alone with Wi. Then causing Wi
to strip off his cloak, he made him lie down and rubbed
him all over with seal-oil. Also with a sharp flint and
a shell ground to a fine edge, slowly and painfully he cut
his hair short, so short that it could give no hold to Henga's
hand, and this done greased what remained of it with the
seal-oil. Next he bade Wi sleep awhile and left the hut,
taking with him Wi's stone axe, also his spear, that with
which he had killed the wolf, and his flint knife that
was hafted with two flat pieces of ivory rubbed down
from a walrus tusk and lashed on to the end of the flint.

Outside the hut he met Aaka, who was wandering to
and fro in an ill-humour. She made as though she
would pass him, setting her face towards the hut.

" Nay," said Pag, " you do not enter."

" Why not ? " she asked.

" Because Wi rests and must not be disturbed."

" So a misshapen monster, a wolf-man, hated of all,
who lives on bounty, may enter my husband's hut, when
I, the wife, may not," she said furiously.

" Yes, for presently he goes upon a man's business,
namely, to kill his enemy or be killed of him, and it is
best that no woman should come near to him till the thing
is ended."

" You say that because you hate women, who will
not look on you, Pag."

" I say it because women take away the strength of
men and suck out their courage and disturb them with
weak words."

She leapt to one side as though to rush past him, but
Pag leapt also, lifting the spear in his hand, whereon she
stopped, for she feared the dwarf.

" Listen," he said. " You do ill to reproach me,
Aaka, who am your best friend. Still, I do not blame

you overmuch, for I know the reason of your hate. You
are jealous of me because Wi loves me more than he
does you, as does Foh, if in another fashion."

"Loves you, you abortion, you hideous one!" she
gasped.

"Yes, Aaka, who, it seems, do not know that there
are different sorts of love; that of the man for the woman
which comes and goes, and that of man for man which
changes not. I say that you are jealous. Only this day
I told Wi that if he had not taken me with him hunting
but had left me to watch Foa, she would not have been
stolen and killed by yonder cave-dweller. It was a
lie. I could have refused to go hunting with Wi and
he would have let me be, who knows that always I have
a reason for what I do. I went with him because of words
that you had spoken which you will remember well. I
told you that Foa was in danger from Henga the cave-
dweller and that I had best watch her, and you said that
no girl-child of yours should be watched by a wolf's cub
and that you would take care of her yourself, which you
did not do. Therefore because you goaded me I went
hunting and Foa was taken and killed."

Now Aaka hung her head, answering nothing, for
she knew that his words were true.

"Let that be," went on Pag; "the dead are dead, and
well dead, perchance. Now, although I speak wisely to
you, you would thwart me again and go in to awaken
Wi, even when I tell you that to do so may turn the fight
against him and bring about your death, and Foh's as
well."

"Does Wi sleep?" asked Aaka, weakening a little

"I think he sleeps, because I bade him, and in such
matters he obeys me. Also last night he slept little. But
the road is open and I have said my say. Go and look
for yourself. Go wake him and ask if he is asleep and
wear him out with your woman's talk, and tell him
what dreams have come to you about Foa and the gods,
and thus make him ready to fight the devil-giant, Henga."

"I go not," she said, stamping her foot, "lest if Wi

fall, your poisoned tongue should put it about that I
was the cause of his death. But know, misshapen,
outcast Wolf-man, that should he conquer and live, he
must choose between you and me, for if he takes you
to dwell with him in the cave, then I stay here in the hut."

Pag laughed deep down in his throat after his fashion,
and answered,

" That would be peace indeed, were it not, as I remember, that if Henga dies he leaves behind him sundry fair
women who also live in the cave and doubtless will be
hard to dislodge. Still, in this matter, as in all others,
do what you will. Only I tell you, Aaka, that you do
ill to revile me, whom you may need presently to help
you out of the world."

Then ceasing from his mockery and the rolling of his
great head from side to side as was his habit when he
mocked, he looked her in the face with his one bright eye
with which folk said he could see in the dark like a wild-
cat, and said quietly :

" Why do you reproach me because I am hideous ?
Did I make my own shape or was it the gift of a woman ?
Did I throw away my right eye or did a woman dash it
out against a stone ? Afterwards, did I leave the camp
to starve in the winter, or did women drive me out because
I told them the truth ? Why are you angry with me
because I love Wi who saved me from the cruelty of
women, and your son Foh whom Wi caused to be ? Why
will you not understand that although I be misshapen,
yet I have more wisdom than all the rest of you and a
larger heart, and that the wisdom and the heart are the
servants of Wi and those with whom he has to do ? Why
should you be jealous of me ? "

" Would you know, Pag ? Because you speak truth.
Because you are more to Wi than I am—yes, and to
Foh also. When one comes whom Wi loves better than
he does you, then we may be friends again, but not
before."

" That may happen," said Pag reflectively. " Now
trouble me no more, who go to make ready Wi's weapons

for this fight and who have no time to waste. Go now
to the hut—as I have said, the way is open—and tell
your own tale to Wi."

Aaka hesitated, then she said,

" Nay, I come to help you with the weapons, for my
fingers are defter than yours. Let there be peace between
us for an hour, or gibe on if you will and I will not answer."

Again Pag laughed his great laugh, saying,

" Women are strange, so strange that even I cannot
weigh or measure them. Come on ! Come on, the edges
of the spear and axe need rubbing and the lashings are
worn."

For a while did Pag and Aaka, with the lad Foh to
help them, fetching and carrying or holding hide strips,
labour at the simple weapons of Wi, pointing the spear
and grinding the edge of the axe. When it was as sharp
as they could make it, Pag weighed the thing in his hand
and cast it down with a curse.

" It is too light," he said. " What chance has this
toy against the club of Henga ? "

Then he rose and ran to his hovel at the back of the
hut, whence he returned bearing in his hand a glittering
lump fashioned to the shape of an axe.

" See here," he said. " This is not much larger, yet
it has thrice the weight. I found it on the mountain
side, one of many shattered fragments, and last winter
working by the light of seal-oil, I fashioned it."

Aaka took it in her hand, which it bore to the ground,
so heavy was it. Then she felt its edge, which was sharper
than that of new-flaked flint, and asked what it was.

" I don't know," answered Pag. " Outside it looks
like stone that has been in hot fire, but see, within it
shines. Also it is so hard that I could only work it with
another piece of the same stone, hammering it after it
had lain in fire until it turned red, and polishing it with
fine sand and water."

Here it may be stated that although he knew it not,
this substance was meteoric iron that had fallen from
heaven, and that Pag by the light of nature had become

one of the first blacksmiths. When, finding that he could not touch it otherwise because of its hardness, he thrust that lump into a hot fire until it turned red, and beat it upon a stone with another lump, he learned the use of iron and thus took one of mankind's earliest and greatest steps forward.

" It will not break ? " said Aaka doubtfully.

" No," answered Pag, " I have tried. The blow that shatters the best stone axe leaves it unmarked. It will not break. But that which it hits will break. I made it for myself, but Wi shall have it. Now help me."

Then he produced the handle that, like the blade, was of a new sort, being fashioned with infinite patience and labour from the solid lower leg-bone of a gigantic deer that he had found, blackened and half-fossilised, when digging in a bog by the banks of a stream to make a water-hole ; doubtless that of the noble creature that is now known as *cervus giganteus* or the Irish deer, which once roamed the woods of the early world. Having cut off a suitable length of this bone, he had made a deep slot, dividing the end in two, to receive the neck of the axe, which it exactly fitted, projecting two inches or so over this neck. Now with wonderful skill, helped by the others, he set to work and with sinews and strips of damp hide cut from the skins of reindeer, he lashed haft and blade together, knotting the ends of the strips again and again. Then, having heated fossil gum, or amber, of which there was plenty to be found on the shore, in a shell till it melted, he poured the resin over and between the hide strips, and as it cooled rubbed it smooth with a piece of stone. This done, he plunged the finished axe into ice-cold water for a while till the resin was quite solid, after which he held it in the smoke of the fire that burned near by to dry and shrink the hide strips by heat. Lastly, in case the first should have cracked, he poured on more resin, cooled it with a handful of snow, dried it in the smoke and polished it.

At length all was finished and with pride swelling in his heart Pag held up the weapon, saying,

" Behold the finest axe the tribe has ever seen ! "

" The bone will not shatter ? " asked Aaka the doubtful.

" Nay," he answered, as he rubbed the smoke-dulled resin. " I have tested it as I tested the blade. No man and no shock can break it. Moreover, see, to make sure, I have lashed it about with hide at every thumb's-length. Now let me go and wake Wi and arm him."

Still polishing the axe and its handle with a piece of skin as he went, Pag entered the hut very quietly leaving Aaka without. Wi slept on like a child. Pag laid the axe upon the skin covering of his bed, and going to the head of the hut, hid himself in the shadow. Then he scraped with his foot on the floor, and Wi woke. The first thing his eyes fell on was this axe. He sat up, lifted the axe and began to examine it with eager eyes. When he had noted all its wonders—for to him it was a most marvellous thing made of a glittering stone such as he had never seen, that was thrice heavier than any stone, hafted with black bone as hard as walrus ivory, with a knob at the end of it fashioned by rubbing down the knuckle joint, to save it slipping through the hand, lashed about here and there with neatly finished strips of hide, double-edged and sharper than a flint flake, balancing in the grasp also—Oh, surely he dreamed, for this was such a weapon as the gods must use when they fought together in the bowels of the ice !

Pag waddled forward out of the shadow, saying,

" Time to arise, Wi. But tell me first, how do you like your new axe ? "

" Surely the gods made it," gasped Wi. " With it I could kill a white bear single-handed."

" Yes, the gods made it ; it is a gift to you from the gods—how they sent it I will tell you afterwards—that with it you may kill, not the white brute that prowls in the darkness, but a fiercer beast who ravens by day as well as by night. I tell you, Wi, that this is the Axe of Victory ; holding it you cannot be conquered. Hearken to me, Wi. Henga will rush at you with his great club.

Leap to one side and smite with all your strength at his
hands. If the blow from this axe falls upon them, or
upon the handle of the club where he grasps it, they
or it will be shorn through. Then if his hands remain, he
will rush at you again, striving to seize you and crush
you in his grip, or to break your back or neck. If you
have time, smite at his leg or knee, cutting the tendons or
crippling him. Should he still get a hold of you, do your
best to slip from his grasp, as being greased perhaps you
may, and before he can catch you again, hew at his
neck, or head, or backbone, as chance may offer, for this
axe will not only bruise, it will sink in, and slay him.
Above all do not lose hold of the axe. See, there is a
thong tied to its handle ; twist it doubly round your
wrist thus and it will not come off. Nay, to make sure
I will tie it there with a deer's sinew ; hold out your hand.''

Wi obeyed, and while very deftly Pag made the thong
fast with the sinew, answered,

"I understand, though whether I shall be able to do
all or any of these things I do not know. Still, it is a
wondrous axe and I will try to use it well."

Then Pag rubbed more oil all over Wi, looked once more
at the axe to make sure that the damp thongs had dried
and shrunk tight upon the haft in the warmth of the
fire and that the amber-resin had set hard, then, having
given Wi a piece of dried fish soaked in seal-oil to eat and
a little drink of water, he threw a skin cloak over his
shoulders and led him from the hut.

Aaka was waiting outside and with her Wi's brother,
Moananga. She stared at Wi and asked,

"Who has cut off my man's hair ? ''

"I have," answered Pag, "for a good reason."

She stamped her foot, saying coldly,

"How dare you touch his hair, which I loved to see
him wear long ? I hate you for it."

"Since you are minded to pick a quarrel with me,
why not hate me for this as well as for anything else ?
Yet, Aaka, you may have cause to thank me for it in the
end, though if so it will only make you hate me more.''

"That cannot be," said Aaka, and they went on towards the meeting-place.

Here all the tribe was gathered in a ring, standing silent because they were too moved for speech. On the issue of this fight hung their fate. Henga they feared and hated, because he used them cruelly and brought any who murmured to their death, while Wi they liked well. Yet they dared say nothing, who knew not how the fight would go and thought that no man could stand against the strength of the giant Henga, or save himself from being crushed beneath his mighty club

Still they stared wonderingly at the new axe which Wi bore and pointed to it, nudging each other. Also they marvelled because his hair had been cut off, for what reason they did not know though they thought it must be as an offering to the gods.

The time came. Although because of the cold mist that hung over sea and shore the sun could not be seen, all knew that it was within an hour of its setting, and grew more silent than before. Presently the voice of one who watched on the outskirts of the crowd, called,

"He comes! Henga comes!" whereon they turned and stared towards the cave.

Emerging from the shadow of the cliff the giant appeared, walking towards them with a heavy tread but unconcernedly. Wi stooped down and kissed Foh his son, beckoning to Aaka to take charge of him. Then, followed by Moananga his brother and by Pag, he walked to the centre of the open space where Urk the Aged, the Wizard, whose duty it was to recite the conditions of the duel in the ancient form, stood waiting. As he went, Whaka, the Bird of Ill-omen, called to him,

"Farewell, Wi, whom we shall see no more. We shall miss you very much, for I know not where we shall find so good a hunter or one who brings in so much meat."

Pag turned, glowering at him, and said,

"Me at least you shall see again, croaking raven!"

Taking no note, Wi walked on. As he went it came

into his mind that while he lay asleep in the hut he had
dreamed a beautiful dream. He could not remember
much of it, but its substance was that he was seated in a
rich and lovely land where the sun shone and water
rippled and birds sang, where the air was soft and warm
and the wild creatures wandered round him unafraid
and there was plenty of fragrant food to eat. Then in
that sweet place came his daughter Foa, grown very
fair and with a face that shone as moonlight shines upon
the sea, and set a garland of white flowers about his
neck.

This was all he could recall of the dream, nor indeed
did he search for more of it, for this vision of Foa, the
cruelly slain, brought tears of rage to his eyes. Yet of
a sudden his strength seemed to double and he swore that
he would kill Henga, even though afterwards he must
enter that happy land of peace in which she seemed to
wander.

Now the thief stood before him wearing his cloak of
tiger skin and holding the great club in his left hand.

" It is well," muttered Pag to Wi. " Look, he is
swollen ; he has eaten all the salmon ! "

Henga, who was followed by two servants or slaves,
stopped at a little distance.

" What," he growled, " have I to fight this manikin's
friends as well as himself ? "

" Not yet, Henga," answered Moananga boldly.
" First kill the manikin ; afterwards you can fight his
friends."

" That will be easy," sneered Henga.

Then Urk advanced waving a wand, and with a proud
air called for silence.

CHAPTER VI

THE DEATH OF HENGA

FIRST, as master of the ancient customs of the tribe, Urk set out at great length the law of such combats as that of Wi and Henga. He told how the chief only held his office and enjoyed his privileges by virtue of the strength of his body, as does the bull of a herd. When a younger and stronger than he arose, he might kill the chief if he could, and take his place. Only, according to the law, he must do so in fair and open fight before the people, each combatant being armed with a single weapon. Then, if he conquered, the cave was his with those who dwelt there, and all would acknowledge him as chief ; whereas if he were conquered his body would be thrown to the wolves, such being the fate of those that failed.

In short, though Urk knew it not, he was setting out the doctrine of the survival of the fittest and the rights of the strong over the weak, as Nature preaches them in all her workings.

At this point Henga showed signs of wishing to have done with Urk's oratory, being for reasons of his own quite certain of a speedy victory over an enemy whom he despised, and anxious to return to the cave to receive the praises of his womenfolk and to sleep off the salmon which, as Pag guessed, he had devoured almost to the tail. But Urk would not be silenced. Here he was master as keeper of the oral records ; head official and Voice of the ceremonies of the tribe, who naturally regarded any departure from established custom as one of the worst of crimes.

Everything must be set out, Urk declared in a high and indignant voice, otherwise how would he earn his fee of the robe and weapons of the defeated? Here he cast covetous looks at Wi's strange axe, the like of which he had never seen before, although his withered arm could scarcely have found strength to lift it for a blow. He announced loudly that once before in his youth he had assisted his father, who was the First Wizard before him, to go through this ceremony, and the cloak he still wore—here he touched the shiny, hairless and tattered hide upon his shoulders—had been taken from the body of the conquered. If he were interrupted now, he added, as Wizard he would pronounce his most formidable curse upon the violator of tradition and privilege, and what that meant probably both of them would understand.

Wi listened and said nothing, but Henga growled out, " Be swift then, old fool, for I grow cold and soon there will not be enough light for me to see so to smash up this fellow, that even his dog would not know him again."

Then Urk set out the reasons that caused Wi to challenge, which, being angered by Henga's description of him as " old fool," he did with point and acidity. He told how Wi alleged that Henga oppressed the people, and gave startling instances of that oppression, all of them quite true. He told of the kidnapping and murder of Wi's daughter, Foa, which Wi lay at the door of Henga, and of how the gods were wrath at such a crime. Warming to his work, indeed, he began to advance other grievances not strictly connected with Wi, whereupon Henga, able to bear no more, rushed at Urk and sent his frail old body flying with a kick of his huge foot.

As Urk picked himself up and hobbled off, calling down on Henga's head his wildest if somewhat confused wizard's curse, Henga threw off his tiger-skin cloak, which a slave removed. As Wi did likewise, Pag, who took the garment, whispered to him,

" Beware ! He has something hidden in his right hand. He plays a trick."

Then he hobbled off with the cloak, leaving the giant.

and the hunter facing each other at a distance of five paces.

Even as Pag went, Henga lifted his arm and with fearful force hurled at Wi a flint knife set in a whale's tooth for handle, which he had hidden in his great paw. But Wi, being warned, was watching, and as a shout of " Ill-done ! " went up from the crowd, dropped to the ground so that the knife whizzed over him. Next instant he was up again, charging at Henga, who now grasped the club with both hands and swung it aloft to crush him.

Before it could fall, Wi, remembering Pag's counsel, smote with all his strength. Henga sloped the club sideways to protect his head. Wi's axe fell on it half-way up the handle and the sharp steel, forged in Heaven's furnace, shore through the tough wood, so that the thick part of the club fell to the ground, a sight that caused the people to shout with wonder.

Henga threw the handle at Wi, striking him on the head, and as he staggered back, picked up the thick end of the club. Wi paused to wipe the blood out of his eyes, for the broken stick had grazed his skin. Then again he charged at Henga and keeping out of reach of the short-ened club, strove to smite him on the knee, once more following the counsel of Pag. But the giant's arms were very long and the handle of Wi's axe was short, so that the task was difficult. At length, however, a blow went home and, although no sinew was severed, it cut into Henga's flesh above the knee so deeply that he roared aloud.

Maddened with rage and pain, the giant changed his plan. Dropping the club, as Wi straightened himself after the blow, he leapt at him and gripped him in his huge arms, purposing to break his bones or hug him to death as a bear does. They struggled together.

" All is over," said Whaka. " That man whom Henga embraces is dead."

Pag, who was standing beside him, smote him on the mouth, saying,

" Is it so ? Look, Raven, look ! "

As he spoke Wi slipped from the grasp of Henga
as an eel slips from a child's hand. Again Henga caught
him by the head, but Wi's hair having been cut and his
scalp greased, he could not hold him. Then the giant
smote at him with his great fist, a mighty blow that struck
Wi upon the forehead and felled him to the ground. Before
he could rise Henga hurled himself on to him and the
two struggled there upon the sand.

Never before had the tribe seen a fight like this, nor did
tradition tell of such a one. They writhed, they twisted,
they rolled over, now this one uppermost, and now that.
Henga tried to get Wi by the throat, but his hands would
not hold on the oiled skin ; always the hunter escaped
from that deadly grasp and twice or thrice found
opportunity to pound Henga's face with his fist.

Presently they were seen to rise together, the giant's
arms still about Wi, whom he dared not loose because
he was weaponless, while the axe still hung to the Hunter's
wrist. They wrestled, staggering to and fro, covered with
blood and sand and sweat. The watchers shook their
heads, for how, thought they, could any man stand
against the weight and strength of Henga ? But Pag,
noting everything with his quick eye, whispered to Aaka
who, forgetting her hate in her trouble and fear, had
drawn near to him,

" Keep courage, Woman. The salmon does its work.
Henga tires."

It was true. The grip of the giant loosened, his breath
came in great gasps ; moreover, that leg into which the
axe of Wi had cut began to fail and he dared not put
all his weight upon it. Still, gathering up his strength,
with a mighty effort he cast Wi from him with such
force that the Hunter fell to the ground and lay there a
moment, as though he were stunned or the breath had
been shaken out of him.

Now Moananga groaned aloud, waiting to see Henga
spring upon his foe's prostrate form and stamp him to
death. But some change came over the man. It was

as though a sudden terror had taken him. Or perhaps he thought that Wi was dead. If so he did not wait to look, but turning, ran towards the cave. Wi, recovering his wits or his breath or both, sat up and saw. Then with a shout he leapt to his feet and sped after Henga, followed by all the people; yes, even by Urk the Aged, who hobbled along leaning on his wand of office.

Henga had a long start but at every step his hurt leg grew weaker and Wi sped after him like a deer. At the very mouth of the cave he overtook him, and those who followed saw the flash of a falling axe and heard the thud of its blow upon the back of Henga, who stumbled onward. Then the pair of them vanished into the shadow of the cave, while the people halted without awaiting the issue, whatever it might be.

A little while later there was a stir in the shadows; out of them a man appeared. It was Wi, who bore something in his hands, Wi with the red axe still hanging from his right arm. He staggered forward; a ray from the setting sun pierced the mists and struck full upon him and that which he carried. Lo! it was the huge head of Henga.

For a moment Wi stood still like one bemused, while the tribe shouted their welcome to him as chief by right of conquest. Then he swooned and fell heavily into the arms of Pag who, seeing that he was about to fall, thrust himself past Aaka and caught him.

Because it was nigh at hand, Wi was carried into the cave whence, now that he was fallen, the body of the giant Henga was dragged as though it had been that of a dog. Afterwards, by the command of Wi, it was borne to the foot of the glacier and, as he had vowed, laid there as an offering to the Ice-Gods. Only some of those whom he had wronged and who hated him took his head, and climbing a dead pine that stood near by, of which the top had been twisted out by the wind, stuck it upon the jagged point of the broken tree, where it remained, its

long locks floating on the wind, grinning with empty
eyes at the huts below.

When they entered it, the cave, which was very great,
was found to be full of women who, although he was
still senseless, hastened to do reverence to Wi as their
future lord, and hung about him till with the help of
Moananga and others, Pag drove them all out, saying
that if the Chief Wi wanted any of them back again
he could send for them. He added that he did not
think this probable because they were all so ugly, which
was not true. So they went away seeking shelter where
they could, and were very angry with Pag, more because
he had said that they were ugly than because he had
driven them out, which they guessed he had done because
he did not trust them and feared lest they, Henga's
wives, should do Wi a mischief by poison or otherwise.

Wi being laid upon Henga's bed in a side cave near
to a brightly burning fire, soon recovered from his swoon,
and having drunk some water that one of the slaves of
the place gave to him—for these were not driven out with
the women—asked first for Foh, whom he embraced, and
next for Pag, whom he bade to find Aaka. But Aaka,
learning that he was recovered and little hurt, had gone,
saying that she must attend to the fire in her hut, lest
it should go out, but would return in the morning.

So Pag and Moananga fed Wi with food they found
in the place, among it a piece of that salmon which Henga
had left to eat after the fight. Having swallowed this,
Wi turned over and went to sleep, being utterly outworn
so that he could not even speak. Foh crept on to the
bed by his side, for he would not leave his father, and did
likewise.

Wi slept all night and woke in the morning to find
himself alone, for Foh had gone He was very stiff and
bruised, with a lump on the back of his head where he
had fallen when Henga threw him to the ground. Also
he was sore all over from the grip of the giant's hands,
there was a long deep cut on his forehead where the
handle of the club had struck him, and his skin was

scratched by Henga's claw-like nails. Still, he knew within himself that no bone was broken and that his body was sound and whole. Thankfulness filled his heart that this should be so when he might well have been as Henga was to-day.

To whom did he owe this safety—to the Ice-Gods? Perhaps. If so, he thanked them, he who did not desire to die and felt that he had work to do for the people. Yet the Ice-Gods seemed very cold and far away, and although the stone fell, it might have been by chance, so that he wondered whether they troubled themselves about him and his fate. Pag thought that there were no gods and perhaps he was right. At least this was clear, that if it had not been for Pag the gods would not have saved him yesterday from Henga the giant, the mightiest man that was told of in the tale of the tribe, even by Urk and others who made up stories and sung them by the fire on winter nights, Henga who once had caught a wild bull by the horns and twisted its neck with his hands.

Pag it was who had oiled him all over and cut off his hair so that Henga could not hold him. Pag it was who had made and given to him the wonderful axe that lay on the bed beside him, its thong still about his wrist, without which he never could have smitten Henga down as he gained the safety of his cave, or dealt him that deep cut upon the leg which caused him to give up the fight and run even when he, Wi, lay prostrate on the ground; caused him also to limp and stumble in his flight so that he could be overtaken. Pag it was, too, that had put a great heart into him, telling him not to be afraid for he would conquer on that day, words which he remembered even when all seemed finished. And now Henga was dead, for after he fell, smitten on the back, two blows of the wonderful axe had hewed right through his thick neck as no other weapon could have done. Foa was avenged, Foh and Aaka were saved, and he, Wi, was Lord of the Cave and Chief of the People. Therefore he, Wi, swore this, that Pag, though a dwarf deformed whom all hated and named " Wolf-man," should be next to him among them and his counsellor. Yes, he swore it, although he knew that it would please Aaka little because of her jealous heart.

Whilst he lay and thought thus, by the light that crept into the cave Wi noted that three of the women, the youngest and fairest among them, had returned to the place and were standing at a distance, talking and looking towards him. Presently they came to some decision, for they advanced very quietly, which caused Wi to grip his axe. Seeing that his eyes were open, they knelt down and touched the ground with their foreheads, calling him lord and master, saying that they wished to stay with him who was so great and strong that he had killed Henga, and swearing to be faithful to him.

Wi listened astonished, not knowing what to answer. Least of all things did he wish to take these women into his household, if for no other reason, because anyone whom Henga had touched was hateful to him ; yet, being kind-hearted, he did not desire to tell them this roughly. While he was seeking for soft words one of the women crept forward, still upon her knees, seized his hand, pressed it against her forehead and kissed it. It was at this moment that Aaka appeared, followed by Pag. The women sprang up and running a few paces, huddled themselves together, while Pag laughed hoarsely and Aaka, drawing herself to her full height, said,

" It seems that you soon make yourself at home in your new house, Husband, since already I find Henga's cast-offs kissing you in love."

" Love ! " answered Wi. " Am I in a state for love ? The women came—I did not seek them."

" Oh yes, without doubt they came knowing where they would be welcome, Husband ; indeed, perhaps they never went away. Of a truth I perceive that there will be no room for me in this Chief's Cave. Well, I am glad of it, who love my own hut better than such a darksome hole."

" Yet often, Wife, I have heard you say, when the

wind whistled through the hut in winter, that you wished you lay safe and warm in the Chief's Cave."

"Did I? Well, I have changed my mind who had never seen the place, not having been one of Henga's family."

"Peace, woman," said Pag, "and let us see how the Chief Wi fares. As for those slaves, I have hunted them out once and presently will do so again. Chief, we bring you food. Can you eat?"

"I think so," answered Wi, "if Aaka will hold me up."

Aaka looked wrathfully at the women and still more wrathfully at Pag, so that Wi thought that she was about to refuse. If so, she changed her mind and supported Wi, who was too stiff to sit up alone, while Foh, who had now returned, fed him with pieces of food, chattering all the while about the fight.

"Were you not afraid for your father," asked Wi at length, "who must fight a giant twice his size?"

"Oh no," said Foh cheerfully. "Pag told me that you would win in the end and that therefore I must never be afraid, and Pag is always right. Still," he added, shaking his head, "when I saw you lying on the ground and not moving and believed that Henga was about to jump on you, then I began to think that for once Pag might be wrong."

Wi laughed and lifting his hand with difficulty, patted Foh's curling hair. Pag in the background growled,

"Never think that I am wrong again, for the god lives on the faith of his worshippers," words that Foh did not in the least understand.

Nor did Aaka quite, but guessing that Pag was comparing himself to a god, she hated him more than ever and frowned. Although she believed in them after her fashion because her forefathers had done so before her, she was not a spiritual woman and did not like his talk of gods who, if in fact they existed at all, were, she was sure, beings to be feared. It was true that she had sent Wi to worship the Ice-Gods in which he put faith and to watch for the sign

of the falling stone, but that was because she had
made up her mind that the time had come for him
to fight Henga and avenge the death of Foa if he could,
taking the risk of being killed, and knew that at this
time of year at sunrise a stone was almost certain to
fall from the crest of the glacier, which was strewn with
hundreds of them, and that without some sign he would
not move. Indeed, she had made sure that one or more
of these stones would fall upon that very morning.

Also she had some gift of foresight with which women
are often endowed, especially among northern people, that
told her Wi would conquer Henga. She said that something of this had been revealed to her in a dream wherein
Foa appeared to her, and it was true enough that she
had dreamed that Foa had appeared and told her that
Wi would work vengeance upon Henga, because the
thirst for vengeance and desire for the death of Henga
were always present to her mind.

Therefore she frowned and told Foh that it was foolish
to believe sayings because they came out of the mouth
of Pag.

" Yet, Mother," answered Foh, " what Pag said was
true. Moreover, he made the wonderful sharp axe and
he oiled Father's skin and cut off his hair, which none of
us thought of doing."

Now Pag, wishing to stop this talk, broke in,

" These things are nothing, Foh, and if I did them
it is only because a hideous deformed one such as I am,
who was born different from others, must think and
protect himself and those he loves by wisdom, as do the
wolves and other wild beasts. People who are handsome,
like your father and mother, do not need to think, for
they protect themselves in different ways."

" Yet perhaps they think as much as you do, Dwarf,"
said Aaka angrily.

" Yes, Aaka, doubtless they think, only to less purpose.
The difference is that such as I think right and they think
wrong."

Without waiting for an answer Pag waddled off very

swiftly on some business of his own. Aaka watched him
go with a puzzled look in her fine eyes, then asked,

" Is Pag going to live with you in this cave, Husband ? "

" Yes, Wife. Now that I am Chief, he to whom I
owe so much, he the Wise and the Axe-giver, will be my
Counsellor."

" Then I shall live in my hut," she answered, " where
you can visit me when it pleases you. I hate this place ;
it smells of Henga and his slave-women. Bah ! "

Then she went away, to return later, it is true. Yet
as to sleeping in the cave, she kept her word—that is,
until winter came.

CHAPTER VII

THE OATH OF WI

BEING very strong and healthy, Wi soon recovered from this great fight, although for a time he suffered from festering sores where he had been scratched by Henga, whose nails it would seem were poisonous as are a wolf's teeth. Indeed, on the following day he came out of the cave and was received by all the people, who were waiting without to give him welcome as the new chief. This they did very heartily, then, through the mouth of Urk the Ancient, went on to set out their grievances of which they had prepared a long list. These they suggested he, the present ruler, should redress.

First they complained of the climate, which of late years had grown so strangely cold and sunless. As to this, he answered that they must make prayer to the Ice-Gods, whereon someone cried out that if they did, these gods would only send them more ice, of which they had enough already, an argument that Wi could not combat. He said, however, that perhaps the weather had changed because of the evil-doings of Henga, and now that he had gone it might change again.

Next they spoke of a delicate and domestic matter. Women, they pointed out, were very scarce among them, so much so that some men, although they were prepared to marry the ugliest or the most evil-tempered, could find no wives and make no homes. Yet certain of the strongest and richest took as many as three or four into their households, while the late chief, by virtue of his rank and power, had swallowed up from fifteen to twenty of the youngest and best-looking, whom they supposed Wi intended to keep for himself.

On this point Wi replied that he intended nothing of the sort, as he would make clear in due season, and for the rest, that women were few because of their habit of exposing female children at birth, rather than be at the pains of rearing and feeding them.

Then they passed to other questions, such as the pressure of taxation, or its primeval equivalent. The chief took too much, they said, and gave too little. He did no work himself and produced nothing, yet he and all his great household expected to be supported in luxury and with the best. Moreover, he seized their wives and daughters, raided their stores of food or skins and occasionally committed murder.

Lastly, he favoured certain rich men among them—here Urk looked hard at Turi the Food-hoarder, the Avaricious, and at Rahi the Wealthy One, the trader in fish-hooks, skins and flint instruments which he caused to be manufactured by forced labour, only paying the makers with a little food in times of want. These rich men, they alleged, were protected in their evil-doing by the chief, to whom they paid a heavy tithe of their ill-gotten goods, in return for which he promoted them to positions of honour and gave them fine names, such as Counsellor, ordering that others should bow down to them.

Wi said that he would look into these practices and try to put a stop to them.

Finally they called attention to the breaking of their ancient customs, as when he who had killed an animal or trapped it in a pit, or found it dead, or caught it fishing, and proposed to lay it up for the winter, was robbed of it by a horde of hungry idlers who wished to live on the industrious without toiling for themselves.

Into this matter also Wi said that he would inquire.

Then he announced that he summoned the whole tribe to a gathering on the day of the next full moon, when he would announce the results of his deliberations, and submit new laws to be approved by the tribe.

During the time which elapsed between this meeting and that of the full moon, namely, seventeen days, Wi

thought a great deal. For hours he would walk upon the
shore, accompanied only by Pag, whom Aaka contemptuously named his "shadow," with whom he consulted
deeply. Towards the end of the time, also, he called in
Urk the Aged, Moananga his brother, and two or three
other men, none of the latter of much prominence but
whom he knew to be honest and industrious.

The rest of the tribe, devoured by curiosity, tried to
wring from these men what it might be that the chief
talked of with them. They would say nothing. Then
they set the women on to them, who, being even more
curious, did their best by means of many wiles to find
out what all wanted to know. Even Tana, Moananga's
wife, the sweet and gentle, played a part in this game,
saying that she would not speak to him or even look at
him until he told her. But he would not, nor would
the others, whereupon it was decided that Wi, or Pag,
or both of them, must have some great magic, since it
sufficed to bridle the tongues of men even when women
tempted them.

Now a strange thing had happened. From the day
that Wi became chief the weather mended. At length
the cold, snowy-looking clouds rolled away; at length the
piercing wind ceased to blow out of the north and east ;
at length, though very late, the spring, or rather the
summer came, for that year there was no spring. Seals
appeared, though not in their usual quantity, the salmon
which seemed to have been icebound, ran up the river
in shoals, while eider and other ducks arrived and nested.

"Late come, soon gone," said Pag, as he noted
these things. "Still, better that than nothing."

Thus it came about that on the appointed day the
tribe, full of food and in high good-humour, met its
chief whom it felt to be an auspicious person. Even
Aaka was good-humoured and when Tana, who was her
relation both by blood and because she was the wife of
Wi's brother, asked her what was about to happen,
answered laughingly,

"I don't know. But no doubt we shall be told some

nonsense which Wi and that Wolf-man make up together,
empty words like the cackling of wild geese, which makes
a great noise and is soon forgot."

"At any rate," said Tana inconsequently, "Wi is
behaving very well to you, for I know that he has sent
away all those women slaves of Henga."

"Oh yes, he is behaving well enough, but how
long will it last? Is it to be expected, now that he has
become Chief, that he will be different to other chiefs,
seeing that one man is like the rest? They are all the
same. Moreover," she added acidly, "if he has sent
away the women, he has kept Pag."

"What can that matter to you?" asked Tana,
opening her big eyes.

"Much more than all the rest, Tana. If you could
understand it, which you cannot, it is of Wi's mind that
I am jealous, not of anything else about him, and this
dwarf has his mind."

"Indeed!" said Tana, staring at her. "That is
a strange fancy. For my part, anyone is welcome to
Moananga's mind. It is of him that I am jealous and
with very good reason, not of his mind."

"No," said Aaka sharply, "because he has not got
one. With Wi it is otherwise; his mind is more than
his body, and that is why I would keep it for myself."

"Then you should learn to be as clever as Pag,"
answered Tana with gentle irritation as she turned to
talk to someone else.

The people were gathered at the Talking-place in
front of the cave, that same spot where Wi had conquered
Henga. There they stood or sat in a semi-circle, those of
the more consequence in front, and the rest behind.
Presently Wini-wini blew a blast on his horn, a strong and
steady blast for this time he feared no harm from stones,
or otherwise, to announce the appearance of the chief.
Then Wi, clad in the tiger-skin cloak that Henga used to
wear, which, as Aaka remarked, was too big for him and
much frayed, advanced, followed by Moananga, Urk,

Pag and the others, and sat down upon a stool made from
two joints of the backbone of a whale lashed together,
which had been placed there in readiness for him.

" Is all the Tribe gathered here ? " asked Wini-wini
the Herald, to which spokesmen answered that it
was, except a few who could not come.

" Then hearken to the Chief Wi, the great Hunter,
a mighty man, the Conqueror of Henga the Evil—that is,
unless anyone wishes first to fight him for his place,"
and he paused.

As nobody answered—for who in his senses wished to
face the wonderful axe that chopped off the great head
of Henga, whereof the hollow eyes still stared at them
from the broken trunk of a neighbouring tree—Wi rose
and began his address, saying,

" O People of the Tribe, we believe that there are no
others like us anywhere, at least we have seen none
upon the beach or in the woods around, though it is
true that in the ice yonder, behind the mighty Sleeper is
something that looks like a man. If so, he died long
ago, unless indeed he is a god. Perhaps he was a forefather of the tribe who went into the ice to be buried
there. Being therefore the only men and, though it
is true that in some ways, they are stronger than we are,
much greater than the beast people, for we can think and
talk and build huts, and do many things that the beasts
cannot do, it is right that we should show how much
better we are than they by our conduct to each other."

As it had never occurred to the people to compare
themselves relatively to the animals around them, these
lofty sentiments were received in silence. Indeed, if
they thought about the matter at all, most of them,
comparing men and the beasts, would have been inclined
to give the palm to the latter.

Could any man, they would have said and in fact did
say in private argument afterwards, match the strength
of the aurochs, the wild bull of the woods, or of the whale
of the waters ? Could any man swim like a seal or fly
like a bird, or be as swift and savage as the striped tiger

that dwelt or used to dwell in caves, or hunt in packs like the fierce ravening wolves, or build such houses as the birds did, or fly through the air, or do many other things with the perfection of the creatures which lived and moved in the seas and sky or upon the earth? While, as for the other side of the matter, were not these creatures in their own way as clever as man was? Also, although their language was not to be understood, did they not talk together as men did and worship their own gods? Who could doubt it that had heard the wolves and dogs howling at the moon? But of all this at that time they said nothing.

Having laid down this general rule, Wi went on to say that he had given ear to the complaints of the people, and after consulting with sundry of the wisest among them, had determined that the time had come to lay down new laws which all must bind themselves to obey. Or if all would not, then those who refused must give way to the majority who consented to them, or if they rebelled must be treated as evil-doers and punished. If they agreed to this, let them say so with one voice.

This they did, first because they were tired of sitting still and it gave them an opportunity of shouting, and secondly because they had not heard the laws. Only one or two of the most cunning exclaimed that they would like to hear the laws first, but these were over-ruled by the cries of general approbation.

To begin with, continued Wi, there was the matter of the scarcity of women, which could only be remedied to some extent by every man in future binding himself to be content with a single wife, as he, Wi, was prepared to do, swearing by the gods that he would keep to his oath and calling down on his own head and on the heads of the people of which he was the chief, the anger and the vengeance of the gods, should he break it and should they allow him to do so.

Now in the silence which followed this amazing announcement, Tana whispered to Aaka delightedly,

" Do you hear, sister? What do you think of this law ?"

" I think that it amounts to nothing at all," answered Aaka contemptuously. "Wi and the other men will only obey it until they see someone who makes them wish to break it ; moreover, many of the women will find it hateful. When they grow old will they wish to have to do all the work of the household and to cook the food for the whole family ? That for this law, which is foolish like all new things." Here she snapped her fingers. "Still, let it go on, seeing that it will give us a stick with which to beat our husbands when they forget it, as doubtless Wi himself will find out before all is done, the silly dreamer who thinks that he can change the nature of men with a few words. Unless indeed it was Pag who put it into his head, Pag who is neither man nor woman, but just a dwarf and a wolf-hound."

" Wolf-hounds are very useful sometimes, Aaka," said Tana reflectively, then turned to listen to the voices about her.

These, as it happened, were many, for as soon as the meaning of Wi's startling proposal had come home to the minds of his audience, great tumult arose. All the men who had no wives, or wished for those of others, shouted for joy, as did many of the women who were members of large households and therefore much neglected. On the other hand, some of the lords of those households protested with vigour, whereas others acquiesced with a shrug and a smile.

Long and loud was the debate, but at length it ended in a compromise, the polygamists agreeing to the proposal, provided that they were allowed to keep that wife whom they liked best, also to change her when they wished by mutual consent of all concerned. As public opinion among the tribe, an easy-going folk, was tolerant on such matters, ultimately this solution was accepted by all except by Wi himself. He, with the new-born enthusiasm of the reformer and as one who wished to set an example, rose and exempted himself solemnly from the arrangement.

"Others may do what they will," he said, "but be it known that I, the Chief, will never change my wife while she lives, No, not even if she desires me to do so, which can scarcely happen. Hearken, O People: once more I swear by the gods that I will take no other wife, and pray the gods to lay their curse upon me if I break this, my oath. Moreover, lest at any time I should grow weak and foolish and be tempted so to do, I pray the gods, if that chances, to lay their curse upon the people also, all of them, from the oldest to the youngest——"

Here some of his audience grew uneasy and a voice shouted out,

"For what reason?"

"Because," answered Wi in his burning zeal, "knowing the evil that my ill-doing would bring upon your heads, never would I yield to folly, I who am your chief and your protector. Also, if I went mad and did such a thing, you could kill me."

Silence followed this remarkable declaration, in the midst of which Hotoa the Slow-speeched at last got out a question.

"How would killing you help us, Wi, if the curse for which you have been asking had already fallen upon our heads? Moreover, who is likely to try to kill you while you have that wonderful axe with which you chopped Henga in two?" he asked.

Before Wi could think of a suitable answer—for the question was shrewd and the point one which he had not considered—the general argument broke out again, many women taking part in it at the top of their voices, so that he lost his opportunity. At length three men were thrust forward, a somewhat ominous trio, as it happened: Pitokiti the Unlucky, Hou the Unstable and Whaka the Bird of Ill-omen, of whom Whaka was the spokesman.

"Chief Wi," he said, "the people have heard your proposals as to marriage. Many of us do not like them because they overthrow old customs. Still, we acknowledge that something must be done lest the tribe should come to an end, for those who have many wives bring up no more children than those who have but one. Also the unmarried turn into murderers and thieves both of women and of other property. Therefore we accept the new law for a period of five summers, which will give us time to see how it works. Also we note your oath that you will take no other wife while Aaka lives and that you call down the curse of the gods upon yourself if you do so. We do not think that you will keep that oath, for being a chief who can do what he likes, why should you ? But when you break it we shall wait to see if the curse falls upon you. As for the rest, that you call it down on the people also, with that we will have nothing to do, nor do we believe it. For why should the people suffer because you break an oath ? If there are gods, they will be avenged upon him who does the wrong, not on others who are innocent. Therefore, speaking on behalf of the people, I say that we accept your law, though for myself I add that I am sure no good can ever come of the changing of ancient customs. Indeed, I daresay that the curse will fall upon you and that soon you will be dead."

Thus spoke Whaka the Bird of Ill-omen, fulfilling his repute, and retired with his companions.

By now it was growing dark for all this debate had taken a long time ; moreover, many of the people had slipped away to try to make fresh arrangements in view of this sudden and unexpected revolution in their matrimonial law. Therefore Wi adjourned the discussion of the next rule of his new code, that which dealt with the exposure of unwanted female infants, till the morrow, and the tribal conference broke up.

That night he slept in the hut where he lived before he became chief, and at the evening meal tried to open a discussion with Aaka on his great new law. She listened for a minute, then remarked that she had heard enough of it that afternoon, and if he wanted to talk more of the matter instead of eating his food and discussing what was of real importance, namely, how she should lay up her winter stores now that he was the chief, he had better do so with his counsellor, Pag.

This retort angered Wi, who said,

"Do you not understand that this law makes women taller by a head than they have been, for now they are the equals of men who give up much?"

"If so," answered Aaka, "you should first have asked us whether we wished to grow taller. Had you done so, you would have found, I think, that the most of us were content to remain the same size, seeing that we do not desire more work and more children. Still, it matters little, for your law is all nonsense, one made by fools, of whom I should hold you the biggest did I not know that you speak with the mouth of Pag the woman-hater and the cutter-down of old trees." (By this she meant the destroyer of ancient customs). "Man is man and woman is woman and what they have done from the beginning, they will continue to do. Nor will you change them by talking, Wi, although you think yourself so clever. Yet I am glad to learn that I shall have no pert girls thrust into my household—or so you swore, calling down curses on your own head in the presence of many witnesses, like a fool, for when you break the oath you will find them troublesome to deal with."

Then with a sigh Wi grew silent. He had thought to please Aaka, whom he loved and had suffered much to win, and who, he knew, loved him in her fashion, although often she treated him so roughly. Still he noted that it was her purpose to take advantage of this law so far as she was concerned, and to keep him for herself alone. But why, he wondered, did she despise and belittle that by which she meant to benefit, a thing which no man would do? Then he shrugged his shoulders and began to talk of the winter food and of the plans which he and Pag had made, whereby all would be assured of plenty.

That night towards dawn they were awakened by a great tumult. Women shrieked and men shouted. The boy Foh, who slept on the other side of the hut behind a skin curtain, crept out to see what was the matter, thinking perhaps that the wolves had carried off someone. Presently he returned and reported that there was fighting going on, but he did not know what about.

Now Wi wished to rise and look into the matter, but Aaka bade him lie still, saying,

" Keep quiet. It is your new law at work, that is all."

When morning came this proved to be true enough. Some wives of old husbands had run away from them to young lovers, and some men who had no wives had captured or tried to capture them by force, with the result that there was much fighting, in which one old man had been killed and others, male and female, injured.

Aaka laughed at Wi about this business, but he was so sad that he did not try to answer her, only he said,

" You treat me hardly of late, Wife, who am trying to do my best and who love you, as I proved long ago when I fought a man who wished to take you against your will, and killed him, which brought much anger and trouble on me. Then you thanked me and we came together and for years lived happily. At last Henga, who hated me and had always desired to take you into the cave, caught our daughter, Foa, and killed her, and from that time you who loved Foa more than you do Foh, have changed towards me, although that this happened was no fault of mine."

" It was your fault," she answered, " for you should have stayed to watch Foa instead of going out to hunt to please yourself."

" I did not hunt to please myself, I hunted to get meat. Moreover, if you had asked me I would have left Pag to watch the girl."

" So the dwarf has been telling you that tale, has he ? Then know the truth. He did offer to stay with Foa, but I would not have the hideous beast guarding my daughter."

" Pag has told me no tale, though it is true that, doubtless to shield you, he reproached me for having

taken him out hunting when there was danger from
Henga. Wife, you have done ill, for if you hate Pag,
yet he loves me and mine, and had you allowed him to
bide with Foa she would have been alive to-day. But
let that be, the dead are dead and we shall see them
no more. Afterwards I prayed to the gods as you wished,
and challenged Henga, and killed him, taking vengeance on
him, as you also wished, Pag helping me with his wisdom
and by the gift of the axe. And now I have driven away
all the chief's women who were mine by right of custom,
and made a law that henceforth a man shall have but
one wife. Also that I might set an example as chief, I have
called down curses on my head and, that I might never
weaken in this matter, on the tribe, too, if I myself
should break that law. Yet you are still bitter
against me. Have you then ceased to love me ? "

"Would you know the truth, Wi ? " she answered,
looking him in the eyes. " Then I will tell you. I have
not, I who never had a thought towards another man
I love you as well as I did on the day when you killed
Rongi for my sake. But hearken—I love not Pag who
is your chosen friend, and it is to Pag that you turn, not
to me. Pag is your counsellor, not I. It is true that
since Foa was killed all water is bitter to my taste and
all meat is sprinkled with sand, and in place of my heart a
stone beats in my breast, so that I care for nothing and
am as ready to die as to live, which I thought I must do
when the huge cave-dweller hurled you down. Yet I
say this to you—drive out Pag, as you can do, being
chief, and so far as I am able I will be to you what I
was before, not only your wife but your counsellor.
Choose then between me and Pag."

Now Wi bit his lip as was his fashion when perplexed,
and looked at her sadly, saying,

"Women are strange, also they know not the thing
that is just. Once I saved Pag's life and because of
that he loves me ; also because he is very wise, the
wisest I think of all the tribe, I listen to his words.
Further, by his craft and counsel, and with aid of the

gift he gave me," and he looked at the axe hanging from his wrist, " I slew Henga, who without these should now myself be dead. Also Foh our son loves him, and he loves Foh, and with his help I have fashioned new laws which shall make life good for all the tribe. Yet you say to me—' Drive out Pag your friend and helper,' knowing that if he ceased to sit in my shadow the women, who are his enemies, would kill him, or he must wander away and live like a wild beast in the woods. Wife, if I did this I should be a treacherous dog, not a man, and much less a chief whose duty it is to do justice to all. Why, because you are jealous of him, do you ask such a thing of me ? "

" For my own reasons, Wi, which are enough. Well, I ask, and you do not grant, so go your road and I will go mine, though among the people it need not be known that we have quarrelled. As for these new laws, I tell you that they will bring you trouble and nothing else. You seek to cut down an old tree and to plant a better in its place, but if it ever grows at all you will be dead before it keeps a drop of rain from off you. You are vain and foolish and it is Pag who has made you so."

Thus they parted, Wi going away full of sadness, for now he was sure that nothing he could say or do would change Aaka's heart. Had he been as were the others of the tribe he would have rid himself of her and taken another wife, leaving her to take a new husband if she chose. But Wi was not like his fellow tribesmen ; he was one born out of due time, a forerunner, one with imagination who could understand others and see with their eyes. He understood that Aaka was jealous by nature, jealous of everyone, not only of other women. That which she had she wanted to keep for herself alone ; she would rather that Wi should lack guidance and help than that he should find these in the dwarf Pag or in other men. She was even jealous of her son Foh because he loved him, his father, better than he did her. Now with Foa it was otherwise, for although he loved her so much, she had taken less note of her father and clung closer to her mother.

So when Foa was killed Aaka had lost everything ; moreover, she knew that she herself was to blame, for when Wi went out hunting, as he must, she would not suffer Pag to protect the child, both because she hated him and because Foa liked Pag. Therefore, through her own folly she had lost her daughter, and knew that this was so, and yet blamed not herself but Wi, because Pag was his friend, which caused her to hate Pag so much that she would not suffer him to guard Foa. From that moment, as she had said, water had become bitter to her, and all meat full of sand ; she was soured and different to what she had been ; indeed, another woman.

In the old days with a kind of trembling joy she had thought how one day Wi might become Chief of the Tribe ; now she did not care whether he were chief or not ; even to have become the first woman in the tribe gave her no pleasure. For the blow of the death of Foa, although she knew it not, had fallen on her brain and disturbed her reason, the more so because she was sure that she would bear no other children. Yet deep in her heart she loved Wi better than she had ever done and suffered more than she could have told, because she feared lest some other woman should appear to whom he might turn for the fellowship and comfort she would no longer give

Now all these things Wi knew better than Aaka did herself, because by nature he was a man with an understanding heart, although but a poor savage who as yet had no pot in which to boil his food. Therefore he was very sad though determined to be patient, hoping that Aaka's mind would right itself and that she would change her face toward him.

When Wi reached the cave he found Pag waiting for him with food which Foh, who had gone before him at the break of day, served with much stir and mystery. Eating of this food—it was a small salmon new run from the sea—Wi noted, idly enough, that it was cooked in a new fashion and made savoury with salt, shell-fish and certain herbs.

" I have never tasted the like of this before," he said. " How is it prepared ? "

Then with triumph Foh pointed out to him a vessel hollowed from a block of wood which stood by the fire, and showed him that in this vessel water boiled.

" How is it done ? " asked Wi. " If wood is placed upon fire it burns."

Next Foh raked away some ashes, revealing in the heart of the fire a number of red-hot stones.

" It is done thus, Father," he said ; " for days I have been hollowing out that block of black wood, which comes from the swamp where it lay buried, by burning it, and when it was charred, cutting it away with a piece of that same bright stone of which your axe is made. Then when it was finished and washed I filled it with water and dropped red-hot stones into it till the water boiled. After this I put in the cleaned fish with the oysters and the herbs and kept on dropping in red-hot stones till the fish was cooked. That's how it is done, Father, and—is the fish nice ? " and he laughed and clapped his hands.

" It is very nice, Son," said Wi, " and I would that I had more stomach to eat it. But who thought of this plan, which is clever ? "

" Oh, Pag thought of it, Father, but I did nearly all the work."

" Well, Son, take away the rest of the fish and eat it, and then go wash out your pot lest it should stink I tell you that you and Pag have done more than you know and that soon you will be famous in the tribe."

Then Foh departed rejoicing, and afterwards even took the pot to his mother to show her all, expecting that she would praise him. But in this he was disappointed, for when she learned that Pag had hit upon the plan, she said that for her part she was content with food cooked as her forefathers had cooked it from the beginning, and she was sure that seethed flesh would make those who ate of it very sick.

But it did not make them sick and soon this new

fashion spread. Indeed the whole tribe might have been seen burning hollows in blocks of wood, cutting away the char that was left with their chipped flints, and when the pots were finished, making water boil with red-hot stones and placing in it meat that was tough from having been stored in the ice, or fish or eggs, or whatever they needed to cook. Thus those who were old and toothless could now eat again and grew fat ; moreover, the health of the tribe improved much, especially that of the children, who ceased to suffer from dysentery brought on by the devouring of lumps of flesh charred in the fire.

CHAPTER VIII

PAG TRAPS THE WOLVES

ON the afternoon of this day of his quarrel with Aaka and of the boiling of the salmon, Wi and his counsellors again met the tribe in front of the cave to declare to them more of his new laws. This time, however, not so many attended, because as a fruit of the first law a number of them were laid by hurt, while others were engaged quarrelling over the women, or if they belonged to the unmarried, in building huts large enough to hold a wife.

At once, before the talk began, many complaints were laid as to the violence worked upon the previous night, and demands for compensation for injuries received. Also there were knotty points to be decided as to the allotment of women. For example, when three or four men wished to marry one girl, which of them was to take her?

This, Wi decided, must be settled by the girl choosing which of them she would, an announcement that caused wonder and dismay. Never before had a woman been allowed to make choice in such a matter, which was settled by her father if he were known, or more frequently by her mother. Sometimes, if there was none to protect her, she was dragged off by the hair of her head by the strongest of her suitors after he had killed or beaten the others.

Soon, however, Moananga and Pag pointed out to him that if he stopped to hear and give judgment on all these cases, no more new laws would be declared for many days. Therefore he adjourned them till som future time, and set out the second law which declared that in future no female child should be cast forth to be taken by the wolves or to perish of cold, unless it were deformed. This decree caused much grumbling because, said the grumblers, the child belonged to the parents, and especially to the mother, who had a right to do with their own as they wished.

Then an inspiration seized Wi and he uttered a great saying which afterwards was to be accepted by most of the world,

" The child comes from Heaven and belongs to the gods whose gift it is, and who will require account of it from those to whom it has been lent," he said.

These words, so amazing to the people who had never even dreamed their like, were received in astonished silence. Urk the Aged, sitting at Wi's side, muttered that he had never heard anything of the sort from his grandfather, while Pag the Sceptic behind him, asked,

" To what gods ? "

Again an inspiration came to Wi, and he answered aloud,

" That we shall learn when we are dead, for then the hidden gods will become visible."

Next he went on hastily to declare the punishment of the breaking of this law. It was terrible ; namely, that the casters-forth should themselves be cast forth to suffer the same fate and that none should succour them.

" But if we had no food for the children ? " cried a voice.

" Then if that is proved to be so, I, the Chief, will receive them and care for them as though they were my own, or give them to others who are barren."

" Surely soon we shall have a large family," Aaka remarked to Tana.

" Yes," said Tana. " Still, Wi has a great heart and Wi is right."

At this point, as though by general consent, the meeting broke up, for all felt that they could not swallow more than one law a day.

On the following afternoon they came together again, but in still fewer numbers, and Wi continued to give out laws, very excellent laws, which did not interest his audience much, either because, as one of them said, they were " full to the throat with wisdom," or for the reason that, like other savages, they could not keep their attention fixed for long on such matters.

The end of it was that none came to listen, and that the laws must be proclaimed throughout the tribe by Wini-wini with his horn. For days he went from hut to hut blowing his horn and shouting out the laws into the doorways, till at last the women grew angry and set the children to pelt him with egg-shells and dried cods' heads. Indeed, by the time that he had finished, those in the huts where he began had quite forgotten of what he was talking. Still, the laws, having been duly proclaimed without any refusal of them, were held to be in force, nor was ignorance of them allowed to be pleaded as excuse for their breaking, every man, woman and child being presumed to know the laws, even if they did not obey them

Yet Wi discovered that it is much easier to make laws than to force people to keep them, with the result that soon, to his office of law-giver, he must add that of Chief Magistrate. Nearly every day he was obliged to sit in front of the cave, or in it when the weather was bad, to try cases and award punishments, which were mostly inflicted by certain sturdy fellows who wielded whips of whalebone. In this fashion a knowledge of the code and of what happened to those who broke it grew by degrees. Thus when Turi the Food-hoarder managed to secure more than his share of the spread of stock-fish by arriving earlier than the others, his hoard was raided and most of it distributed among the poor, after which he was more careful in the hiding of his ill-gotten gains.

Again, when Rahi, the rich trader, was proved to have supplied bad bone fish-hooks, broken at the point or weak in the shank, in exchange for skins which had been

received by him in advance, Moananga went with some
men and, digging beneath the floor of his hut, found
scores of hooks wrapped up in hide, which they took and
distributed amongst those of the tribe who had none.
Great was the outcry of Rahi, but in this case few joined
in it, for all loved to see one who battened on the poor
in the hour of their necessity, forced to disgorge some of
his gain.

Moreover, although he offended many who murmured
and plotted against him, on the whole Wi gained great
credit for those good laws of his. For now the people
knew that he who dwelt in the cave was no murderer
or robber as Henga and other chiefs had been, but a
man who, was honest, taking from them as little as might
be, and, although often, as they thought, foolish, one
who strove for the good of all. Therefore by degrees
they came to obey his laws, some more and some less,
and, although they abused him openly, in private they
spoke well of him and hoped that his rule would continue.

Yet at last trouble came. It chanced that a certain
sour-natured woman named Ejji bore a female child,
and not wishing to be troubled with it, forced her husband
to lay it on a stone at the edge of the forest where the
wolves came every night, that it might be devoured by
them. But this woman was watched by other women
set about the business by Pag, who knew her heart and
suspected her; as was her husband, who was seized when
he had laid the child upon the stone at nightfall, even
as he told his wife Ejji what he had done and received
her thanks.

Next morning both of them were brought before Wi,
who sat dealing out justice at the mouth of the cave.
He asked them what had become of the girl-child that
was born to them within a moon. Ejji answered boldly
that it died and its body had been cast away according
to custom. Thereon Wi made a sign and a foster-mother
was led from the cave bearing the child in her arms,
for thither it had been taken, as Wi had promised should
be done in such cases. The woman Ejji denied that it

was her child, but the husband, taking it in his arms, said otherwise, and on being pressed, admitted that what he had done was against his will and for the sake of peace in his home.

Then when the finding of the child had been proved, Wi, after reciting the law, ordered that these two, who were rich and not driven by need, should be taken at sunset and tied to trees by that stone upon which they had exposed the child, that the wolves might devour them. At this stern sentence there was much trouble among the tribe, most of whom had thrown out female infants in their time, and threats were made against Wi.

Yet he would not change his word, and at nightfall, amidst lamentations from their relatives and friends, the pair were taken out and tied to the trees. Thereon they were abandoned by all as evil-doers who had been unlucky enough to be found out.

During the night growlings and cries were heard rising from the direction of the trees, which told the tribe that Ejji and her husband had been devoured by the wolves, which always wandered there at a distance from the huts where, unless they were very hungry, they dared not come because of fires and the pitfalls. The death of these two made the people angry, so much so that many of them ran up to the cave to revile Wi, by whose order it had been brought about, shouting out that the killing of men and women because they wished to be rid of a useless brat was not to be borne. Greatly were they astonished when, there in the mouth of the cave, they saw three dead wolves and, standing behind them, bound hand and foot, Ejji and her husband.

Then waddled forth Pag, holding a red spear in his hand, who said,

"Listen! This pair were justly condemned to die by the death that they would have given to their child. Yet went forth Wi the Chief, and Moananga his brother, and I, Pag, with some dogs, and waited in the night close by, but where they could not see us. Came the wolves, six or eight of them, and flew at these two.

Then we loosed the dogs and at risk to ourselves attacked the brutes, killing three and wounding others so that they ran away. Afterwards we unbound Ejji and her husband and carried them here, for they were so frightened they could scarcely walk. Now by the command of Wi I set them free to tell all that if another girl-child is cast forth, those who do the deed will be left to die and none will come to save them."

So Ejji and her husband were loosed and crept away covered with shame, but for his dealings in this matter Wi gained great honour, as Moananga and even Pag did also.

After this no more girl-children were thrown out to die or be devoured, but on the other hand several were brought to Wi because their parents said they could not support them. These infants, as he promised he would do, he took into the cave, setting aside a part of it near to the light and fires for their use, which, as the place was large, could be done easily. Here the mothers must come to feed them, till they were old enough to be given into the charge of certain women whom he chose to tend them.

Now all these changes caused much talk in the tribe, so that two parties were formed, one of which was in favour of them, and one against them. However, as yet no one quarrelled with Wi, whom all knew to be better and wiser than any chief told of in their tradition. Moreover, the people had other things to think of, since now in the summer months was the time when food must be stored for the long winter.

At this business Wi and his Council made everyone work according to his strength, even the children being set to collect the eggs of sea-birds and to spread out the cod and other fishes, after cleaning them, to dry in the sun in a place watched day and night, where the wolves and foxes could not come to steal them. A tithe of all this food went to the chief for his support and for that of those dependent on him. Then half of what remained was stored against days of want, either in the cave or, to keep it fresh, buried deep in ice at the foot of the glaciers, with great stones piled upon the top of it to make it safe from the wolves and other beasts of prey.

Thus did Wi work from dawn to dark, with Pag to help him, directing all things, till often he was so tired that he fell asleep before he could lie down—he who hitherto had spent most of his days hunting in the open air. At night he would sometimes rest in Aaka's hut, for she kept her word and would not come into the cave because Pag was there. Thus they lived in seeming agreement and talked together of small matters of daily life, but no more of those over which they had quarrelled.

The boy Foh, however, although he slept in his mother's hut at night as he was commanded to do, lived more and more with his father, because there he was so welcome. For Aaka was jealous even of Foh, and this the lad knew, or felt.

The winter came on very early; indeed, that year there was little autumn. Of a sudden on one calm day when a sun without heat shone, Wi, who was walking on the shore with Urk the Aged, Moananga and Pag— for he was so busy that thus he was forced to take counsel with them—heard a sound like thunder and saw the eider-duck rise in thousands wheel round and fly off towards the south.

"What frightened them?" he asked, and Urk answered,

"Nothing, I think; but when I was a boy over seventy summers gone, I remember they did just the same thing at about this time, after which came the hardest and longest winter that had been known, when it was so cold that many of the people died. Still, it may happen that the fowl were frightened by something, such as a shaking of the earth when the ice stirs further north at the end of summer. If so, they will return. If not, we shall see them no more till next spring."

The duck did not return, although they left so hurriedly that hundreds of flappers which could scarcely fly remained behind and were hunted down by the children of the tribe, and stored in the ice for food. Also the breeding seals that came up from the south, and other creatures went away with their young, as did most of the fish. Next night there was a sharp frost, warned by which Wi set men to drag in firewood from the edge of the forest, where firs blown down by storms lay in plenty. This was a slow and toilsome task because they had no saws with which to cut up the trees, or rid them of the branches, and could only hack them to pieces slowly with flint axes. From long experience they counted on a month of open weather for this wood-harvest before the snow began to fall, burying the fallen trees so that they could not come at them, for this fuel-dragging was their last task ere winter set in.

That year, however, snow fell on the sixth day, although not thickly, and the heavy sky showed that there was more to come. Noting this, Wi set the whole tribe to work and, neglecting everything else, went out with them to make sure that all did their share. Thus it came about that in fourteen more days they had piled up a greater store of wood than Urk had ever seen in all his life, and with it much moss for the lamp-wicks and many heaps of seaweed left by the high tides which, if kept dry under earth, burned even better than did the wood.

The people grumbled at this incessant toil carried on in sleet or lightly-falling snow. But Wi would not listen to their complaints, being frightened of he knew not what, and made them work through all the hours of daylight and even by that of the moon. Well was it that he did so, for scarcely were the last trunks dragged home, the boughs brought in and piled by the boys and girls, and all the heaps of seaweed earthed up, when a great snow began to fall, which continued for many days, burying the land feet deep, so that it would have been impossible to come to the fallen trees or to collect the moss and seaweed. Then after the snow came frosts, great frosts that continued for months.

Never had such a winter been known as that which began with this snowfall, especially as the daylight seemed to be shorter than in the past, though this they held was because of the continual snow-clouds. Before it was done, indeed, even the greatest grumbler in the tribe blessed Wi who had laid up such vast stores of food and fuel, without which they must have perished. As it was, many who were old or weakly died, as did some of the children, and because it was not possible to bury them in the frozen earth, were taken away and covered with snow, whence presently the wolves dug them up.

As the months went on these wolves became very terrible, for being unable to find food they ravened boldly round the village, and even rushed into the huts at night, dragging out some of their inmates, while in the daytime they lay in wait to catch children. Then Wi caused steep snow-banks to be made as a protection, and at certain places kept fires burning, doing all he could to scare the beasts. Great white bears from the sea-borne ice appeared also, roaming round and terrifying them, though these creatures seemed to be afraid of man and did not kill any people. Drawn by the smell, however, they dug up some of the buried stores of food and devoured them, which was a great loss to the tribe.

At length the attacks of these wolves and other wild beasts grew so fierce and constant that Wi, after consulting with Moananga and Pag, determined that war must be waged against them before more people were devoured. Now in the ice-topped hills behind the beach, where the huts stood, was a certain high-cliffed hole whence there was no escape as it could only be entered by a narrow gorge. This was the plan of Wi, the cunning hunter—to drive all the wolves into that great rock-surrounded hole, then to build a wall across its mouth over which they could not climb, and thus to be rid of them. First,

however, he must accustom them to enter that place
lest they should break back. This he proposed to do in
the following fashion :

At the beginning of the winter a dying whale, of which
the tongue was torn out by thrasher sharks, had drifted
ashore, or rather into shallow water, and when it was
dead the tribe was set to work to cut it up for the sake
of its blubber and meat. This they did, piling up on
certain rocks that rose out of the water, great lumps of
flesh and blubber which they purposed to drag away
after the ice had formed. Whilst they were still engaged
upon this task there came terrible snowstorms and gales,
so that they must abandon it, and after these a thaw,
with more gales, had prevented them from coming to the
rocks.

When at last the weather abated they went there to
find that the whale's flesh had become rotten during the
thaw, so that it was useless and must be left where
it lay. Now, when everything was frozen, Wi determined
to fetch this flesh, or as much of it as they could carry,
and place it in the great rock hollow, whither the wolves
would certainly be drawn by its smell. Having planned
all this he called the chief men of the tribe together and
told them what must be done.

They listened very doubtfully, especially a party of
them led by Pitokiti the Unlucky and Whaka the Bird
of Ill-omen, who said that wolves attacked men, but
never had they heard such a thing as that men should
attack the host of the wolves in the dead of winter when
these were fierce and terrible.

" Listen," said Wi. " Will you rather kill the wolves
or be killed by them with your women and children ?
For know that it has come to this, the brutes being mad
with hunger."

Then they wrangled for a long time, so that the
matter could not be settled that day but must be put
off till the morrow.

As it chanced, that very night the wolves made a
great attack upon the huts, a hundred or more of them,

scrambling over the snow-banks and rushing past the fires, so that before they could be driven off a woman and two children were torn to pieces, while others were bitten. After this the elders accepted the plan of Wi, because they could see no other.

So first of all the strongest men were sent to the mouth of the gorge, where they dragged together loose stones, of which there were hundreds lying about though many of them they could not move because the frost held them fast. These stones they built into a wall with a broad bottom and twice the height of a man, filling in the cracks with snow which soon froze solid, but leaving a gap in the middle through which the wolves might enter, also other piled-up stones wherewith it could be closed very swiftly. Then they went down to the sea-shore and crossing the ice, or if it was broken, wading through the shallow water, came to those rocks on which the whale's flesh was stored, and scraped the deep snow off the heaps.

Now, however, they found themselves beaten, for notwithstanding the covering snow, the frost had frozen the outer lumps of flesh and blubber so hard that they could not stir them; therefore, their labour lost, they returned home, Whaka announcing loudly that he knew all the while that this would be so.

That night Wi and Pag talked long and earnestly, but wise though they were they could find no plan to overcome this trouble. Wi thought of lighting fires upon the heaps to thaw them, but Pag pointed out that if they did this the blubber would catch and all be burned. So at last they ceased talking and Wi went to Aaka, who now had changed her mind and slept in the cave because of the cold and the wolves, and asked her counsel.

" So when Pag fails you, you come to me for wisdom," she said. " Well, I have none to give. Seek it of the gods, for they alone can help you."

As it came about, the gods, or chance, did help, and in a strange fashion. In the darkness towards dawn a great noise of grunts and growlings was heard out at sea, and when at last light came, Wi saw a whole troop of the great white bears crawling away through the snow mists. When they had all gone, calling Pag and some others, he made his way over the ice to the rocks where the whale's flesh was piled up, and found that with their sharp claws and giant strength the bears, scenting food now that the snow had been removed, had torn the heaps open and scattered them, so that the centres of them, which were not frozen so hard because of the protection of the snow, lay exposed. Much they had eaten, of course, but more remained.

Then Wi said to Pag,

"I thought that we must leave the pit unbaited and try to drive the wolves into it as best we could, but it is not so, for the gods have been good to us."

"Yes," said Pag, "the bears have been very good to us, and for aught I know the gods may be bears, or the bears gods."

Then he sent to summon all the men of the tribe before the exposed flesh turned to solid ice. They came, scores of them, many with hide ropes which they made fast to great lumps of meat, and others with rough reed-woven baskets. Setting to work, before night fell again they had carried tons of the flesh into the rock pit, which was round and may have measured a hundred paces from side to side, where they left it to freeze so that the wolves could not drag it away, or eat it easily.

That night, watching by the moonlight, they saw and heard many wolves gathered at the mouth of the gully and walking to and fro filled with doubt and fear of traps. At last some entered, though only a very few of them, and were suffered to go away unhindered when they had gorged themselves. Next night more entered, and next night more, though now they could make small play with the flesh because the frost had turned it into stone. On the fourth day Wi called up the tribe, and before sunset sent all the younger men, led by Moananga,

into the woods, making a great half-circle round those
places where they knew the wolves had their lairs,
ordering them to hide there, several together so that
they might not be attacked, and not to stir till they
saw a fire burn upon a certain rock. Then with shoutings
they were to advance, driving all the wolves before them
towards the mouth of the gorge.

So the men went, for now they knew that either they
must conquer the wolves or the wolves would conquer
them.

Then it was that Pag behaved very strangely, for
after these men had started, he said,

" This plan is of no use, Wi, for when the wolves
hear the shoutings they will not run towards the gorge,
but will break and scatter by ones and twos, this way
and that, slipping through the drivers, or round the ends
of the line before it closes."

" If you think that why did you not say so before ? "
asked Wi angrily.

" For my own reasons. Hearken, Wi. All the women
call me a wolf-man, do they not, one who changes into a
wolf and hunts with the wolves? Well, that is a lie,
and yet there is truth mixed up with this lie. You know
that soon after I was born my mother cast me, or caused
me to be cast out into the forest where she was sure the
wolves would eat me, but afterwards my father found
me and brought me back. What you do not know is
that this was ten days from the time when I was cast
out. Now how did I live during those days ? I cannot
tell you, who have no memory, but I hold that some wolf
suckled me, since otherwise I must have died."

" I have heard of such things," said Wi doubtfully,
" but always set them down as winter-fire tales. But
why do you think this one to be true ? Perchance your
father found you the day that you were cast out."

" I think it to be true, because in after time, when she
was dying, my mother whispered this tale into my ears.
She said my father, who himself was killed by wolves
not long afterwards, told her secretly, for he dared not

speak of the matter openly, that when he came upon
me in the forest whither he had gone to seek my bones
and, if any of them could be found, bury them, he discovered me in such a nest as wolves make when they
bear their young, and saw a great grey wolf standing
over me with her teat in my mouth, one that had lost
her cubs, mayhap. She growled at him but ran away,
and seizing me he also ran, bearing me home. This,
my mother swore to me."

"A dying woman's fancy," said Wi.

"I think not," answered Pag, "and for this reason.
When for the second time I was driven out by the women,
or, rather, by Henga's father, whom they persuaded that
I was a bewitcher and unlucky, having nowhere else to
go and all hands being against me, I wandered into
the woods, that there the wolves might kill me and
make an end. The day began to die and presently
wolves gathered round me, for I saw them moving
between the tree-trunks, waiting till night fell to spring
upon me. I watched them idly, caring nothing, since
I had come there to be their meat. They drew near,
when suddenly a great grey she-wolf ran up as though
to seize me, then stopped and smelt at me.

"Thrice she smelt, then licked me with her tongue,
and leaping round, rushed at those other wolves, snarling
and open-jawed, her fur starting up on her back. The
dog-wolves ran away from her, but two of the she-wolves
stood, being hungry. With these she fought, tearing
the throat out of one and mauling the other so that it
limped off howling. Then she, too, went away, leaving
me amazed till I remembered my mother's story, after
which I wondered no more, being sure that this old wolf
was she that had suckled me and knew me again."

"Did you see more of her, Pag?"

"Aye. Twice she returned, once after five days,
and once after six more days, and each time she brought
me meat and laid it at my feet. It was filthy carrion,
torn from some dead deer that she had dug up from
beneath the snow, but doubtless the best that she could

find. Moreover, although she was thin with hunger and this was her portion, still she brought it to me."

" And did you eat it ? " asked Wi, astonished.

" Nay, why should I, who had crept into that hole to die ? Moreover, my stomach turned at the sight of it. Then you found me and carried me into your hut and I have met that foster-mother of mine no more. Yet she still lives, for more than once I have seen her ; yes, this very winter I have seen her who now is the leader of all the wolf-people."

" A strange story," said Wi, staring at him. " Surely if you have not dreamed it, you, who slay many of them, should be more tender towards wolves."

" Not so, for did they not kill my father and would they not have killed me ? Yet to this wolf I am tender, as I shall show you, for in payment of what I would do I ask her life."

" And what would you do ? " asked Wi.

" This. Now, before the fire is lighted, I will go down into the forest and find that wolf, for she will know me again and come to me. Then, when the shouting begins and the brutes grow frightened, she will follow me and all the other wolves will follow her, and I will lead them hither into the trap. Only her will I save from the trap, for that is my bargain."

" You are mad," said Wi.

" If I come back no more, then call me mad, or if my plan fail. But if I live and it succeeds, then call me wise," answered Pag with a low, guttural laugh. " There is yet an hour before the lighting of the fire when the edge of the moon covers yonder star. Give me that hour and you shall learn."

Then without waiting for more words, Pag slipped down the rock on which they were standing and vanished into the gloom.

" Without doubt he is mad," said Wi to himself, " and without doubt this is the end of our fellowship."

Presently, waiting there in the cold frost and watching his breath steam upon the still air, Wi's mind went back to this matter of Pag. Now that he came to think of it, it was very strange that all the tribe believed Pag to be a companion of wolves. What was accepted by all, he had noted, was generally true. If one person smelt a fox he might be mistaken, but if everybody smelt it, surely there was a fox. It was certain also that Pag never had any fear of wolves; he would go down into the forest when they were howling all around, as quietly as another would walk into his hut, and take no harm, whereas from bears or other wild beasts he would run like the rest.

Further, now Wi remembered having heard the tale told in his youth, that when Pag was cast out by his mother shortly after birth, for some reason that he forgot, fifteen days went by before his father went to seek his bones to bury them. Yet he found him living and strong, because of which, so ran the tale, the people held Pag to be not human, but a monster sprung from one of those evil spirits that might be heard howling round the huts at the dead of night.

So perhaps what Pag said was true. Perhaps his father had found him in a wolf's den and seen her suckling him. Perhaps, too, food had been brought to him by that same wolf when he was cast out for the second time. For these beasts were known to live very many years, especially if the spirit of a dead man were in them, as Urk and other aged ones declared happened from time to time both in the case of wolves and of other creatures, such as the great-toothed tiger.

Well, he would learn presently; meanwhile the moment drew near when he must light the signal fire.

A while later Wi looked at the moon and saw that the star was vanishing in the light of its edge; then he whispered to Foh, who had now come to him and crouched at his side, watching all things eagerly as a boy does. Foh nodded and slipped away, to return presently with a smouldering brand that he had brought from a little fire which was burning out of sight further down the hillside.

Wi took it and going to the pile of dried wood that had been prepared upon the rock, he blew it to a flame and set it among some powdered seaweed at the base of the pile. The seaweed caught readily, as this sort does when dry, giving out a blue light, and presently the pile was ablaze. Then Wi bade Foh go home to the cave, which he pretended to do, but did not, for desiring above all things to see this great wolf-hunt, he hid himself away behind a rock.

Thinking that Foh had departed, Wi crept down to where the old men, to the number of fifty or more under the command of Hotoa the Slow-speeched, lay hidden among the stones, down-wind so that the wolves might not smell them, and near to the mouth of the gully that save for a gap in the middle, was built up with a wall of snow-covered boulders, as has been told. These men he bade be ready, and when the wolves had gone through the gap and they heard his command, but not before, to rush forward, each of them carrying a large stone, and fill it up, so that the wolves could not come out again. Meanwhile they must keep stirring the stones lest the frost should fasten them to the ground.

These men, many of whom were shivering with cold or fear, or both, listened dully. Whaka said that his heart told him that no good would come of this business ; Hou the Unstable asked if they could not change their plan and go home ; Ngae the Magician announced that he had sought an omen from the Ice-Gods, whose priest he was, and had dreamed a very evil dream in which he had seen Pitokiti sleeping in the belly of a wolf, signifying, no doubt, that they were all about to be killed and eaten ; news at which Pitokiti moaned and wrung his hands. Urk the Aged shook his head and declared that no such plan as this had ever been made from the beginning ; at least his grandfather had never told him of it. and what had not been done before could not be done now. Only Hotoa, a man of good heart though stupid, answered at length that the stones were ready and that for his part he would build them up if and when the wolves were in the pit, even if he had to do so alone.

Now Wi grew angry.

"Hearken!" he said. "The moon is very clear and I can see all. If one man runs, be sure I shall note him and will dash out his brains now or later. Yes, the first man who runs shall die," and he lifted his axe and looked at Hou and Whaka.

After this all grew silent, for they knew that what Wi said, that he would do.

Presently wolves began to appear, looking like shadows on the snow, and by twos and threes louped past with lolling tongues and vanished through the cleft into the pit beyond.

"Stir not," whispered Wi. "These are not driven, they come to eat the whale's flesh as they have done before."

This was true enough, for soon from within the pit the watchers heard the sound of growls and of the teeth of the starved beasts grating on the frozen flesh.

At length from far away came a noise of shouts and they knew that the drivers had seen the fire on the high rock and were at their work. A long time went by. Then—oh! then those watchers saw a terrible sight, for behold, the snow slope beneath them grew black with wolves, more wolves than they had ever counted; hundreds of them there seemed to be, all coming on in silence, slowly, doggedly, like a marshalled host. And lo! in front of them trotted a huge, gaunt, grey she-wolf and, either running at her side, holding to her hair, or mounted on her back, which they could not be sure because of the shadows, was Pag the Dwarf, Pag the Wolf-man!

The watchers gasped with fear, and some of them hid their eyes with their hands, for they were terrified. Even Wi gasped, for now he knew that Pag had spoken truth and that wolf's milk ran in his blood as the wolf's craft lived in his brain.

Into the shadow of the cleft passed the great grey

mother-wolf; Wi could see her glowing eyes and her worn yellow fangs as she trotted beneath him, and with her went Pag. Lo! they entered the gap in the stone, snow-covered wall, and as they entered the she-wolf raised her head and howled aloud. All the multitude which followed her, that for a moment had seemed to hesitate, raised their heads and howled also, making such a sound as the people had never heard, so terrible a sound that some of them fell to the ground, swooning. For this was the cry of the mother-wolf to the pack, the call that they must obey. Then the multitude pressed on after her, scrambling upon each others' backs to be first into the pit.

All were in, not one of the hundreds remained outside, and the time had come to close the breach. Wi opened his lips to utter the command, then hesitated. Pag was there in the pit, and when the wolves found that they were trapped, certainly they would tear him to pieces, and the mother-wolf also which had led them to their death. He must speak; yet Pag was in the pit! How could he command the death of Pag? Oh, Pag was but one man and the people were many, and if once those wolves broke out again, mad with rage, none would be left living.

"To the wall!" he said hoarsely and, himself lifting a large stone, sprang forward.

Then it was that through the cleft came the great mother-wolf and with her Pag unharmed. He bent down, whispered into the ear of the she-wolf, and it seemed to them, the watchers, that she listened and licked his face. Then suddenly like an arrow she sped away.

In her path was Pitokiti the Unlucky, who turned to fly. With a growl she nipped him, tearing a great hole in his flank, fled on, and was no more seen.

"Build up!" cried Wi. "Build up!"

"Aye, build you up," echoed Pag, "and swiftly if you would see the sun. I go, my work is finished," and he shambled through them who even then shrank away from him.

Wi rushed to the cleft and flung down his stone, as did others. A wolf's head appeared above the rising pile ; he brained it with his axe so that it fell backwards dead, and there was a sound of its being torn to pieces and devoured by those within. This gave them a breath of time. The stones rose higher, but now at them came all the weight of the wolves. Some were killed or driven back, for even the most timid fought desperately with their stone spears, clubs and axes, knowing that if once the prisoned horde climbed or broke through the wall it would have the mastery of them. So some built and others fought, while yet others brought baskets filled with damp grit or snow taken from deep holes, which they poured on to the stones, where immediately it ran down into the cracks and froze, turning them to a fortress wall.

Yet some of the wolves got over by mounting on to each other's backs and leaping thence to the crest of the wall before it reached its full height. The most of these fled away to be the parents of other packs in years to come, but certain of the fiercest fought with the men beyond and mauled them, so that one old fellow died of his wounds.

In all this noise and confusion, suddenly Wi heard a cry for help which caused him to turn round, for he thought he knew the voice. He looked, and by the bright moonlight shining on the snow saw Foh, his son, fighting a great wolf. With a snarl the brute sprang. Foh bent himself and received the weight of it upon the point of his flint-headed spear. Down went the lad with the wolf on the top of him. Wi bounded forward, thinking to find him with his throat torn out. He reached the place too late, for both Foh and the wolf lay still. Putting out his strength he dragged the brute away. Beneath it lay Foh covered with blood. Thinking him sped, in an agony Wi lifted him, for he loved this boy better than anyone on the earth. Then suddenly Foh slipped from his arms, stood upon his feet and gasped as his breath returned to him.

" See, Father, I killed the beast ! My spear broke—
but see—the point of it sticks out of his back. His teeth
were on my throat when all at once his mouth opened
and he died."

" Get you home," said Wi roughly, but in his heart
he thanked the Ice-Gods because his only son had been
saved alive.

Then he rushed back to the wall, nor did he leave it
until it had been built so high that it could not be leapt
over by any wolf in the world. Nor could it be scaled,
for the topmost stones were set so that they curved
towards the great pit within. There, then, Wi waited
till the damp sand and the snow froze hard, and he knew
that before the spring came nothing could stir them.

At length the work was done, and in the east broke the
dawn of the short winter day. Then Wi climbed to the
top of the wall and looked into the pit beyond. It was
still full of darkness, for the moon had sunk behind the
hills, but in the darkness he could see hundreds of fierce
eyes moving, while the mountains echoed with the
howlings of the imprisoned beasts.

So they howled for days, the strongest devouring
those that grew weak, till at length there was silence in
that darksome place, for all were dead.

CHAPTER IX

WI MEETS THE TIGER

Two days had gone by, for the most of which time Wi had slept. Indeed, after this great battle with the wolves he was weary almost to death, not with the work or the fighting, but through amazement at the sight of Pag keeping awful fellowship with the great she-wolf, and agony of mind because of what he had suffered when he thought that the throat of Foh was torn out ; also when he believed that the whole host of the wood-dwellers would break through or over the wall, and tear him and his companions to pieces.

When at times he woke up from that sleep Aaka was kind to him, more so than she had been since Henga had murdered Foa. For she was proud of his deeds and fame that were in every mouth, and now that he had risen from his bed she brought him food and spoke to him softly, which pleased Wi, who loved Aaka, the wife of his youth, although of late her face seemed to be turned away from him. While he ate, Aaka giving him his food piece by piece, as was the fashion of wives among the tribe, Moananga joined them and began to talk in his light manner of that night of fear.

" All the good of it was with you, Brother," he said, " for we tramped through the forest cutting our feet and breaking our shins against trunks of trees and boughs half buried in the snow, for no purpose at all."

" Did you not see any wolves ? " asked Wi.

" Not one, though we heard them howling in the distance. It seems that they had all gone on before, led by a certain friend of ours who can charm wolves,

if what I hear is true," and he shrugged his shoulders.
" Yet we saw something else."

" What was that ? " asked Wi.

" We saw the great striped beast of which we have
learned from our fathers ; the tiger with teeth like spear-
heads, a like beast to that whose skin, or what remains
of it, is your cloak to-day, which has been worn by the
Chief of the Tribe from the beginning."

Now this was true, since for generations those who
dwelt in the cave one after another wore that cloak,
though none knew how it had come to the first of them.
Moreover, although tradition told of this great tiger
beast, which was once the terror of the tribe, hitherto
none living had seen it, so that although they still talked
of it, men thought that its race was dead, or had left
their land.

" What did it do ? " said Wi, much stirred, as a
hunter would be.

" It appeared from between the trees and walking
forward boldly, leapt on to a rock and stood there staring
at us and lashing its tail, a mighty brute tall as a deer
and longer. We shouted, thinking to scare it away
but it took no heed, only stood and purred like a wild
cat of the woods, watching us with its glowing eyes.
Now in front of it, with others, was the man named
Finn, whom Henga hated and swore to kill, so that he
must hide himself in the woods, whence he only came out
again after you had slain Henga. Suddenly the tiger
ceased purring and fixed its eyes on Finn. Finn saw it
and turned to run. Then the tiger leapt, such a leap as
has never been seen. Right over the heads of the others
it leapt, landing on to the back of Finn, who fell down.
Next instant the tiger had him in his jaws and bounded
away with him as the wild cat bounds with a bird which
it has seized. That was the last we saw of it, and of Finn."

" Strange that the tiger should have chosen him who
was hated of Henga, the Tiger-man," said Wi.

" Yes, Wi, so strange that all the people hold that
the spirit of Henga has entered into this tiger."

Now Wi did not laugh at this saying, because it was the belief of his folk that the ghost of an evil man often passed into the shape of some terrible beast that could not be killed, and in that form took vengeance upon those whom that man had hated in life, or on his children. Therefore he only said,

"If it be so, it seems that I must guard myself, seeing that if Henga hated Finn, he hated me ten times more, and with good reason, as perhaps he knows to-day. Well, I slew Henga, and I swear that, if it troubles us more, I will slay this tiger also, though whence the beast came I cannot guess."

At this moment Pag appeared, whereon Aaka, who had been listening to the tale of the death of Finn, turned and went away, saying over her shoulder,

"Here comes one who perchance can show you how to lead the tiger into a trap. For what is a tiger but a big striped wolf?"

Others, too, shrank to one side as Pag advanced, because, although they were grateful to him for what he had done, they who had always feared Pag now feared him a great deal more. Yes, even Moananga shrank and made a place for him.

"Fear not," said Pag mockingly. "The grey wolf-mother has fled afar and no more of her kin follow after me and her. Indeed, I come from watching them. They fight and devour each other there in the pit, and ere long, I think, all will be dead, for that wall they can neither climb nor tunnel."

"Tell us, Pag," said Moananga boldly, after his fashion, "what are you—a man, or a wolf fashioned to the shape of a dwarf?"

"You knew my father and my mother, Moananga, and therefore should be able to answer your own questions. Yet in all men there is something of the wolf and, for certain reasons that Wi has heard, in me perhaps more than in most."

"So the people think, Pag."

"Do they, Moananga? If so, tell them from me

that I am not a wolf that can be caught in any trap ; also that if they will leave me alone, I will leave them alone. But if they will not, then they may feel my fangs."

" How did you lead the wolves, Pag ? "

" Why should you ask secrets, Moananga ? Yet if you would know, I will tell you that you may tell it to others. The mother of them all is my friend. I went into the wood and called and she came to me. Then I bade her follow me as a dog does. She followed, and the rest followed her ; that is all."

Moananga looked at Pag doubtfully and answered,

" I hold that there is more behind, Pag."

" Aye, Moananga, there is always more behind everything, for those who can find it. We cannot see far and know very little, Moananga—not even what we were before we were born, or what we shall be after we are dead."

Now there was something so grim about Pag's talk that although he was curious Moananga asked him no more questions ; only he said,

" If there be something of a wolf in man, there may be something of man in a tiger," and he repeated to him that tale which he had told to Wi.

Pag listened earnestly and answered,

" When one cloud passes, another comes ; the wolves have gone, the tiger follows. Whether Henga dwells in this beast I do not know. But if so, the sooner it is slain the better," and he glanced at Wi, and at Foh who was now standing by his father, his arm thrown about him. Then he went to fetch his food, for he was hungry.

Now from that day forward the tiger became as great an ill to the tribe as the wolves had been, although it was but one and these had been many. It lurked around the village in the dark of the night, and when light came and people crept out of their huts, it rushed in, seizing now one and now another and bounding away with its prey in its mouth. No fence would keep it out, nor would it tread on any pitfall, while so swift were its movements that none could hit it with a spear. It was noted, moreover, that all those who were taken had been men whom Henga hated, or their children, or perchance women who had been his and now were married to others. Therefore the people grew sure that in this tiger dwelt the spirit of Henga. Also Ngae the Priest and Taren his wife, having taken counsel with the Ice-gods, returned from the glacier and declared that this was so.

Pondering these things, Wi was much afraid, though more for Foh than for himself. Certainly soon or late the lad would be seized, or perchance his own turn would come first. The people lived in terror also and now none of them would come out of his hut till it was full day, much less walk beyond the village unless there were many of them together.

Very slowly and very late, at length the spring came ; the snows melted and the horned deer appeared in the woods. Now Wi hoped the huge tiger with the flashing teeth would cease from killing men and fill itself with venison, or perhaps go away altogether whence it came, wherever that might be, to seek a mate there. Yet the tiger did none of these things. Almost it seemed that it was the last of its race, who could find no mate because none was left living on the earth. At least it stayed in the great woods that bordered the beach, living now in one place and now in another; moreover, it continued to find victims, for between the spring and the first month of summer three of the tribe were dragged away, so that the end of it was that they dared not go out to seek food, never being sure but that the striped beast might spring upon them from some lair where it lay hid, for it appeared to watch all their movements and to know where they would come.

The end of it was that the people gathered at the meeting-place and sent Wini-wini the Shudderer to pray Wi to speak with them. He came accompanied by Pag. Then by the mouth of Urk the Aged they addressed him, saying,

" This tiger with the great teeth, whom we believe

to be Henga in the shape of a beast, kills us. We demand that you who slew Henga and turned him into a tiger, you who are a mighty hunter and our chief by right of conquest, should slay the tiger, as you slew Henga."

"And if I cannot, or will not, what then?" asked Wi.

"Then, if we are strong enough we will kill you and Pag and choose another chief," they replied through Wini-wini the Mouth. "Or if we cannot, at least we will obey you and your laws no more, but will go away from this place where we have lived since the beginning, and seek another home far from the tiger."

"Mayhap the tiger will go with you," said Pag darkly, a grin upon his ugly face, which saying did not please them, for they had not thought of such a thing.

Before any of them could answer, however, Wi spoke in a slow, sad voice,

"It seems that among you I have many enemies," he said; "nor do I wonder at this, for in sundry ways the past winter has been most evil, with fiercer cold and longer snows than were ever known, whence have come much death and sickness. Also a number of us have been killed, first by the wolves, which are now destroyed, and afterwards by this tiger; nor, although we have made offerings, do the gods who live in the ice yonder help us at all. Now you tell me that I must kill the tiger, or that you will kill me if you can and find another chief, which by the ancient custom you have a right to do. Or if you cannot, that you will leave me and go hence to seek a new home far from where you were born.

"Hearken, People of the Tribe. I say to you it is not needful that you should wander away perhaps to find worse dangers than those which you have left. Soon I go out to seek this tiger and match myself against it, as I did against Henga, whose spirit you believe lives in its skin. Perhaps I shall kill it, or more probably it will kill me, in which case you must fight with the beast as best you can, or, if it should please you better, flee away. In any case it is not needful that you should try to kill me, for learn that I am weary of this chieftainship. A while ago I rid you of a tyrant who murdered many of you, as he did my own daughter, and since then, labouring day and night, I have worked for the good of all and done my best to serve you. Now, as you hold that I have failed, and I am of the same mind—for otherwise you would love me better—it is my wish to lay down my chieftainship, or if custom will not allow of this, to stand here unarmed while he whom you may choose to succeed me, puts an end to my life with his club and spear.

"Therefore choose the man, that I may submit myself to him. Yet, if you will take my last counsel as your chief, when you have done so, command him to spare me a little while that I may go forth to kill the tiger if I can. Then, if perchance it does not kill me, I will return and you can deal with me as you will, either by suffering me to live on as one of you, such as I was before I became your chief, or by putting an end to me."

When the people heard these words and understood their nobleness, they were ashamed. Also they were perplexed, for they knew not whom to choose as chief, if indeed there was anyone who would take that office. Moreover, Pag did not comfort them by announcing loudly that this new chief would find one to challenge him, and that within an hour, namely, Pag himself. Indeed, at this saying they looked aside, or rather those among them who had cast eyes of longing on the cave did so, for although Pag was a dwarf his strength was terrible. Besides, he was a wolf-man who could doubtless summon powers to help him from the earth or air, perhaps the grey wolf-mother, or ghosts that howl in the night. Still one voice did call out the name of Moananga, whereon he answered,

"Not so, fool. I stand with my brother Wi, and tell you that if you thrust him out it will be because the gods have made you mad; for where can you find one who is braver or wiser or more honest ? Why do you not go up yourselves against the tiger and kill it ? Is it perchance that you are afraid ? "

None answered. For a while they murmured together confusedly; then as though with one voice cried out,

"Wi is our Chief. We will have no other Chief but Wi."

So that trouble ended.

That night Wi and Pag took counsel as to how they might make an end of the tiger. Earnestly they debated, but for a long while could see no light. Everything had been tried. The brute would not walk over their most cunning pitfalls; it would not eat the meat poisoned with the juices of a certain fish that when rotten was deadly; it feared no fires and could not be driven away. Twice men in numbers had gone out to attack it, but once it hid itself and the next time it charged them, smote down a man with its great paw, and vanished, after which they would go no more.

"You and I must fight it alone," said Wi, but Pag shook his head.

"Our strength is not enough," he answered. "Before you could smite a blow with your axe it would have killed us both. Or perchance if the ghost of Henga dwells in it, as all the people think, it would not face that axe again, but would hide itself."

Then he walked to the mouth of the cave and idly enough stared up at that broken tree where, as the moonlight showed, the blackened head of Henga was still fixed, its long locks waving in the wind. He returned and said,

"That tiger must be very lonely, having none of its kind with which to talk or mate. Will you lend me your Chief's cloak, Wi? If it is lost I will promise you a better."

"What for?" asked Wi.

"That I will tell you afterwards. Will you lend me the cloak, and the necklace of tiger-claws?"

"Take them if you wish," said Wi wearily, knowing that it was useless to dig for secrets in the dark heart of Pag. "Take them and the chieftainship also, if it pleases you, for of all these I have had enough, who would that once again I were a hunter and no more."

"A hunter you shall be," said Pag, "the greatest of hunters. Now talk no more to me of tigers for a while, lest I should smell them in my sleep."

After this for several days Pag was missing for hours at a time, and when he returned at night always seemed to be very weary. Also Wi noticed that other things were missing, namely, his tiger-skin cloak, with the necklace, and the head of Henga from the broken tree outside the cave, that now was nothing but skin and bone. Aaka asked him why he did not wear his cloak. He answered,

"Because winter passes and it grows too warm."

"I do not find it warm," said Aaka. "And why do you not wear the necklace?"

"Because in spring the skin is tender and it scratches me."

"Surely Pag is a good master to you," said Aaka. "Himself he could not have answered with a smoother tongue. But where does Pag go so secretly?"

"I do not know, Wife. I was about to ask you, who watch him well, if you could tell me."

"That I think I can, Wi. Without doubt he goes to hunt with the old mother-wolf, as he must do when she calls him, which is why he comes home so tired. I hear that certain of our dead have been dug out of the snow lately and eaten."

"That has not been reported to me," said Wi.

"Even a Chief is not told everything, especially of those he loves," answered Aaka, and walked away laughing.

Two nights later Pag went to the mouth of the cave and by wetting his finger and holding it in the wind, tested its direction very carefully. Then he came to Wi and whispered,

"Will you rise an hour before dawn and come with me to kill the tiger?"

"Had we not better take others also?" asked Wi, hesitating.

"Nay. Only fools share their meat with strangers; let the glory be ours alone. Now ask me no more in this place where there are many ears."

"Good," said Wi. "I will come with you, to—kill the tiger, or be killed by it."

So a little more than an hour before dawn the two of them might have been seen slipping from the cave like shadows. But before he went Wi kissed Foh, who lay fast asleep at his side, because he did not think to see him again. Also he looked at the place where Aaka slept and sighed sadly. He was fully armed with his heavy axe of bright stone, two flint-headed spears and a knife also of flint. Pag likewise carried two spears and a knife.

When they were clear of the huts and picking their way towards the wood by the light of the moon, now near her death, and of the stars, Pag said that the gale which had been raging for days seemed to have blown itself away, and the stars shone so brightly that he prophesied fair weather. Then Wi grew angry, exclaiming,

"Have done with your talk of the weather and the stars, and tell me whither we go and to what end. Am I a child that you should keep me thus in the dark?"

"Yes," answered Pag, "I think you are something of a child, out of whom women can suck secrets, which cannot be said of me."

"I return home," said Wi, stopping.

"Yet," went on Pag quietly, "if you would hear the tale it is short. Only do not stand there like a girl looking after her lover, but come on, for our time is also short."

"That I can well believe," muttered Wi as he walked forward.

"Listen," said Pag. "You know the two rocks yonder near the edge of the forest that people call Man and Wife because they are so close together and yet divided ? "

" Yes, I know them. Once we thought of digging a pit there, but did not do so because the bases of the rocks slope inward and doubtless meet just under the ground."

" Those who would know must first look to see," said Pag. " I heard that talk about the pit, heard also Urk declare that his grandfather had tried to dig one there, but could not because the rocks met. Then because I knew that Urk's grandfather must have been a great liar—or perhaps it is Urk who is the liar—I went to try for myself with a sharpened stake and found that the rocks do not meet. I found another thing also —that the tiger used this path. So to scare him away for a while I hung up cast-off skin garments with a man's scent on them. Then I set to work and dug my pitfall ; a very nice pitfall, narrow like a grave, and placed sharp stakes in it and lit a fire at the bottom of it to take away the smell of man. Next I laid pine boughs over it which smell of themselves, and covered it with fine sand like to that around, which I carried there in a skin filled with a shell so that my hand never touched a grain of it, and did all other things that might deceive a tiger."

" This tiger cannot be deceived," said Wi gloomily, " for is it not as cunning as a man ? How many pitfalls have we made, and has it not walked round every one of them ? "

" Yes, Wi, that tiger is cunning, but it is also lonely, and when it sees that another tiger has crossed the pit and is waiting for it on the further side, then perhaps it will follow ; at least I hope so."

" Another tiger ! What do you mean ? "

" That you shall learn presently. And now, Wi, I pray you to forget that you are a good chief and to remember that you are a better hunter, and be silent, for then there is naught to fear, because the wind blows straight down the cleft and the tiger cannot smell us."

Presently they came to the pit, where there was a

gap in a rocky ridge of the height of a tall pine, which gap was wider at the top than at the bottom, worn so by ice or water, perhaps. Indeed, at its foot it did not measure more than two paces across. To one side of this cleft lay some stones, large stones, and among these Pag told Wi to hide, whispering,

" Be swift and lie close, for the dawn is near and if, as I hope, the tiger comes, it will be soon. Have your axe ready also."

" What are you going to do ? " asked Wi.

" That you shall learn. Be not astonished at anything you may see, and do not stir unless you are attacked or I call to you."

Then Pag slipped away into the darkness, and kneeling on the ground Wi watched between a crack in the stones. By such light as there was, having been a hunter from his youth and therefore accustomed to see in the gloom, as wild beasts can, he perceived that on the snow-sprinkled bottom of the cleft—for here in this shaded place the snow had not melted—appeared footmarks, such as are made by a tiger's pads of which the claws cut lines in the snow, and thought to himself that Pag was too late, for the brute had already passed here. Then he remembered that this could not be, because if it had, it would have fallen into the pit which was dug beneath.

Whence, then, came the footprints, he wondered. Soon he wondered much more, for almost beneath him in the shadow of the rock and on the hither side of the pitfall, appeared the tiger. Yet how could the tiger be there, for had they not just come to the place across open land where there were no trees, such as grew in plenty on the further side of the cleft, and so must have seen it ? Yet it was the tiger, for he could distinguish its striped hide, or some of it. Moreover, it growled as do beasts of prey, and appeared to be tearing with its jaws at something that lay before it on the snow just where the pitfall should end.

Now, thought Wi to himself, if I spring down suddenly

and hit with all my strength, perhaps I may break this brute's neck, or dash out its brains with a blow of my axe before it turns upon me.

Then he remembered that Pag had said that he must not stir except to defend himself, unless he, Pag, called to him ; also that Pag boasted that he never spoke without a reason. So Wi stayed where he was and watched.

The first grey light of dawn began to gather, and though the tiger was still hid in the shade, it fell upon that which it seemed to be devouring, something black and round from which hung hair.

By the gods ! it was the head of Henga. Now Wi understood everything. Pag was the tiger ! Yes, inside that skin, fashioned from the Chief's cloak set out to a tiger's shape upon a framework of twigs covered with dried grass or seaweed, was Pag, in front of whom lay the dried head of Henga which he pretended to devour. And to think of it ! A few moments past he had proposed to smite this sham with his axe, thereby killing Pag. The blood of Wi ran cold at the thought ; then he forgot it, and all else.

For on the further side of the cleft, creeping up slowly, belly to ground, with waving tail, flashing fangs and bristling hair, appeared the monstrous creature they had come out to seek. There it stood, for now it had risen to its full height, which seemed to be that of a deer ; doubtfully it stood, glaring in front of it with glowing eyes.

The other tiger beneath, or rather, Pag in its skin, growled more fiercely, tearing at the head of Henga. The monster pricked its ears and growled back, but in a friendly fashion. Then suddenly it seemed to smell the head of Henga and glared down at it. It stepped forward, arched its back, and leapt as a wolf cub or a puppy leaps to seize that which it desires for its play. The tiger rose into the air and with gathered paws landed on to the covering of the pit, which broke beneath its weight. Down into the pit it went, and after it rolled the head of Henga. Roar upon roar rent the air as the sharp stakes which Pag had set at the bottom of the pit, pierced deep into the beast beneath the pressure of its bulk.

Wi leapt from his hiding-place and ran forward to Pag, who having cast off the stuffed-out tiger-skin, stood staring into the pit, a spear in his hand. Wi looked down and saw the huge tiger, its eyes glowing like lamps, twisting on the stakes. Suddenly it ceased its awful roarings and for one moment they thought that it was dead. The next Pag cried,

" Beware ! The brute comes."

As he spoke, the tiger's claws appeared over the edge of the grave-like pit, followed by its great flat head. It had freed itself from the stakes and with all its mighty strength was drawing itself from the hole. Pag drove at it with his spear, wounding it in the throat. It caught the handle with its teeth and bit it in two.

" Smite ! " he said, and Wi brought down the axe upon its head, crushing its skull—a great blow.

Yet even this did not kill the tiger. Wi struck again and shattered one foreleg. It heaved itself upwards and now it was out of the pit. It reared up and smote at him with its uninjured paw. Wi ran back, bending so that the blow went over his head, and Pag slipped to one side. The tiger followed Wi, towering above him on its hind feet, for because of its hurts it seemed that it could not spring. Wi struck again with the axe, which he wielded in both hands, and the sharp blade sank into the beast below the breast. He strove to withdraw the axe, which was firmly fixed in the tough hide, but before he could do so the brute fell on him and down he went beneath it, and lay there covered by its carcase.

Pag ran up and drove his remaining spear into its side, behind the fore-arm. Yes, again and again he pushed with all his weight upon the spear. Then the tiger, which had opened its mouth to seize the head of Wi and crush it, uttered a moaning noise ; its jaws closed, its head dropped on to the face of Wi. its claws contracted, scattering the sand, a shiver ran through its whole length, and it lay still.

Again Pag thrust at the spear, driving it in yet further, until he knew that it must have reached the beast's heart. Then he seized one forepaw and putting out all his great strength, dragged at it till the dead tiger rolled over upon its back, revealing Wi beneath, painted red with blood.

Pag, who thought that he was dead, uttered a low cry of grief, but as he did so Wi sat up gasping, for the breath was pressed out of him.

" Are you torn ? " asked Pag.

" I think not," grunted Wi. " I think the claws missed me."

" Perhaps after all there are some gods," said Pag.

" At least there are devils," answered Wi, looking down at the dead monster.

" You will have a fine new cloak, a cloak of glory," said Pag.

" Then it should cover your shoulders," answered Wi.

CHAPTER X

THE BOAT AND ITS BURDEN

Wi and Pag, leaning on each other—for though neither
was hurt, now, after all was over, both felt very tired—
walked back to the cave, for with the carcase of the huge
tiger they could do nothing by themselves. But first
Pag shook the seaweed and withies with which it had
been stuffed, out of the Chief's cloak wherein he had
played the part of a tiger, and as Wi would not wear it
because he was too filthy with blood and dirt, threw it
over his shoulder. But the head of Henga he left where
it lay. It had served its turn; also Pag swore that never
again did he wish to have it so close to his nose and
teeth.

When they reached the huts it was still so near to the
dawn that no one was about, for since the people learned
that the great tiger attacked at this hour, they had become
late-risers. Therefore Wi and Pag came to the mouth
of the cave unnoticed.

Here, however, they found some waiting for them, as
Aaka, having been awakened early by Foh who came to
tell her that his father was gone from their bed, rose to
look for him. For in this matter Aaka was strange:
although so sharp with Wi when he was present, she kept
a watch on all his movements and grew disturbed when
she could not see him, and did not know where he might
be or why he had gone away. This mood was strong on
her that morning because she was sure in herself that
danger was near to him, especially when she learned that
Pag was also missing from the cave. Therefore, although
the tiger might be on the prowl, she bade Foh run swiftly
to the hut of his uncle Moananga and bring him to her.

So Moananga came and with him Tana, who would not
be left alone in the hut, also others whom he summoned,
for because of the tiger if people stirred at this hour when
it was known to be abroad, a company of them always
went together. They reached the cave and Moananga
asked what was the trouble. Aaka answered that she
desired to know if they had seen Wi, whom she could not
find, or Pag who doubtless was with him, or if they knew
where he had gone.

Moananga answered No, and spoke calm words to her
for she was much disturbed, saying that Wi had many
duties to attend of which he told no one, and doubtless one of these had called him away. Or perhaps,
he added, he had gone to the glacier to make prayer to
the Ice-Gods or to seek some sign of them.

While he was speaking thus, Foh pointed with his
finger and behold! out of the morning mists appeared
Wi, painted from head to heel with blood and leaning
upon the shoulder of Pag the dwarf as a lame man
leans upon a stick.

" Not for nothing was I troubled," said Aaka. " See,
Wi is wounded, and sorely."

" Yet he walks well and his axe is as red as his skin,"
answered Moananga.

Then Wi came up to them and Aaka asked,

" Whose blood is that which covers you, Husband ?
Your own or another man's ? "

" Neither, Wife," answered Wi. " It is the blood of
the great-toothed tiger which Pag and I have been
fighting."

" Yet Pag's skin is white and yours is red, which is
strange. But what of the tiger, husband ? "

" The tiger is dead, Wife."

Now they stared at him and Aaka asked,

" Did you slay it ? "

" Nay," he answered, " I fought it, but I think Pag
was its slayer. He made the plan, he dug the trap,
he set the bait and it was his spear that reached the
brute's heart at last, ere my head was bitten off."

"Go look at the tiger's skull," said Pag, "and see whether Wi's axe fits into the hole there. Look at its forearm also and judge what weapon shattered it."

"Pag! always Pag! Is there nothing that you can do without Pag, Husband?"

"Oh yes," answered Wi bitterly. "Perchance I might kiss a woman, if I could find one who was fair and gentle-hearted."

"Why don't you?" mocked Aaka.

Then he went past her into the cave and called for water to wash himself, while Pag sat down in front of it and told the tale of how Wi had slain the tiger to all who would listen to him, but of his part in that play saying nothing at all.

Led by Moananga, men went out, a score of them or more, and carried in the beast, which they laid down in a place where it could be seen by everyone. That day all who could stand upon their feet, from the oldest to the youngest of the tribe, came to stare at the dead monster which had worked them so much mischief, while Pag sat by grinning, and pointed out how the axe of Wi had shattered its skull and wellnigh hewn off its great forepaw.

"But who gave the wound that pierced its heart?" asked one.

"Oh, Wi did that too," answered Pag. "When the beast charged him with its last strength, he leapt aside and thrust his spear through its heart, after which it fell on top of him and tried to bite off his head."

"And what did you do all this time?" asked Tana, the wife of Moananga.

"I? Oh, I looked on. No, I forgot, I knelt down and prayed to the gods that Wi might conquer."

"You lie, Wolf-man," said Tana, "for both your spears are buried in the beast."

"Perhaps," answered Pag. "If so, it is an art I have learned from women. If you have never lied, Tana, for good ends or bad, then reproach me; but if you have, leave me alone."

Then Tana was silent, for although she was sweet and loving, it was well known that she did not always tell the truth.

After this, when he was recovered from his weariness and shaking and his crushed ribs ceased to ache, all the people came up and worshipped Wi who had rid them of the tiger as he had rid them of the wolves, declaring that he was one of the gods who had come out of the ice to save them.

"So you say when things go well and danger passes. But when they go ill and it hangs over your heads then you tell another tale about me," answered Wi, smiling sadly. "Moreover, you give praise where it is not due, while you withhold it where it is due."

Then to be rid of all this clamour he slipped away from them and went out quite alone to walk upon the beach, while Pag stayed behind to skin the tiger and to dress its hide. For now that the wolves were dead and the tiger was dead, and Henga the murderer was dead, all slain by Wi, man or woman or child might walk the beach in safety and alone, especially as the bears seemed to have gone away, though whether this was from fear of the tiger or lack of food none knew.

The great gale from the south, which that spring had raged for very many days and almost up to the night when Wi went out to fight the tiger, had now quite blown itself out, leaving behind it a clear grey sky, though of sun that spring there seemed to be even less than during the year that was gone. Indeed, the air remained very cold, feeling as it does when snow is about to fall, though this was not the time for snow ; the flowers which should have been making the woodlands and the hillsides bright had not yet bloomed, nor had the seals and the birds come in their wonted numbers. But though the wind was gone there was still a great swell upon the sea, and big waves, upon which floated blocks of ice, broke sullenly upon the beach.

Wi walked towards the east. Presently he came to

the mouth of the glacier-cleft, and though he had not purposed to go up to the face of the ice or to look upon the shape of the Sleeper, something seemed to lead him there ; indeed, he felt as if an invisible cord was drawing him towards this gloomy, yet to him sacred spot, because in it dwelt the only gods he knew. Moreover, he remembered that during the mighty frosts of the past winter, and especially at the time of the big gale, great noises had been heard in the ice, which caused the tribe to think the gods were stirring.

He reached the head of the cleft and there, poor savage that he was, covered his eyes with his hands and kneeling down, prayed after his fashion. He thanked the gods because they had delivered him and the people in his charge from great peril, giving him strength to kill the evil Henga, and by the help of Pag to do away with the most of the wolves, also with the awful tiger that the tribe believed contained the spirit of Henga still lingering upon earth. He prayed also that the laws which he had made might prosper ; that there might be plenty of food ; that Foh his son might grow and be strong, ceasing to cough ; that Aaka might be gentle towards him, who felt so lonely and companionless and who by the law that he had made, was forbidden to seek any other wife. Lastly he prayed that the sun might shine and the weather become warm.

Then, as had happened to him before in this spot, something seemed to speak in his heart, reminding him that he had brought no offering, also that it was too late to find one, especially as now that the wolves were gone, he could not slay a beast as he had done before, and set its head upon a stone that the gods might smell blood.

Well, if so, what did it matter ? How could the blood of wolves be of any service to gods ; and if it were so, was it good to worship beings who rejoiced in blood and suffering ? If they lived and had power, must they not desire a very different sacrifice ? What sacrifice ? A thought came to him. Surely that of the heart, that of repentance for past evil, that of promise to do better.

A gust of passion seized him. He flung himself upon his face, muttering,

" O gods, let me be the sacrifice. Give me strength to see and understand, to bring blessing upon the heads of all, to protect and nurture all, if only for a little while, and then, if you will, take my life in payment for your gifts."

Thus prayed poor Wi, and for a moment thought that he was better than those among whom he lived, since he knew that not in the heart of one of them would this prayer have been born, except perhaps in that of Pag, if Pag had believed in anything, which he did not. For even then Wi understood that he who does not believe cannot pray. A boy, so long as he thinks he sees something, or smells it, or hears it move, will throw stones in the hope that he may hit it ; but when he is certain that there is nothing beneath the water or in the tree, for how long will he go on throwing the stones ? Now this was the difference between them : although he could not see it, Wi thought that there was something beneath the water or in the tree, and therefore continued to throw his stones of prayer, whereas Pag was sure there was nothing at all, and therefore kept his stones and saved his strength.

Then Wi remembered that after all he had no cause to boast himself. He prayed for the people. But why did he do so ? Oh, the answer was plain : it was not for the people and their woes that he was sorry, but for his own, in which he saw theirs reflected by the mirror of his heart, as images are seen in clear water. His little daughter had been taken from him in a cruel fashion. He had avenged her death upon the murderer, thinking thus to satisfy his soul. Yet it was not satisfied, for he had learned that there is no comfort in vengeance. What he needed was his daughter, not the blood of her butcher. Therefore he hoped that some land unseen lay beyond that of life where he might find her and others whom he had loved, which was why he prayed to the gods. He was sorry for others who had lost their children, because he could measure something of their suffering by his own, but at bottom he was most sorry for himself. So it was with everything. By his own unhappiness he measured that of others, and when he feared for them, really he feared for himself and those he loved, feeling for all with the ache of his own heart and seeing all by the light of his own eyes.

These thoughts crushed Wi, who by help of them now understood that even the sacrifice which he offered for others was full of selfishness, because he desired to escape from trouble and at the same time to earn merit and to leave a hallowed name behind him, he who did not know that than this no higher measure is given to man, for if it were he would cease to be man and become a god.

Of a sudden Wi abandoned prayer. He had thrown the spear of his mind at the skies, and lo ! it stood there fixed in the ground before his feet. Since he could never get away from himself, what was the use of praying ? Let him do those things that lay to his hand as best he might ; let him bear his burdens as far as he could and cease from importuning help from he knew not whence ; he who in this bitter moment of understanding for a while became sure that man could not hunt the gods, since it was they who hunted him, paying no more heed to his petitions than he, Wi, did to the groanings of any seal that he pursued, as it strove impotently to reach the sea where it would be safe.

He rose from the ground to look at the face of the glacier and discover how far it had moved forward during the fierce winter that was gone. He stared at it and started back, for there in hideous imagery stood his own thought portrayed. In that clear ice he had been accustomed to see the dim form of the Sleeper and behind it, rather to one side, a yet dimmer form, thought to be that of a man who pursued the Sleeper, or perchance of one of the gods taking his rest with it. Now, behold ! all this was changed. There stood the Sleeper as before, but by magic, or perhaps by some convulsion of the ice, the figure that had been behind was now in front. Yes, there it stood with not more than one pace length of ice between Wi himself and it, a weird and awful thing.

It was a man, of that there could be no doubt, but such a man as Wi had never seen, for his limbs were covered with hair, his forehead sloped backwards and his great jaw stood out beyond the line of his flat nose. His arms were very long, his legs were bowed and in one of his hands he held a short, rough staff of wood. For the rest his sunk but open eyes seemed to be small, his teeth large and prominent, while his head was covered with coarse matted hair and from his shoulders hung a cloak, the skin of some animal of which the forepaws were knotted about his neck.

On this strange and hideous creature's face there was stamped a look of the wildest terror, telling Wi that he had died suddenly and that when he died he was very much afraid. Of what had he been afraid? Wi wondered. Not of the Sleeper, he thought, because until some movement of the glacier had thrust him forward during the past winter he had been behind the Sleeper, as though he were pursuing it. No, it was something else that he feared.

Suddenly Wi guessed what it was. Long, long ago this forefather of the tribe—for, knowing no other men, Wi thought that so he must be—thousands of winters ago, perhaps, this man had been flying from the ice and snow, when in an instant they rushed down and swallowed him up, so that there he choked and died. He was no god, but just a poor man, if indeed he were altogether a man, whom death had taken in this fashion and whom the ice had preserved with his story written on his hideous face and fleeing form.

Then was the Sleeper a god, or was he only some huge wild beast that lived when the man lived and perished when the man perished and in like fashion, roaring open-mouthed to the heavens for help? So much for the gods! If they dwelt here in the glacier, as perhaps they dwelt everywhere, it was not in the shapes of this enormous brute, or of the man who also looked like a brute, for as

Wi had never seen an ape he did not know that this was
what he really resembled.

Whatever their end may have been, as he stared at
them a fancy, or a vision, came to Wi. That man was
himself, or all men, and the huge brute behind was Death,
who pursued, and the ice around was Doom, which
swallowed up both Life and Death. Vague thoughts of
all this mystery got hold of his untutored mind and over-
came it, so that presently he turned to creep, shivering
and terror-struck, from these relics and emblems of a
tragedy he could not comprehend.

Coming to the beach again, Wi continued to walk
eastwards past the smaller hills and ice-filled valleys,
for he desired to visit a certain bay beyond them where
the seals were wont to gather when they arrived,
hoping to see the first of them come up from the south
to breed. Like the rest of the tribe, Wi thought
more of seals than he did of anything else, because these
furnished the most of their winter food and of the other
things that they needed. On he went, till turning a
spur of cliff which here ran down to the sea to the east of
the glacier field, he came to the bay that was bordered by
a broad stretch of white sand and backed by a barren,
rocky plain. Ceasing to ponder upon the Sleeper and
the man, and the deeper things that the sight of them had
awakened in his heart, Wi searched the shore with his
keen hunter's eyes, and the water of the bay and the
ridge of rock whereby at low tide it was almost enclosed,
that ran at some four spear-casts from the shore ; but not
one seal could he see.

" They are even later this spring than they were last
year," he muttered to himself and was about to make
his way homeward when, on the further side of the ridge
where the waves broke, he caught sight of some strange
object that was stranded among the surf, a long thing
which seemed to be pointed at both ends At first he
thought that it might be a dead animal of a sort new to
him, washed up by the sea, and was turning to go when
the surf lifted the object and he saw that it seemed to be

hollow and that there lay in it what looked to him like a human form.

Now Wi's curiosity was awakened, and he wished that he could come nearer. This, however, was impossible, as at each end of the ridge of rocks was open water through which the tide raced swiftly; or rather it was not possible except by swimming out from the shore of the bay. It is true that Wi was a great swimmer, but the water was bitterly cold for in it still floated many lumps of drift ice, so cold that there was much danger to a swimmer, who might, moreover, be cut or bruised by the sharp edges of the ice. Also the swim would be long for the ridge was far away. So again he thought that he would go home and not give himself up to more fancies about someone who lay in that hollow thing, which was strange to him, for Wi had never seen a boat. Indeed, he turned to do so and walked a few paces.

Then for a second time that day it seemed to him as though a rope were drawing him, this time not to the glacier-face but to the ridge of rock and that which lay upon its further side. Supposing that there was a man—or woman—yonder? It seemed impossible, because no other men or women lived except those upon the beach, of whom he was chief. What he saw was some drift log splintered white by rolling upon stones, or perhaps a great fish dead and rotten. Yet how could he say that there were no other men and women, he who had just looked upon the corpse of a man who must have lived thousands of years ago, when the ancient ice that wrapped him round, was born in the womb of the distant mountains whence it had flowed? How could he be sure that he and his people were the only two-legged creatures on the earth, which perhaps was bigger than they knew?

Oh, he would go to look, for if he did not he would be sorry all his life. Should he be cramped in the cold water and drowned, or should the pack-ice strike him so that he sank—after all it would not matter very much. Then doubtless Pag would become chief, or perhaps he would make Moananga chief and be the whisperer in his ear, which would please the people better. Either of them would look after Foh, or if they did not Aaka would, especially when he was gone and she could no longer be jealous because the boy loved him more than he did her. Probably, too, there at the bottom of the sea was peace without fears or hopes, questionings or disappointments. Also fate was always behind them as the huge Sleeper was behind that wild, hairy creature that was once a man.

So thought Wi, and as he thought he threw off his cloak and laid it on a rock, hiding the axe beneath it, so that if he did not return, Pag and the others might learn that the sea had taken him. Then he plunged into the water very swiftly lest his courage should desert him, and struck out for the reef. At first that water was bitterly cold but as he swam with great strokes, stopping now and again to push aside the blocks of floating ice or to feel them with his hand beneath the surface, lest on them should be sharp points that would cut him, he grew warmer.

Also the joy of the quest, the hope of adventure caused his blood to flow more quickly than it had done there upon the beach, where he was filled with so many sad thoughts and haunted by the memory of the strange and hideous man with whom he had come face to face in the ice of the glacier. Now he felt as he had done when as a boy he had climbed the mountain crag on which none had ever dared to set foot, to rob the great eagle's nest, and had brought down its young one in a basket on his back, while the parent eagles screamed round him, striking at his head and tearing him ; which young one he had pinioned and kept for years, till at last the dogs killed it. Yes, once more he was a fearless boy, untroubled by memories of yesterday or fears for to-morrow, and seeking only what the hour might bring him.

At length Wi reached the reef uncramped and unhurt. Crawling on to it, he shook himself as a dog does, then very cautiously picked his way among its stones and peered down at the spot where, from the height of the shore, he had seen that strange, sharp-pointed thing in which a figure seemed to be lying. It was gone! No, there it was, right beneath him, lifted up towards him by the send of the surf. It was something made by man to float upon the water, much larger than he had thought for five or six people could have sat in it, hollowed, it would seem, from a big tree, thicker than any that he knew, for there were axe marks in the red-hued wood. Moreover, his eyes had not deceived him for behold, within this shaped log lay a figure covered with a cloak or blanket of white fur which hid it all, even the head that rested at the raised end of the log No, not quite all, for outside of the cloak lay a tress of hair, long hair, yellow as the marsh flowers that came in spring, also a white arm and hand, which hand grasped a wooden implement, that from its shape he guessed must be used to drive the hollowed log through the water.

Wi stared and stared, and while he stared became aware that this hand was not that of a dead woman—for from its delicate shape he knew it to be a woman's—because although blue with cold, presently the little finger moved, bending itself inwards. Noting this he pondered for a moment. What could he do? To swim to the beach bearing a senseless woman was impossible; moreover, she would die in the icy water. If she might be brought there at all, it must be in that in which she lay. Yet to drag that great log across the reef was beyond his strength. Therefore there was but one thing to be done. It had come ashore but a little distance from the western channel, by which the sea flowed in and out of the bay. The tide had turned, he noted it as he swam, and was now running shorewards. If he pushed the log to the channel it would float to the beach. He leapt into the surf and thrust it forward; being light it moved easily and as it drew but very little water, not more than four hand-breadths it would seem, he could guide it through the surf and shallows out of reach of the breaking waves.

Pushing it in front of him, presently he came to the

lip of the race down which the tide began to run strongly
shorewards. Here he paused a moment, purposing to
take to the water once more and swim behind the hollow
tree, guiding it with his hand. Then he remembered
that the water was dreadfully cold, that the way was
long, and that before he covered it cramp might seize him,
so that he sank and went to find out the truth about the
gods and many other matters

Perhaps this might be well for him, but if he were
drowned what would happen to her who lay there?
Without doubt she who must already be near to death
would die also; for except to kill seals, of which as yet
there were none, no one came to this lonely, far-off
bay; or if perchance some did and saw a strange woman
lying in a hollowed tree, they would run away, thinking
that she was a witch of the sea such as was told of in
legends. Or perhaps they would kill her lest she should
be the bearer of a curse.

Then he thought to himself, why should he not get
into the log and guide it ashore with that which lay in
the stranger's hand? Often when the sea was calm and
the weather warm he, with others of the tribe, would
bestride a piece of wood and paddle it by help of a bough
to a certain sandbank that swarmed with fish, there to
catch them on a line. Therefore he could guess the use of
what she held and knew how it should be handled.

Taking the paddle very gently from her hand, Wi
entered the canoe, for such it was, and seating himself
at the woman's feet pushed it off into the centre of the
race. Here the tide took it and bore it forward, so that
all he need do, at any rate at first, was to keep the bark
straight, and after they were out of the race and in the
bay, with gentle strokes of the paddle, that he dipped
into the water first on one side and then on the other,
as he was accustomed to do when out fishing on a log, to
drive it shorewards, avoiding the lumps of floating ice.

Thus this naked, savage man and the shrouded woman,
upon whose face he had not yet dared to look, partly
because he was naked and partly because he feared what

he might behold beneath that cloak—a sea-witch perhaps, who would drag him into the deep water—came safely to the shore.

When awhile before Wi had looked upon the Sleeper in the ice and the hairy one who seemed to flee in front of it, in his heart he had compared these two to man being hunted of Fate in a most fearful form. He did not know that Fate has many shapes and that some of them are very fair. He did not guess that there, stretched before him, lay *his* fate, a fate as deadly as the monstrous Sleeper would have been to the hairy man who had lived and died thousands of years ago.

CHAPTER XI

LALEELA

WI leapt to the beach, and seizing the canoe by a hide rope which was attached to its prow, dragged it over the hard wet sand, as being very strong he could do easily enough, till it was well above high-water mark. Then he ran to the rock and clothed himself swiftly in his girdle of dressed seal-fur, and his hooded cloak of grey wolf-skin which he wore when out hunting, slipping his hand through the loop of the axe, for after all, who knew what might lie beneath that covering ? Also about his shoulders he hung the bag in which, when he went abroad, he kept food for a day or two and his tools for making fire. Then he returned to the canoe and with a beating heart, for like all savages he was frightened of the unknown, drew off the fur wrapping from her who lay senseless there beneath it.

Next instant he staggered back, for never had he seen, never had he even dreamed of a woman so beautiful as this that the sea had brought to him. Tall she was and shapely. Young, too, and all about her hung the tangled masses of her yellow hair. Though somewhat blue with cold and reddened where the weather had caught it, her skin was of the whiteness of snow ; her face was oval and her features were fine and well cut. Her eyes he could not see because they were shut, at which he rejoiced, for had they been open he would have known that she was dead ; but he noted the long curling eyelashes which lay upon her cheek, also that they were not yellow like her hair, but dark, indeed almost black in hue.

She was clothed, but in a fashion that was strange to him, for beneath her breast, supported by straps across her shoulders, was a long garment blue in colour made of he

knew not what, that was tied in at the waist with a girdle
of fur to which were sewn polished stones and beautiful
little shells that glittered. Also about her neck was a
string of amber, rounded into beads and pierced, while
on her feet were sandals made fast with broidered thongs.
Lastly, from her shoulders hung a long cloak, also deep
blue in colour and of the same soft unknown stuff as was
her gown, and with this a bag worked like the sandals.

Yes, Wi staggered back, muttering,

" The Sea-witch! The Sea-witch herself! She who
brings curses; no woman. Now what says the tale—
that such should be thrust back into the sea, taking their
curse with them. I will thrust her back into the sea."

He drew near again and touched her cheek with his
finger-tip, as though expecting to find it vapour, which he
did not, for he said to himself,

" This one has flesh like women   Have sea-witches
flesh like a woman's? "

Just then the Sea-witch shivered and made a little
moaning noise.

" And can they shiver," went on Wi, " they who
are said to live upon the ice? Surely first I should warm
her who can suffer, and bring her back to life. I can
always kill her afterwards if I find that she is a witch
and not a woman. That is, unless she kills me."

He looked about him. At the back of the beach was
a sloping cliff of soft stone, and in it a little cave hollowed
out by water; indeed, a spring of pure water bubbled
beside it, of which Wi had often drunk when he sheltered
in this cave, weary with the hunting of seals. Now he
bethought him of this place, and stooping down encircled
the Sea-witch's shape with his strong arms, lifted her,
and although she was heavy, if somewhat wasted perhaps
with want and cold, carried her over the beach to the cave,
where he laid her down upon a bed of dried seaweed which
he himself had used at the last seal-hunting. Then he
began to rub her hands and arms and as still she did not
wake, he lifted her again and held her against his breast
that she might gather warmth from him

Still she swooned on, although he clasped her fast, so once more he laid her down and covering her with both his cloak and her own, bethought him of another plan. In this cave, amongst other things used by the hunters, was a store of driftwood for making fires on which to cook seal's-meat. Wi took from his bag his fire-sticks, and setting one between his feet and on it a pinch of dry touchwood powder from his pouch, twirled the other sharp-pointed hard-wood rod between the palms of his hands more quickly perhaps than ever he did before. The spark appeared, the touchwood lighted; Wi blew on it and on little pieces of crumbled seaweed that he added, till there was a tiny flame, on which he placed more dried seaweed and more and more. Then he set the burning seaweed beneath the wood that he had built up ready, leaving a hollow in its centre, and presently there was a great blaze.

He paused, admiring his own work after his simple fashion, and wondering dimly why two pieces of wood rubbed together produced fire which, if it were allowed to grow and spread, would burn a forest, as every day he wondered about many things that he could not under-stand. Then bringing his mind back to the matter with which he had to deal, he lifted the Sea-witch and laid her down upon her fur rug quite close to the fire, being careful first to arrange the masses of her tumbled hair so that no spark could fall among them. Thus she lay awhile, the heat beating on her and her beautiful face illumined in the strong light of the flames, and Wi watching her entranced, wondered whether she would live or die. He hoped that she would live, though he felt that if she died perhaps it would be better for him, for then he would be left with the company of a marvellous memory, yet without fear of trouble to be born.

" Which way will you have it ? " asked Wi of Fate, and sat still by the fire awaiting the answer.

Presently it came, for the Sea-witch was strong and did not mean to die. She needed nothing but warmth to call her back to life, and on his breast and by his fire Wi had given her warmth. She opened her eyes, and with a little catching of the breath Wi noted that they were large and dark—not black, but of the hue of those woodland flowers that we call violets, and very tender. Next she sat up, resting her weight upon one hand, and stared at the fire, muttering something in a soft voice and holding her other hand towards it. Thus she remained a space, drinking in its glorious warmth, then began to look about her, first out towards the sea, then round the little cave.

So her eyes fell upon Wi, a dark, massive figure, a perfect shape of developed manhood, who now was on his knees bending towards her with his hands outstretched a little, silent, motionless, like to the statue of one who is lost in prayer. She started, then began to study him with those great eyes of hers. Slowly her glance travelled up and down him, resting for a long while upon his face. Then it fell upon the shining axe on his wrist and for a moment grew fearful. Back from the axe it flew to his face, and reading there that she had nothing of which to be afraid, for it was a most earnest, kindly face, wild enough but not ill-looking after its fashion, she shook her head and smiled, whereon in a slow and doubtful fashion he smiled back at her.

Next she touched her lips and her throat with her long fingers. For a moment Wi was puzzled. Then he understood. Leaping up, he ran from the cave and at once returned with his joined hands full of water, for these were his only cup. She smiled again, nodding, then bent her head and drank the water till all was gone, and by a little sign asked for more. Thrice he went and thrice returned, till at last her thirst was satisfied.

Again she lifted her fingers, this time laying them upon her teeth, and again Wi understood. Seizing his bag he drew from it a handful of dried codfish, and explaining that it was good, took a little piece, chewed and swallowed it. She considered this food doubtfully, showing him that it was one to which she had not been accustomed, then, overcome by hunger, accepted a fragment and made trial. Apparently she liked it well enough, for she

asked for more and more till she had eaten a good meal,
after which she signed to him to bring her another drink
of water.

By the time this strange feast was done the light
began to fail. She noted it and pointed to the sky,
then spoke, asking some question, but what she said
he could not understand, nor could she understand what
he said to her. Now Wi was much perplexed. Night
fell and the village was far away, nor was it safe to try to
walk thither in the darkness because of wild beasts and
other dangers.

Moreover, this Sea-witch must be very tired and need
rest, if witches ever rested. So he signed to her to lie down
to sleep, and made a bed for her of dry seaweed, near to
the fire. Also, taking more seaweed, he piled it outside
the mouth of the cave, and by pointing first to himself and
then to it, showed her that he would sleep there. She
nodded to tell him that she understood, whereon Wi
left her for a time and by the light of the dying day
walked some distance round the spur of the cliff which
almost encircled the bay, and beyond it, to discover if
perchance Pag had followed him, tracking his footsteps as
sometimes he did.

But Pag, who was working on the skin of the tiger and
thought that Wi would return at nightfall, had not done
so. Therefore, finding neither Pag nor anyone else,
Wi walked back again. Coming to the mouth of the cave
he peeped in and saw that the Sea-witch had lain down
and was asleep, or at any rate that her eyes were closed.
He went away and covering himself with seaweed,
lay down also, but sleep he could not, for it was cold
there outside the cave and he was hungry, who would
not touch the dried fish because the Sea-witch might
need more of it at any moment and the supply was small.
Indeed, that he might not fall into temptation he had
left the bag in which it was carried at her side.

Yet perhaps cold and hunger would not have kept
him awake, who was hardy and like all savages accustomed
to privations. Perhaps it was the thought of the strange

adventure that had befallen him and of the wonderful beauty of the woman creature whom he had saved from death—that is, if she were a woman and could die; also of all that these things might mean to him, which caused him to toss from side to side with open eyes.

Already he knew that whatever chanced—though she were taken away as swiftly and as strangely as she came—he would never be able to forget this Witch of the Sea who even now seemed to draw his heart towards her. And if she were not taken away, what then? With what eyes would the people look on her, and how would Aaka receive her, and where was she to live? In the old days before the making of the new law all would have been simple, for if she were willing, then there was nothing to prevent him, the Chief, or indeed any other man, from taking a second wife; indeed even were she not willing, she might pass as such and have the shelter of the cave. But there was the new law and he had sworn an oath that might not be broken, for if it were, shame, mockery and disaster would come upon him, and perhaps on others.

Thus mused Wi from hour to hour, striving to climb this slippery mount of doubt and fear first from one side and then from the other, but always failing, until his head swam and he gave up the quest. Twice he rose and crept into the cave to replenish the fire lest that fair sleeper should grow cold. This he did with his eyes turned from her, because according to the customs of the tribe it was not seemly that he should look upon a maiden while she lay asleep. Yet, although he did not look at her, he was sure that she looked at him, for he could feel, or thought that he could feel, her eyes upon him.

After his second visit to the cave he did at length sink into a troubled sleep, only to be awakened suddenly. Glancing upwards but without stirring, he saw what had wakened him. It was the Sea-witch who stood there, tall and stately, considering him with earnest eyes. He lay quite still feigning slumber, till at length, having, as he thought, made up her mind that really he was asleep,

she moved a little way and looked upwards, searching the
skies. Presently she found what she sought, for between
a rift in the clouds appeared the faint shape of the waning
moon. Thrice she bowed to it, then, kneeling down,
with uplifted hands spoke aloud, making some sweet-
voiced prayer.

" Evidently she is a witch," thought Wi, " for she
worships the moon, which no one does among the people.
And yet, is it more witch-like to pray to the moon that
gives light, than to kneel and make offerings before the
Ice-Gods and him who sleeps in the ice ? Perhaps if she
saw me do that she would say that I was a wizard."

She rose, again bowed thrice, turned and glanced at
Wi as though in farewell, and glided away across the
beach.

" She is going back into the sea, as a witch would.
Well, let her go, for perhaps it is better," thought Wi
again.

She came to the canoe and stood by it, thinking ;
then she bent herself and pushed at it, but by now it had
sunk into the wet sand, and being water-logged was too
heavy for her to move.

" I will help her," said Wi, and rising he followed
her.

She looked at him without astonishment, apparently
also without fear ; it was as though she knew already that
he would never harm her. By signs he made it clear that
if she desired it, he would bale out the canoe and push it
into the water for her, which seemed to surprise her a
little. Most earnestly she studied his face, noting
perhaps that it was very sad and that what he offered
to do was not because he wished to be rid of her. Then
muttering some words and waving her arms she
looked upwards again at the dying moon like one who
seeks a sign. Presently she came to some decision,
for suddenly she shook her head, smiled a little and,
taking him very gently by the hand, led him back towards
the cave, which she entered, leaving him without.

" So the witch means to stay," thought Wi. " If so,

it is her own choice, for I have done my best to help her back to the sea."

Day came at last, grey and dull, as all the days seemed to be that year, but without snow or rain. The witch appeared at the mouth of the cave and beckoned to Wi, who sat shivering without. For a little while he hesitated, then entered to find that she had heaped wood upon the fire, which burned gloriously. In front of it she sat upon the seaweed of her bed that she had gathered to a pile, changed indeed from what she had been when first he saw her lying at the bottom of the hollowed log.

Looking at her he thought that she must have washed herself at the spring before he saw her praying to the moon, for there was no longer any brine upon her face or arms, also her blue cloak and other garments were dry, and to his sight, who had never seen such robes, splendid. Moreover, she was drawing through the masses of her yellow hair something with many sharp points made of horn or bone, which doubtless she had taken from her bag; a new thing to Wi, for combs were unknown in the tribe, though now when he looked upon it and saw its use, he wondered that they had not thought of them before.

While she was still engaged upon this task and the long yellow waving hair that had been so matted and tangled, separated itself till it hung about her glittering in the firelight, a garment in itself that hid her to the waist, Wi stood before her awkwardly, for he was amazed.

Then he bethought him that by now she must be hungry again, and lifting his bag that lay near by, he poured out more of the shredded codfish and offered it to her. She began to eat heartily enough, till some thought seemed to strike her, and she pointed first to the codfish, then to Wi's mouth, also lower down, saying as plainly as signs could do that he too must be hungry.

He shook his head, pretending that this was not so, but she would not be deceived, and held out a piece of the fish towards him, refusing to eat any more until it was swallowed.

The end of it was that together they finished all remaining in the bag, eating alternately.

It was just as Wi was offering the last fragment to the Sea-witch, that Pag appeared at the mouth of the cave and stood staring at them outlined against the bright background of the fire, as though he believed them to be ghosts.

The Sea-witch, glancing up, perceived this squat, bow-legged form, great head and ugly one-eyed face, and for the first time was frightened. At least she grasped Wi's arm and looked at him in inquiry, whereon, not knowing what else to do, he smiled, patted her hand and spoke to Pag in a commanding voice, of which she understood the tones, if not the words.

" What are you doing here ? " Wi asked.

" I wonder ! " answered Pag reflectively, " for in this cave there seems to be no place for me. Still, if you would know, I followed your footprints hither, fearing lest harm had befallen you—as I think it has," he added still more reflectively, fixing his one bright eye upon the Sea-witch.

" Have you brought any food with you ? " asked Wi, who to tell the truth desired to fend off explanations for a while. " If so, give it me ; for this maiden," and he nodded to the Sea-witch, " has fasted long and is still hungry."

" How do you know that she is not married and that she has fasted long ? " asked Pag inconsequently, adding, " Can you talk her language ? "

" No," answered Wi, seizing upon the last part of the question and ignoring the rest. " I found her floating in a hollow log which lies yonder on the beach, and brought her back to life."

" Then you found something that was worth finding, Wi, for she is very beautiful," said Pag ; " though what Aaka will say about her I do not know."

" Nor do I," answered Wi, rubbing his brow, " or the people either."

" Perhaps she is a witch whom you would do well to kill Urk and Ngae tell of such, Wi."

"Perhaps, Pag; but witch or woman, I do not mean to kill her."

"I understand that, Wi, for who could kill anything so lovely? Look at her face and shape and hair, and those great eyes."

"I have looked at them already," replied Wi with irritation. "Cease your foolish talk and tell me what I am to do."

Pag pondered awhile and replied,

"I think that you had better marry her and tell the people that the Ice-Gods, or the Sea-Gods, or any other gods, gave her to you, which indeed they seem to have done."

"Fool! how do I know that she would marry me who am so far beneath her? Also there is the new law!"

"Ah!" said Pag, "I always misdoubted me of that law and now I understand why I did so. Well, if you will not kill her and will not marry her, you must bring her to the village; and since she cannot live with Aaka or in the cave, or in any place where there is another woman, you must set her in a hut by herself. There is a very fine one empty quite near the mouth of the cave, so that you could look at her whenever you liked."

Wi, who was thinking of other things, asked in an absent-minded way what hut was empty.

"That of Rahi the Miser who, you remember, died last week, as some said from fear of the tiger, but as I believe of grief because you ordered him to divide up his fish-hooks and flint knives with those who had none."

"Yes, I remember," said Wi, "and by the way, have you got the fish-hooks?"

"Not yet, Wi, but I shall have them soon, for I am sure that old woman who lived with Rahi and who has run away from the hut, buried them in his grave, as he ordered her to do. Presently I will catch her and find out. Meanwhile there is the hut all ready."

"Yes," said Wi, "and the women who nurse the children in the cave can look after this Sea-witch."

Pag shook his head doubtfully and remarked he did not think that any woman would look after her, as the young ones would be jealous and the old ones afraid.

"Especially," he added, "as you say that she is a witch."

"I say no such words," exclaimed Wi angrily ; "Sea-witch I named her because she came out of the sea and I know no other."

"Or because she is a witch," suggested Pag. "Still, let us try to learn how she calls herself."

"Yes," said Wi, "it is well to do that, for if the women refuse her I shall give her into your care."

"I have known worse tasks," answered Pag.

Then he turned to the Sea-witch, who all this while watched them steadily, guessing that they were talking of her, and clapped his hands as though to awake her, which was not needful. Next he tapped Wi upon the breast and said, "Wi." Then he tapped his own breast and said "Pag." Several times he did this, then tapped her arm and pointing his finger at her, looked a question.

At first she seemed puzzled, but after the third repetition of the tappings and the names she understood, for she smiled, a quick, bright smile, then pointing at each of them, repeated . "*Wi-i, Pa-ag.*" Lastly she set her finger on her breast and added, "*La-lee-la.*"

They nodded and exclaimed together, "La-lee-la," whereon she nodded back and, smiling again, repeated "*Laleela.*" Then they talked about the canoe, and taking her to it, showed her by signs that they proposed to hide it in the cave, to which she seemed to assent.

So, having emptied the water out of it, they dragged the canoe to the cave, and after Pag had examined it with much interest—for in this strange and useful thing he saw a great discovery—they hid it beneath piles of seaweed, burying the paddles, of which they found two, in the sand of the cave. This done, Wi took her by the hand and as best he could showed her that she must accompany them. At first she seemed afraid and hung back, but presently shrugged her shoulders, sighed, looked imploringly at Wi as though to ask him to protect her, and walked forward between them.

An hour or more later Aaka, Moananga, Tana and Foh, who were watching on the outskirts of the village, being frightened because Wi had not returned, caught sight of the three of them walking towards them.

" Look ! " cried Foh as they came into view from round the spur of the glacier mountain. " There are Father and Pag and a Beautiful One."

" Beautiful she is indeed," said Moananga, while his wife stared open-eyed. But Aaka only exclaimed,

" You call her beautiful, and so she is, but I say that she is a witch come to bring evil upon our heads."

Tana watched this tall stranger advancing with a gliding step across the sands ; noted her blue cloak and amber necklace, her yellow tresses and, when she came nearer, her great dark eyes set in a face that was pink as the lining of a shell. Then she said,

" You are right, Aaka ; here comes a witch, if not of the sort you mean, such a witch as you and I wish that we could be."

" Your meaning ? " asked Aaka.

" I mean that this one will draw the hearts of all men after her and earn the hate of all women, which is what every one of us would do if she could."

" So you say," said Aaka, " but I hold otherwise."

" Yet you will walk the same road as the rest of us, although you hold your head sideways and pretend that it is different—you who tell us that Wi is nothing to you and who treat him so badly, and yet always watch him out of the corners of your eyes," said Tana, who never loved Aaka overmuch and was very fond of Wi.

Now Aaka would have answered sharply enough, but at this moment the three came up to her. Foh dashed forward and threw his arms about his father, who bent down and kissed him. Moananga uttered some word of welcome, for he, who loved his brother, was glad to see him safe, and Tana smiled doubtfully, her eyes fixed upon the stranger's marvellous robe and necklace. Wi offered some greeting to Aaka, who answered,

"Welcome, Husband; we feared for you, and are glad to see you safe, and your shadow with you"—here she glanced at Pag. "But who is this third in a strange robe? Is it a tall boy whom you have found, or perhaps a woman?"

"A woman, I think," answered Wi. "Study her and you will see for yourself, Wife."

"It is needless, for doubtless you know, Husband. But if so, where did you find her?"

"The story is long, Wife, but the heart of it is that I saw her floating in a hollow log yesterday, and swimming out, brought her to shore in the Bay of Seals."

"Is it so? Then where did you sleep last night? As I have said, we feared for you."

"In the cavern at the Bay of Seals. At least, the woman Laleela slept there after I had brought her back to life."

"Indeed, and how did you learn her name?"

"Ask Pag," said Wi shortly. "He learned it, not I."

"So Pag's hand is in the business as in every other. Well, I hope that this witch, whom he has brought to you, is not one of his grey wolves turned to the shape of woman."

"I have said that I found her myself and carried her to the cave, where Pag came to us this morning. Laugh if you will, but it is true, as Pag can tell you."

"Doubtless Pag will tell me anything that you wish, Husband. Yet——"

Here Wi grew angry and exclaimed,

"Have done. I need food and rest, as does this stranger Laleela."

Then he walked forward with Laleela and Pag, who grinned as he went, the others following, except Tana, who had run on ahead to tell the people what had happened.

CHAPTER XII

THE MOTHER OF THE CAST-OUTS

THE news spread fast, so fast that when they reached the village, even from the huts that were furthest off, folk were rushing to look on this Witch-from-the-sea whom Wi had found ; for a witch they knew she must be, because they of the tribe were the only people who lived or ever had lived in the world. Of course there was the Dead One who stood in the ice with the Sleeper, but if he were a man, of which they were not sure, doubtless he was one of their forefathers. Therefore this was no woman whom Wi and Pag brought with them, but a ghost or a spirit.

When they beheld her walking between the pair in such a calm and stately fashion, like a stag indeed, as one of them said, and noted her long yellow hair and the whiteness of her skin, her height, taller than any of them by a head except Aaka, and her wonderful blue cloak and other garments, the broidered sandals on her feet, the amber necklace on her breast, and everything else about her, not forgetting her large dark eyes, liquid and soft as a deer's yet somewhat scornful, then of course they knew that they were right and that this was in truth a witch, for no woman could look like that. They stared, they gaped, they pointed ; some of the children ran away and—here was proof of the worst— so did certain of the dogs that had bounded forward barking, but on seeing and smelling that at which they barked, had turned tail and fled, as it was their custom to do from ghosts who pelted them with invisible stones. So, a dirty, unkempt, half-clothed crowd, they stared on while, guarded on either side like a captive by Wi and

Pag, Laleela glided through them, glancing now to right
and now to left with unchanging face and saying nothing.

At first they were silent, then, when she had passed
and with her the fear that she would shoot a curse at them
with a glance of those dark eyes, whispered debate broke
out among them as, huddled together, they followed
on her footsteps.

" She is a very ugly witch," said one woman, " who
has hair the colour of sunlight and such long arms."

" I wish you were as ugly," answered her husband
rudely, and thus the argument began to rage, all the
women and some of the old men holding that she was
vile to look on, while the young men, also the children
as soon as they grew used to the sight of her, thought her
beauteous.

" Where will Wi take her ? " asked one.

" Nowhere," answered Urk the Aged, " because she
will vanish away," and as the point was disputed, he hastily
invented a tale.

His grandfather, he said, had been told by *his* grandfather that such a witch as this, probably the same witch
since witches never grew old, once visited the tribe,
coming to the shore standing upon an ice-floe that was
pushed by white bears with their noses. Knowing her
for what she was, the people tried to kill her with
stones, but when they threw the stones, these fell back
upon their heads and killed them ; also the bears attacked
them. So she came ashore and sat in the cave for six
days singing, till the chief's son, a bold and dissolute
youth, fell in love with her and tried to kiss her, whereon
she turned him into a bear and mounting on to his
back, went out into the sea again and was no more
seen.

Now some believed this tale and some did not, yet it
worked well for Laleela, since all made up their minds
that they would be on the safe side and neither try to
stone nor to kiss this witch, lest they also should be
turned into bears or otherwise come to harm.

As the three drew near to the cave Aaka and

Moananga overtook them, also Tana who, having spread
the news, had rejoined her husband, very breathless.

"What are you going to do with the witch, Husband?" Aaka asked, looking at her sideways.

"I am not sure," he answered, then added in a
hesitating voice, "perhaps you, Wife, would take her
in to our old hut, seeing that now you sleep in the cave
and are only there during the day."

"Not so," answered Aaka firmly. "Have I not
enough troubles that I should add a witch to them?
Also, now that the winter is gone I, who hate that cave
and the crying of the children, intend to sleep in the
hut again."

Wi bit his lip and stood thinking.

"Brother," broke in Moananga, "we have two huts
side by side, and in the second we only keep our food.
This Sea-woman might live in it and——"

He got no further, for Tana cut him short.

"What are you saying, Husband?" she asked.
"That hut is needed for the dried fish, the firewood and
the nets, also by me for the cooking of our food."

Then Wi walked on, leaving Moananga and Tana
disputing. At the mouth of the cave stood those women
who tended the girl-children that would have been cast
out to perish, but were saved under Wi's new law. Some
of these were young and nursed the children at the
breast, while others were old and widows, who watched
them when the nurses were not there. Addressing them,
Wi bade them choose one of their number to wait upon
and cook for this stranger from the sea. They heard,
they looked at the stranger, and then they ran away,
into the cave or elsewhere, so that Wi saw no more of
them. Now Wi turned to Pag and said:

"All things have happened as you told me, and the
women refuse her from the sea who is named Laleela
and comes we know not whence. What is to be done?"

Pag spat upon the ground, Pag stared upwards with
his one eye, Pag looked at Laleela and at Wi. Then he
answered,

"When a cord is knotted and cannot be unravelled, the best thing is to cut it through and knit up the ends afresh. Take the witch into the cave and look after her yourself, Wi, as Aaka and the others will not receive her and she cannot be left to starve. Or if this does not please you, kill her, if she can be killed."

"Neither of these things will I do," answered Wi. "Into the cave she cannot come because of my oath. Starve she shall not, for who could refuse food even to a dog that creeps hungry to the hut door? Kill her I will not; it would be murder and bring the sky on to our heads."

"Yes, Wi; though if she were old and hideous the sky might remain where it is, since perhaps for an ancient hag it would not fall. But as all these things are so, what next?"

"This, Pag. Take her to the hut of Rahi who is dead. Command some of my servants, men not women, to make it ready for her, to light a fire and to furnish food from my store. Then go you and dwell in the out-house against the hut which was Rahi's workshop where he shaped flints, and the place where he kept his goods and traded in them, and by day and night be the guard of this beautiful one whom the gods have sent to us."

"So I am to become a witch's nurse. Well, I thought that would be the end of the story," said Pag.

Thus it came about that Laleela, the Beautiful One who had risen from the sea, went to dwell in the hut of Rahi the dead miser, and there was tended by Pag the dwarf, the hater of women. Without a word she went, patiently submitting to all things as one who feels herself to be swept along by the stream of Fate, and waits for it to bear her whither it will, caring little how that journey might end. Pag, too, went patiently to fulfil his strange and unaccustomed task of guard and servant to one whom all the tribe held to be a witch, providing for her needs, teaching her the customs of the people and protecting her from every harm.

All these things he did, not only to please Wi but
for a certain reason of his own. He, who saw further
than the rest, except perhaps Wi himself, understood from the first that this woman was no witch,
but one of some people unknown to them. He saw also
that this unknown people had many arts which were
strange to him and he desired to learn those arts, also
where they lived and everything else about them. Of
what was the blue cloak made ? How came it that the
stranger woman travelled across the sea in a hollowed
log, and how was that log made fit to bear her ? What
knowledge was hid in her which she could not utter
because her tongue was different ? All this and
much else Pag, who was athirst for wisdom, desired to
learn. Therefore when Wi commanded him to be the
guide and companion of Laleela, the Risen-from-the-Sea,
he obeyed without a word.

Strange was the life of Laleela. There she sat in the
hut and cooked the food that Pag brought to her after
new fashions that were unknown to him. Or sometimes
she walked abroad followed and guarded by Pag, taking
note of the ways of the people, and after she had learned
these, up and down upon the beach, with her eyes ever
fixed upon the sea, looking southwards. Or when the
weather was bad, by signs she caused Pag to give her
dressed skins and sinews, also splinters of ivory from the
tusks of the walrus. These splinters she fashioned into
needles, boring an eye in the head of them with a sharp
and heated flint, and threading the sinews through them,
then began to sew in a fashion such as Pag had never seen.
Of this sewing he told the women of the tribe who,
gathering in front of the hut, watched her with amazement and later prayed Pag to ask of the witch to make
them needles like her own, which she did, smiling, till
there was no more ivory.

Then Pag, since he could not understand hers, began
to teach her his own language, which she learned readily
enough, especially after Wi came to join in the lessons.
Within two moons, indeed, she could ask for what she

wanted and understand what was said to her, and within four, being very apt and eager, could talk the tongue of the people well enough, if but slowly.

Thus at last it came about that Wi and Pag learned as much of her history as she chose to tell them, which was but little. She said that she was the daughter of a Great One, the ruler of a tribe that could not be counted, who lived far away to the south. This tribe dwelt for the most part in houses that were built upon tree-trunks sunk into the mud in the waters of a lake, though some of them made their homes upon the shores of the lake. Fish and game were their food; also they cultivated certain herbs, the seeds of which they gathered and ate, after grinding them between stones and making them into a paste that they cooked in clay heated with fire. They had implements also, and weapons of war beautifully fashioned from flint, ivory and the horns of deer, and they wove cloth, such as that of her garments, from the wool of tame beasts, and dyed it with the juices of herbs, different from those that bore the seeds which they ate.

Moreover, where they lived, although much rain fell, the sun shone more brightly and the air was warmer than here in the home of the tribe.

To all of these tales, gathered painfully word by word, Wi and Pag listened with wonder; then at last Wi asked,

" How comes it, O Woman Laleela, that you left a land where you were so great and where you lived in such plenty and comfort ? "

" I left it because of one I hated and because of a dream," they understood her to answer.

" Why did you hate this one and what was the dream ? " asked Wi.

She paused awhile as though to master his question, which she seemed to be translating in her mind, then answered,

" The one I hated was my father's brother My father was going away " (by this she meant dying), " the brother wished to marry me and become king. I hate him. Taking boat with much food, I row down river to the sea at night."

Wi nodded to show that he understood, and asked again,

"But what of the dream?"

"The dream told me to go north," she replied, "and a great wind blow me north for days and days, till I fall asleep and you find me."

"Why did the dream tell you to go north?" asked Wi with the help of Pag.

She shook her head and answered with a set face,

"Ask of the dream, O Wi." Nor would she say any more.

From this time forward Laieela began to learn the language of the tribe very fast, so that soon she could speak it quite well, for she was quick and clever, and Pag, who was also clever, taught her continually. In the evenings when his work was done Wi would come to her hut, and sitting there with Pag he asked her many things, and especially about her country. She answered as before that it was much warmer than his own, although there was a great deal of rain, if little snow; also that it lay a long way off, for she had been days and nights in the boat driven by the gale before she fell asleep.

"Could you find your way home?" asked Wi.

"I think so," she answered, "because all the time I was seldom out of sight of the shore, and I marked the headlands and know the mountains between which the river runs that leads to my country. I mean that I should know all this if once I were out of the ice that floats upon your sea. For it was after I passed the last headland and came across open water into the ice, that I fell asleep."

"Then that headland cannot be so very far away," said Wi, "for if it were, the cold would have been your death before I found you."

So this talk ended, but Wi thought much of it afterwards and often he and Pag spoke together of the matter.

A little while later Laleela began to grow restless and to say that she lacked work, she who had been a big woman among her people with much to do.

Pag thought over her words for a time, then one day when Wi was out upon some business he took her to the cave and showed her the little girl infants which were nurtured there, telling her their story; how they had been cast out to perish, or rather, how they would have been cast out, had it not been for Wi's new law.

" Your mothers are very cruel," she said. " In my country she who did this would herself be cast out."

Then she took up some of the infants and after looking them all over, said that they were ill-tended as though by hirelings, and that two of them were like to die.

" Several have died," said Pag.

Now, although they did not see him, Wi, having returned to the cave, stood in the shadow watching them and listening to their talk. Presently he stepped forward and said,

" You are right, Laleela; these babes need more care. After the first few weeks their mothers neglect them, I think to show that they were fated to die and that for this reason they wished to cast them out; nor do the other women nurse them as they should. Yet I am help-less, who lack time to see to the business, and when I complain I find all the women leagued against me. Will you help me with these children, Laleela ? "

" Yes, Wi," she answered, " though if I do so the women of your tribe will become even more bitter against me than they are now. Why does not your wife, Aaka, see to the matter ? "

" If I walk one way Aaka walks another," answered Wi sadly. " See now," he added, " I make you, Laleela, the Stranger-from-the-Sea, head-nurse of these babes, with authority to do what you will for their welfare. This I will proclaim, and with it my word that any who disobey you in your duty shall be punished."

So Laleela, the Witch-from-the-Sea, became the

"Mother of the Cast-outs," with other women set under her, and filled that office well. There she would sit by the fire among these little creatures, feeding them with such food as was known to this people, and in a low, sweet voice singing songs of her own country that were very pleasant to hear. At least Wi thought them pleasant, for often he would come into the cave and, seated in the shadows, would watch and listen to her, thinking that she did not know he was there, though all the while she knew this well enough. At length, finding out that she knew, he came from the shadows and, seated on a log of wood, would talk to her, who by now understood his language.

Thus he learned much, for though she would not speak about herself, in broken words she told him of her country, and of how around it lived many other peoples with whom they made war or peace, which astonished him who had believed that the tribe were the only men upon the earth. Also she told him and Pag of such simple arts as they practised, whereof these heard with wonder. But of why she fled from these folk of hers, trusting herself to the sea in an open boat to be driven wherever the winds would take her, she would or could tell him little or nothing. Moreover, when he asked her whether she wished to return to her own country, she answered that she did not know.

Then after a while Wi began to talk to her as a friend and to tell her of his own troubles, though of Aaka he said nothing at all. She listened and at length answered that his sickness had no cure.

"You belong to this people, Chief," she said, "but are not of them. You should have been born of my folk."

"In every company one walks quicker than the rest," answered Wi.

"Then he finds himself alone," said Laleela.

"Not so, because he must return to guide the others."

"Then before the hilltop is gained, night will overtake them all," said Laleela.

" If a man gain that hilltop, what can he do by himself ? "

" Look at the plains below, and die. At least it is something to have been the first to see new things, and some day those who follow in his footsteps will find his bones."

From the time that Wi heard Laleela speak thus, he began to love her with his heart and not only for her beauty's sake, as he had always done since first he looked upon her in the boat.

Soon Aaka noted all this and laughed at him.

" Why do you not take the witch to yourself, as it is lawful that you should do ? " she asked ; " for whoever heard of a chief with only one wife ? I shall not be jealous of her, and you have but a single child left."

" Because she is far above me," he answered. " Moreover, I have sworn an oath upon this matter."

" That for your oath ! " said Aaka, snapping her fingers.

Yet when she spoke thus Aaka did not tell all the truth. As a wife she was not jealous of Wi, because of the customs of her people. Yet in other ways she was very jealous, because in old times she and no other had been his counsellor. Then she became bitter towards him because he set their children before her, and left him to go his own way. Thereon he turned to Pag and made a friend of him and hearkened to his words, and for this reason she hated Pag. Now the Witch-from-the-Sea had come with her new wisdom which he drank up as thirsty sand drinks up water, and behold ! she hated her even more than she had done Pag, not because she was fair but because she was clever.

Moreover, although he had liked Laleela well enough at first and guarded her as her friend, Pag began to hate her also, and for the same reason. The truth was that, notwithstanding his faults, which were many, Wi was one of those men who is beloved by all who are near to him, even when they do not understand him, so much so that those who love him grow jealous of each other. But this

Wi himself never knew, any more than he did that it
was because he entered into the hearts of all, reading
them and their joys and sorrows, that he drew the hearts
of all after him.

So Wi made a friend of Laleela, telling her his troubles,
and the closer he drew to her the further away moved
Aaka and Pag. Laleela listened and advised and comforted, and being a woman, in her heart wondered why
he did not come still nearer, though whether or not she
would have been glad if he had, she did not know. At
least she would have wondered, had not Wi told her of
the new law that he had made, under which, because
women were so few among the tribe, no man might take
more than one wife, and of the oath that he had sworn that
this law he would keep himself, calling down upon his
head the curse of the Ice-Gods whom he worshipped,
should he break it, and not on his head only, but also
upon those of the people.

Now Laleela did not believe in the Ice-Gods, because
she was a Moon-worshipper. Yet she did believe that a
curse invoked in the name of one god was just as terrible
as that invoked in the name of another. In fact she put
more faith in the curse than she did in the gods, because
if the gods were invisible, always evil could be seen.
Therefore she was not angry because Wi, who was so near
to her in mind, still remained as far away from her as
though he were her brother, or her father ; nor did she
try to draw him closer, as, had she wished, she knew well
enough that she could do.

Meanwhile it is to be told that this year all things
went ill with the tribe. There was no spring, and when
the time of summer came the weather remained so cold
and sunless that always it felt as though snow were
about to fall, while the wind from the east was so bitter
that but little could grow. Moreover, only a few seals
appeared from the south to breed, not enough to furnish
the food of the people or their garments for the winter.
With the duck and other wildfowl, and the fish, especially
the salmon, the story was the same, so that had it not

been for the chance that four whales of the smaller sort, coming in with a high tide, were left stranded in the Bay, which whales they cut up, preserving their flesh as best they could by smoking it and otherwise, there would have been little for them to eat until the spring of another year.

At the cutting up of these whales, also at the collection of all food that could be found, Wi laboured very hard. Yet the people, who had been accustomed to plenty in the summer season, however tight they must draw their belts in winter, murmured and walked about with sullen, downcast faces, grumbling and asking each other why such trouble should come upon them, the like of which even Urk the Aged could not remember. Then a whisper began to run from ear to ear among them, that it was because the beautiful Witch-from-the-Sea had brought evil on them out of the sea, changing the face of heaven, and driving away the seals and the fowls and the fish that would not come where no sun shone.

If she were gone, said the whisperers, the sun would shine again and the beasts and birds would return, and their stomachs would be full and they could look up to the ridge-poles of their huts and see them bending beneath the weight of the winter food, as they used to do in the old days. Why could she not go back into the sea in her hollow log, or, if she would not, why could she not be cast out thither living, or if need be—dead ? Thus they said one to another by signs, or speaking in hints ; but as yet, whatever he might guess, Wi knew nothing of their talk.

CHAPTER XIII

THE LESSON OF THE WOLF-MOTHER

ON a certain day Aaka saw Pag shambling past her hut, his eyes fixed upon the ground.

"The Wolf-man is sad," she said to herself, "and I know why he is sad. It is because Wi up there at the cave, is taking counsel with that yellow-haired Laleela about big matters and asking no help from him."

Thus she thought, then called to Pag to come to her and offered him a dish of food, mussels cooked in a shell. Pag, who was hungry, looked at it, then said,

"Is it poisoned, Aaka?"

"Why do you ask that, Pag?" she answered.

"For two very good reasons," said Pag. "First, because I never remember the day that you offered food to me out of kindness; and secondly, because you hate me, Aaka."

"Both those things are true, Pag. Because I hate you I have never offered you food. Yet one hate may be driven out by a larger hate. Eat the mussels, Pag. They are fresh and good, for Foh brought them to me this morning, though not so fat as they used to be in past years."

So Pag sat down and devoured that dish to the last mussel, smacking his thick lips, for he was a large eater and food had been scarce of late, because by Wi's command all that could be spared was being saved for the coming winter.

Aaka, handsome, solemn, black-browed, deep-eyed, watched him as he ate, and when he had finished, said,

"Let us talk."

"I wish there were some more mussels," said Pag,

licking the shell, "but if they are finished, then, if you
have anything to say about Laleela, talk on, for I am sure
it is of her you wish to speak."

"Now, as always, you are clever, Pag."

"Yes, I am clever; if I were not I should have been
dead long ago. Well, what of Laleela the Beautiful?"

"Oh, nothing much, except"—here she leant forward and whispered in his ear—"that I wish you would
kill her, Pag, or bring it about that she is killed. This,
being a man, or something like one, you can do, whereas
for us women it is impossible because it would be set
down to jealous hate."

"I understand," said Pag. "And yet, why should
I kill Laleela, whom I like very much, and who knows
more than all the rest of us put together?"

"Because she has brought a curse upon the tribe,"
began Aaka, whereon Pag stopped her with a wave of his
big hand.

"You may think that, Aaka, or choose to say that
you think it, but why waste breath in telling such a tale
to me, who know it to be a lie? It is the skies and the
season that have brought a curse upon the tribe, not
this fair woman from the sea, as the people believe."

"What the people believe is always true," said
Aaka sullenly. "Or at least they think that it is true,
which is the same thing. Hearken: if this witch is
not killed, or driven away to die, or put in her hollow log
and sent out to sea, so that we look on her no more, the
people will kill Wi."

"Worse things might happen to him, Aaka. For
instance, he might live on, hated, to see all his plans
fail and all his friends turn against him, as it seems some
have done already," and he looked at her hard, adding,
"Come, speak your mind, or let me go."

"You know it," said Aaka, staring at the ground with
her fine eyes.

"I think I know it," answered Pag. "I think that
you are so jealous of Laleela that you would like to be
rid of her. Yet why are you jealous, seeing that Wi by

his new law has built a wall between himself and her ? "

" Talk not to me of Wi's foolish laws, for I hate them and all new things," interrupted Aaka impatiently. " If Wi wishes more wives let him take them. That I could understand, for it is our custom. What I do not understand is that, seated with her by the fire, he should make a friend and a counsellor of this witch, leaving me, his wife, standing outside the hut in the cold while she is warm within ; me—and you also, Pag," she added slowly.

" I understand it well enough," said Pag. " Wi, being wise and in trouble, seeks wisdom to help him out of his trouble. Finding a lamp to his hand, he holds it up to search the darkness."

" Yes, and while he stares at this new light his feet will fall into a pit. Listen, Pag. Once I was Wi's counsellor. Then you, the Wolf-man and outcast whom he had saved, came and took him from me. Now another has come and taken him from both of us. Therefore we who were foes should be friends and rid ourselves of that other."

" To find ourselves enemies again afterwards. Well, there is something in what you say, Aaka, for if you can be jealous, so can I. Now what you want me to do is to bring about the death of Laleela, either by causing her to be killed, or by driving her into the sea, which is the same thing. Is that so ? "

" Yes, Pag."

" You wish me to do this, not with my own hand, because you know that I would never strike down with an axe or a stone one whom I have been set to watch and who has always been kind to me, but by stirring up the people against her."

" Perhaps that might be the better plan," said Aaka uneasily, " since it is the people upon whom she brings the curse."

" Are you sure of that, Aaka ? Are you sure that if you leave her alone she will not bring a blessing on the

people in the end, seeing that wisdom is always strong,
and that she has more of it than the rest of us put
together ? "

" I am sure that she would be best out of our path,"
answered Aaka, scowling, " and so would you be if you
had a husband whom you loved and who was being led
aside."

" How should a wife show love to her husband, Aaka ?
I ask you because I do not know. Is it by being always
rough to him and finding fault with all he does, and
turning her back on him and hating his friends ? Or is
it by being kindly and loving and trying to help him in
his troubles, as such a one as Laleela would do ? Well,
who am I to talk of such matters, of which as a wolf-
man I can know nothing ? Friendship and its duties
I understand, since even a dog may care for its master,
but love and its ways have never been mine to know.
Still, it is true that, like you, I am jealous of this Laleela
and should not be sorry to see her back. Therefore I
will think over all that you have said, and afterwards
we will talk again. And now I will be going, that is, if
you have no more mussels, Aaka."

So, as there were no more mussels, Pag went, leaving
Aaka wondering, for she was not sure what he would do.
She knew that he was jealous of Laleela who had taken
his place in Wi's counsel, and therefore surely he must
wish to be rid of her, as she did. And yet Pag was very
strange, and who could be certain ? He was only a twisted
dwarf, wolf-suckled they said ; yet he seemed to have
the mind of a man, and how could men be counted on,
especially where a woman was concerned ? She might
have bewitched him also. Notwithstanding his wrongs
he might turn round and take her side. Now she almost
wished she had not paid so much heed to Pag's grumblings
and opened her secret heart to him ; for after all, Pag
was a man, and how was it possible to trust men, mad
people, most of them, who thought quite differently to
women, and could be turned from their ends and
advantage by all sorts of silly reasons ?

Pag went away, far into the woods, for he knew that Wi was taking counsel with Laleela and would not want him. At a certain place in the woods, a secret place where the trees were very thick and, save himself, no man had ever come, he cast himself down upon his face and lay thinking.

It had come to this, that he hated Laleela, of whom he used to be so fond, almost as much as Aaka did, and for the same reason, because she had robbed him of the heart of Wi. If he caused her to be killed, as Aaka had suggested, which he could do well enough by stirring up the people against her, who thought that she had brought a curse upon them, then he would be rid of her and Wi's heart would come back to him, because his nature was such that he must have someone to trust and to care for him, and the boy Foh was not yet old enough for him to lean upon. Only if ever Wi learned that he, Pag, had loosed the stone that crushed Laleela, what then? He would kill him. Nay, that was not Wi's way. He would look over his head and would never see him more, even when he sat on the other side of the fire, or stared him in the face. Yes, Wi would despise him and in his heart call him dog.

Pag thought till he could think no more, for his mind went up and down, first this way and then that, like a stick balanced on a stone and shaken by the wind. At last a kind of savagery entered into him, who grew weary of these reasonings and wished that he were as the beasts are who obey their desires and question not. He set his hand to his big mouth and uttered a low howling cry. Thrice he uttered it and presently—far, far away in the distance—it was answered. Then Pag sat silent and waited, and while he waited the sun went down and twilight came.

There was a patter of feet stirring the dried pine needles. Then between the trunks of two trees appeared the head of a grey wolf glaring about it suspiciously. Pag howled again in a lower note, but still the wolf seemed doubtful. It moved away till such wind as there was

blew from Pag to it, then sniffed thrice and leaped forward, and after it ran a cub. It came to Pag, a great
gaunt creature, and rearing itself up, set its forepaws
upon his shoulders and licked his face, for it knew him
again. Pag patted it upon the head, whereon the old
she-wolf sat herself down beside him as a dog might do,
then with low growls called to the young one to come
near as though to make it known to Pag, which it would
not do, for man was strange to it. So Pag and the wolf
sat there together, and Pag talked to the wolf that many
years ago once had suckled him, while she sat still as though
she understood him, which she did not. All she understood was that by her was one whom she had suckled.

" I have killed your kin, Grey Mother," said Pag to
the she-wolf, or rather, to himself, " if not all of them,
for it seems that somewhere you have found one to mate
with you," and he looked towards the cub lurking at a
distance. " Yet you can forgive me and come at my
call, as of old, you that are a brute beast, while I am a
man. Then if you, the beast, can forgive, why should
not I, the man, also forgive one who has done me far
smaller wrong ? Why should I kill this Witch-from-the-
Sea, this Laleela, because for a while she has stolen the
mind of one whom I love, being wiser than I am and
knowing more ; being a very fair woman also and therefore armed with a net which I cannot cast ? Oh, old
Mother-wolf, if you, the savage beast, can forgive and
come at my call because once you gave me of your milk,
why cannot I forgive who am a man ? "

Then the great gaunt she-wolf, that understood
nothing save that he, her fosterling, was troubled, licked
his face again and leaned against him who had planned
the murder of all her kin and used her love to decoy
them to their doom.

" I will not kill Laleela, or cause her to be killed,"
said Pag at length aloud. " I will forgive as this grey
wolf-mother of mine forgives. If it is in Aaka's mind
to kill her, let her work her own evil, against which I
will warn Laleela ; yes, and Wi also. I thank you for

your lesson, Grey Mother; and now get you back to your cub and your hunting."

So the old she-wolf went away and presently Pag went also.

Next morning Pag sat at the mouth of the cave, watching Laleela at her work among the cast-out female babes, going from one to another, tending them, soothing them, talking to those who nursed them, bravely, sweetly, gently, lovely to look on and in all her ways.

At length her tasks were finished and she came to Pag, sat herself down beside him, glanced at the grey, cold sky, drew her robe closer about her shoulders, and shivered.

"Why do you stop in this cold place, Laleela?" asked Pag; "you who, I understand, come from a country where the sun shines and it is warm."

"Because I must, or so it would seem, Pag."

"Then would you go away if you could, Laleela?"

"I do not know; I am not sure, Pag. The great sea is a lonely place."

"Then why did you cross it to come hither, Laleela, you who tell us that you are a chieftainess in your own land?"

"Because no woman can rule alone; always there must be one who rules her, Pag, and I hate him who would have ruled me. Therefore I became a death-seeker, but instead of finding death I found this place of ice and cold and you who dwell here."

"And here once more have become a chieftainess, Laleela, seeing that you rule him who rules us. Where is Wi?"

"I think he has gone out to quell some trouble among the people, Pag. There is always trouble among your people."

"Yes, Laleela; empty bellies and cold feet make bad tempers, especially when men and women are afraid."

"Afraid of what, Pag?"

" Of the sunless skies ; of lack of food and of the cold black winter that draws on ; also of the curse that has fallen upon the tribe."

" What curse, Pag ? "

" The curse of the Witch-from-the-Sea, the curse of a fair woman called Laleela."

" Why am I a curse-bearer, Pag ? " she asked, staring at him open-eyed and turning pale.

" I don't know, Laleela, seeing that from the look of you blessings should come in your basket, not curses, you whose eyes are kind and who do kind deeds with your hands. Yet the people hold differently, because they believe that they are the only men and women on the earth and think that therefore you must be a witch born of the sea. Also, since you came there has been nothing but misfortune ; the sun has hidden itself, those beasts and birds and fishes on which we fed have kept away, and even the berries do not grow upon the bushes in the wood, while now in the early autumn we hear winter marching towards us, for on the mountain-tops already rain turns to ice, as it does in the dark of the year. Yes, winter is always with us. Listen ! There is one of his footsteps," and he held up his hand, while from the hills behind them came the terrible rending sound of mighty masses of ice being thrust forward by other new-formed masses that had gathered above them.

" Can I command the sun ? " asked Laleela sadly. " Is it my fault if the season is cold and the seals and the fowl do not come, and it snows on the mountain-tops when it ought to rain, and the rest ? "

" The people think so," answered Pag, nodding his great head, " especially since *you* have become Wi's chosen counsellor, which was once my office."

" Pag, you are jealous of me," said Laleela.

" Yes, that is true ; I am jealous of you, yet I would have you believe that I try to judge justly. I have been urged to kill you, or to bring about your death, which would be easy. But this I do not wish to do, because I like you too well, who are fairer and wiser than

any of us, and have shown us how to sew skins together,
with other arts ; also because it would be wicked to put
a stranger to death who has come among us by chance,
for well I know that you are no witch, but just a stranger."

" To kill me ! You have been urged to kill me ? "
she exclaimed, staring at him with big, fearful eyes as
a seal does when it sees the club above its head.

" I have said it, also that I will have no hand in this
business ; but others may be found who think differently.
Therefore, if you will listen I will give you counsel to
take or to leave."

" When the fox told the raven how to draw the bolt
of its cage, the raven listened, so says the tale of my
country, but it forgot that the hungry fox was waiting
outside," answered Laleela, casting a doubtful look at
Pag. " Still, speak on."

" Have no fear," said Pag grimly, " since perhaps the
counsel that I shall give you, if taken, would leave this
fox hungrier than he is to-day. Hearken ! You are in
danger. Yet there is one way in which you can save
yourself. Become the wife of Wi, which, although he
hangs round you with his eyes fixed upon your face, it
is well known you are not. None dare to touch Wi,
who, if he is grumbled against, is still beloved, because,
it is known that all day and all night he thinks of others,
not of himself, and because he killed Henga and the
great-toothed tiger, and is mighty. Nor would any
dare to touch one who was folded in his cloak, though
while she is outside his cloak it is otherwise. Therefore,
become his wife and be safe. Yes, I say this, although I
know that when it happens I, Pag, who love Wi better
than you do, if indeed you love him at all, shall be driven
far from the cave and mayhap shall go to live in the
woods, where I can still find friends of a sort, who will
not turn on me even when they are mating ; or at any
rate one friend."

" Marry Wi ! " exclaimed Laleela. " I do not know
that I wish to marry Wi ; I have never thought of it.
Also Wi is married already, to Aaka. Also, never has

he sought to marry me. Had such been his desire,
surely he would have told me, who speaks to me of no
such matters."

" Men do not always talk of what they desire, or
women either, Laleela. Has not Wi told you about his
new laws ? "

" Yes, often."

" And do you not remember that because women are
so few among us, the first of these was that no man
should have more than one wife ? "

" Yes," said Laleela, dropping her eyes and
colouring.

" May be, also, he has told you that he called down
a curse upon his head and on all the tribe if he broke
that law."

" Yes," she said again in a low voice.

" Then perhaps it is because of this oath that Wi,
although he is always so close to you and sees no one else
when you are near, has never spoken to you of coming
closer, Laleela."

" Now would he, having sworn that oath, Pag."

Nor Pag laughed hoarsely, saying,

" There are oaths and oaths. Some are made to be
kept and some made to be broken."

" Yes, but this one is coupled with a curse."

" Aye," said Pag, " and there comes the trouble.
Choose now. Will you make Wi marry you, as being
so beautiful and clever, doubtless you can do if you wish,
and take the chance of the curse that follows broken
oaths falling upon his head and yours, and that of the
tribe, and be happy until it falls, or does not fall ?
Or will you not marry him and continue as his counsellor
with your hand in his but never round his neck, until
the wrath of the tribe strikes you, stirred up by your
enemies, of whom perhaps I am the worst——"

Here Laleela smiled.

" —and you are killed or driven out to die ? Or
will you perhaps be pleased to return to your own people,
as doubtless you can do in that magical boat of yours—or so

declares Urk the Aged, who says that he knew a great-grandmother of yours who was exactly like you."

Laleela listened, wrinkling her fair, broad brow in earnest thought. Then she answered,

" I must think. I do not know which of these things I shall do, because I do not know which of them will be the best for Wi and all his people. Meanwhile, Pag, I thank you for your kindness to me since the Moon led me here—you know I am a Moon-worshipper, do you not, like all my forefathers before me ? If we should not talk again, I pray you to remember that Laleela, who came out of the sea, thanks you for all your kindness to her, a poor wanderer, and that if she continues to live upon the earth, often she thinks of you, or if the Moon takes her and she has memory in the houses of the Moon, that thence she looks down and still thanks and blesses you."

" What for ? " asked Pag gruffly. " Is it because I hate you who have robbed me of the company and the trust of Wi, whom alone I love upon the earth ? Or is it because with one ear I have listened to Aaka, who urges me to make an end of you ? Do you thank me for these things ? "

" No, Pag," she answered in her quiet fashion ; " how can I thank you for that which is not ? I know that Aaka hates me, as it is natural that she should and therefore I do not blame her. But I know also that you do not hate me ; nay, rather that you love me in your own fashion, even if I seem to have come between you and Wi, which, if you knew all, in truth I have not done. You may have listened to Aaka with one ear, Pag, but your finger was pressed hard upon the other ; for you know well that you never meant to kill me or to cause me to be killed, you who in your goodness have come to warn me against dangers."

Now hearing these gentle words, Pag stood up and stared at the kind and beautiful face of her who spoke them. Then, seizing Laleela's little hand, he lifted it to his thick lips and kissed it. Next he wiped his one eye with the back of his hairy paw, spat upon the ground, muttering something that might have been a blessing or an oath, and shambled away, while Laleela watched him go, still smiling sweetly.

But when he had gone and she knew that she was alone, she smiled no longer. Nay, she sat down, covered her lovely eyes with her hands, and wept.

That evening when Wi returned she made her report to him as to the babes whom he had set in her care, speaking particularly of two who were ailing that she thought needed watching and chosen food.

" What of it ? " asked Wi in his pleasant fashion, " seeing that you watch them and give them their food, Laleela ? "

" Oh, nothing," she answered, " except it is well that everything should be known to two, since always one might be ill, or forget. And that puts me in mind of Pag."

" Why ? " asked Wi, astonished.

" I do not know, and yet it does—oh, it was the thought about two. You and Pag were one, and now you have become two, or so he thinks. You should be kinder to Pag, Wi, and talk more to him, as it seems you used to do. Hark ! That sick baby is crying ; I must go to it. Good-night, Wi, good-night."

Then she went, leaving him wondering, for there was something about her manner and her words which he did not understand.

CHAPTER XIV

THE RED-BEARDS

NEXT morning Laleela was missing. When Wi noticed this, as he was quick to do, and inquired of her where-abouts, one of the women who helped her in the care of the cast-out babes, answered that the "Sun-haired-White-One," as she called her, after she had prepared their food that morning, had told her that she needed rest and fresh air. She added, said the woman, that she was going to spend the day in the woods and therefore none must trouble about or search for her, as she would be back at nightfall.

"Did she say anything else?" asked Wi anxiously.

"Yes," answered the woman. "She spoke to me of what food should be given to those two sick babes and at what hours, in case she should make up her mind to spend the night in the woods, which, however, she was almost sure she would not do. That was all."

Then Wi went away to attend his business, of which he had much in hand, asking no more questions, perhaps because Aaka had come into the cave and must have overheard them. Yet that day passed slowly for him, and at nightfall he hurried home to the cave, thinking to find Laleela there and to speak to her sharply, because she had troubled him by going out thus, without warning him so that he could cause her to be guarded against dangers.

But when he came to the cave as the day died, there was no Laleela.

He waited awhile, pretending to eat his food, which he could not touch. Then he sent for Pag. Presently Pag shambled into the cave, and looking at Wi, asked,

" Why does the Chief send for me, which he has not
done for a long while ?   It was but just in time, for as
I am never wanted nowadays I was about to start for
the woods."

" So you too desire to wander in the woods," said
Wi suspiciously, and was silent.

" What is it ? " asked Pag.

Then Wi told him all.

Now as Pag listened he remembered his talk with
Laleela and was disturbed in his heart.   Still, of that
talk he said nothing, but answered only,

" There is no cause for fear.   This Laleela of the
Sea is, as you know, a Moon-worshipper.   Doubtless she
has gone out to worship the moon and to make offerings
and prayer to it according to the rites of her own people."

" It may be so," said Wi, " but I am not sure.'

" If you are afraid," went on Pag, " I will go out to
search for her."

Wi studied the face of Pag with his quick eyes, and
said.

" It comes into my mind that you, Pag, are more
afraid than I am, and perhaps with better reason.   But
whether this be so or not, nobody can search for Laleela to-
night, because the moon is covered with thick clouds and
rain falls, and who can find a woman in the dark ? "

Pag went to the mouth of the cave and looked at the
sky, then came back and answered,

" It is as you said.   The sky is black ;   rain falls
heavily.   No man can see where to set his foot.   Doubtless Laleela is hid in some hole or beneath thick trees,
and will return at dawn."

" I think that she has been murdered, or has gone away,
and that you, Pag, or Aaka, or both of you, know where
and why she has gone," said Wi in a muttering, wrathful
voice, and glaring at him.

" I know nothing," answered Pag.   " Perhaps she is
at the hut of Moananga.   I will go to see."

He went, and a long while afterwards returned with
the rain-water running off him, to say that she was not

in Moananga's hut, or in any other that he could find,
and that none had seen her that day.

All that night Wi and Pag sat on either side of the
fire, or lay down pretending to sleep, saying nothing,
but with their eyes fixed upon the mouth of the cave.
At length dawn came, a wretched dawn, grey and very
cold, although the rain had ceased. At the first sign of
it Pag slipped from the cave, saying no word to anyone.
Presently Wi followed, thinking to find him outside, but
he had vanished, nor did any know where he had gone.
Then Wi sent out messengers and inquired for Laleela.
These returned in due course but without tidings. After
this he despatched people to search for her, yes, and
went himself, although Aaka, who had come up to the
cave, asked him why he should be so disturbed because
a witch-woman had vanished, seeing that it was well
known that this was the fashion of witch-women when
they had done all the ill they could.

" This one did good, not ill, Wife," said Wi, looking
at the foundling babes.

Then he went out to the woods, taking Moananga
with him.

All that day he searched, as did others, but found
nothing, and at nightfall returned weary and very sad,
for it seemed to him as though Laleela had torn out his
heart and taken it with her. Also that night one of the
sick babes which she had been nursing died, for it
would not take its food from any hand but hers. Wi
asked for Pag, but no one had seen him ; he too had
vanished.

" Doubtless he has gone with Laleela, for they were
great friends, although he pretended otherwise," said
Aaka.

Wi made no answer, but to himself he thought that
perhaps Pag had gone to bury her.

A second dawn came, and shortly after it Pag crept
back to the cave, looking very thin and hungry, like a
toad when it crawls out of its hole after winter is past.

" Where is Laleela ? " asked Wi.

" I don't know," answered Pag, " but her hollow log
has gone. She must have dragged it down to the sea
out of the seal-cave at high tide, which is a great deed
for a woman."

" What have you been saying to her ? " asked Wi.

" Who can remember what he said days ago ? "
answered Pag. " Give me food, for I am as empty as a
whelk-shell upon the midden."

While Pag ate Wi went down to the seashore. He did
not know for what reason he went, unless it was because
the sea had taken Laleela from him, as once it gave her
to him, and therefore he wished to look upon it. So
there he stood staring at the grey and quiet sea, till
presently, far away upon the edge of the mist that covered
it, he saw something moving.

A fish, he thought to himself, but I don't know what
kind of fish, since it stays upon the top of the water,
which only whales do, and this fish is too small to be
a whale.

There he stood gazing idly and caring nothing what
sort of fish it might be, till suddenly he noted, although
it was still so far away and so hidden by mist wreaths,
that the thing was not a fish at all. Yet it reminded him
of something. Of what did it remind him ? Ah, he
knew—of that hollow log in which Laleela had drifted
to this shore. But it was not drifting now ; it was being
driven beachwards by one who paddled, one who paddled
swiftly.

The gathering light fell on this paddler's hair and he
saw that it glinted yellow. Then Wi knew that Laleela
was the paddler, and ran out into the sea up to his
middle. On she came, not seeing him until he hailed her.
Then she paused breathless and the canoe glided up to
him.

" Where have you been ? " he asked angrily. " Know
that I have been much troubled about you."

" Is it so ? " she gasped, looking at him in an odd
fashion. " Well, we will talk of that afterwards. Meanwhile learn, Wi, that many people descend on you,

coming in boats like this, only larger. I have fled away from them to warn you."

"Many people?" said Wi. "How can that be? There are no other people, unless they be yours that you have brought upon us."

"Nay, nay," she answered, "these are quite different; moreover, they come from the north, not from the south. To shore now, to shore quickly, for I think that they are very fierce."

Then she paddled on beachward, Wi wading alongside of her.

They reached the shore, where some who had seen the canoe had gathered, among them Moananga and Pag. It was dragged up on the sand and Laleela climbed out of it stiffly, helped by Wi. Indeed she sank down upon the sand as though she were very tired.

"Tell us your story," said Wi, his eyes fixed upon her as though he feared lest she should vanish away again.

"It is short, Chief," she answered. "Being weary of the land, I thought that I would float upon the sea for a while. Therefore I took my boat and paddled out to sea for my pleasure."

"You lie, Laleela," said Wi rudely. "Still, go on."

"So I paddled far, the weather being calm, towards the end of the great point of rocks which lies out yonder, though perhaps you have never seen it," she continued, smiling faintly.

"There, last evening at the sundown, suddenly I saw a great number of boats coming from the north and rounding the point of rock as though they were following the shore line. They were big boats, each of them holding many men, hideous-looking and hairy men. They caught sight of me and yelled at me with harsh voices in a talk I did not understand. I turned and fled before them. They followed after, but the night came down and saved me. Sometimes, however, the moon shone out between the clouds and they caught sight of me again. Then at last her face was covered up and

I paddled on through the mist and darkness, having seen the outline of these hills and knowing which way to row. I think that they are not far off. I think that they will attack you and that you must make ready at once. That is all I have to say to you."

"What do they come for?" asked Wi, amazed.

"I do not know," answered Laleela, "but they looked thin and hungry. Perhaps they seek food."

"What must we do?" asked Wi again.

"Fight them, I suppose," said Laleela; "fight them and drive them off."

Now Wi looked bemused, for this thought of folk fighting against each other was strange to him. He had never heard of such a thing, because the tribe, until Laleela came, believed themselves to be alone in the world and therefore had no need of defence against other men. Then Pag spoke, saying,

"Chief, you have fought wild beasts and killed them; you fought Henga and killed him. Well, it seems that this is what you and all of us must do against this people who attack us. If Laleela is right, either they will kill us or we must kill them."

"Yes, yes, it is so," said Wi, still bemused, then added, "Let Wini-wini summon all the tribe and bid them bring their weapons with them. Yes, and let others go with him, that they may hear more quickly."

So certain of those who had gathered there on the beach departed, running their hardest. When they had gone Wi turned to Pag and asked,

"What shall we do, Pag?"

"Do you seek counsel of me while Laleela stands there?" answered Pag bitterly.

"Laleela, a woman, has played her part," said Wi. "Now men must play theirs."

"It always comes to that in the end," said Pag.

"What can we do?" asked Wi.

"I don't know," answered Pag. "Yet low tide draws on and at low tide there is but one entrance to the bay, through the gap in the rocks yonder. These strangers

will not know that and if they come on, presently their
boats will be stranded, or only a few of them will get
through the gap. These we must fight, also any who
remain upon the reef. But what do I know of fighting,
who am but a dwarf? There is Moananga your brother,
one who is strong and tall and brave. Let him be captain
and manage the fighting, but do you, Wi, keep behind it
to look after the people, who will want you ; or if need
be, to fight any of the strangers who get on shore."

"Let it be so," said Wi. "Moananga, I make you
captain. Do your best and I will do my best behind
you."

"I obey you," said Moananga simply. "If I am
killed and you live, look after Tana and see that she
does not starve."

Just then, summoned by the furious trumpetings of
Wini-wini, and by rumours that flew from mouth to
mouth, the people came running up, each of them armed
in a fashion, some with stone axes, some with flint-headed
spears and knives, some with stakes hardened in the
fire, or with slings.

Wi addressed them, telling them that devils who came
floating on the sea from the north, were about to attack
them, and that they must fight them unless they wished
to be killed with their wives and children ; also that
Moananga would direct them. Then there arose a great
noise, for the women who had run up with the men,
began to wail and cling to them, till in the end these were
driven away. After this Hou the Unstable began to
argue loudly, saying that Laleela was a liar, that there
were no men in boats and that therefore there was no
need for all this making ready. Also Whaka, the Bird
of Ill-omen, declared that if there were such men, there
was no use trying to fight against them, because if they
did they would all be killed, since men in boats must be
very strong and clever. So the only thing to do was to
run away and hide in the woods.

This counsel seemed to move many ; indeed, some
departed at once. Noting this, Wi went up to Whaka

and knocked him down with a blow of his fist. Also he strove to serve Hou in the same way, but seeing him come, Hou escaped. After this he called out that the next man who ran he would catch and brain with his axe, whereon all the rest stayed where they were. Still Hou went on talking from a distance, till presently there was a shout—for there on the misty surface of the sea appeared a great number of large canoes, manned, some of them, by as many as eight or ten paddlers. These canoes rowed on towards the bay, knowing nothing of the falling tide or of the reef of rocks. So it happened that presently six or eight of them struck those rocks upon which waves broke and there overturned, throwing the men in them into the water, where some were drowned. But the most of them reached the rocks to the right and stood upon them, jabbering in loud voices to their companions in the other boats outside the reef, who jabbered back to them.

At length these men paddled forward gently, which, the sea being calm, they could do well enough, not to the gap where those boats that went first had been overturned, but to the rocks upon its right side, on which many of them landed, leaving some in each canoe to hold on to the seaweed that grew upon the rocks. When they had gathered there to the number of a hundred or more they began to talk, waving their long arms and pointing to the shore with the spears they carried that seemed to be tipped with walrus ivory or white stone.

Wi, watching them from the beach, said to Pag at his side,

"Surely these strangers are terrible. See how tall and strong they are, and behold their skins covered with fur and their red hair and beards. I think that they are not men but devils. Only devils could look like that and travel about without women or children."

"If so," answered Pag, "they are very hungry devils, for that big fellow who seems to be their chief opens his mouth and points down it, also at his stomach, and then waves his hand towards the shore, thus telling the

others that there they will find food. Likewise they
are devils who can drown," and he nodded towards the
corpses of one or two of them who had been in those canoes
that were overset, which corpses now were rolling to and
fro in the shallow water. " For the rest," he added after
a pause, " wives can always be stolen," and he glanced
towards the women of the tribe who were gathered in
little companies behind them, all talking together at
once, or screaming and beating their breasts, while the
children clung to them terrified.

" Yes," said Wi. Then he thought for a moment and
called certain men to him.

" Go," he said, " to Urk the Aged, and bid him lead
the women, the children, and the old people to the woods
and hide them there, for how this business will end I
do not know and they will be better far away."

The men went and there followed much screaming and
confusion. Some of the women began to run towards
the woods ; others would not move ; while others threw
their arms about their husbands and tried to drag these
away with them.

" Unless this wailing stops soon the hearts of the men
will melt like blubber over a fire," said Pag. " Look, some
of them are creeping away to the women."

" Go you and drive them to the woods," said Wi.

" Nay," answered Pag, " I, who never liked the
company of women overmuch, stay where I am."

Now Wi took another counsel. Seeing Aaka standing
at a distance between the women and the men, or most
of them, whom Moananga was marshalling as best he
might, he called to her. She heard and came to him,
for Aaka did not lack courage.

" Wife," he said, " those red devils are going to
attack us and we must kill them or be killed."

" That I know," answered Aaka calmly.

" It is best," went on Wi looking down and speaking
in a rapid voice, " that the women should not see the
fighting. I ask you therefore to lead them all to the woods
and hide them away, together with the old people and

children and those who have run there already. Afterwards you can return."

"What is the use of returning to find our men dead? It is better that we should stay here and die with them."

"You would not die, Aaka. Those Red wanderers may want wives. At least you would not die at once, though in the end they might kill and eat you. Therefore I command you to go."

"Surely the Witch-from-the-Sea who guided these wanderers to attack us should go also before she works more treachery," answered Aaka.

"She did not guide them; she fled before them," exclaimed Wi angrily. "Still, take her with you if you will, and Foh also. Only drive back any men. Go now, I command you."

"I obey," said Aaka, "but know, Husband, that although we have grown away from each other, if you die, I die also, because once we were close together."

"I thank you," answered Wi. "Yet if that should happen, I say—live on, rule the tribe, and build it up afresh."

"Of what use are women without men?" replied Aaka, shrugging her shoulders.

Then she turned to walk away and as she went Wi saw her wipe her eyes with the back of her hand. She reached the women and cried out something to them in a fierce voice, repeating it again and again, till presently they began to move away with the aged, dragging the children by the hand, or carrying them, so that at last the tumult died and that sad company vanished among the first of the trees.

All this while the Red-men had been jabbering together, making their plans. At last these seemed to be settled, for by the help of their boats a number of them crossed the mouth of the bay and gathered upon the line of rocks to the left that now at low tide also stood bare above the water. Others, too, in some of the boats set themselves in order between these jaws of rock, as though preparing to paddle towards the shore.

Pag noted this and cried out exultingly,

"That they cannot do, for their boats will overset upon the reefs that lie beneath the waves, and they will be drowned in the deep holes between, like those fellows," and he pointed to the bodies rolling about in the surf.

But such was not the purpose of the Red-men, as presently he was to learn.

As he spoke Wi heard the crunching of little shells in the sand behind him and looked round to see who came. Behold, it was Laleela, clad in her blue cloak and holding a spear in her hand.

"Why are you here?" he asked angrily. "Why have you not gone to the woods with the other women?"

"Your orders were to the tribe," she replied in a quiet voice. "I am not of the tribe, so I hid in a hut till all were gone. Be not wrath, Chief," she went on in a gentle voice, "for I, who have seen other tribes and their fightings, may be able to give good counsel."

Now he began to speak angry words to her and bid her begone, of which, standing at his side, she took no heed, but only looked out at the sea. Then suddenly with a cry of: "I thought it!" she leapt in front of Wi, whose face was shoreward, and next instant staggered back, falling into his arms as he turned. He stared at her, as did Pag, and lo! they saw that in her cloak stood a little spear with feathers on it which had struck her just above the breast.

"Pull it out, Pag," she said, recovering her feet. "It is an arrow which other peoples use, and well was it for me that this cloak is so good and thick."

"Had you not sprung in front of me, that little spear would have pierced me," exclaimed Wi, gazing at her.

"It was by a chance," answered Laleela with a smile.

"You lie," said Wi, at which she only smiled again and drew the cloak more closely about her. Aye, while Pag pulled she still smiled, though he noted that her lips turned pale and twitched. At length the arrow came out and he noted something else, namely, that on its bone

barb there was blood and a little piece of flesh, though,
being wise, of this he said nothing.

" Lie down, Chief," said Laleela, " there, behind that
rock ; and you also, Pag, for so you will be safer. I
also will lie down," and she did so. " Now hearken
to me," she went on. " Those Red-beards, or some of
them, have bows and arrows, as we have just learned,
and their plan is to shoot at you from the boats until
the tide is quite low, and then to climb along both lines of
rock and attack you."

At this Moananga came up and was also made to
lie down.

" Perhaps," said Wi ; " and if so we had better draw
out of the reach of the little spears."

" That is what they want you to do," answered
Laleela, " for then they will climb along the lines of rock
quietly and without hurt. I have another counsel, if
it pleases you to hear it."

" What is it ? " said Wi and Moananga together.

" This, Chief : you and all the people know those
rocks and where the deep-water holes are between them,
since from childhood you have gathered shell-fish there.
Now divide your men into two companies, and do you
command one while Moananga commands the other.
Clamber along those rocks to the right and left with the
companies and attack the Red-men on them, for when they
see you coming so boldly some of them will get into the
boats. The others you must fight and kill ; nor will
those in the boats who have bows and arrows, be able
to shoot much at you for fear lest they should hit their
own people. Do this, and swiftly."

" Those are good words," said Wi. " Moananga,
do you take the left line of rocks with half the men, and
I will take the right with the rest. And, Laleela, I bid
you remain here, or fly."

" Yes, I will remain here," said Laleela rather faintly,
and turning on her face so that none should see the stain of
blood soaking through her blue robe. Yet as they went
she cried after them,

"Bid your people take stones, Wi and Moananga, that they may cast them into the boats and break their bottoms."

Coming to the men of the tribe who stood in knots, looking very wretched and afraid, most of them, as they stared at the hairy Red-men upon the rocks and in their boats, Wi addressed them in few hard words, saying,

"Yonder Red-beards come from I know not whence. They are starving, which will make them very brave, and they mean to kill us, every one, and to take first our food and then our women, if they can find them ; also perhaps to eat the children. Now we count as many heads as they do, or even more, and it will be a great shame to us if we allow ourselves to be conquered, our old people butchered, our women taken and our children eaten by these wanderers. Is it not so ? "

To this question the crowd answered that it was, yet without eagerness, for the eyes of most of them were turned towards the woods, whither the women had gone. Then Moananga said,

"I am chief in this matter. If any man runs away I will kill him at once if I can. And if not I will kill him afterwards."

"And I," added Pag, "who have a good memory, will keep my eye fixed on all and remember what every man does, which afterwards I will report to the women."

Then the force was divided into two companies, of whom the bravest were put in the rear to prevent the others from running away. This done they began to scramble along the two horns of rock that enclosed the little bay, wading round the pools that lay between the rocks, for they knew where the water was deep and where it was shallow.

When the Red-men saw them coming they made a howling noise, wagging their heads so that their long beards shook, and beating their breasts with their left hands. Moreover, waving their spears, they did not wait to be attacked, but clambered forward down the rocks,

while those of them in the boats shot arrows, a few of
which hit men of the tribe and wounded them.

Now at the sight of blood flowing from their brothers
whom the arrows had struck, the tribe went mad.   In
an instant they seemed to forget all their fears ; it was
as though something of which neither they nor their
fathers had thought for hundreds of years came back
to their hearts.   They waved their stone axes and flint-
pointed spears, they shouted, making a sound like to
that of wolves or other wild beasts ; they gnashed their
teeth and leapt into the air, and began to rush forward.
Yet moved by the same thought, Wi and Moananga made
them stay where they were for a while, for they knew
what would happen to the Red-men.

This happened : These Red-beards, also leaping
forward, slipped upon the seaweed-covered rocks and
fell into the pools between them.   Or if they did not
fall, they tried to wade these pools, not knowing which
were deep and which were shallow, so that many of them
went under water and came up again spluttering.   Then
Wi and Moananga shouted to the tribe to charge.

On they went, bounding from rock to rock, as they
could do readily enough, who from boyhood had known
every one of these stones and where to set their feet
upon them.   Then coming to the pools into which the
Red-men had fallen, they attacked them as they tried
to climb out, breaking their skulls with axes and stones ;
thus killing a number without loss to themselves.

Now the Red-beards scrambled back to the ends of
the two horns of rock, purposing to make a stand there,
and here the tribe attacked them, led by Wi and Moananga.
That fight was very hard, for the Red-men were strong
and fierce, and drove their big ivory-pointed spears
through the bodies of many the tribe.   Indeed it
looked ill for the tribe, until Wi with his bright axe
that Pag had made, that with which he slew Henga,
killed a great fellow who seemed to be the Chief of the
Red-beards, cutting his head in two so that he fell down
into the water.   Seeing this, the Red-men wailed aloud

and seized by a sudden panic, rushed for the boats, into
which they began to scramble as best they could. Then
Wi and Moananga remembering the counsel of Laleela,
gave commands to the tribe to throw the heaviest
stones they could lift into the boats. This they did,
breaking the bottoms of most of them, so that water
flowed in and they sank.

The men in those boats swam about till they drowned,
or tried to come to the shore, where they were met with
spears or stones, so that they died, every one of them.
The end of it was that but five boat-loads got away, and
these rowed out to sea and were never seen again. That
night a wind blew in which they may have foundered ;
or perhaps, being so hungry, they starved upon the sea.
At least the tribe saw no more of them. They came
none knew whence, and they went none knew whither.
Only the most of them remained behind in the pools of the
rocks or sunk in the deep sea beyond the rocks.

Thus ended the fight, the first that the tribe had ever
known.

CHAPTER XV

WI KISSES LALEELA

WHEN all was over, Wi and Moananga, having come together on the shore, bearing the hurt with them, counted their losses.   They found that in all twelve men had been killed and twenty-one wounded, among whom was Moananga, who was hit in the side with an arrow, though not badly.   Of the Red-beards, however, over sixty had died, most of them by drowning ; at least this was the number that they found after the next high tide had washed up the bodies.   There may have been more that were taken out to sea.

" It is a great victory," said Moananga as Wi washed the wound in his side with salt water, " and the tribe fought well."

" Yes," answered Wi, " the tribe fought very well."

" Yet," interrupted Pag, " it was the Witch-from-the-Sea who won the fight by her counsel, for I think that had we waited for the Red-men to attack us on the beach, it would have ended otherwise.   Also it was she who taught us to throw stones into the boats."

" That is true," said Wi.   " Let us go to thank her."

So they went, all three of them, and found Laleela lying where they had left her behind the rock, but face downwards.

" She has fallen asleep, who must be very weary," said Moananga.

" Yes," said Wi.   " Yet it is strange to sleep when death is so near," and he looked at her doubtfully.

Pag said nothing ; only, kneeling down, he thrust

his long arms underneath Laleela and turned her over on to her back. Then they saw that the sand beneath her was red with blood and that her blue robe was also red. Now Wi cried out aloud and would have fallen, had not Moananga caught him by the arm.

" Laleela is dead ! " he said in a hollow voice. " Laleela, who saved us, is dead."

" Then I know one who will be glad," muttered Pag. " Still, be not so sure."

Then he opened her robe and they saw the wound beneath her breast, which still bled a little. Pag, who was skilled in the treating of hurts, bent down and examined it, and while he did so Moananga said to Wi,

" Do you understand, Brother, that the little spear gave her this wound while she was talking to us, and that she hid it so that none of us knew she had been pierced ? "

Wi nodded like one who will not trust himself to speak.

" I knew well enough," growled Pag, " I who drew out the arrow."

" Then why did you not tell us ? " asked Moananga.

" Because if Wi had known that this Witch-from-the-Sea was smitten in the breast, the heart would have gone out of him and his knees would have become feeble. Better that she should die than that the heart of our Chief should have turned to water while the Red wanderers gathered to kill us."

" What of the wound ? " asked Wi, paying no heed to this talk.

" Be comforted," answered Pag. " Although she has bled much, I do not think that it is deep, because this thick cloak of hers almost stopped the little spear. Therefore, unless the point was poisoned, I believe that she will live. Stay now and watch her."

Then he shambled off towards certain bushes and sea-herbs that grew upon the beach, and searched among them till he found one that he sought. From this he plucked a number of leaves, which he put into his mouth and chewed between his great teeth. He returned, and taking the green pulp from his mouth, thrust some of it into Laleela's wound, and the rest into that of Moananga.

"It burns," said Moananga, wincing.

"Aye, it burns out poison and staunches blood," answered Pag as he covered Laleela with her cloak.

Then Wi seemed to awake from the deep thought into which he had fallen, for stooping down, he lifted Laleela in his arms as though she were a child and strode away with her towards the cave, followed by Pag and Moananga, also by certain of the tribe who waved their spears and shouted. By this time the women were returning from the woods, for some of the younger and more active of them had climbed tall trees and watching all, though from far away, had made report to those below who, learning that the Red wanderers had fled or been killed, trooped back to the huts, leaving the aged and the children to follow after.

The first of all came Foh, running like a deer.

"Father!" he cried in an angry voice as he met Wi, "am I a child that I should be dragged off to woods by women when you are fighting?"

"Hush!" said Wi, nodding his head at the burden in his arms, "hush, my son. We will talk of these matters afterwards."

Then appeared Aaka, calm-faced and stately although, if the truth were known, she had run also and with much swiftness.

"Welcome, Husband," she said. "They tell me that you have conquered those Red-men. Is it true?"

"It seems so, Wife; at least they have been conquered. Afterwards I will tell you the tale."

As he spoke he strove to pass her by, but she stepped in front of him and asked again,

"If that Witch-from-the-Sea has been killed for her treachery, why do you carry her in your arms?"

Wi gave no answer, for anger made him speechless. But Pag laughed hoarsely and said,

"In throwing stones at the kite you have hit the dove!

Aaka. The Witch-from-the-Sea whom Wi clasps upon his breast has not died for treachery. If she be dead, death came upon her in saving Wi's life, since she leapt in front of him and received into her bosom that which would have pierced him through, and this not by chance."

" Such things might have been looked for from her, who is ever where she should not be. What did she among the men, who ought to have accompanied the women ? " asked Aaka.

" I don't know," answered Pag. " I only know that she saved Wi's life by offering up her own."

" Is it so, Pag ? Then it is his turn to save hers if he can ; or to bury her if he cannot. Now I go to tend the wounded of our own people. Come with me, Tana, for I see that Moananga's hurt has been dressed and that we are not wanted here," and tossing her head she walked away slowly.

But Tana did not follow her, being curious to learn the tale of Laleela ; also to make sure that Moananga had taken no harm.

Wi bore Laleela into the cave and laid her down upon the bed where she slept near to the cast-out children. Tana took Moananga away and Pag went to make broth to pour down Laleela's throat, so that Wi and Laleela seemed to be left alone, though they were not, for the women who nursed the cast-outs watched them from dark places in the cave. Wi threw fur wrappings over her, and taking her hand, rubbed it between his own. In the warmth of the cave, where fire still burned, Laleela woke up and began to talk like one who dreams.

" Just in time ! Just in time ! " she said, " for I saw the arrow coming, though they did not, and leapt into its path. It would have killed him. If I saved him all is well, for what matters the life of a stranger wanted of none, not even of him ? "

Then she opened her eyes and, looking upward, by the light of the fire saw the eyes of Wi gazing down upon her.

" Do I live ? " she murmured, " and do you live, Wi ? "

Wi made no answer ; only he bent his head and kissed her on the lips, and although she was so weak she kissed him back, then turned away her head and seemed to go to sleep. But asleep or awake Wi went on kissing her, till Pag came with the broth, and after him the women with the cast-out children appeared from their hiding-places, chattering like starlings before they flight in autumn.

Presently Wi looked up from his task of watching Laleela, who, having swallowed the broth, seemed to have fallen asleep, and saw Aaka standing by the fire and gazing at them both.

" So the Witch lives," she said in a low voice, " and has found a nurse. When are you going to marry her, Wi ? "

Wi rose and came to her, then asked,

" Who told you that I was going to marry her ? Have I not sworn an oath upon this matter ? "

" Your eyes told me, I think, Wi. What are oaths against such service as she has done you ?—though it is strange that I should live to learn that Wi made use of a woman's breast as a shield in battle."

" You know the truth of that," he answered.

" I only know what I see, who pay no heed to words ; also what my heart tells me."

" And what does your heart tell you, Wife ? "

" It tells me that the curse which this witch has brought upon us has but begun its work. She goes out to sea in her hollow log and returns leading a host of Red wanderers. You fight these wanderers and drive them away, for a time. Yet many of the tribe are dead and wounded. What she will do next I do not know, but I am sure she has worse gifts in her bag. For I tell you that she is a witch who has been seen staring at the moon and talking with spirits in the air, and that you would have done well to leave this darling of yours to die upon the beach, if die she can."

" Some wives might have held that these are hard words to use of one who had just saved their man from

death," said Wi. " Yet if you think so ill of her, kill
her, Aaka, for she is helpless."

" And bring her curse upon my head ? Nay, Wi, she
is safe from me."

Then, able to bear no more, Wi turned and left the
cave.

Outside on the Gathering-ground he found much
tumult, for here the bodies of the dead had been carried
and everybody was come together. Women and children
who had lost their husbands or fathers wailed, making
a great noise after the fashion of the tribe ; men who had
been wounded but could still walk, moved about, showing
their hurts and seeking praise or comfort, while others
who had come through unscathed boasted loudly of
their deeds in the great fight with the Red-beards, the
devils who came out of the sea.

Here and there were groups, and in the centre of each
group a speaker. In one of them Whaka, the Bird of
Ill-omen, was telling his hearers that these Red ones
whom they had fought and conquered, were but the
forerunners of a great host which would descend upon
them presently. At a little distance Hou the Unstable,
while rejoicing in the victory of the tribe, declared that
such good fortune could not be trusted ; therefore
the best thing to do would be that they should all run
away into the woods before it turned against them.
Meanwhile Wini-wini the Shudderer went from corpse
to corpse, followed by the mourners, blowing his horn
over each and pointing out its wounds, whereon all the
mourners wailed aloud in chorus.

The most of the people, however, were collected round
Urk the Aged who, his white beard wagging upon his
chin, mumbled to them through his toothless jaws that
now he remembered what he had long forgotten, namely,
that his great-grandfather had told his, that is Urk's,
grandfather, that his—Urk's—great-grandfather's great-
grandfather had heard from his remote ancestors that
once just such Red-beards had descended on the tribe
after the appearance among them of a Witch-of-the-Sea,

very much like to the lady Laleela who was beloved of
Wi their Chief, as was known of all, for had not he, Wi,
been seen kissing her ?

" And what happened then ? " asked a voice.

" I cannot quite remember," answered Urk, " but I
think that the witch was sacrificed to the Ice-Gods,
after which no more Red-men came."

" Do you mean that Laleela the White Witch should
also be sacrificed to the Ice-Gods ? " asked the voice.

Confronted with this problem, Urk wagged his long
beard, then answered that he was not sure, but he thought
that on the whole it might be wise to sacrifice her if the
consent of Wi could be obtained.

" For what reason ? " asked the voice again, " seeing
that she warned us of the coming of the Red-men, and
afterwards took into her own breast the little spear that
was aimed at Wi."

" Because," answered Urk, "after a great event,
such as had happened, the gods always sought a sacrifice,
and as none of the Red-beards had been taken alive it
would be better to offer up to them the Witch-from-the-
Sea, who was a stranger, rather than any one of their
own people."

Now Moananga, who was among those that heard this
speech, limped up to Urk, for the wound in his side made
him walk stiffly, and seizing his beard with one hand,
slapped him in the face with the other.

" Hearken, old Vile-one who call yourself a wizard,"
he said. " If any should be sacrificed I think that it is
you, because you are a liar who feed the people upon
false tales of what has never been. Well you know
that this Laleela whom you urge us to kill, is the noblest
of women and that had it not been for her, Wi, my brother
and our chief, would now be dead ; indeed that we should
all be dead, since she warned us of the coming of the Red
wanderers. She it was, too, who after the little spear
had found her breast—the spear she bade Pag drag out
with her flesh upon it, saying no word, as I who was
present know—gave us counsel that told us how to master

the Red-Beards by attacking them and throwing stones into their boats, which afterwards we did, thus killing the most of them. Yet now you would egg on the people to sacrifice her to the Ice-Gods, dog that you are."

Then Moananga once more smote Urk upon the face, tumbling him over on to the sand, and limped away, while all who heard shouted applause of his words, as just before they had done of those of Urk, for such is the fashion of crowds.

Just then Wi appeared, whereon Urk rose from the sand and began to praise him, saying that there had been no such Chief of the Tribe since the days of his great-grandfather's great-grandfather. Then all the people ran together and took up that song of praise; yes, even those of the wounded who could walk, for in their hearts they knew, every one of them, that it was Wi who had saved them from death and their women from even a worse fate. Yes, however much they might grumble and find fault, they knew that it was Wi who had saved them, as they knew also that it was Laleela, the Witch-from-the-Sea, who had saved Wi by springing in front of him and receiving the little spear into her own breast, and who, after she was stricken, yet had given good counsel to him, to Pag and to Moananga.

Wi heard all their praises, but answered nothing to them. Nay, he pushed aside those who crowded round him and the women who strove to kiss his hand, forcing a way through them to where the dead lay, upon whom he looked long and earnestly. Then, having given orders for their burial, he went on to visit those who had deep wounds, still saying nothing. For the heart of Wi was heavy in him and the words of Aaka had pierced him like a spear. Remembering his oath he knew not what he should do, and even now, in the hour of his victory. he wondered what fate had in store for him and for Laleela who had saved his life, which he wished that she had not done.

So from that time forward day by day Wi went about his tasks very silently, saying little to any one because

his heart was sore and he feared lest, should he open his
lips, its bitterness would escape from them. Therefore
he kept apart from others and walked much alone, or
accompanied by Foh only, for this son of his seemed all
that was left to him. Also he went out hunting as he
used to do before he killed Henga and became the Chief,
letting it be known that sitting so much in the cave took
away his health and spirits, also that meat being needed
he held it his duty as the best huntsman of the tribe
to kill deer if he could, though this was not often, since
because of the bad season the most of the deer seemed
to have left the woods.

One day Wi followed a doe far into the forest, and
having lost her there, turned homewards. His road led
him past a little pocket in the hillside where the fir-trees
grew thickly. This cleft or pocket was not more than
thirty paces deep by about as many wide. All round
it were steep walls of rock and its mouth was narrow,
perhaps three paces across, no more. Outside of it was
a patch of rain-washed rock of the size of a large hut, which
rock ended in a little cliff about four spear-lengths high.
Below this cliff lay a patch of marsh, such as were common
in the forest, a kind of hole filled with sticky red slime, in
the centre of which a spring bubbled up that could be
seen beneath the growth of marsh briars that grew on the
red mud, which mud spread out for many paces every
way and at its edge was ringed round with fir-trees.

As Wi drew near to this pocket he heard a snorting
sound that caused him to stand still and take shelter
behind the bole of a big tree, for he did not know what
beast made that noise.

Whilst he stood thus, out of the narrow entrance of
the cleft there stalked a huge aurochs bull, so great a
beast that a tall man standing by its side could not have
seen over its shoulder. It stood still upon the patch of
rock, looking about it and sniffing the air, which caused
Wi to fear that it had smelt him and to crouch close behind
the tree.

But this was not so, for the wind blew from the bull

to him. Now Wi stared at the aurochs as he had never stared at anything, except at Laleela when first he saw her in her hollow log. For although such beasts were told of among the tribe, they were very rare, being quite different from the wild cattle, and he had never seen but one of them before, a half-grown cow. It was a mighty creature with thick curved horns and its body was covered with black hair, while down its spine ran a long grey streak of other lighter-coloured hair. Its eyes were fierce and prominent, its legs were short, so that its dewlap hung nearly to the ground, and it had big, cleft hoofs.

A great desire took hold of Wi to attack that beast, but he restrained himself because he knew that he could not prevail against it, for certainly it would toss and trample him to death. Whilst he watched it the bull turned and went away from him down the ledge of rock and presently he heard it crashing a path through the forest, doubtless to seek its feeding-ground.

When it had gone Wi crept to the mouth of the cleft and looked in, searching the place with his eyes. Then as he could neither see nor hear anything, with a beating heart he entered the cleft, keeping close to the left-hand wall of rock, and worked his way round it, slipping from tree to tree. It was empty, but at its end grew some large firs, and beneath them bracken, and here from many signs Wi learned that the aurochs bull had its lair. Thus the trunks of the trees were polished by its hide as it rubbed itself against them, which showed him that this was its home; also the ground was trodden hard with its feet, and in certain places where it was soft, torn by its horns which it thrust deep into the sandy soil to clean and sharpen them.

Wi came out of the cleft and stood still, thinking. He turned and looked over the edge of the little cliff at the morass beneath. Then he climbed down the cliff, and, by help of a fallen tree, some few feet out upon the morass, where he tested the depth of the mud with his spear.

It was deep, for he must drive in the spear to its full

length and the arm that held it to the elbow before he touched the rock or hard ground that formed its bottom. Scrambling along the fallen tree he did this thrice, and always found the bottom at the same depth. Then he climbed the cliff again, and standing before the mouth of the cleft, Wi, the brave and cunning hunter, thought to himself thus :

That mighty bull rests in the daytime in yonder hole. But when evening draws on it comes out to feed. Now if when it came out, or when it returned in the morning, it found a man standing in front of it, and that man threw a spear into its face, what would it do ? Certainly it would charge him. And if the man leapt aside, what would happen ? It would fall over the cliff and be bogged, and there the man might go down and fight it.

Thus thought Wi, his nostrils spreading themselves out and his eyes flashing as he pictured the great fight which might be between a hunter and this bull of bulls wallowing together there in the slime. Then he thought again,

The odds are great. The bull might catch the man with a sweep of its horns and be too cunning to rush over the cliff, which it knows well. Or being so mighty, when they were struggling in the mud it might break out and come on to him, and there would be an end. Yes, there would be death.

A third time Wi thought,

Am I so happy that I should fear to face death ? Have I not wondered many a time of late whether it would not be well to stumble among the rough roots of the trees and to fall by chance upon the point of my spear ? And were it not for Foh, should I not have stumbled thus—by chance—and been found pierced with the spear ? For when the spear had done its work might there not be peace for one who has tried and failed and knows not which road to take ? What better end could there be for a hunter than to die covered with glory fighting this mighty beast of the forest, which no man of his people has ever yet dared to do ? Would not

the tribe make songs about me which they would tell
on winter nights by the fire in the days to come ; yes,
they and their children after them for more generations
than Urk can remember ? And would not Aaka, the wife
of my youth, then learn to think of me tenderly ?

Thus said Wi to himself and hastened homewards
through the twilight. Indeed, as the way was far and
the path difficult, the darkness had fallen ere ever he came
to the cave.

Entering silently from the shadows he saw Aaka
standing by the fire, and noted that her face was troubled,
for she was staring into the darkness at the mouth of the
cave. By the fire also sat Pag polishing a spear-head,
and near to him Foh, who was whispering into his ear.
At a distance by the other fire Laleela, now recovered
from her wound but still somewhat pale, went about
among the cast-out babes, seeing that their skin rugs
were wrapped round them so that they might not grow
cold in the night. With her was Moananga. He whispered into her ear and she smiled and seemed to answer
aimlessly, for her eyes too were fixed upon the darkness
at the mouth of the cave.

Wi came forward into the firelight. Aaka saw him
and instantly her face changed, for on it seemed to fall
its usual mask of haughtiness.

" You are late, Husband," she said, " which, as you
were alone "—here she glanced first at Laleela and
next at Pag, the two of whom she was so jealous—" is
strange and caused me to fear, who thought that perhaps
you might have met more Red wanderers."

" No, Wife," he answered simply. " I think that we
shall see no more wanderers on this shore. I wounded a
doe with my spear, which stuck in its side, and followed it
far, but it escaped me, who have no fortune nowadays,
even at the only craft I understand," he added with a
sigh. " Now I am tired and hungry."

" Did the deer carry away the spear, Father ? "
asked Foh.

" Yes, Son," he replied absently.

"Then how comes it that it is in your hand, Father?
For when you sent me back this morning you had only
one spear."

"If fell from the doe's side and I found it again
amongst the rocks, Son."

"Then if it fell among rocks, why is the shaft covered
with mud, Father?" asked Foh, but Wi made no answer.

Only Pag, who had been watching him with his one
bright eye, rose and taking the spear, began to clean it,
noting as he did so that there was no dry blood upon its
point.

Before she went away to her hut, where the fancy
had taken her to sleep again for a while, because she
said that the crying of the cast-out children disturbed
her, Aaka brought Wi his food. This she did because
she feared that otherwise Laleela might take her place and
serve him with his meat.

On the following day Wi stopped at home and did
those things that lay to the hand of the Chief. There
was much trouble in the tribe. The time of autumn
had come and the weather remained cold and cheerless,
as it had done during that of summer. Food was scanty
and by the order of Wi, the most of what could be won
was being saved up against the coming winter. Even here
there was trouble, because many of such fish as could be
caught, being laid out on the banks in the usual way
for curing, went bad owing to the lack of sun to dry
them, so that much labour was wasted. Moreover those
women whose husbands or sons had been killed in the
fight with the Red-beards, forgetting the perils from which
they and all the tribe had been saved, began to grumble
much, as did those whose men had been wounded and
were not recovered of their hurts. This was their cry—

That Laleela, the fair, white Witch-from-the-Sea,
she who was the love of Wi, had brought all these ills
upon them, she who had led the Red-men to their shores,
and that therefore she ought to be killed or driven away.
Yet none of them dared to lift a finger against her, first
because, as they supposed, she was the lover of Wi whom

every one of them feared and honoured ; and secondly because all did not think as they did. Thus many of the men clung to Laleela, some for the reason that she was sweet and beautiful, others because they knew that she had saved Wi from death, offering up her own life for his.

Also there were women who sided with her. For instance, the mothers of the cast-out children whom she nursed night and day ; for although they had cast them out, the most of those mothers still loved their children and came to nurture them, in their hearts blessing Wi who had saved them from death, and her who tended them in their helplessness. Moreover, although this was strange, however much she may have plotted against her and desired her death in the past, and however much in a fashion she hated her through jealousy, in secret Laleela's greatest friend and protector was Aaka.

For, although she would never say so, Aaka knew that had it not been for this woman whom she called " Witch-from-the-Sea," there would have been no Wi left living. Also she honoured Laleela, knowing too that if she, who was so sweet and beautiful, chose to stretch out her hand and to look on him with the eyes of love, she could cause Wi to forget his oath and to take her to himself, which she did not do. Therefore, although she spoke rough words of her openly and turned her back upon her, and mocked at Wi about her, still in secret she was Laleela's friend.

Further, Laleela had another friend in Moananga, who, after Wi, was the most beloved and honoured of any in the tribe, especially since he had borne himself so bravely against the Red-men. For from the moment that Moananga had seen Laleela leap in front of Wi to receive the arrow in her breast, he had fallen in love with her, although it was not in front of him that she had leapt. This folly of his made trouble in his house, because although his wife, Tana, like Aaka, was jealous-natured, if in a gentler fashion, still he loved Laleela, and what was more, said so openly.

Indeed he tried to win her, announcing that he was bound by no laws which Wi had made. But in this matter he failed, for although Laleela answered him very sweetly, she would have none of him, about which, when she came to learn of it, Tana mocked him much. Yet so kindly did Laleela push him away from her, that he remained the dearest and closest of her friends, mayhap because he knew that it was Wi who stood between them, Wi his brother whom he loved more than he did any woman. Still, he found Tana's mockery hard to bear, though the more she mocked the closer he clung to Laleela, as did Tana, because she held that Laleela had taught Moananga a lesson that he needed.

Taking heed of none of these things which meant naught to them, the common people of the tribe grumbled and moaned in their distress, and because they could find no other at whose door to lay these troubles, they bound them on to the back of Laleela, saying that she had brought them with her out of the sea and that their proper place was on her shoulders. For being but simple folk they did not understand that, like the rain or the snow, evil falls upon the heads of men from heaven above.

CHAPTER XVI

THE AUROCHS AND THE STAR

On the second morning Wi, who had made all things
ready to his hand, rose while it was still dark, kissed Foh
who lay fast asleep at his side, and slipped from the
cave, taking with him three spears and the bone-hafted
axe of iron that Pag had made and fashioned, the same
with which he had slain Henga. As he went, by the
flickering light of the fire he saw Laleela sleeping among
the babes, looking most beautiful with her long bright
hair lying in masses about her. Sweet was her face as
she lay thus asleep, and yet, as he thought, sad and
troubled. He stood still looking at her, then sighed
and went on, thinking that she had not seen him, for
Wi did not know that after he had passed Laleela sat
up and watched him till he was lost in the shadows.

Outside the cave, tied to a stake beneath a rough shelter
of stones, was his dog, Yow, a fierce, wolf-like beast that
loved him only, which often he took with him when he
went a-hunting, for it was trained to drive game towards
him. Loosing Yow, who whimpered with joy at the
smell of him, he struck it on the head with his hand, thus
telling the beast that it must be silent. Then he started,
pausing a little while by the hut in which Aaka slept ;
indeed almost he entered it, but in the end did not because
he knew that she would question him closely. For the
night was too far gone for him to come to sleep with her
in the hut as he did sometimes, while it was too early
for him to be stirring when all were still asleep, so
guessing that he planned some adventure, she would
try to wring out of him what it might be.

Wi thought to himself that if only Aaka was as she

had been in past years he would not now be starting to
fight the aurochs single-handed ; and so thinking, for the
second time that morning he sighed.   Yet he was not
angry with her, for well he knew what had caused this
change.   It was the death of her child, Foa, murdered
by the brute-man Henga, that had turned her heart sour
and made of her another woman.   For he knew also that
secretly she blamed him and laid Foa's death upon his
shoulders, as Pag had laid it upon her own.

Always Aaka, for a long time before he did so, desired
that he should challenge Henga, and this not only because
she wished that he should become Chief of the Tribe.   Nay,
there was a deeper reason.   Something within her warned
her that if Henga continued to live he would bring
calamity upon her and her House.   Therefore, knowing
Wi's strength and skill and being sure in herself that
however mighty Henga might be, he could conquer him,
again and again she had urged Wi to give him battle,
though she hid from him the true reason for her urging.
This he would not do, not because he was afraid, but
because he shrank from thrusting himself forward and
causing all to talk of him, being a man of very modest
mind ;   also because he feared lest Henga should overcome him, being so terrible a giant, in which case not
only would he be killed, a matter of no great moment, but
Aaka and his children would be at the mercy of the
tyrant, and unless they slew themselves must bear his
vengeance.

Therefore, not until Foa had been butchered through
Aaka's own fault and jealousy of Pag, whom she hated
because Wi loved him so much, would he consent to
stir in this business that he might avenge his child's
blood upon Henga, if so he could.   Even then he would
not act until she had sent him to take counsel with the
Ice-Gods and watch for the omen of the falling stone,
which stone she knew well would fall, for secretly she had
climbed to the crest of the glacier on the day before he
went and thrust sundry of the loose stones to its very
edge, whence she knew that one or other of them must slip

on the following morning when the rays of the risen sun struck upon the ice.

Or if perchance none fell, then she would make some other plan to bring about that which she desired, for always, be it remembered, she was sure in herself that Wi, whom she looked upon as greater and stronger than any who lived, as half a god indeed, would deal out death to Henga if once he could be brought to face him; and now that Foa had been murdered she had but one aim in life—to see Henga dead ere he killed Wi and Foh also.

Much of all this Wi knew, and more he guessed, though some things were hid from him, such as the placing of the stones upon the lip of the glacier. Oh, all had gone awry between Aaka and himself, and now Laleela had come clothed in beauty, wisdom and sweetness, to tie the threads of their lives to a knot that he knew not how to loosen. Surely he would be better dead, leaving Moananga to become chief after him. At least so he held. If the gods had decreed otherwise, then let them give him the strength to conquer the bull of bulls.

Thus did he take these matters out of the rackings of his troubled mind and lay them in the hands of Fate, that Fate might decide them as it would. If he killed the aurochs, or could not find it again, then he would know it was a sign from the gods who decreed that he must live on; if otherwise, then his troubles would be over. So he departed from the hut, thinking that Aaka would never learn how he had stood there in the darkness filled with such musings and memories, and presently was on the seashore and clear of the village.

Here he stayed awhile until the sky turned grey and there was light sufficient to enable him to thread his way through the forest.

This he did slowly at first, but afterwards more quickly, following a different road to that which he had taken after he had first seen the aurochs, one which ran along the edge of the beach, where in places blown sand still lay among the fir-trees. This he did because he feared the bull might have scented him after he left its lair two days before, and be watching and waiting on his track. At length he struck up hill, for although he had never walked that path, the hunter's sense within him told him where to turn, and striking the foot of the little marsh, skirted round it till he came near the bottom of the low cliff, along the top of which ran the rocky path that bordered the den of the aurochs. Here he rested awhile, hiding himself in the brambly undergrowth, because he did not know at what hour the bull returned to its lair after its nightly feed, and feared lest he might meet it on the rocky path.

He had sat still thus for perhaps the half of an hour or more, idly watching certain birds that had gathered together on the branches of a dead fir near-by, preparing to flight south long before their accustomed time. Presently, after much twittering, the birds rose in a cloud and flew away to warmer climes, though as Wi knew nothing of any other country, he wondered why they went, and whither. Next a rabbit ran past him, screaming as it ran and, as though bewildered, took shelter behind a stone, where it crouched. Presently he saw why it screamed, for after it, running on its scent—swift, thin, terrible, silent—came a weasel. The weasel also vanished behind the stone where the rabbit had crouched. There was a sound of scuffling and of more shrill screams, then the weasel and the rabbit rolled out together from behind the stone, the weasel with its sharp teeth fixed in the rabbit's neck.

Behold Death hunting all things! thought Wi. Behold the gods hunting man, who flees and screams, filled with terror of he knows not what, till they have him by the throat!

Suddenly the dog, Yow, that had taken no heed of the rabbit, being too well trained, half rose from where he crouched hidden in the thick bushes at his master's side, lifted his fierce head, sniffed the wind which blew towards them from the direction of the aurochs' den and, looking upward, uttered a growl so low that it could scarce be heard.

Wi also looked upward and saw what it was at which Yow growled.

For there, but a few paces above him with the morning light glancing from its wide, polished horns, came the huge aurochs, returning, full-fed, to its lair. Wi shivered when he saw it, for viewed thus from beneath with its shadow magnified by the low light, showing enormous on the rocky wall beyond, the beast was terrifying as it marched past him majestically, shaking its great head and lashing its flanks with its bushy tail ; so terrifying indeed that Wi bethought him that it would be wise to fly while there was yet time.

Oh, could any man prevail against such a brute as this ? Wi wondered, and turned to go.

Then he remembered all the purpose that had brought him thither ; also how great would be his future glory if he could kill that bull, and how noble his end if the bull killed him. So he sat down again and waited awhile, another half-hour perhaps, to give the aurochs time to settle itself in its lair and forget its vigilance, so that if it were disturbed it might come out bewildered by sleep. Also Wi waited till the sun which, as it chanced, shone that morning, should reach a certain height, when he hoped that its rays striking full in the beast's eyes, would confuse it as it issued forth.

At length the moment was at hand when he must either dare the deed, or leave it undared and return home ashamed, making pretence that he had gone forth to hunt deer which he had not found, and perhaps to be laughed at for his lack of skill by Pag, whom of late he had forbidden to follow him because he wished to be alone ; or to be asked by Aaka for the venison which she knew he had not brought.

Remembering these things, Wi rose up, stretched his arms, straightened himself, and climbed the little cliff to give battle to the aurochs.

Stripping himself of his skin robe he laid it on one side, hanging it to the bough of a tree, so that now he was clothed only in an under-garment of fawn's hide which came down

to above his knees. Then, having thrust his left wrist
through the loop of his axe, he took one of the short heavy
spears in his right hand, holding the other two in his
left. Next he peered into the cleft, but could see nothing
of his game, which doubtless was lying down under the
trees at the further end. The hound, Yow, smelt it there
indeed, for it began to slaver at the mouth and its hair
stood up on its back. Wi patted it upon the head and
made a motion with his arm. Yow understood and
leapt into the cleft like a stone from a sling. Before Wi
could count ten there arose a sound of wrathful bellowing
and of crashing boughs, telling him that the bull was
up and charging at Yow.

Nearer came the bellowing and the crashings, and now
he saw the great brute. Yow was leaping to and fro in front
of it, silently, after its fashion, keeping out of the reach
of its horns, while the aurochs charged again and again,
tearing up the ground and stamping with its feet, but
never touching Yow, that thus led it forward as it had
been trained to do. At length when it was quite close
to the mouth of the cleft, Yow sprang, and seizing it by
the nose, hung there.

Out they came, the pair of them, the aurochs tossing
its head and trying to shake off Yow that would not leave
go, rearing up also as it swung the dog from side to side
and striking at it with its fore feet, but without avail. Now
it was alongside of Wi, who stood waiting with raised
spear, like to a man of stone. It dropped its head, hoping
to rub Yow on the ground and free itself.

Wi saw his chance ! Quick as a stooping hawk he sprang
at it and drove the flint spear through the bull's right eye,
then thrust upon it with all his strength. The spear-
head vanished in the bony socket of the eye ; with a
roar of rage and pain the aurochs tossed up its head so
mightily that the spear shaft broke close to the pierced eye,
and Yow was hurled far away, torn from its hold upon
the nose, though never had the brave hound unlocked
its jaws. The bull smelt the man and charged at him
along the narrow path, Wi flattening himself against the

rock. It could not see him with its blinded eye and rushed past him, though the long horn touched his chest. It wheeled round. Wi saw and scrambled up the face of the rock to twice the height of a man, where he stood upon a little ledge, steadying himself with his left elbow against the root of a fir.

Now the aurochs caught sight of him, and rearing itself up on its hind legs strove to reach him with its horns. Wi took a second spear in his right hand, letting fall the third, and with his left that was now free, gripped the root of the fir. The great mouth of the aurochs appeared over the edge of the ledge, but because of this ledge it could not touch him with its horns. It opened its mouth, roaring in its mad rage. Wi, bending forward, thrust the second spear down that cavern of a mouth and deep into the throat beyond. It was wrenched from his grip. Blood running from its muzzle, the aurochs drove furiously at the ledge on which Wi stood. Its horn caught underneath the ledge, and so great was its strength, that it broke a length of the soft rock away from the cliff face, that length on which Wi stood, leaving him hanging to the root.

Now Wi became aware that Yow had re-appeared, for he heard its low growls. Then the growling ceased and he knew that it must have fixed its fangs into the hind parts of the bull. Down went the aurochs, seeking to kill the hound, leaping along the path and kicking, and down went Wi also, for his root broke. He landed on his feet, turned and saw the bull a few paces to the left, almost doubled into a ball in its efforts to be rid of Yow that clung to its flank or belly. Wi picked up his last spear which lay upon the path. The bull came round, and as it came, saw him with its unharmed eye. It charged, dragging Yow with it ; Wi hurled his last spear, which struck it in the neck and there remained fixed. Again Wi leapt aside, but this time to the right because he must, for the bull rushed along close to the bank from which he had fallen. The brute saw, and wheeling, came at him. Wi caught it by the horns with both hands

and hung there, being swung to and fro in the air over
the swamp beneath. The rotten ground gave and
down went Wi, the aurochs, and Yow into the mud
below !

. . . A little while after Wi had left the cave Pag
was wakened by someone who shook him by the shoulder.
He looked up and in the low light of the fire saw that it
was Laleela, her blue eyes wide open, her face distraught
as though with fear.

" Awake, Pag," she said. " I have dreamed a very
evil dream. I dreamed that I saw Wi fighting for his life,
though with what he fought I do not know. Listen !
Before it was day I woke up suddenly and by the light of
the fire I saw Wi leave the cave carrying spears, and
presently heard Yow whimper as he loosed it from its
kennel. Then I went to sleep again and dreamed the
evil dream."

Pag sprang up, seizing his spear and his axe.

" Come with me," he said, and shambled from the
cave to the place where Yow was tied up at night.

" The dog is gone," he said. " Doubtless Wi has taken
it with him to hunt in the woods. Let us search for him,
for perhaps you who are wise dream truly."

They sped away, heading for the woods. As they
passed Moananga's hut he came out of it just awakened,
to look at the promise of the dawn.

" Bring axe and spear and follow," called Pag
" Swift, swift ! Stay not to talk."

Moananga rushed into his hut, seized his weapons,
and raced after them. As the three of them went Pag told
the story.

" A fool's dream," said Moananga. " With what
would Wi be fighting ? The tiger and the wolves are dead
and wild cattle have left the woods."

" Have you never heard of the great bull of the forest
before which no man dare stand ? It is about, as I know,
for I have seen its signs and where it lies, and although
I hid it from him, perhaps Wi knew it also," answered Pag

in a low voice to save his breath. Then in the gathering
light he pointed to the ground, saying,

" Wi's footmark and the track of Yow walking at
his side, not an hour old," and putting down his big head
he fixed his one eye upon the ground and followed the
trail, while after him came the others.

Swiftly they ran, for the light was good and the trail
across the sand clear to Pag the wolf-man, who, it was said,
could run by scent alone. Following the footprints at
length they came to the foot of the marsh that lay beneath
the little cliff. Still running on the track, they turned
to skirt it as Wi had done. Suddenly Laleela uttered a cry
and pointed with her hand.

Lo ! there in the mud of the swamp, wallowing feebly,
was the terrible bull ; there athwart its neck sat Wi,
holding to its horn with one hand, and with the other still
smiting weakly at its head with his axe, while crushed
beneath appeared the hind-quarters of the dead dog.

As they looked the aurochs made a last effort. It reared
itself up, tearing its shoulder from the sticky mud ; it turned
over, bearing Wi with it. Wi vanished beneath the mud ; the
bull moaned and lay still ; its flesh quivered, its eyes shut.

Pag and Moananga rushed round the marsh till they
came to the foot of the cliff near to which Wi and the bull
were bogged. They leapt on to the body of the aurochs.
Pag, whose strength was great, dragged the huge head
aside. Beneath it lay Wi !

Laleela came. She and Moananga, standing up to
their middles in the mud where they found a footing,
tugged at him ; mightily they strove till at last he
was free. They dragged him to the edge of the swamp,
they laid him on his face and waited. Lo, he moved.
Lo, he coughed ; red mud was pouring from his mouth.
They had come in time—Wi lived !

The tribe was in a tumult. These three, Laleela, Pag
and Moananga, had brought Wi back to the village,
half-supporting, half-carrying him. Then the tribe
learning what had happened, had rushed out to the

swamp beneath the little cliff, and thence by main force had dragged the aurochs and the dog Yow, which in death still clung to it with locked jaws.

They washed the mud off the beast with water and saw the spears of Wi, one fixed deep in its eye-socket and one in its throat at the root of the tongue. They noted how Wi had hacked at the beast's head with his axe, striving to sever its neck-bone, which he could not do because of the thickness of the mane and hide, but at length battering it till it died. They marvelled at its mighty horns, one of which it had splintered when it tore the ridge of rock upon which Wi stood. They measured its bulk with wands and reported it to Urk the Ancient, who was too old to go so far but said that in the days of his grandfather's grandfather a still bigger bull had been killed by his great-uncle's great-uncle, who threw over it a net of withies and pounded it to death with rocks while it struggled to be free. Someone asked him how he knew this, whereon he answered that his great-great-grandmother, when she was a hundred winters old, had told it to his grandmother, who had told it to him when he was a little lad.

So the bull was skinned, the meat on it was divided up and the hide brought home to be a mat for the cave. Also the head was brought, carried upon poles by four men and tied to that tree upon which had been hung the head of Henga until Pag used it as a bait for the great-toothed tiger. Yes, it was brought with one of Wi's spears fixed in the eye-socket, and another, whereof the shaft was champed to pieces, fast in its throat. There it hung and the people came up and stared at it. Wi also, when he had vomited out all the red mud and rested himself, sat in the mouth of the cave and stared at the great head hanging on the tree, wondering how he had found strength to fight that beast while it lived.

There Aaka spoke with him.

"You are a mighty man, Husband," she said, "so mighty that long ago you might have made an end of

Henga if it had pleased you, and thus saved our daughter
from death. I am proud to have borne the children of
such a man. And yet, tell me, how came it that Pag and
Moananga were there to drag you from the mud when the
bull rolled over on to you ? "

"I don't know, Wife," Wi answered, "but I hear that
Laleela had something to do with the business. She
dreamed something, I know not what, which she told to
Pag and Moananga, and they ran out to seek me. Ask
her whom I have not seen since I woke up."

"I have sought her, Husband, but she cannot be
found. Yet I do not doubt that being a witch her
witchcraft was at work here, as always."

"If so, in this case you should not grumble, Wife."

"I do not grumble ; I thank her who has preserved
alive the greatest man that is told of among the people.
I say more. I think that you should marry her, Wi, for
she has earned no less. Only first you must find her."

"As to this matter of marriage, I made a new
law," answered Wi. "Shall the maker of laws be also
the breaker of laws ? "

"Why not ? " said Aaka, laughing, "seeing that he
who makes can also break. Moreover, who will find
fault with the man that single-handed could slay this
bull of bulls ? Not I for one, Wi."

"Two of us slew it," answered Wi, looking down.
"The hound Yow and I slew it together. Without Yow
I should have been slain."

"Aye, and therefore glory be to Yow. If I were a
law-maker like you, Wi, I should choose Yow to be a
god among us."

Then she smiled in her dark fashion and went away to
talk with Pag and Moananga, for Aaka desired to learn
the truth of all this matter.

Wi sat in the mouth of the cave, eating his food and
telling the tale of the fight to Foh, his son,who listened with
open mouth and staring eyes. Then he sent Foh to help to
peg out the skin of the bull, and when he was gone slipped
from the cave to seek for Laleela who could not be found.

Not knowing where to look, he walked, very stiffly
at first, along the shore by the mouth of the great glacier
and round the headland beyond, past the hills and smaller
glaciers towards the Seal Bay. There, if anywhere, he
thought that he might find Laleela, since thither, after
the fight with the Red wanderers, her boat had been
brought back and hidden in the little cave at the head of
the bay. Late in the afternoon he reached the place
and there, seated at the mouth of the small cave, he
found Laleela as though she were waiting for the sun to
set or for the moon to rise. She started, looking down
but saying nothing.

" Why are you here ? " he asked sternly.

" I came to be alone to give thanks to the moon that I
worship, because of a certain dream which was sent to
me, and to make my prayer to the moon when she appears."

" Is it so, Laleela ? Are you sure that you did not
come for another purpose also ? " and he looked towards
the cave where her boat was housed.

" I am not sure, Wi. All hangs upon the answer that
is sent to my prayer."

" Hearken, Laleela," he said in a voice that was thick
with rage. " Unless you swear to me that you will
not try to depart for the second time, I will drive
my axe through the bottom of that boat of yours,
or burn it with fire."

" To what end, Wi ? Cannot the seekers of Death
travel to him by many roads ? If one be blocked a hundred
others still remain."

" Why should you seek death ? " he asked passionately.
" Are you then so unhappy here ? Do you hate me so
much that you wish to die ? "

Now Laleela bent her head and shook her long hair
about her as though to hide her face, and spoke to him
through its meshes, saying very softly,

" You know that I do not hate you, Wi, but rather
that I hold you too dear. Yet, hear me. Among my
own folk I am named a prophetess, one believed to have
gifts that are not given to all, and in truth sometimes I

think that I have such gifts. Thus when I left my own
land, I was sure that I must do so that I might find one
who would be more to me than all others ; and did I not
find him ? Yet now that gift is upon me again, and it
tells me that I should do well to go away, because if I
bide here I shall bring evil upon the head of one who is
more to me than all others.''

"Then stay, Laleela, and together let us face this
evil that your heart foretells.''

"Wi, we may face nothing quite together. Have you
not sworn an oath, and would you break that oath ?
I think not. Yet if you should be weak, must I therefore
cease from being strong ? Nay, draw not near to me, lest
madness take you, for here and now *I* swear that oath for
you afresh. Never will I live to see you mocked of Aaka
and of your people, as a man who has broken his oath
for a woman's sake. Nay, rather would I die twice over.''

"Then it is finished,'' said Wi with a groan.

Laleela lifted her head and looked upward. In the
sky appeared the evening star, and on this star she
fixed her eyes, then answered,

"By what right do you say that it is finished between
us, or indeed that anything is ever finished ? Listen, Wi.
Among my folk are wise men and women who hold
that death is not the end of all—indeed that it is but the
beginning—and that yonder, beyond that star, the life we
lay down here will spring fresh, and that in this new life
all which we have lost will be found again. I am of that
company, I who am called a prophetess—and so I believe,
who hold therefore that this world is of small account,
and that if once we find thereon that which we were sent
forth to seek, for us it has served its purpose and may
be well forgot.''

Wi stared at her, then asked,

"Do you mean that somewhere beyond death there is
a home where we shall find those whom we have lost,
where I shall find Foa my child and the mother who
suckled me, and—and others, and there be in joy and
peace with them ? ''

" Yes," answered Laleela, looking him in the face, and her eyes were bold and happy.

" At times," said Wi, " aye, not often, but now and again, such hope has come to me, only to fade away. If I could but be sure that I who am but what you see, a beast that thinks and talks . . . Oh, tell me of this faith, Laleela ! "

So, speaking low and earnestly, she set it out to him, a simple faith indeed, such as has been held by chosen ones throughout the earth in all the generations, yet a pure and a comfortable, while he drank in her words and his heart burned with a new fire.

" Now I understand why you were sent to me, Laleela," he said at length. " Tell me no more to-night. I must think, I must think."

She smiled at him very happily, and as they rose to go, said this,

" Wi, there was more in that dream that came to me this morning than I told to Pag or any. That dream said to me that you went out secretly in the darkness, almost hoping that you would not return in the light."

" Perhaps," he answered briefly, " for I was unhappy."

" Who now are happy again, Wi. See, I have promised you that no more will I flee from you back into the mists whence I came, but through good and ill will stand at your side till the end, which is the beginning, though not hand in hand. Do you promise me as much, Wi ? "

" I do, Laleela."

" Then all is well, Wi, and we can laugh at troubles."

" Yes, Laleela. But there is one thing. You know that I love Foh, my only child, and always I am afraid for Foh. I am afraid lest the brother should follow the sister, Laleela."

" Cease to be afraid, Wi. I think that one day Foh will be a great chief over a great tribe."

" How do you know that ? " he asked eagerly.

" Have I not told you that I am named a prophetess, or a Witch-from-the-Sea, as your people call me ? " she answered and smiled at him again.

CHAPTER XVII

WI DEFIES THE GODS

THIS great talk of theirs, the "light-bringing" talk, as
Wi named it, was the first of many such between him and
Laleela. From the cup of her wisdom he drank deeply
until his heart was as full of it as is a hiving bee with honey.
Soon what she believed he believed, so that their souls
were one. Yet never did he break the oath that he had
sworn to the people, and never did she tempt him so to
do by look or touch or word.

Wi changed. He who had been gloomy and full of
care, always looking over his shoulder to see the evil
behind him, became happy-faced and full of cheerful,
pleasant words. Aaka stared at him amazed, who no
longer even fretted or troubled her about the health and
safety of their son Foh, but said outright that he had
no fear for him any more; that he knew all would be
well with him. At first Aaka was sure that while keeping
his oath to the outward eye, in secret he had taken Laleela
to wife, but when she found that certainly this was not
so, she felt bewildered. At length she could bear no more,
and questioned Wi in such fashion that he must answer.

"All things go ill," she said; "there is little food, and
the cold, even now at the beginning of winter, is such as
has not been known. Yet you, Wi, are as happy as a
boy who fishes on a rock in the sunshine and catches
fishes many and great How does this come about,
Wi?"

"Would you know, Wife? Then I will tell you. I
have discovered a great truth, namely, that we live on
after death, and that not for nothing did I bury her toys

with Foa, for when all is finished I shall find her playing with them elsewhere."

"Are you mad?" asked Aaka. "Do the Ice-Gods promise us any such thing? Do Urk and the ancients teach any such thing?"

"No, Wife. Yet what I tell you is true, and if you would be happy you will do well to learn the same lesson."

"Who is to teach it to me, Wi?"

"I, Wife, if you will listen."

"Or rather, to begin at the beginning," she went on, "who taught it to you? Was it Laleela?"

Now Wi, who found that he could no longer lie as perhaps he would have done in the old days, answered simply,

"Who else, Wife? I have learned the wisdom of her people. Believe me, I am not mad, and hers is a true wisdom, which has made me happy who was wretched, which has made me brave who was full of terrors."

For a while Aaka was silent, for words choked in her throat. Then she said coldly,

"Now I understand. That Witch-from-the-Sea has made a wizard of you. She has not been content to take you as a fair woman might have done with little blame. No, she has poisoned your heart. She has turned you from our ancient gods. Little wonder that they are wrath and bring misfortune upon us, when the Chief of the People and a Witch-from-the-Sea join together to mock and reject them and to turn to I know not what. Tell me, what is it that you two worship when you stand staring at the skies at night, as I know you do?"

"That which dwells in the skies, Wife; That which waits to receive us in the skies."

Now the cold and stately Aaka trembled with wrath.

"Shall I bandy words with a wizard, one who spits upon our fathers' gods?" she asked, and turning, left him.

From that hour began the great trouble. The winter

was terrible, none had known such a winter; even
Urk the Aged declared that weather so fierce had not been
told of since the days of his grandfather's great-grandfather.
The winds howled continually from the north and east,
and whenever they sank a little, snow fell till it was piled
up in great drifts out of which in places only the tops of
the firs appeared, drifts that almost swallowed up the
huts, so that men must throw aside the snow from day
to day to come to each other. The sea, too, was more
frozen than ever it had been before, and through the pack-
ice moved great bergs like mountains, crashing their
road southward, on which bergs might be seen numbers
of terrible white bears that scrambled from them to the
shore, seeking what they might devour. For if any of
the seals on which they lived were left, these were hidden
beneath the ice where the bears could not come at them.

From month to month the people lived upon such food
as Wi in his wisdom had stored up for them, though now
and again, led by him and Moananga, they must go out
against the bears that, made mad by hunger, even
strove to tear a way through the sides and roofs of the
huts. In these fights a number of them perished, being
mauled by the bears, or dying of the cold while they
waited for them. Also many of the old people and young
children died of this same cold, especially in those huts
where, notwithstanding Wi's orders, enough wood and
dried seaweed had not been stored. For now no seaweed
could be got, and because of the snow-drifts and the
blizzards it was impossible to go to the forest and thence
to bring more wood.

During all this time of suffering and of terror Wi went
to and fro with a smiling face, doing the best he could to
help even the humblest, sheltering them in the cave,
sharing the Chief's food with them, and even the fuel, of
which he had gathered so great a store. Laleela, too,
cherished the outcast babes and wept as one by one they
died of the bitter frosts that poured into the open mouth
of the cave and struck them through their wrappings.

At last the black winter months passed away, giving

place to those of spring Yet no spring came. The
snow, it is true, ceased to fall and the pack-ice off the
shore grew thinner ; also the rivers began to run turbidly,
filled with brine rather than water, and the trees of the
woods appeared again out of their white beds, blackened
and dead for the most part. But there was no green
where there should have been grass, no spring flowers
bloomed, the fir-buds did not burst, no seals or birds
appeared, while the cold remained like to that of a
winter when Wi was a lad.

Great murmuring went up from the tribe. Tales
had gone about from mouth to mouth.

" The curse has come upon us," said these tales,
" a curse brought by the fair Witch-of-the-Sea."

Moreover, there spread a rumour that Wi, their chief,
had deserted the Ice-Gods whom all had worshipped
since the days of Urk's grandfather's great-grandfather,
and perhaps even earlier ; that now he bent the knee to
some other god, that of the Witch-of-the-Sea. As Aaka
would say nothing, although perchance already she had
said too much, and as they dared not ask the truth of
Wi, he who had slain Henga and the great-toothed tiger,
and the bull of bulls, and was therefore more than a
man, chosen ones from among the people waylaid Pag,
who was Wi's chief counsellor, and questioned him.
He listened grimly, wrapped up in his skin rugs and
watching them with his one eye, then answered,

" I know nothing of this matter of gods, I who put
no faith in any gods. All I know is that the weather has
changed for the worse ; also, that as for the oath which
Wi swore, he has kept it well, seeing that although a
very fair one lay to his hand, he has taken no other wife,
which he might have done, for she whom he has does not
treat him kindly. For the rest, if you are not content
to die quietly, as it seems that we must do, and would
find out what is the will of the gods, go and ask it of those
who dwell in the ice yonder. Ay, let all those who
complain gather themselves together, and let Wi and those
who cling to him, of whom I am one, gather themselves

together also. Then let us go up and stand before the
Ice-Gods, in whom you put faith, and make sacrifice to
them—if there be anything left to offer—and ask them
for an oracle."

Thus spoke Pag in bitterness and mockery, never guessing that those poor, tortured and bewildered folk would
pay heed to his words. Yet this they did, for these seemed
to them a tree to cling to as they were swept away by the
flood of misery. Surely the gods to whom their fathers
had bent the knee from the beginning must exist ; surely,
if the people appeared before them and offered them
sacrifice, they would listen and cause the ice to melt and
the spring to come.

The people took counsel together, and at last sent some
of their number to the mouth of the cave to speak with
Wi, Ngae, he who made charms, the Priest of the Ice-
Gods, and Pitokiti and Hou and Whaka among them.
So they went up to the cave, having chosen Hotoa the
Slow-speeched and Urk the Ancient as their spokesmen,
and at the mouth of the cave Wini-wini the Shudderer
blew three blasts upon his horn according to the old
custom when the people desired to talk with the Chief.

Wi came forth wearing his robe that was made of the
hide of the long-toothed tiger which he had killed, and
saw the spokesmen standing before him, shamefaced
and with downcast eyes, while behind them, gathered
upon the meeting-place where he had fought Henga, the
mass of the people, or those who were left of them, were
huddled together miserably

"What would you with me ? " he asked.

"Chief," mumbled Urk, "we are sent to say that the
people can no longer bear the curse which has fallen upon
them. We hear that the Witch-from-the-Sea, who
brought the curse, has changed your heart, so that you
have ceased to worship the ancient gods who dwell in
the ice, and have set up some other god in your heart,
wherefore the Ice-dwellers are angry. We ask you if
this be true."

"It is true," answered Wi steadfastly. "No longer

do I worship the Ice-Gods, because there are no such gods. Those that dwell in the ice are but a great beast and a man, both of whom have been dead from the beginning."

Now the messengers looked at each other and shivered, for to them these words were horrible, while Ngae the Priest waved his hands and muttered prayers or spells. Then Urk went on,

"We feared that this was so. Hearken, Chief. It has been handed down to me from my forefathers that once when the people were starving because of bad seasons the chief offered up his son as a sacrifice to the Ice-Gods. Yes, he killed his son before them, whereon the gods were appeased, the seasons changed, the seals and the fish returned in plenty and all was well."

"Do you demand that I should sacrifice my son?" asked Wi.

"Chief, Ngae, the Priest of the Ice-Gods, like his father before him, the Weaver of spells, and Taren his wife, the Seeress, have made divination, and wisdom has come upon them. Yes, a Voice has spoken to them from the roof of their hut in the dead of night."

"And what said the Voice?" asked Wi, leaning on his axe and looking at Ngae. "Tell me, you to whom it spoke."

Then the lank, evil-faced Ngae piped an answer in his thin voice,

"Chief, the Voice said that the Ice-Gods must have their sacrifice and that this sacrifice must walk upon two legs."

"Did it name the sacrifice, Ngae?"

"Nay. Yet it said that it must be chosen by the Chief from the Chief's household, and thereafter be offered with his own hand, yonder in the holy place before the face of the gods."

"Name my household," said Wi.

"Chief, there are but three of them. Aaka your wife, Foh your son, and the Witch-from-the-Sea who is your second wife."

"I have no second wife," answered Wi. "In that

matter as in all others I have kept the oath which I made
to the people."

" We hold that she is your second wife ; also that she
has brought the curse upon us, as she brought the Red
wanderers," replied Ngae stubbornly, while the others
nodded their heads in assent. " We demand," he went
on, " that you choose one of these three to be offered to
the Ice-dwellers at sunset on the night of full moon, which
is the appointed hour of sacrifice, when the sun and the
moon look at each other across the sky."

" And if I refuse ? " said Wi quietly.

Now Ngae looked at Urk, and Urk answered,

" If you refuse, Chief, this is the decree of the people ;
this is their message to you. They will kill all these
three, Aaka your wife, Foh your son, and the Witch-
from-the-Sea your second wife, so that they may be sure
that the one dies who should have been chosen. This
they will do whenever and wherever they can
catch them, by day or by night, waking or sleeping,
walking or eating ; and having slain them, they will take
their bodies and lay them as an offering on the threshold
of the Dwellers in the Ice."

" Why not kill me ? " asked Wi.

" Chief—because you are the Chief, who may only be
slain by one who is stronger than he, as you slew Henga ;
and who is there that is stronger than you are, or who dare
stand before you ? "

" So, like wolves, you would kill the weak and let
the mighty be ? " said Wi with scorn. " Well, Messengers—well, Voices of the people, go back to them and say
that Wi the Chief will take counsel with himself as to this
matter which you have brought before him. To-morrow,
at this same hour of midday, return to me and I will
speak my heart to you and to the people, so that to-morrow
night at the setting of the sun the sacrifice, if sacrifice
there must be, may be accomplished, when the sun and
the full moon look at each other across the skies."

Then they went, shrinking before his eyes, which
seemed to burn them like fire.

Now of this talk Wi said nothing to any, no, not even
to Aaka or Pag or Laleela, though perchance they all
knew of it, for when they met him they looked upon him
strangely, as did even Foh his son, or so it seemed to
him. That afternoon, going to the mouth of the cave
he saw that a large fire had been lit down among the
huts and that round it many were gathered as though
at a feast.

" Perhaps they have found a dead seal and cooked it,"
said Wi to himself.

As he stood there wondering, Pag and Moananga
came up and he noted that Moananga was bruised as
though he had been fighting.

" What passes yonder ? " asked Wi.

" This, Brother," answered Moananga, and there
was horror in his voice. " Those of the people who have
eaten all their store, to whom by your orders no more
may be given till after the night of full moon, and who are
therefore starving, have slaughtered two girl-children,
and cook and devour them. I tried to stay them, but
they felled me with clubs, for they are fierce as wolves
and more savage."

" Is it so ? " said Wi in a low voice, for his heart was
sick in him.

" Shall we gather men and fall on them and kill them ? "
asked Moananga

" Of what use to shed more blood ? " answered Wi.
" They are starving brutes and such will fill themselves.
Hearken. I go out to think. Let none follow me, for
I would be alone. Fear not, I shall return. Yet keep
watch over the other children, for there are many famished
yonder."

So Wi went along the base of the hills that this
spring were covered with thick ice, such as had never
been seen upon them before. This ice, indeed, had crept
down from the glacier above almost to the sea-shore,
and he noted that where it ended its thickness was that
of the height of three spears tied one to another, and
wondered what it might be in the clefts further up the

slope of the hills. Wi came to the valley that was called
the Home of the Ice-Gods and went up it.

Lo! the great glacier had moved forward, for the
last wand that he had set to measure its advance was
covered, and the rocks that the ice had pushed in front
of it, were piled into a heap or ridge that separated the
valley into two parts, a larger part to the left as he faced
the glacier in front of the Sleeper and the man whom
now it seemed to pursue, and a smaller part to the right
where the ice was not so steep. Wi looked at the Sleeper
and the man. It seemed to him that they were nearer
than ever they had been before, for he could see them
both more clearly, although they were also higher up in
the ice.

"These gods travel," he said to himself, and
crossing the ridge of piled-up stones, sat himself down
upon a rock to think, as more than once he had done
before.

Then he had come thither because the place
was holy to him. Now it was no longer holy, but he
sought it because he knew that he would be alone, for
none dared enter it at nightfall. Wi watched the edge of
the sun sinking towards the west and the edge of the moon
rising in the east, and began to pray.

"O That which Laleela worships and has taught me
to worship, hear me," he prayed. "Behold! I am
helpless. Those poor starving folk seek to kill the ones
I love and say to me, ' Choose the victim,' and if I choose
not they will kill them. They say that the Ice-devils
demand a sacrifice and that this sacrifice must be given
to them. O That which Laleela worships, tell me what
I must do."

Thus he prayed in rough and simple words, with his
heart rather than with his lips, and having prayed, fell
into thought, communing with his own soul.

The place was very silent. The frozen air hung
heavily; on either side rose the black rock walls of the
gulf; in front was the blue ice full of reflected lights,
and above to the left of him were the grim figures of the

dead man of long ago being hunted from age to age by the enormous, shadowy, unknown beast. In this dread house of the gods of his people Wi bowed his head and communed with his soul, and not only with his own soul, but as it seemed to him with the souls of all who had begotten him. For he sought not his own wisdom only, but that of his race.

What now should he do ? The tribe believed in the Ice-Gods, as their forefathers had done, back and back for ever, and though he had come to reject those gods as gods, still he also believed in them as devils, the bearers of misery. The tribe believed that if the sacrifice in which ran the blood of man were made to the gods, these would cease from tormenting them and that once more they would have plenty and live as their ancestors had lived.

It might be so. It might be that devils could only be made kind by blood offerings, and that the devils were near while the real gods were far away. At the least so held the people who were starving and desperate, and whose soothsayers had declared that one of his own household must be offered to these, their gods from generation to generation, as legend told had been done in the past by chiefs who ruled before him. Moreover, if that offering were not made, they would make it for themselves by murder. Therefore an offering must be made, and on him was laid the burden of this dreadful choice.

Who then should he give up to be butchered ? Aaka, the wife of his youth whom he still loved although she treated him so roughly ? Never ! The very thought of such a deed made him burn with shame even in that cold. Laleela, the Sweet One from the South, whose beauty was that of a star and whose breath was as the balm from fir-trees, she whose wisdom had given him peace, she who had offered her life for his ? Never ! Then who remained ? Only Foh his son, the one child that was left to him, the bright, brave lad of promise, who, as Laleela had prophesied, might live on to become a better and more famous man than he had been, and to beget children to succeed him. Should he stand by and see the throat of Foh cut before the Ice-Gods that the smoke of his blood might rise to their nostrils and give them pleasure ? Never !

Who then remained of his household to satisfy the hunger of the gods and to take away the fear of the people? One only. He, Wi himself, whom they dared not touch because he was Chief and too strong for them.

A while ago in his wretchedness he had gone up to fight the great bull of the woods, half hoping that the bull would prevail against him, who had no more desire to live. Afterward Laleela had taught him certain lessons, amongst others that it was wrong to die thus to please himself, and to cast the burdens from his back upon the backs of those who came after him. But Laleela had never taught him that it was wrong to die for others ; indeed, she herself had shown that she was ready to do this very thing when she leapt in the path of the little spear, and when she rowed out to sea to perish there in her hollow log, that he might be no more reproached or mocked.

Perchance if he died the devils whom once he thought to be gods, would be appeased and the sun would shine again as it used to do, the snows and ice would melt, the beasts and the birds would return and give the people food. Was it not well that one should die for the sake of many ? Should he hold back his own life, if by the giving of it many might be helped, or even believe that they would be helped ? Surely this must be given, nor should he grieve overmuch, to whom Laleela had taught certain lessons, except that for a little while he would be called upon to leave Foh and her behind him.

Such were the counsels that the soul of Wi gave to Wi there in the icy silence of the glacier.

Wi rose up and laughed aloud. He stood upon the pile of ice-borne stones, a tiny form in that tremendous place, and shook his axe at the Sleeper and him whom the Sleeper hunted, and at the shadowy shapes that seemed to crowd about these in the moonlight, the towering, changeful shapes that the people held to be those of gods.

" I defy you ! " he cried, his voice echoing strangely

from the mighty ice-cliff and the walls of rock. " Ye
shall have your sacrifice. My blood shall steam before
you. Ye shall feed on death. Then, being full, ye and
those that worship you, those from whom ye draw your
strength, shall come face to face with That which is
greater than ye are. Yes, ye, the Demanders of Sacrifice,
shall yourselves be sacrificed to That which is greater
than ye are ! "

Thus cried Wi in his madness, scarce knowing what
it was he said, or why such words broke from him.

But from the Ice-Gods there came no answer. Still
the Hunter and the Hunted stared at him, still the frost
bit and the deep silence reigned, and the moon shone
on above, as he, a defeated, desperate man, crept, half-
frozen, back to whence he came.

When Wi reached the cave he saw crouched in front
of it a single figure wrapped up in furs. It was Pag who
awaited him.

" What counsel from the Ice-dwellers ? " asked Pag,
eyeing him strangely.

" Out of nothing comes nothing," answered Wi.
" What do you here ? "

" There are three within whom I watch," said Pag.
" Hearken. I know all as do the others, and if the Ice-
dwellers are dumb, I have counsel. It is that we three—
you, Moananga and I—fall upon certain ones whom you
know, those who spoke with you to-day, now in the
night, and slay them. Then, lacking leaders, the rest
will scatter and hide their heads, for they are cowards."

" I will shed no blood," said Wi, " not even that of
those who hate me, for misery makes them mad."

" Then other blood will be shed—that of those who
love you."

" I think not," said Wi. " Still, watch them well
who walk in the midst of hungry wolves."

Then he entered the cave and laid himself down
between Foh and Aaka. For he had sent command to
Aaka that she must no more sleep alone in her hut.

CHAPTER XVIII

THE SACRIFICE

NEXT day at the hour of noon Wini-wini came and, as before, blew three blasts upon his horn. Wi went to the mouth of the cave, and there without stood old Urk and the messengers, they who spoke as the tongue of the people.

" What of the sacrifice ? " asked Urk. " Chief, we await your word."

" It seems that one has been offered, yonder among the huts, and that the bellies of some of you are full of strange meat," answered Wi sternly.

They cowered before him and muttered together. Then Hotoa, the Slow of Speech, spoke and the words fell from his lips heavily, like stones thrown into water one by one,

" Chief, we starve and must have food. The old gods, whom you deny, starve also and must have blood. Name the sacrifice from among the chosen three, or we will kill them all and thus be sure that the appointed one has died."

" Am I not also of the household of the Chief, Hotoa ? " asked Wi. " And if you would make sure, should I not be killed with them ? See, I am but one, while you are many. Come, kill me that your gods may have their sacrifice."

One leapt out of the darkness of the cave and stood at his side. It was Aaka.

" Kill me also," said Aaka, " for I would go with my man. Shall we who have slept together for so many years lie in different beds at last ? "

The messengers shrank back from them.　Indeed, Hou and Whaka ran away, for they were cowards.

" Hearken, Dogs, who like dogs devour the flesh of men," said Wi in a great voice.　" Get you back to the people and say to them that since they will have it so, I will meet them at sunset in the Home of the gods.　There we will stand together before your gods, I and my household upon the one side and you and the people upon the other.　There too perchance shall the sacrifice be named and made.　Till then I am silent.　Dogs, begone ! "

For a moment they stood staring at him, and he stared back at them with flashing eyes.　A mighty man he was in his robe of tiger-skin and gripping the heavy axe ; so mighty that their hearts turned to water and their knees shook.　Then they slunk away like foxes before a wolf.

Aaka looked at him and there was pride in her face.

" Tell me, Wi," she said, " are you born of the same blood as these two-legged beasts, or did some god beget you ?　Tell me also what is your plan ? "

" I tell you nothing, Wife," he answered sternly.

" Is it so, Wi ?　Then perchance the Sea-Witch has your counsel, for as we all know she is wiser than I am."

" Upon this matter I take no counsel from Laleela, Wife."

" Then perchance it is Pag who whispers in your ear, Pag the wolf-man, who is my enemy and your friend, who teaches to your heart the craft of wolves ? "

" That stone was ill-aimed," said Pag, who stood by. " Last night I whispered such counsel as I think would have pleased you, but Wi would have none of it, Aaka."

" What counsel ? " she asked.

" The counsel of axe and spear ; the counsel of dogs left dead before their own doors as a warning to the pack.　Wolf's counsel, Aaka."

" Here is wisdom where I little thought to find it," she said.

Then before Pag could answer Wi stamped his foot, crying,

"Have done! Before the moon rides high to-night all shall learn who is wise and who is foolish. Till then, give me peace."

Wi went into the cave and ate, talking with Foh as he ate and telling him tales of wild beasts and how he had slain them, such as the lad loved to hear. But to Aaka and Laleela he spoke no word, nor to Pag either, for spear in hand Pag kept guard at the mouth of the cave, and Moananga with him. Yet Laleela, watching him from far off, wondered what his soul had said to Wi yonder in the Home of the gods. Or perhaps she did not wonder. Perhaps his soul had told her soul and she knew.

After he had eaten Wi lay down and slept awhile. When it drew towards sunset he rose and called to Aaka and Laleela, to Foh and to Pag, also to Moananga and his wife Tana, to cover themselves with their fur cloaks, for the air was cold, and to accompany him to the Home of the gods. Then he wrapped himself in his tiger-skin robe, took his axe, Pag's gift, and two spears, and led the way past the white hills that rose above the beach, to the gulf in the mountain where the blue ice shone and the Sleeper slept.

As he passed from the cave he noted that the most of those who were left of the people, were come together on the Gathering-ground where he had fought Henga, and watched him, a strange and silent company. Presently, looking back, he saw that they were following him, still silent, much as a pack of hungry wolves follows a little herd of deer. Yes, that was what they looked like upon the white snow which this season would not melt, a pack of wolves creeping after a little herd of deer.

Wi came to the glacier gulf and climbed up it, followed by his household, till he reached the foot of the ice. Then he bade them stand on the right of the little ridge of stones that the ice had pushed before it, where there was a narrow strip or bay of ground between these stones and the rock-wall of the cleft which was not overhung by the ice. For here the rocky gulf bulged outwards, so that

on it no ice could lie, the mighty glacier being to the west
on the left of the stones.

" This is a strait place, Husband," said Aaka, " which
gives us but little standing room."

" We are few, Wife," he answered, " and those who
come are many. Moreover, standing here where the
rock slopes outwards, we can be seen and heard of all
who gather before the face of the ice."

Led by the elders the people came, and as they came
Wi pointed with his spear, showing them that they should
take their place to the left of the stones where the valley
was broad and in summer a stream ran from the ice,
which stream was now frozen. So there they gathered
on the bed of the stream, family by family, for all the
tribe that could walk had come to see this sacrifice to
the ancient gods.

At length all were there and stood still. Wi climbed
upon a rock in the little bay of the eastern cliff and
stood before them, a figure of fire, for the light from
the sinking sun struck full upon him, while the great
company of the people were in shadow.

" I, Wi the Chief, am here and my household with me,"
he cried, and in that great cold silence his voice echoed
from the walls of ice and rock. " Now tell me, O People,
what is your will with me and mine ? "

Then out of the shadows answered the piping voice of
Ngae the Diviner, the Priest, the Weaver of Spells, saying,

" This is our will, Chief : that you choose for sacrifice
one of your household, that the gods of our fathers may
smell the blood and lift from off us the curse that has
been brought upon us by Laleela, the Witch-from-the-
Sea, whom against your oath you have taken to wife."

" On that matter I have answered you already,"
cried Wi across the gulf, " but let it be. Now do you,
O People, put up your prayer to your gods, and when that
prayer is finished, if to it no answer comes I will name the
sacrifice."

Then Ngae in his thin piping voice began to pray to
the gods out of the shadows.

" O Ice-dwellers," he said, " you whom our fathers have worshipped from of old, hearken to our tale. A while ago he who is our chief, made new laws, and because the women among us were very few, decreed that no man should take more than one wife. Also he swore that he himself would keep his own law, and should he break it he called down your curse upon his head and upon those of all the tribe.

" O ye ancient gods, there rose out of the sea a very fair witch whom this chief of ours has taken to wife, breaking his oath. Therefore the curse that he created in your names is fallen upon us ; therefore the seasons have changed, the seals and the fish do not come, there are no fowl and no deer in the woods, and where there should be grass and flowers there is naught but ice and snow. Therefore, too, we starve and die and must fill ourselves with the flesh of our own children because ye, O gods, are wrath with us.

" Now hearken, O ye gods. It has come down to us from the former days, father telling the tale to son through many generations, that in the far past such evils have happened to those who begat us and are now forgotten. For then, too, ye were wrath with us because of the wickedness of those who ruled over us, turning their backs on you, ye gods. Yet afterwards that wrath of yours was appeased by a sacrifice chosen from among the household of the chief, and thus the curse was lifted from us, and again we were full of food. But never did any chief of ours sin so greatly against you as does this Wi who rules over us to-day, and who is so mighty a man that none of us may stand against him to fight and kill him. Thus has he sinned, O ye gods from of old. Not only has he broken his oath but, led of the Witch-from-the-Sea, he has rejected you and reviled you, saying that ye are no gods, but devils, and that he worships another power without a name to whose feet he has been led by the magic of the Witch-from-the-Sea.

" Therefore we, your servants from the beginning, have made known and declared to him that no common sacrifice will satisfy his sin, but that the blood to be shed must be that of one of his own family, aye, the blood of a wife, or that of his son. Such is the case that we lay before you, O ye gods, we, your servants from of old. Now let Wi, the mighty man, our chief who rejects you, make answer to it if he is able. And then let the sacrifice be offered that your curse may be lifted from off us, and that we who perish with cold and hunger may live again."

The piping voice of Ngae died and for a while there was silence. Then, standing on the rock, Wi made answer.

"O ye Ice-dwellers whom once I worshipped as good gods, but whom now I know to be devils and bearers of evil, hear my words. Your priest said that I have sworn an oath, and it is so. Yet he is a liar, for that oath I have not broken. True it is that a curse has fallen upon us because the seasons have changed their course, yet that curse began to fall ere ever the woman whom they name Witch-from-the-Sea set foot upon our shore. Now the tribe demands a sacrifice of blood to be named by me from among my household, believing that by virtue of this shed blood the curse will be lifted from them, and spring and summer will return as aforetime, bringing plenty.

"O ye Ice-dwellers, that sacrifice is ready to be offered. I, Wi, am that sacrifice! I, Wi, name myself as the victim whose blood must flow. Yet first, ere I fall upon my spear or stretch out my throat to the Priest, I make prayer to That which is above both you and me. Hear me now, O Power without a name, O Power in whom I have learned to trust; is it your will that I should die as an offering to these devils, the Dwellers in the ice? Answer, for I am ready. The people are in misery; they are mad. I blame them not, I into whose hand they were given to feed and guide. If by the shedding of my blood their woes can be washed away, then let it be outpoured. Judge then, O Power, between me and the people for whom I have laboured vainly, and the

evil gods they worship who rejoice in misery and desire
death. Judge, O Power without a name. Turn the
hearts of these men, if they can be turned, and break the
bonds that bind them. But if this may not be, if, having
heard me, still the people desire sacrifice, or by my
blood their miseries can be washed away, then let me
die for them."

Thus prayed Wi to the Strength that dwelt above
and to the folk whom he had cherished here upon the
earth, asking for no sign nor for any vengeance, putting
up no plea for pity, yet hoping that this Strength might
find a way to turn them from their bloody purpose, so
that no longer in the name of their gods they should
demand the life of him or his. As he prayed the light of
the dying sun faded from him standing there in the bay of
the cliff, so that his last words were spoken out of the deep
gloom, while the light of the rising moon grew and gathered
upon the glacier's face and on the savage horde beneath,
who stared up towards him upon the rock.

He ceased, and for a while there was a great silence.
Through that silence there came home to the heart
of Wi the Hunter, Wi the wild man, knowledge that he
played his part in a war of gods, yes, in the eternal fight
between the Evil and the Good. Suddenly he knew that
those Ice-dwellers whom the people worshipped, as once
he had done, were naught but the Evil in their own hearts
given form and name, and that the Unknown One whom
now he worshipped was the Good in their hearts, and in his
heart of which Laleela had opened the doors so that it
might enter there, the Good which now he saw and felt
but which, as yet, they did not understand. Which,
then, would prevail, he wondered. Yes, wondered
calmly, even coldly, as though he judged another's case,
and in that great wonder all fear left him, and with it
the thought of the agony of death and of the loves that
he must leave behind.

He looked down upon the people and by the shim-
mering moonlight watched their faces. They were disturbed ; they began to whisper one to another ; they grew

sad-eyed and some of the women wept. He caught
snatches of their talk.

" He has been kind to us," they said ; " he has done
all that man can do ; he is not the Lord of the Seasons,
he does not cause the birds to fly or the seals to swim.
Why should he not take another wife if it pleases him ?
Can the gods demand his blood or that of his wives or
son ? Why should he be sacrificed, leaving us leaderless ? "

Such were the words that they murmured one to
another

The Good conquers, the Ill goes down, thought Wi,
still judging of the case as though it were not his own.

But Ngae, the Weaver of Spells, who hated him,
also saw and heard. He ran out from among them, he
stood facing them with his back to the ice-slope ; he cried
in his thin, piercing voice,

" Hear me, the priest of the Ice-Gods, as were my
fathers before me ; hear me, ye People. Wi, the oath-
breaker, Wi through whom the curse has fallen on you,
pleads with you for his life. If he is afraid to die, then
let him give another to the gods. Let him give Aaka
the proud, or the white Witch-from-the-Sea, or Foh his
son. Did we ask for *his* blood ? Would we kill him, the
Chief ? Not so. If he dies it is by his own choice and of
his own will. Therefore let not your hearts be softened by
his pleadings. Remember what he is. Out of his own
mouth he has declared himself a reviler of the gods. He
has set up another god and in their very presence makes
prayer to it, naming them devils. Surely for this he is
worthy of death. Surely because of this blasphemy
the gods will be avenged. Yet we seek not his life. Let
him give to us one of the others ; let him give to us that
white Witch-from-the-Sea that we may bind her and cause
her to die, here and now. I tell you, people, I who am
the priest and to whom the gods talk, that if you go hence
having robbed them of their sacrifice you shall starve.
Yes, you shall die, as many of us have died already, of
sickness and want and cold. More, you shall eat one
another and kill one another till at last none is left.

Will you starve ? Will you see your children devoured ?
Look ! " and he turned, pointing behind him at the
shadows which the moonlight caused to appear in the deep,
clear ice; " the gods are moving ; they gather waiting
for their feast   Will you dare to rob them of their
feast ? Do so and you shall become, every one of you, like
that dead one who flies before the Sleeper. Do you not
see them moving ? "

Now a groaning cry went up from the people

" We see them ! We see them ! "

" And will you rob them of their feast ? " asked the
fierce-faced Ngae again.

" Nay," they shouted, taking fire. " Let the sacrifice
be sacrificed. Let us see the red blood flow ! Let the
Ice-Gods whom our fathers worshipped smell the red
blood ! "

" Wi, you have your answer," piped Ngae as the
shouting died. " Now come hither and die if you dare.
Or if you dare not, then send us one of your household."

Aaka, holding Foh by the hand, Laleela, Pag, Moananga and his wife clustered together as though to take
counsel. Wi prepared to descend from his rock, perchance to fall upon his spear, perchance to give himself
up to be butchered by the people and their priest.

Then it was that something, at first none knew what,
began to happen that caused all to stand silent, each in
his place, like men that had been smitten to stone.
From high up in the air, although no wind blew, there
came a moaning sound, as if out of sight countless great-
winged birds were flying. The air seemed to change ;
it grew more icy cold, men's breath froze upon it. The
shadows in the ice shrank and grew in the wavering
moonbeams. They advanced, they flitted back quickly,
and departed, only to appear again here and there high
above where they had been. The hairy man who stood
before the Sleeper seemed to move a little. Surely they
saw him move !

The earth trembled as though it were filled with
dread, deeper and yet deeper grew the silence, till

suddenly it was broken by a fearful crack like˜to that of
the fiercest thunder. As its echoes died away, out of
the bowels of the ice rushed the Sleeper and he whom it
appeared to hunt. Yea, the white-tusked Sleeper rushed
like a charging bull ; it sped forward like a stone from
a sling. The frozen man was thrown far and vanished,
but the mighty Sleeper fell full on to Ngae the priest,
who still stood staring upwards, crushing him to powder,
and passing on, ploughed a red path through the folk
beyond.

Again for a moment there was silence, and in that silence
Wi said, speaking out of the darkness as one who dreams,

" It would seem that the Ice-Gods have taken their
sacrifice ! "

As the words died upon his lips, with an awful rending
sound, companioned by whirlwinds, the great glacier
moved forward in a slow and deadly march. It flowed
down the valley, thrusting rocks in front of it, heaving
itself into waves like a tumultuous sea, digging up the
solid ground, while before it great boulders leapt and
danced. The boulders danced through the people, the
ice flowed over them. Yes, as they turned to fly it
flowed over them, so that presently where they had been
there was nothing but a deep sea of tumbled, heaving
ice that travelled towards the beach.

Wi leapt from his rock. With those of his household he
huddled further back into the little bay of the mountain-
side, and there, protected by the walls of cliff, watched
the river of ice grind and thunder past them. How
long did they watch ? None ever knew. They saw it
flow. They saw it creep into the sea and there break
off in sharp-topped hills of ice. Then as suddenly as
it had begun to move it stopped, and the night was as
the night had been, only now the valley of the gods was
a valley of ice, and where the glacier had been were
slopes and walls of smooth black rock.

When all was over Wi spoke to the little company
who clung to him, saying,

"The Ice-Gods have given birth. The old devil-gods
have taken a great sacrifice of all who served them, but
That which I and another worship has heard our prayer
and preserved us alive. Let us go back to the cave."

So, Wi leading them, they climbed out of the bay in
the mountain-side up on to the steep cliff of tumbled ice
that had flowed down the valley, filling it from side to
side, purposing to return to the village. But when
they reached its crest and looked towards where the
beach should be and the huts of the people, they sank
down amazed and terrified. For behold! no beach
was left. Behold! the ice gathered upon the smaller
hills behind the village also had flowed down over it
into the sea, so that where the dwelling-places of the
people had been, now there was nothing but a rough
slope of tumbled ice washed up by the waves of the
troubled sea The tribe that had dwelt upon this beach
for ages was gone, and with it, its habitations that now
lay buried for ever, swept from the face of the world.

Aaka, leaning upon Wi, studied all things in the cold
moonlight. Then she said,

"The curse brought by that fair witch of yours has
worked well, Husband; so well that I wonder what
remains for her to do."

"After all that has passed, Wife, such words seem
to me to be evil," answered Wi. "The people who called
upon the Ice-dwellers, where are they? Surely they
have become dwellers in the ice. Yet I who learned
another lesson from her whom you reproach, I who
thought by this time to be a sacrifice, remain alive,
and with me all my House. Is this, then, a time for
bitter words, Wife?"

Then Pag spoke, saying,

"As you well know, Wi, never did I put faith in the
Ice-Gods because our people have made sacrifice to them
and have danced before them for a thousand years.
Now I believe in them less than ever, seeing that those who
worshipped them are swept away, while those who rejected
them live on. The people have gone; not one of them

remains alive except this little company, a handful out of hundreds. They have gone ; they lie buried in the ice, as thousands of years ago the great Sleeper that fell on Ngae and crushed him, and he who hunted it or by it was hunted, were buried. There they lie who perchance in their turn will become gods in a day to come, and be worshipped by the fools that follow after us. Yet we still breathe and, all the rest being dead, how shall we save ourselves ? The children who were born of the marriage of those Ice-Gods have eaten up our homes ; the beach is no more. Nothing remains. Whither, then, shall we go who, if we stay here upon the ice, very soon must perish ? "

Wi covered his eyes with his hands, making no answer, for he was broken-hearted.

Then for the first time spoke Laleela, who hitherto had been silent, saying nothing at all, even when Wi offered himself as the sacrifice.

" Be pleased to hear me," she said. " As the moonlight shows you, the ice has flowed down over the beach and the huts and the woods beyond. Yet on the further side of the ridge that bounds the valley of the gods, and the little hills beyond, it has not flowed ; for there the ice sheet is flat beneath the snow and cannot stir of its own weight. Yonder to the east there is a little cave, that in which the boat lies that brought me to this land, and there I have hidden food. If it pleases you, let us go to that cave and shelter there."

" Ay, let us go to the cave, for if we stay here upon the ice we shall perish," said Pag.

So, climbing round the foot of the mountain and the hills beyond, they came at length to the open beach where lay some snow but no ice, and walked by the edge of the sea to the little cave.

Pag and Moananga, going first, reached it before the others. Pag, peering in, started back, for he saw large eyes looking at him out of its darkness.

" Have a care," he called to Moananga, " here are bears or wolves."

The sound of his voice frightened the beasts in the cave and, moving slowly, these came out on to the beach, whereon they saw that they were not bears or wolves, but two seals, a large cow with her half-grown cub, that had refuged there, perhaps because they were frightened by the sound of the glaciers rushing into the sea. They leapt upon the clumsy beasts and before these could escape, killed them with their axes.

" Here at least is meat enough to last us for a long while," said Pag when the seals were dead. " Now let us skin them before they freeze."

So helped by Foh they set to the task in the moonlight, and had well-nigh finished it before Wi came up with the women. For Tana was so frightened by the horrors she had seen that Aaka and Laleela must support her, and thus they could only walk slowly through the snow.

Then having searched the cave to make sure that now it was empty, they entered it and lit a fire, round which they crouched to warm themselves, silent and full of terrors.

CHAPTER XIX

WHICH ?

BEFORE the coming of the dawn Wi left the cave and climbed a little hill behind it, that was built up of ancient ice-borne rocks and drift in which this hollowed cavern lay. This he did because he wished to look at the land and the sea when the light came ; also to be alone and think. Yet he found that he was not alone, for kneeling behind one of the rocks was Laleela praying, with her face turned towards the sinking moon. When she saw who it was that came she did not stir but went on praying, and kneeling at her side he prayed with her, for now they had one worship, though neither of them altogether understood who or what they worshipped.

Their prayers finished they spoke together.

" Strange things have happened, Laleela," said Wi, " and my heart is pierced because of the people who are dead. I would have offered myself as a sacrifice if they sought it, knowing they believed that thereby a curse would have been taken from them, and that what is believed often comes to pass. Yet I live on and they are slain, every one of them, and I say that my heart is broken," and for the first time since Foa was murdered Wi bowed his head and wept.

Laleela took his hand and comforted him, wiping away his tears with her hair. Then she said in her gentle voice,

" Things have come about as they were decreed, and those who sought blood have died in blood, crushed to powder by the gods they worshipped, whether by chance or by the will of That which dwells yonder, I do not know or seek to learn. Only, Wi, you did ill to wish to slay yourself or suffer yourself to be slain, and," she added with a thrill of fear in her voice, " who can be sure that what has been offered to Heaven, Heaven will not take at its own time ? "

" Not I," answered Wi. " Yet, Laleela, what would you have had me do ? If I refused any sacrifice to those mad folk they would have done what they swore, and murdered Aaka and Foh and you, all three. Therefore a blood offering must be furnished out of my household, and would you have had me name one of you and myself remain alive ? "

" I brought the trouble, Wi ; surely I should have paid its price. Indeed, I would have given myself up to them who hated me and sought my blood, not yours, had not a voice speaking in my breast told me that in some way you would be spared. Also at the last I felt that a terror was at hand, though what it might be I did not know."

" So I think did all of us, Laleela, for last night the air was big with death. But you do not answer. What would you have thought of me when the spear was at your throat, had I said, ' Take yonder Laleela, whom you declare a witch. Offer her to your gods and be content ? "

" I should have thought you a wiser man than you are, Wi," she said, smiling sadly. " Yet, believe me, I thank you who are noble ; nor, should I live ten thousand years, shall I forget. No, never, never shall I forget."

" If you live ten thousand years, Laleela, perhaps I shall also—where there is less trouble."

" I am sure that it will be so," she replied simply.

The dawn came, and standing side by side in silence they watched it come. It was a strange and splendid dawn full of red light which shone upon the little clouds that floated in the quiet sky, turning them to shapes of glory. Yes, it was as though Nature, having done her worst, now lay resting in perfect peace. But oh, what a sight was revealed to them ! Where the village had been was ice piled so high that they could see its tumbled

mass and pinnacles over the shoulder of the hill between.
The great woods also, where Wi had killed the aurochs
bull, that swelled upwards from the beach westward,
had vanished beneath the flood of ice which flowed down
upon them from the mountains that lay behind, which
now showed black, robbed of their white cloak.   In front,
too, far as the eye could reach, the sea was covered with a
sheet of solid ice, so pressed together by the weight of
the glaciers that had plunged into it from the hills and
the valley of the gods, that it seemed quite smooth and
immovable as rock, being held in place by the headland
round which the Red wanderers had come in their canoes.
All the white world was a desolation and a waste.

"What has chanced?" said Wi, staring about him.
"Is the world about to die?"

"I think not," answered Laleela.   "I think that the
ice is moving south, that is all, and that where men lived,
there they can live no more, neither they nor the beasts."

"Then we must perish, Laleela."

"Why so? My boat remains and a store of food, and
I think that it will hold us all."

"Your boat cannot float upon ice, Laleela."

"Nay, but being hollowed from one tree it is very
thick and strong, so that we can push it before us until at
length we come to open water, over which we can row away."

"Where to, Laleela?"

"Down yonder to the south, across a stretch of sea
that lies beyond that headland, is the home of my people,
Wi.   It lies in a very pleasant land, full of woods and
rivers where I think the ice will not reach, because that
sea which borders it, even in winter, is always warm.
Indeed sometimes ice mountains from the north float
into it, for I have seen them from far away, but there at
once they melt.   My people are not as your people, Wi,
for they have tamed creatures like to the bull you slew,
and others, from which they draw milk and on whose
flesh they feed.   Also they are a peaceful folk who for
a long while past have waged no war and live quietly
till death takes them."

" Yet you fled away from these people, Laleela."

" Yes, Wi, and now I understand why I fled ; but let that be. Also, although I fled, I think that should I return they would welcome me, who am a great woman among them, also any whom I brought with me. Still, the way is far and yonder ice is rough and cold, and who knows ?—perchance it would be better to bide here."

" That we cannot do," answered Wi. " Look, all the shore is ice, all the woods are ice, and all the sea whence we won the most of our food, is ice ; while behind us is nothing but a wilderness of black rock upon which nothing grows, as I know, who in past days have hunted the reindeer across it. Also to the east yonder is a wall of mountains that we cannot climb, for they are steep and on them the snow lies thick. But let us talk with the others."

So they descended the hillock of piled-up stones and at the mouth of the little cave found Aaka standing there like one who waits.

" Are your prayers to the new god finished, Wi ? " she asked. " If so, I would learn whether its priestess gives us leave to eat of the food which she has stored here, while so many who now are dead, were starving."

Hearing these words, Wi bit upon his lip, but Laleela answered,

" Aaka, all in this place is yours, not mine. Yet of that food, know that I saved it from what was served out to me, for a certain purpose—namely, to store my boat when I fled away from where I was not welcome."

Now Pag, who was standing by, grinned, but Wi said only,

" Have done and let us eat."

So they ate, who had tasted nothing since noon on the yesterday, and when they had filled themselves, after a fashion, Wi spoke to them, saying,

" The home of our forefathers is destroyed, and with it all the people, of whom we alone are left. Yes, the ice that has piled itself above us for many years, has broken its bounds, and rushing to the sea has buried them, as I for one who marked its course from winter

to winter, always thought that it would do some day
Now what is left to us ? We cannot stay where there is no
food. Moreover, doubtless driven of the ice, wolves
and great bears will come down from the north and devour
us. Therefore this is my word : that we fly south over
the ice, dragging the boat of Laleela with us till we reach
open water, and then travel across that water to find some
warmer land where the ice has not come."

"You are our master," said Aaka, "and when you
command we must obey. Yet I hold that the journey we
make in Laleela's boat will end in evil, for us if not for her."

Then Pag spoke, saying,

"Nothing can be worse than the worst. Here certainly we die. Yonder we may live, who in the end
cannot do more than die."

"Pag's words are mine," said Moananga when Wi
looked towards him, but Tana was silent because fear
had robbed her of all spirit and Laleela also held her
peace. Only while they still stared at the ground the
boy Foh cried out,

"The Chief my father has spoken. Is it for us to
weigh his words ? "

No one answered, so they rose up and laded the canoe
with the food that Laleela had stored, and the cut-up
flesh of the two seals, which now was frozen stiff. The
skins of the seals, although these were undressed, they
used for coverings, lashing them over the food with the
paddles and some wood of which others might be
made. Lastly, at Laleela's bidding they took a young fir-
tree that lay in the cave, over which in former days the
seal-pelts had been hung to dry, that it might serve to
make them a mast ; though except Laleela none of them
knew anything of the use of masts. Also upon their
backs they bound loads of dry wood and seaweed for the
making of fire, wrapped up in such hides as lay in the cave.

These things done, they dragged the boat over the snow
to the ice that covered the sea and away out on to the
ice southward, Laleela walking ahead to guide them and
carrying a pole in her hand with which she tested the ice.

Thus then did Wi and the others bid farewell to the home of their fathers which they were never to see again.

For some hours they dragged the boat thus, making but little progress, for the face of the packed ice was much rougher than it seemed to be when looked at from the shore ; then rested awhile and ate some of their food. When they rose to try to go forward, though by now most of them thought the task hopeless, Foh cried out,

" Father, this ice moves. When we stopped, those rocks on the headland were over against us, and now, look, they are behind."

" It seems that it is so, but I am not sure," said Wi.

While they discussed the matter, Pag wandered back upon their track. Presently he returned and said,

" Certainly it moves. The ice-sheet has broken behind us and there is water filled with hummocks that grind against each other, between us and the shore to which now we cannot return."

Then they knew that a current was bearing them southward and some of them were frightened. But Wi said, " Let us rather be thankful, for so shall we travel faster."

Still they continued to push and drag the boat over the rough ice, though this they did chiefly that they might keep themselves warm, who feared that they would freeze if they remained still for too long. So they toiled all day, till towards nightfall they came to ice upon which snow had fallen and lay deep. Moreover, it began to fall again, so that they must stop and make themselves a kind of hut of snow blocks, as they knew well how to do, in which hut they crouched all night to protect themselves from cold.

Next morning they found that the snow had ceased ; also that now they were out of sight of the mountains that stood at the back of the beach which had been their home, though they could still see snow-covered peaks on the headland to the east of them very far away. Leaving the hut, they dragged the boat forward over the surface of the snow, which had frozen so that now it was easy to

travel, and thus made good progress. All that day,
resting from time to time, they went on thus, till late
in the afternoon the snow began to grow soft and it was
difficult to draw the boat through it. Therefore they
stopped, being tired, and built themselves another snow-
hut, outside of which they lit a fire. On that fire they
cooked some of the seal flesh and ate it thankfully,
then went into the hut and slept, for they were very weary.

Next morning they found that the snow was still
soft and that if they tried to walk on it they sank in
to their ankles, so that it was no longer possible to drag
the boat forward.

" We cannot go forward and we cannot go back,"
said Wi. " There is but one thing to do—to stay here ;
though where that may be I do not know, for the
mountains on the headland have vanished."

Now Tana broke into weeping and Moananga looked
sad, but Aaka said,

" Yes, to stay here till we die ; indeed what other
end could be looked for on such a journey, unless we have
a witch among us who can teach us to fly like the swans ? "
and she glanced at Laleela.

" That I cannot do," answered Laleela, " and the
journey was one that must be tried, or so we all thought.
Nor need we die for a long while, seeing that here we
have shelter in the snow-hut and enough seal's flesh to
last for many days if we are sparing, and snow that we
can melt to drink. Also I hope that always the ice
beneath us is bearing us forward, and it seems to me
that the air grows somewhat warmer."

" Those are wise words," said Pag. " Now let us
make the hut bigger, and since we can do nothing more
for ourselves, trust to the Ice-Gods, or to those that Laleela
and Wi worship, or to any others that there may be."

So they did these things ; also while their fuel lasted
they cooked the most of the seal flesh after a fashion, and
set it aside to eat cold, together with the fat, which they
swallowed raw.

That day Pag and Moananga spoke much with Laleela,

questioning her as to her journey northward and how
long it had taken ; about her own land also and where it
lay, to which she answered as best she could. But Wi and
Laleela talked little together, for whenever they did so Aaka
watched them coldly, which seemed to tie their tongues.

Four more days and nights passed thus, nor during this
weary time was there any change, save one, namely, that
always the air grew warmer, by which they knew they were
being borne southward, so that at last the snow began
to melt and the walls of their hut to drip. On the fourth
day also they saw behind them, but somewhat to the
west, a mountain of ice that they had not noted before.
This mountain seemed to grow bigger and nearer, as though
it were heading towards them, or they towards it, which
told them that all the ice still travelled, though they
could not see or feel it move. During that night they
heard terrible rending sounds and felt the ice shake
beneath them, but, although it was melting, did not dare
to go out of the snow-hut to look whence the sounds came,
for a strong wind had begun to blow from the north,
bringing with it clouds that covered the moon.

Towards dawn the wind fell and presently the sun rose,
shining brightly in a clear sky. Thrusting aside the
block of snow that sealed the entrance hole of the hut,
Pag crept out. Presently he returned, and finding
Wi's hand, without speaking, drew him from the hut,
pushing back the snow block after him.

" Look ! " he said as they rose from their knees, and
pointed to the north.

Wi looked and would have fallen had not Pag caught
him. For there, not more than a hundred paces away,
wedged into the thick floes whereon they floated, was
that great ice mountain which they had seen before they
slept, a tall pinnacle ending in a slope of rough ice. And
lo ! there, half-way up the slope, held up between blocks
of ice and stone, stood the Great Sleeper !

Oh ! there could be no doubt, for the light of the
rising sun struck full upon it. There stood the Sleeper
as Wi had seen it for all his life through the veil of ice, only

now its left foreleg was broken off below the knee. Moreover, this was not all, for among the stones and ice-blocks lay strange, silent shapes shrouded in a powder of snow.

" Here be old friends," said Pag, " if it pleases you to go to look upon them, Wi. Ngae—no, not Ngae, for of him on whom the Sleeper fell little would be left ; but Urk the Aged and Pitokiti and Hotoa, and Whaka—though no longer will he croak of evil like a raven—and many others."

" It does not please me," said Wi.

Then he heard a voice behind him, that of Aaka, who said,

" You thought you had left the old gods behind, but see, they have followed after you, Husband, which I think means no good to Pag and you, who were the first to look upon them whom both of you have rejected."

" I do not know what it means, Wife," answered Wi, " nor do I ask. Still, the sight is strange."

Then the others came. Moananga was silent, Tana lifted her hands and screamed, but Laleela said,

" The evil gods may follow, but we go before them and never shall they come up with us."

" That remains to be learned," said Pag.

As he spoke the ice peak on which they were looking, whereof the base had been melted by the warmer waters into which it had floated, began to tremble and to bow towards them. Thrice it bowed thus, then with a slow and noble motion it turned over. Bearing the Sleeper and its company with it, it vanished into the sea, and where its head had been appeared its foot, spotted all about with great rocks that it had brought with it from the land.

" Farewell to the Ice-Gods ! " said Laleela with a smile, but Wi cried,

" Back ! Back ! The wave comes ! " and seizing Aaka by the hand he dragged her away.

They fled, all of them, and not too soon, for after them followed a mingled flood of ice and water, cast up by the overturning of the berg. Near to their snow-hut it stopped and began to recede. Yet the platform upon which that hut stood rocked and trembled.

In his fear and haste to escape, the lad Foh ran past the hut out on to the snowy plain, whence presently he returned, crying,

" The ice has broken, and far away I see land. Come, Father, and look upon the land."

They followed after him, wading through the snow for some two hundred paces, till before them they beheld a channel of water wide as the mouth of a great river, down which the current ran furiously, bearing with it great blocks of ice. This channel wended its way between two shores of ice, as a river winds between its banks, and seemed to end at last in a blue and open sea where there was no ice.

Far away at the edge of that sea appeared the land of which Foh had spoken ; green hills, between which a large river ran into the sea, and valleys with woods on either side of them that grew upwards from the plains lying at the foot of the hills, clothing their rounded sides. For a few minutes only they saw this green and pleasant land. Then a mist that seemed to arise from where the ice-mountain had overturned drove down wind and hid it.

" Yonder is the shore of my country. I know that river and those hills," said Laleela.

" Then the sooner we come there the better," answered Pag, " for this ice which has borne us so far is breaking up beneath us."

Breaking up it was indeed, having drifted into those warmer waters of which once Laleela had spoken as bathing the coasts of her land. Rapidly it melted beneath their feet. Cracks appeared in it. One opened beneath the snow-hut, which fell to a shapeless heap.

" To the boat ! " cried Wi.

They ran back ; they took hold of the canoe and dragged it forward towards the edge of the ice, that here and there began to yawn. They came to the edge, the women and Foh were thrust in, Moananga followed, and Pag also by the command of Wi, who held the stern of the boat to keep its bow straight in the stream, while Laleela and Moananga got out the paddles. Wi looked at it and saw that it was very heavy-laden ; saw that the water almost ran over the edge of the great hollowed log whereof it was fashioned ; saw too that if another man entered into it and the wind blew a little harder, or if it were struck by one of the lumps of ice that floated past on the swift current, it would fill and overset so that all were drowned.

" Come swiftly, Wi," cried Aaka, and the others also cried, " Come ! " for they found it hard to keep the boat steady.

" I come. I come," answered Wi, and with all his strength thrust at the stern so that the boat darted out into the midst of the channel, and there, being seized by the fierce current, turned and sped away.

Wi went back a few paces and sat himself down upon a floe that was bedded in the sheet-ice, watching. As he went he heard a splash and, turning, saw Pag swimming towards the ice. Being very strong he reached it and by the help of Wi climbed on to its edge.

" Why do you come ? " asked Wi.

" That hollow log is very full," answered Pag, " and there are too many women in it ; their chatter troubles me."

Now Wi looked at Pag, and Pag looked at Wi, but neither of them said anything more. They sat upon the floe watching the canoe being borne down the race between the shores of ice, its head pointing first this way and then that, as though the paddlers were trying to turn it round but could not. The mist grew thick about it. Then, just before it was swallowed up in that mist, they saw a tall woman's shape stand up in the boat and plunge from it into the water.

" Which of them was it ? " asked Wi of Pag in a hollow, groaning voice.

" That we may learn presently," answered Pag.

Then he threw himself down on the ice and shut his eyes like one who wishes to sleep.

Thus the vision ended

CHAPTER XX

THE SUM OF THE MATTER

I, ALLAN QUATERMAIN, woke up, to notice that, as on the previous occasion when Lady Ragnall and I took the *Taduki* together, my trance must have been brief. Although I had forgotten to look at the time, as it chanced I could measure its duration by another method. The *Taduki* herb, as I knew, soon burned itself away, yet when I awoke the last little vapour, so thin and faint that it could scarcely be discerned, was rising from its embers.

Good gracious! I thought to myself, how could all those things have happened in that unknown land and age in much less time than it takes the stump of a cigarette to die?

Then I remembered Good—for although my head seemed rather heavy at first, my brain was clear enough—and looked at him, not without alarm, or rather anxiety, for if anything had happened to Good what would my position be?

There he was in his armchair, his head lying back, staring at me with his eyes half-opened, much as a cat does when it is pretending to be asleep, but is really very wide awake indeed. Also, he resembled something else, a man who was drunk, an effect that was heightened presently by his trying to speak and producing only prolonged stutterings and a word that sounded like " whisky."

" No, you don't," I said. " It is far too soon to drink. Alcohol and *Taduki* might not agree."

Then Good said a word that he should have left unsaid, sat up, shook himself, and remarked,

" I say, Wi—for you *are* Wi, aren't you ?—how in the name of the Holy Roman Empire—or of the Ice-Gods and the Sleeper—did I get out of that canoe; and— where's Laleela ? "

" Before I answer your questions, which seem absurd, might I ask you, Good, what you considered your name to be when you were in the canoe of which you speak ? "

" Name ? Why, Moananga, of course. Dash it all, Wi, you haven't forgotten your own brother, have you, who stuck to you through thick and thin—well, like a brother in a book."

" Then if you were Moananga, why do you not ask after Tana instead of Laleela ? "

" I wonder," said Good reflectively. " I suppose it was because she was out of the picture just then, lying at the bottom of the canoe, overcome with the horrors, or sea-sickness, or something, you know, with that dear boy, Foh, sitting on her. Also you needn't be jealous, old chap, for although I did try to cut in when you were doing the pious over that tom-fool oath of yours and the rest of it, it wasn't the slightest use. She just smiled me out of court, so to speak, and like you, made remarks about Tana. But where's Laleela ? You haven't hidden her away anywhere, have you ? " and he stared round the room in a foolish fashion.

" That's just what I want to know," I answered. " Indeed, to tell you the truth, I never remember wanting to know anything quite so much in all my life."

" Then I can't tell you. The last I saw of her was in the canoe, trying to get the head of the crazy thing round with a paddle, which I didn't know how to do."

" Look here, Good," I said, " this is a serious matter, so pull yourself together and tell me exactly what you remember just before you woke."

" Only this : the canoe was bobbing about, being carried shorewards down that infernal tide-race or current between the two banks of ice, at, I should say, not less than eight or nine knots. Moreover, it was rocking, because that fiddle-headed dwarf, Pag, nearly overset it when he jumped out like a seal from a rock and began to swim towards the ice bank we had left, because he thought we were all going to be drowned, I suppose.

So there remained only Aaka, Laleela, Tana, Foh and myself. Laleela, as I have told you, was trying to get the craft round, Tana was wailing and sobbing, that plucky lad Foh was quite still—I can see his white face and big eyes now—and Aaka, sitting in the bottom of the canoe, gripping the thwarts with both her outstretched hands but still looking very dignified, was making unpleasant remarks to Laleela as to her having murdered you, Wi, Aaka's husband and her lover, or something of the sort, to which Laleela returned no answer. Then just as I was shoving away a lump of floating ice, which cut my hand, everything went out like a candle, and here I am. For heaven's sake tell me where is Laleela."

"I am afraid, old fellow, we shall ask ourselves that question for the rest of our days, yet never learn the answer," I replied solemnly. "Listen. I saw a little more than you did. Pag reached the ice-bank and I pulled him to my side. He said that he had jumped out of the canoe because it was too full and there were too many women in it for his liking. But what the dear chap really meant was that he preferred to return to die with me."

"Good old Pag!" ejaculated Moananga—I mean Good.

"After that," I went on, "the canoe ran into the spindrift which the wind lashed up, and the sea-fog——"

"Always get it with thawing ice," interrupted Good. "Once nearly lost in it myself off the coast of Newfoundland."

"—and for a moment Pag and I lost sight of it. It reappeared between two billows of fog a hundred yards or more away; then—well, then we saw a tall woman spring suddenly from the canoe into the sea. But, as you will remember, both Aaka and Laleela were tall, exactly of a height, indeed, and neither of us could tell which of them it was that the sea took. Next instant the mist closed in again."

" Did you see the woman rise up in the canoe ? Aaka was sitting down, you remember."

" No, we only saw the spring."

" That sounds like Laleela," said Good, " for she was standing up. And yet I do not think it can have been, for she was doing all she knew to try to bring the craft round, thinking to creep back to fetch you by the edge of the ice where the current did not run so fiercely. The last thing she said was to call to me to get out the other paddle and help. Indeed I had it in my hand, but being a land-lubber hardly knew how to use it."

" I don't think Laleela would have done such a thing, Good. Suicide was against her principles. Indeed she reproached me upon that very matter. Also, her own country was just ahead of her and she would wish to reach it, if only to make sure that Foh and Aaka—yes, Aaka—met with a good reception. Yet who knows ? "

" Aaka had a very bitter tongue," remarked Good. " Also, by then Laleela saw that we could never get back against that race and she was mad with grief ; so, as you say—who knows ? " and he groaned, while I . . . well, never mind what I did.

For a time there was silence between us, a very depressing silence, because both of us were overcome. It was broken by Good asking humbly enough if I thought he might have some whisky now.

" I don't know and I don't care, but for my part I mean to risk it," I said, and going to the side table I helped myself freely, as did Good, only more so.

Teetotallers may say what they like, but alcohol in moderation often is a friend in trouble. So at least we found, for as we put that whisky down our spirits rose considerably.

" Look here ! " said Good presently while he lit his pipe and I occupied myself in hiding away that confounded *Taduki* outfit which I both hated and blessed. I hated it because it seemed to be possessed by an imp

which, like a will-o'-the-wisp, led one on and on to the
edge of some great *dénouement*, and then, in the very
moment of crisis, vanished away, leaving one floundering
in a bog of doubt and wonder. I blessed it because the
dreams it gave were, to me at any rate, so very suggestive
and interesting.

"Look here," repeated Good, "you are a clever
old boy in your way, and one who thinks a lot. So be
kind enough to tell me what all this business means. Do
you suggest that you and I have been reading some
chapters out of a former existence of our own ? "

"I suggest nothing," I answered sharply; "the
thing is beyond me. But if you want to know, I don't
much believe in the former existence solution. Does it
not occur to you that we must all of us, perhaps fifty
thousand, perhaps five hundred thousand years ago, have
had just such ancestors as Wi and the rest of them ?
And is it not possible that this drug may have the power
of awakening the ancestral memory which has come down
to us with our spark of life through scores of intervening
forefathers ? "

"Yes, that's right enough. And yet, Allan, in a
way the thing is too perfect. Remember that we understood and used the language of those pre-historic beach-
combers, although we have forgotten every word of it
now—or at least I have. Remember that we saw, not
only our own careers, but those of other people with
whose ancestral memories we have nothing to do ; moreover, that some of those people reminded us, or at any
rate me, of folk whom I have known in this life ; just
as though the whole lot of us had reappeared together."

"That's the very point, Good. Men are queer
bundles of mystery. For the most part they seem quite
commonplace, what might be called matter-of-fact ; yet
I believe that inside there are few who are not stuffed
with imagination, as our dreams show us. Supposing
that we are dealing with our own ancestral pasts ; if that
be so, we could quite well invent the rest, using the stuff
that lies to our hands, namely, our knowledge of others

with whom we have been intimate in life. These would
be the foundation upon which the dreams were built
up, the bits of glass that make the pattern in the kaleidoscope."

" If so, all I have to say is that your kaleidoscope is
an uncommonly clever machine, because anything more
natural than those dirty people upon the beach I never
knew, Allan. Still, one thing seems to support your
argument. Wi, the great hunter of the tribe, who by
birth and surroundings was a most elementary savage,
showed himself much in advance of his age. He made
laws ; he thought about the good of others ; he resisted
his perfectly natural inclinations ; he adopted a higher
religion when it was brought to his knowledge ; he was
patient under provocation ; he offered himself up as a
sacrifice to gods in whom he no longer believed, because
his people believed in them and he thought that his
voluntary death would act as a kind of faith-cure among
them, which is one of the noblest deeds I have ever heard
of among men. Lastly, when he saw that a confounded,
hollowed-out log which by courtesy may be called a
canoe or a boat, was overcrowded and likely to sink in a
kind of ice-packed mill-race, he thrust it out into the
stream and himself remained behind to die, although
it contained all that he cared about—his wife, another
woman who loved him, his son, and, perhaps I may add,
his brother. I say that the man who did these things,
not to mention others, was a hero and a Christian martyr
rolled into one, with something of the saint and Solon,
who I believe was the first recorded law-giver, thrown
in. Now I ask you, Allan, could such a person by any
possibility have existed in paleolithic, or pre-paleolithic
times at that period of the world's history when one of
the Ice Ages was beginning ? Also the same question
may be asked of Laleela."

" You must remember," I answered, " that Wi was
not such a hero as you suppose. He offered to sacrifice
himself chiefly in order to save his family, or one of them,
just as most men would do in like circumstances. As

regards Laleela, she and everything about her were
mysterious : her origin, her noble patience, and especially
her self-control. But it is quite obvious that she belonged
to another stratum of civilisation—I presume that which
we call neolithic, since she told me—I mean Wi—that
her people grew crops, kept cows with other domestic
animals, had some advanced form of religion with a
divinity that was symbolised by the moon, and so
forth.

" Well, there is nothing strange about all this, since now
we know that in prehistoric days races in very different
stages of advancement existed in the world at the same
time. It is quite possible that Wi and his company
lived in their paleolithic simplicity, let us say somewhere
in Scotland (those red-headed wanderers who descended
upon them suggest Scotland), while Laleela and her people
existed perhaps in the south of Ireland or in France, where
the climate was much warmer and the ice did not come."

" Probably. Wi and Co. might have lived anywhere
in a cold district and gone to any warmer shore, perhaps
one washed by the Gulf Stream," answered Good. " At
any rate one thing is obvious. If there is anything in
this dream of ours, it tells of a tragedy that must often
have happened in the world : I mean, the coming of an
Ice Age."

" Yes," I said. " All about the northern shores
there must have been little collections of miserable
people, like to those over whom Wi ruled, each of them
perhaps thinking itself alone in the world ; and time on
time the ice, at intervals of tens or hundreds of thousands
of years, must have descended upon them and crushed
them out, except a few survivors who fled south. Doubtless the tragedy of Wi was common, though nobody
thinks of such things to-day, when for aught we know
we may be living in an interval between two Ice Ages.
Not long ago I was reading of the flint pits at Brandon in
Norfolk, where it is said that in the far past lived tribes
of flint-workers. Then, it seems, came an Ice Age, and
after it was over, appeared other tribes of flint-workers,

separated from the first by untold epochs of time. But one might talk of such things all night."

"And all to-morrow, Allan. But you have not answered my question. How do you account for a man like Wi at that period of the world's history?"

I took a little more whisky and soda to give myself time to think. Then I answered, easily enough, at least to my mind,

"The world, they tell us, has probably been habitable and therefore inhabited by man for millions of years. Now Wi, if he ever existed, by comparison lived quite recently, for he knew how to make fire, how to trap beasts, and many other things. I suggest to you, my dear Good, that we have not really advanced very much since the days of Wi. The skulls that are found of people of or before his period have the same, or sometimes an even larger, brain capacity than our own. All the first and more essential developments of the human race took place infinite ages before the birth of Wi. Some outstanding individuals must have conceived the idea of making and enforcing necessary laws and of putting a stop to infanticide. Why should not Wi have been one of these? He may have gone ahead too fast, as in fact he did, but perhaps the memory of his laws survived through his wife Aaka, or his brother Moananga, or his son Foh, if they escaped, and were repeated and improved upon by future generations of his blood. In short, Good, although I think that men have grown cleverer as a race, I do not believe that the high-water mark of individuals among them has advanced greatly since the times of such as Wi, which after all in the history of the world, and indeed of the human race, are but yesterday. For the rest, in my own life I have known many who are called savages in Africa who knew as little or less than Wi, and yet, in similar circumstances, would have done all that he did, and more."

"That's a new idea," said Good. "Perhaps we civilised people vaunt ourselves too much."

"Perhaps," I answered, "for civilisation as we know

it is very young and a great sham. " I don't know and
it isn't worth bothering about. All I know is that I
wish I had never dreamed that dream, which has given
me a new set of sorrows that cannot be forgotten."

" That's the point," exclaimed Good. " Now there
was Tana. She was a jealous sort of woman and we
quarrelled often, especially when I began to make up to
Laleela. And I—well, I was a natural man, much as I
am to-day, so, as I say, we quarrelled. Yet after all I was
very fond of Tana ; she was my wife for many years and
she bore children whom both of us loved, children that
died, as most children died among the tribe. As for
the rows between us, what do they matter ? Now
that I have come to know her, I can never forget
Tana."

" It is the same here," I answered. " That boy Foh,
and his sister Foa, whom you remember that brute-man
Henga murdered—for example. Well, they may be but
dream-children, but henceforward they are mine. At
this very moment I tell you that I could burst into
tears over the murder of Foa, and that my heart aches
over the loss of Foh, and yet I suppose that they are
only fantasies, drug-born fantasies.

" See what this cursed *Taduki* has done for us !
To the bereavements and miseries of our own lives
it has added another series. It has suggested
to us that we have endured other lives, other
losses and other miseries, and yet it has not helped
us to solve their problems. Shall we ever see any of
these people again ? We who seemed to mix with them
still exist. Do *they* exist, also, and if so, have we any
hope of finding them ? "

" Are you quite certain, Allan, that we haven't found
some of them already, although it was but to lose them
once more ? Now although I never saw him, you have
often told me of the Hottentot called Hans who served
you from your youth until he died, still trying to serve
you by saving your life. Well, isn't there some
resemblance between that Hottentot and Pag ? "

" Undoubtedly there is," I answered, " although Pag,
the Wolf-man, was a. bit more primeval."

" Then as regards Laleela—how about that Lady
Ragnall who left you the fortune which like a donkey
you refused ? Do you see any connection between
them ? "

" Not much," I answered, " except that they were
both priestesses of, or at any rate in some way connected
with the moon. But of course I know very little of
Laleela's life. She appeared from a southern land, but
exactly why she left it I cannot say, because she never
told me. At that time her age must have been—well,
what do you put it at, Good ? "

" Anywhere between twenty-eight and thirty-two,
I should say."

" That's about it. Well, in those days a woman of
her beauty and station must have had lots of private
history behind her at, let us say, thirty. Indeed she
hinted as much more than once. But as she never stated
what it was, there is very little to go on, and identification
becomes impossible.

" Look here, let us stop this before we go cracked.
Under the influence of an African drug we have seen
strange things, or think that we have seen them. We
have seen an ancient, barbaric tribe living at the foot of
the glaciers upon a desolate beach, collecting their food
from year to year as best they could with their primitive
weapons, and evolving a kind of elementary civilisation.

" Thus they were ruled by a chief who might be killed
when any stronger man appeared, as in a herd of game the
old bull is killed by the young bull. We have seen a man of
strength and ability arise, who tried to make new and
better laws and to introduce justice, and who, under the
influence of a foreign and more advanced woman, ultimately turned from the worship of fierce, fetish gods supposed to dwell in the ice they dreaded, to a purer if still
elementary faith. We have seen the fate fall upon him
that overtakes almost all reformers ; also that this ice was
not feared in vain, since it swept down and destroyed his

people, as indeed it must often have done in the history of the world, and perhaps will do again in the future."

"Yes, we have seen all that," said Good, "but if it wasn't real, what is the use of it? Dreams have not much practical value."

"Are you sure about that, Good? Are you sure that life, as we know it, is anything more than a *Taduki* dream?"

"What do you mean, Allan?"

"I mean that perhaps already we may be plunged into and be a part of immortality, and that this immortality may have its nights as well as its days; dream-haunted nights of which this present life of ours is one."

"Steady, old fellow. You are running full steam into strange waters and without a chart."

"Quite true," I answered. "Let us get back into the channel between the lighted buoys. To my mind our experience to-night has been very instructive. Whether it be real or imaginary, it has taught me what must have happened to our forefathers tens or hundreds of thousands of years ago. Let us suppose that it was all a dream or delusion, and think of it as nothing else. Still, it has been a most fascinating dream, a kind of lightning flash, showing us a page of the past. There let us leave it, locking it up as an individual experience not meant for the benefit of others. To advertise what are called hallucinations is not wise."

"I quite agree with you, Allan," said Good, "and I mean to keep my experiences upon that beach, wherever it may have been, very much to myself. Only in my leisure time I intend to take up the study of the Ice Ages and the Glacial Drift.

"And now, about those snipe. It is odd, by the way, that even in those days you seem to have been a sportsman and a hunter. Will you bring your spear—I mean gun—and come to-morrow? . . ."

THE END

If you enjoyed this book and would like to have information sent to you about other Pulp Fictions titles, please write to the address below by completing the coupon or writing clearly on a plain piece of paper. Please enclose an SAE / IRC for response.

In addition to our catalogue you will receive information regarding our creative competition
(see below; closing date 30th June 1999), and will be automatically entitled to :

FREE ENTRY INTO THE PRIZE DRAW!

Twice a year in June and December, coupons will be drawn 'from the hat' and the winner will receive a complete set of Pulp Fictions paperbacks.

Pulp Publications Ltd
PO Box 144
Polegate
East Sussex
BN26 6NW
England
UK.

Full Name ....

Address ....

...........................Postcode................

City/State/Zip....................................

Age........................

Creative Competition: Please send me details of the search for new writing/artistic talent for the millenium ......YES/NO

THESE BOOKS CAN HELP YOU...

thru the GATEWAY
to . . . SUCCESS and a better Jôb.

If you're the type of man who wants to make more money . . . and you've got the ambition and gumption to get ahead . . . and you want the better pay jobs, then these easy-to-understand books will help you . . . and faster, too. Thousands have surged ahead because they used spare time to better themselves. Study these exceptional books, then check the ones you want. You'll see how these books can be YOUR Gateway to Success. When you send your order, ask for our new FREE illustrated catalog. All books sold on MONEY BACK GUARANTEE.

1. **PRACTICAL ELECTRICITY AND HOUSE WIRING:** Excellent for home repair work. Tells all. 200 pages, 227 illus.........**$1.50**
2. **QUICK CONSTRUCTION:** Short cuts and aids to modern building. Handy home book. 250 pages and 670 illus..............**$2.00**
3. **PLUMBING INSTALLATIONS and REPAIR:** For the handy man around the house. Fix everything. 200 pages and 153 illus..**$2.00**
4. **HOUSE PAINTING METHODS:** Shows and tells how to paint houses of any surface. Save . . . do it yourself. 400 pages, 150 illus. **$2.00**
5. **REFRIGERATION SERVICE MANUAL:** Covers every field and shop operation which may be required. Includes domestic types of refrigeration. **$2.00**

MONEY BACK GUARANTEE
Use This Coupon for Your Order

GATEWAY PUBLISHING COMPANY
53 W. Jackson, Dept. P.P.-5, Chicago 4, Ill.

Send the books I've checked, C.O.D. (plus small postage fee. I may return the books within 5 days if they are not completely satisfactory and my money will be refunded.

         1   2   3   4   5

Special: Entire Home Set of 5 Books only $9.00 ($9.50 value).

NAME ....

ADDRESS ....

CITY .... STATE..............

GUITARISTS Burnets Chord Chart shows instantly, on *one master sheet*, exactly how to make over 400 modern chords—Major, Minor, 7th, 9th, Diminished, etc. Diagrams show correct fingering. Price $1.00. **Burnet Publishing Co., Commerce, Texas.**

LEARN MEAT CUTTING
At Home — In Spare Time

Get into the vital meat industry. Concise, practical Home Training based on 25 years proven instruction methods used at National's famous resident school. Prepares you for bigger pay as Meat Cutter, Supervisor, market manager or more money in your own store. Go as rapidly as your spare time permits. Diploma. Start NOW to turn your spare hours into money. Send for FREE bulletin today. No obligation. No salesman will call.
National School of Meat Cutting, Inc., Dept. K-9, Toledo 4, Ohio

HERE'S A NEW AND VITAL BUSINESS!

LEARN ELECTRICAL APPLIANCE REPAIRING

Offers Big Money—Independence

If you are mechanically inclined—can hold and use tools it will pay you to learn electrical appliance repairing. Operate from your garage, basement, etc. Work as many hours as you wish—the appliance repairman is his own boss. On many types of repairs it is usual for a repairman to charge on the basis of $5.00 to $6.00 an hour.

No Previous Experience Needed

Profusely illustrated our new course shows you in simple, easy to understand language plus drawings and photographs, how to make each repair on refrigerators, vacuum cleaners, washing machines, motors, fans, irons, etc., etc. Explains and gives you a working knowledge of electricity, welding, nickel plating, etc. Shows you how to build the power tools you need and how to solicit and keep business coming to you. Not a theory course but an honest to goodness practical course written by and used by repairmen and country over. Price of course is so low that the savings on your own household appliances will pay for it. Act now! Send today for FREE literature. Christy Supply Co., 2835 N. Central Ave., Dept. D-318, Chicago 34, Illinois.

LAW STUDY AT HOME for PERSONAL SUCCESS and LARGER EARNINGS. 35 years expert instruction—over 108,000 students enrolled. LL.B. Degree awarded. All texts furnished. Easy payments. Send for FREE BOOK—"Law and Executive Guidance"—NOW!
AMERICAN EXTENSION SCHOOL OF LAW
Dept. 52-S, 646 N. Michigan Ave., Chicago 11, Ill.

Store Route Plan
PAYS BIG MONEY

SELL COUNTER CARD PRODUCTS
Build a good-paying business of your own. Call on dealers of all kinds; show nationally-advertised Aspirin, Vitamins, Cosmetics and 200 other necessities. Big 5c and 10c retail packages, high quality. Attractive counter display sell goods fast. Free book gives amazing facts. Write!
WORLD'S PRODUCTS CO.,   Dept. 69-H,   Spencer, Ind.

REFRIGERATION
AND AIR CONDITIONING
SERVICE MECHANICS COURSE

Learn at home—how to start your own repair shop on little capital. No previous experience needed. Common school education sufficient. Splendid opportunity for older men. Prepare now for after the war. FREE illustrated booklet.

MECHANICS TRAINING SCHOOL

4701 W. Pico   Dept. R-5   Los Angeles 6, Calif.

RATIONED MOTORISTS

Now Get *EXTRA* GASOLINE MILEAGE

Now you can get up to 30% extra gasoline mileage with a Vacu-matic on your car. Quicker pick-up, smoother running, added power and precious gasoline savings guaranteed.

Automatic Supercharge Principle

Vacu-matic is *entirely different!* Operates on the Supercharge principle. Saves gas. Automatically provides a better gas mixture. Guaranteed to give up to 30% extra gas mileage, more power and better performance.

FITS ALL CARS

Constructed of six parts, fused into a single unit. Adjusted and *sealed at the factory.* Very quickly installed by anyone.

AGENTS TRIAL OFFER

Every car, truck, tractor a prospect. Send name, address on postcard for big money making offer and how you get yours for introducing.

Vacu-matic Co., 7617-1154 W. State St., Wauwatosa 13, Wis.

STOP Scratching
It May Cause Infection

Relieve itching caused by eczema, athlete's foot, pimples—other itching troubles. Use cooling, medicated D. D. D. Prescription. Greaseless, stainless. Calms itching fast. 35c trial bottle proves it—or money back. Ask your druggist for D. D. D. Prescription.

You Can Learn To Be an ARTIST

Trained Artists Are Capable of Earning $30, $50, $75 Weekly. Many of our graduates are now enjoying successful Art careers. By our practical method, famous since 1914, we teach you COMMERCIAL ART, CARTOONING AND DESIGNING in ONE complete home-study course. Two art outfits furnished. Write for details in FREE CATALOG—"Art for Pleasure and Profit," explains course and commercial opportunities for you in Art. State age.

WASHINGTON SCHOOL OF ART

STUDIO 995P

1115-15th Street, N. W.   Washington 5, D. C.

Monastery Secrets

... THE FORBIDDEN KNOWLEDGE OF TIBET

What strange secrets of nature are locked within the mountain fastness of Tibet? What control over the forces of the Universe do these cloistered sages exercise? For centuries the world has sought to know the source of their power—to learn *their mastery of life*, and *their faculty for overcoming problems* with which the masses of mankind still struggle. Have they selfishly deprived humanity of these rare teachings?

WRITE FOR THIS FREE BOOK

Like the streams that trickle from the Himalayan heights to the plateaus below, *the great truths* of these brotherhoods have descended through the ages. One of the preservers of the wisdom of the Orient is the Rosicrucian Brotherhood (not a religious organization). They *invite you* to write today for their FREE Sealed Book, with its amazing revelations about these mysteries of life. Address: Scribe C.M.E.

The ROSICRUCIANS
AMORC
San Jose, Calif.
U.S.A.

a smart man's collar secret

Keeps unruly
collar points down.
Shirts last longer.
19 million sold
to servicemen!

Self-adjusting Spring
Fits all Collars

For collar neatness, Spiffy
is a "Must." Send a few to
your serviceman. Buy several for yourself.
Standard model 25c. Others slightly higher.
At all Drug, Army, PX and Men's stores.

BEFORE

AFTER

Spiffy

INVISIBLE

Collar Stay

CREST SPECIALTY CO., 663 Washington, Chicago 6, Ill.

NO Occupational Restrictions · *NOT Contestable

Triple INDEMNITY
LIFE INSURANCE
POLICY PAYS MAXIMUM BENEFITS
$3000.00

Policy Costs Only $1.00 a Month

Provide for those you love this wise, easy way. Only a few pennies a day will pay for TRIPLE IN-DEMNITY LIFE INSUR-ANCE, backed by Legal Reserves. Old reliable Pioneer Life Insurance Company offers this as-sured protection without restrictions as to your Occupation, Travel or Residence and includes

COMPLETE LIFE PROTECTION
POLICY PAYS
for
LOSS of LIFE
DUE TO
ANY CAUSE!

*valuable Incontestability Clause—all as plainly stated in the policy. Men, women and children from 1 day to 70 years of age eligible. No Red Tape—No Medical Examination! Full details sent by mail. No Agent will call. Write at once for FREE inspection offer. DON'T DELAY!

PIONEER LIFE INSURANCE COMPANY
8612 Pioneer Building ● Rockford, Illinois

SORE FEET FEEL FINE

When You Do This at Night

For 10 minutes tonight, soak your sore, raw, itching feet in the rich, creamy lather of Sayman Wonder Soap—and pat dry with a soft towel. Then smooth on plenty of medicated Sayman Salve—over the watery blisters, the painful cracks, the sore, raw skin. Do this for 10 nights and shout with joy for comforting relief. 25c and 60c. All druggists. Ask for

SAYMAN SALVE

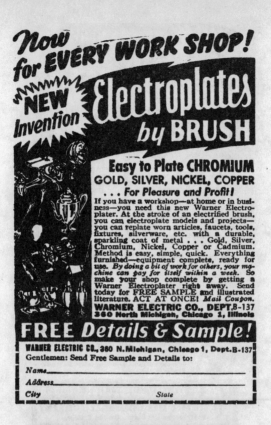

Now for EVERY WORK SHOP!

NEW Invention

Electroplates *by BRUSH*

Easy to Plate CHROMIUM
GOLD, SILVER, NICKEL, COPPER
... For Pleasure and Profit!

If you have a workshop—at home or in business—you need this new Warner Electroplater. At the stroke of an electrified brush, you can electroplate models and projects—you can replate worn articles, faucets, tools, fixtures, silverware, etc. with a durable, sparkling coat of metal ... Gold, Silver, Chromium, Nickel, Copper or Cadmium. Method is easy, simple, quick. Everything furnished—equipment complete, ready for use. *By doing a bit of work for others, your machine can pay for itself within a week.* So make your shop complete by getting a Warner Electroplater right away. Send today for FREE SAMPLE and illustrated literature. ACT AT ONCE! *Mail Coupon.*
WARNER ELECTRIC CO., DEPT.B-137
360 North Michigan, Chicago 1, Illinois

FREE *Details & Sample!*

WARNER ELECTRIC CO., 360 N. Michigan, Chicago 1, Dept. B-137
Gentlemen: Send Free Sample and Details to:

Name_____

Address_____

City_____ State_____

High School Course
at Home   Many Finish in 2 Years

Go as rapidly as your time and abilities permit. Course equivalent to resident school work—prepares for college entrance exams. Standard H.S. texts supplied. Diploma. Credit for H. S. subjects already completed. Single subjects if desired. High school education is very important for advancement in business and industry and socially. Don't be handicapped all your life. Be a High School graduate. Start your training now. Free Bulletin on request. No obligation.
American School, Dpt. H549, Drexel at 58th, Chicago 37

STAMMER?

GET THIS **FREE** BOOK!

This new 128-page book, "Stammering, Its Cause and Correction," describes the Bogue Unit Method for scientific correction of stammering and stuttering—successful for 44 years.
Benj. N. Bogue, Dept. 2966, Circle Tower, Indianapolis 4, Ind.

NOW JUST $1 A MONTH

PROVIDES CASH WHEN YOU NEED IT MOST!

AMAZING NEW GOLD SEAL POLICY

Provides *all-around* protection, cash for almost every emergency! Issued by old-line LEGAL RESERVE company, yet actually *costs less than $1 a month.* Protection you need at a price you can afford!

Pays for ANY and ALL Accidents, ALL Common Sicknesses, as provided, even minor injuries. Disability benefits paid from first day. No waiting period. NO, this is NOT the usual "limited" policy. NO jokers. NO trick clauses. It's *extra liberal!*

NO MEDICAL EXAMINATION

Accumulated CASH BENEFITS

Up To **$6000.00** for Accidental LOSS OF LIFE, LIMBS or SIGHT▪

Up To **$2400.00** for ACCIDENT DISABILITY at rate up to $100 Monthly for as long as 24 months▪

Up To **$300.00** for SICKNESS DISABILITY at rate up to $100 monthly for as long as 3 months▪

Up To **$650.00** for HOSPITAL EXPENSES as a result of either sickness or accident

Policy issued BY MAIL at *big savings.* Ages 15 to 69. Actual policy sent for 10 DAYS' FREE EXAMINATION. Write for it today. No cost! No obligation! No salesman will call. Use coupon below. Do it today—Provide for tomorrow!

FREE 10-Day Inspection Coupon

The SERVICE LIFE INSURANCE COMPANY
453L Service Life Bldg.   Omaha 2, Nebr.
Without cost or obligation, send your GOLD SEAL $1-A-MONTH Policy for 10 DAYS' FREE INSPECTION.

Name_____

Address_____Age_____

City_____State_____

Beneficiary_____

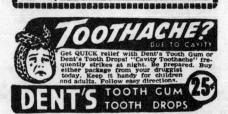

TOOTHACHE?
DUE TO CAVITY

Get QUICK relief with Dent's Tooth Gum or Dent's Tooth Drops! "Cavity Toothache" frequently strikes at night. Be prepared. Buy either package from your druggist today. Keep it handy for children and adults. Follow easy directions.

25¢

DENT'S TOOTH GUM TOOTH DROPS